FOUR SEASONS

FOUR SEASONS

Paperback ISBN 979-8-9883810-1-3

Hardcover ISBN 979-8-9883810-2-0

Ebook ISBN 979-8-9883810-0-6

Printed in 2023

Published in the United States of America
By Brandbureau Consulting LLC
Cheyenne, WY 82001

Book design by Carlos Castellon

For Carlos, Julia and Luis

READING PLAYLIST

1

Groaning, I buried my head under the pillows. My phone was ringing non-stop and I knew it wouldn't end until I picked up.

"It's Saturday, for Pete's sake! It's supposed to be my 'no-phone-calls' day!"

Of course, Salem, my two-year-old black cat, was the first one up, and he meowed at me impatiently from the foot of the bed.

"You, too, go away!" I shouted back.

Salem knew I'd been putting things off on finishing some book editing and was trying to motivate me. But all I wanted to do was stay in bed just a little longer. It was too early for anything else right now.

Unfortunately, Salem wouldn't let it go so quickly this time, and after several more minutes of constant meowing, I yelled, "Okay, I'm coming!" I looked at the yellow-eyed, black-furred menace at the foot of the bed, "You're supposed to be on my side and not working with whoever is on the other end of the line."

Salem gave me a look of disapproval and disbelief. It was almost like he silently said: *'You have got to be kidding me. You have got to be the laziest human in all of existence.'* Salem was quite the character. He loved socializing with humans and other cats, although he can sometimes be

1

aloof and stubborn. He was out most of the day but always returned home after a long day of chasing butterflies or hunting for birds and other critters. Salem, for all his gregariousness, had a tendency to complain and hiss at the slightest provocation, giving him an air of entitlement and hostility. It was as if he believed the world revolved around him, and any deviation from his expectations resulted in a barrage of grumbles and complaints. But no matter what, Salem will always be a loyal friend. Not today, though, as he threw loyalty out of the window and wanted me to settle what caused the noise resulting in the chaos early in the morning.

I sighed in exhaustion as the sound of my phone ringing echoed around the room. Reluctantly, I reached out to pick up the call and blinked at the caller ID. Jenna Huey. Of course. She and her relentless demands for her project to finish yesterday, if not sooner.

"I don't want to sound like a buzzkill, but I'm supposed to start working on my manuscript, and I need the characters for my story," Jenna exclaimed, breaking the peaceful silence of the morning.

As I rubbed my eyes, attempting to shake off the lingering drowsiness, I couldn't help but ask Jenna, "Why do you always wake up so early on weekends?" My voice sounded muffled since I was still lying under the covers.

"Why do you ask?" she retorted sarcastically, implying that she had a deadline to beat with her publisher.

I tried to listen carefully to what she was saying, yet all I could make out were fragmented sentences that seemed almost distant and stifled —like they were coming from another dimension. I forced myself to leave the bed with an exasperated sigh. I put her on speakerphone as I said, "I got your back, Jenna. I'll take care of it." I got to my kitchen and reached   for the Nespresso machine —a small piece of luxury that served me well on days like this when reality refused to let go of its grip.

"I know you will. Hope, I would love to see you at my place when you have the time," she said before ending the call. Finally, some peace and quiet!

The aroma of freshly brewed espresso filled the air as my realization became clear. This morning would be like most days — more writing, taking care of bills, and constantly questioning what the future has in store for me.

I slumped on one of my mismatched chairs in my tiny kitchen-slash-dining room. The room certainly didn't look fit for four people, or even one plus a guest, yet here I am, using it as my virtual conference room setup. I sipped coffee alone at an equally tiny table-chair combo plastered with postcards from Paris which I bought from the old bookshop in Lexington. Over the years, I have learned how to deal with demanding clients, and sometimes it was best just to listen and to give assurance that you will work on it as soon as possible.

Working alone definitely has its advantages. There was no need for second-guessing decisions or discussions on how to work more efficiently. When you're alone, you have complete control over the project, tackling it the way you think best without worrying about compromising with others. I could fully immerse myself in the task without worrying about others interfering with my creative process. I could work at my own pace, set deadlines, and put one hundred percent of my effort into every detail.

Of course, working alone also comes with its own set of challenges. No one will bounce ideas off or help solve the problem when you encounter obstacles. But for me, the benefits of solitude far outweigh the drawbacks.

Ultimately, it was all about finding the right balance between working alone and collaborating with others. Sometimes, the best outcomes come from combining both, and switching between the two is a valuable skill.

———

I forced myself to switch into action mode. However, it seems like today isn't productive, considering how tired I still felt from staying up late last night working on some pending projects. Rather than diving straight into work mode as Jenna probably expected me to, I think taking a breather and getting some fresh air would help me shake off the grogginess. And perhaps I should grab some more caffeine.

"Salem, hop in. We're going Dunkin!" He perched happily atop my shoulder, and off we went to our favorite coffee-on-the-go spot at the corner of 89th, enjoying all the new sights around us while we made our way to our destination.

The morning chill of Autumn in New York was like a gentle reminder to the city-dwellers that winter was on its way. It wasn't too severe — just enough to make you want to bundle up and take an extra minute under the warm sheets before getting out of bed. On this particular day, it seemed every citizen had received the memo because the streets were almost eerily quiet for such a bustling metropolis.

As Salem and I walked down the street, I watched as steam rose from maintenance hole covers and people slowly emerged with their coffee cups in tow. The pedestrians moved at a plodding pace.

I got my Midnight Dunkin' while Salem was content with lying on the coffee table. We spent a few minutes staring out the window, knowing this peaceful scene wouldn't last long. Soon enough, cars and cabs began honking, and buses filled up with commuters heading into work for another day's grind. A couple of minutes more, people walking their pets around the neighborhood appeared as the autumn's chill began, along with its beautiful golden hues adorning every street corner. All these reminded me why New York City was such a fantastic place, even during its most mundane days!

As Salem and I made our way back home, I noticed how different it looked during this time of year. The trees were bare, and leaves were scattered about on the sidewalks rather than rustling above me. Autumn always feels special amid all this commotion. There was still something so calming about embracing this seasonal change in New York City — something that reminded me how much beauty can be found in these small moments throughout life if we only take a moment to notice them.

My neighborhood was a charming mix of quaint shops and bustling streets. Nestled along my street lies everything one could possibly need for a comfortable life. From the old-fashioned diner, Millie's Place, serving up classic American fare, to the Wishy Washy laundromat where I can clean clothes with ease, and even Betty's Baked Goods where I get my daily bagel fix — all are just a few steps away from my doorstep. And when I feel like my apartment needs a pop of color, Veronica's Bloom is a hop and a skip away. The vibrant blooms and luscious greenery bring a sense of tranquility and peace to my dwelling, transforming it into a sanctuary in the middle of the exciting and noisy city life. Every day it comes alive and I love it. People going about their business, chatting outside doorways, or simply taking the time to appreciate each other's company. Even in its hustle and bustle, something undeniably beautiful about this unique area made me feel so connected to my home. It reminded me of why I fell in love with New York City in the first place.

"Hey Salem, would you like to make a quick detour to Charlie's place?" I glanced back at him, hoping he would be up for it. He was always delighted to visit Veronica's Bloom, situated on the ground level of my old yet charming apartment building. The floral shop was owned by my favorite neighbor, Charlie Sung, a 56-year-old immigrant who managed the store with his 22-year-old daughter, Veronica. Entering the shop is like stepping into a fairytale with its vibrant pink walls and rustic wooden shutters that let in the sunshine. Inside, bouquets of brightly colored flowers filled every corner, creating a perfume that envelops you as soon as you open the door and see Charlie's bright smile. Charlie is always friendly and welcoming, taking time to chat with every customer, no matter how busy he is.

Today was no different. There are already people gathering in front of his shop. I spotted Charlie by the flowerpots and Veronica operating the counter. Though his silver grey hair was receding and he had a noticeable bald spot on the top of his head, he had a distinguished look reminiscent of the original Mr. Miyagi from *The Karate Kid*.

I stepped out onto the street, feeling the cold wind on my skin and the gentle breeze in my hair. As I walked towards the flower stand, I could see Charlie's smiling face beaming at me from behind rows of bright tulips.

"Hi, Charlie! How are the tulips today?" I called out, feeling my mood lift even further at the sight of the colorful blooms.

"Hey there, Hope. They are still as lovely as ever, just like you," he said with a grin, reaching out to pet Salem as he perched on my shoulder. "I have something for Salem in the kitchen, by the way."

As if on cue, Salem jumped off my shoulder and wasted no time darting off toward Charlie's kitchen knowing that he'd always find a treat waiting for him there. I couldn't help but chuckle at the sight of his black tail disappearing around the corner. He'll probably spend a few hours with Charlie like usual and find his way back to our place.

When I first moved into this building, I stumbled upon Charlie's flower stand and was immediately drawn to the beautiful blooms in the window display. As I stepped inside, Charlie greeted me with a warm smile, and I could tell that he was more than just a florist — he was a kind soul who had a story to tell.

I soon discovered that Charlie had left Vietnam two decades ago, seeking a better life in the United States. His journey had been anything but easy, and he had faced many challenges along the way. Yet, despite everything he had been through, Charlie remained an optimist, always ready with a kind word and a generous gesture.

As someone with a mixed background — my mom is from New York and my dad originally from Manila — I immediately felt a kinship with Charlie. We bonded over our shared love for Asian folklore and tales of adventure, and our conversations quickly developed from simple pleasantries to deep, meaningful exchanges.

Before I knew it, I had become a regular visitor to Charlie's home, popping in for a cup of tea and an hour of conversation. There, I met his daughter, Veronica. Despite only being five years younger than me, she was a force to be reckoned with when it came to politics and social issues. Her opinions were strong and well-informed, making her seem older beyond her years. She possessed a rare intelligence that set her apart from her peers, captivating all those who had the pleasure of conversing with her. From the moment Veronica and I met, we hit it off instantly. We found ourselves spending more and more time together, talking and laughing on some Tiktok videos, or binge-watching *Queer Eye* and gushing over the charming Antoni Porowski until the early hours of the morning. Soon enough, she was hanging out at my apartment regularly, sometimes, with our neighbor Sara.

I couldn't help but think that Charlie and Veronica had become like family to me, the kind of people who made this city a little bit more like home.

Salem had taken a liking to the Sungs. Whenever he was upset with me, he often sought refuge at Charlie's home. He and Veronica loved having Salem around, and I think Salem enjoyed the extra attention and treats he got from them.

"How's your book coming along?" Charlie asked.

"I don't write books, Charlie," I replied. "I create characters for the books."

"Come on, Hope. You're very talented. Why don't you write your novel instead of working on someone else's?"

"I know, but this job pays well," I said. "At least I can afford the rent and a little extra for Salem and me."

"Don't let economics dictate what you can and can't do," he said with a smile.

"Don't worry, I'll write that book someday," I reassured him. To be honest, I was reassuring myself as much as him. Publishing my book has been my dream since I started reading — it's been my favorite thing to do since childhood. Reading books and writing stories— there's nothing quite like it! Despite my best intentions, I found myself constantly creating story characters or editing someone else's work. It seemed that my own dreams always took a backseat, as if they were not worth pursuing. As time went on, I realized that my plans did not go as smoothly as I would have liked. Obstacles seemed to crop up at every turn, making it difficult to pursue my own passions and desires.

Charlie and I chatted for a bit longer, catching up on the latest news and gossip from the neighborhood. As always, he had a kind word and a warm smile for everyone who passed by his stand. I patted Salem's head while he enjoyed his treats from Charlie, then I gave Charlie a quick peck on the cheek before heading toward my flat. I left the flower stand with a spring in my step, feeling grateful for the simple pleasures of life and the kind souls who brightened up the world around them.

———

As I settled into my modest room, I opened my laptop and got ready to work. I designed this room for writing: a couple of books on the corner shelves, memos and post-its scattered over the walls like stars in the night sky — it was perfect. What I loved most about this tiny, pleasant one-bedroom apartment was its ideal size. I loved the large windows that let in plenty of natural light, the cozy balcony from which I could breathe the fresh air, and the open floor and the space with an air of grandeur that belied its actual size, allowing me to imagine for a moment that it was much larger than it appeared to be. What this apartment may have lacked in luxury, it more than made up for in character. I picked most of my furniture at garage sales. The built-in bookshelves near the balcony created a cozy corner to curl up in with a mug of coffee and a good book. I love how my books were crowded in by my favorite art pieces, photos, and mementos. No matter how small or humble my apartment may be, these shelves reminded me of everything I needed.

As I picked up the old silver-framed graduation photo, nestled amidst a yellow teapot and my collection of Hilary Mantel novels, a wave of nostalgia washed over me. There we were, my friends and I, forever captured within the glass panes — eternally young and carefree. Life in those days revolved around part-time jobs to cover shared-room rent or apartment expenses. For the fortunate ones, parents' credit cards provided a safety net, covering costs without a second thought — no rat race, no student loan repayments. The three of us were college buddies, all grappling with our shared struggles while working at Starbucks between classes.

Jane, the fiery redhead to my right, had married two years prior and now enjoyed a jet-setting life in Florence. Lizzie, my math companion, had chased her dreams by attending law school, ultimately becoming a junior associate at one of Chicago's top law firms. As I gazed at the photo, a sense of disappointment began to loom over me. Reflecting on my own journey, I couldn't help but feel that I had fallen short of the expectations I had set for myself. It appeared that everyone around me was accomplishing their goals and living their best lives, while I remained trapped in a cycle of indecision and uncertainty.

At 27, I was still living a fairly ordinary life and hadn't accomplished as much as I should have for someone in their twenties. I graduated college with honors and briefly worked at an advertising firm as a copy editor before moving to a book publishing firm. Then I found myself working independently with some writers or ghostwriting for them. As the product of an American mother and Filipino father, I looked different, not too American but not entirely Asian. My hair is long and dark with wispy bangs framing my fair complexion, while my brown eyes reveal just how shy I truly am. I resembled my mother in many ways but her green eyes and blond hair were the glaring difference. Sometimes, I wished I had inherited her eyes —hers were bright green ones with specks of grey.

My love and sex life were sadly non-existent, as I hadn't prioritized dating until now. But even so, my little corner of the world gave me solace and peace. Growing up in the diverse city of New York instilled an appreciation for different cultures that I would carry with me to adulthood. While it could not replace what I might be missing elsewhere, perhaps it was a small way of making up for it.

I quickly fixed myself a mug of coffee and brought it to my table, curling up into my chair as I prepared to write. Salem had gone away for his usual afternoon jaunts so, enjoying the quiet respite, I slowly took a sip from the steaming mug. The warm liquid filled me with renewed energy and determination to tackle the task ahead. I turned on my laptop, ready to begin.

I started working on Jenna's book characters — this is one of my most fulfilling writing jobs. It was like having my own witching hour, when I summoned magic and breathed new life into the pages. With every keystroke, I crafted characters that came to life, captivating readers and leaving them spellbound. I wrote until almost sundown and took a break to prepare a peanut butter and grape jelly sandwich. As I munched away at my very late lunch but too early for dinner, Salem returned home like clockwork — just as he always did around twilight. He padded calmly through the door with an air of magic, almost like he had been out casting spells all day. He meowed as if asking what I'd been up to while he was gone and, after giving me one last curious glance, hopped onto his bed in the corner of the room —ready for another evening nap.

I looked at the crisp autumn twilight. The sky over New York City was breathtaking. From my tiny balcony, I can glimpse the horizon far into the distance — a timeless backdrop of soft pink and orange hues against an expanse of deep blue sky. Above me was a sparkling carpet of stars stretching endlessly; and beyond them were fluffy white clouds floating lazily. In the middle of a bustling city, it was serene, with an almost magical quality that never fails to fill me with awe.

It didn't take long before Salem's gentle purring filled up every inch of space in our tiny apartment —how we both liked it: cozy and peaceful.

2

As a freelancer, I've experienced the highs and lows of life away from the 9-to-5 grind. While embracing my independence has its advantages, there are also times when I miss the comfort of having a regular job with a steady income, not to mention the security of paying all those bills on time each month. But ultimately, I don't regret the freedom freelancing affords me. I can work flexible hours, explore new opportunities, and eventually do what I love without constraints or expectations. It's worth more than money, except when unpaid bills are staring at you. So when I received a call from Jenna offering me the opportunity to work with her, I eagerly accepted. Collaborating with Jenna involved various tasks, including character development, copy editing, and occasionally, a touch of developmental editing. Completing a book with Jenna typically took at least five months, sometimes even longer. With this project — in addition to others I was already working on — I could comfortably cover my rent for the next five months!

With my coat draped over my arm, I made my way toward Jenna's place. Despite its outdated transportation system, one of the things I love about New York City is that it's still easy to get around without relying on cabs, Ubers, or Lyfts. It only takes me 7 minutes to walk from 89th to the 86th Street station, where I can catch the 4, 5, or 6 train. The best part is the short walk from Lexington Avenue to the Upper East Side neighborhood — it always feels like a special treat, like a visit to Argosy bookstore, one of the oldest independent bookstores in the city. Of course, today isn't one of those days. With Jenna's deadline looming over my head like a red light, I couldn't afford any detours — no matter how tempting they may be.

Jenna lived in one of the luxurious buildings on the Upper West Side, complete with a marble lobby and doorman. I had always been envious of the people living in this glamorous neighborhood. I passed all the chic shops and bakeries, watched nannies taking care of toddlers, and dog sitters walking their dogs, and I couldn't help but wonder what it would be like to live like them.

What does it feel like when life is nothing more than brunch dates, shopping sprees, and social events? Would my days be filled with peace, or would there also be moments of stress? After all, they say money can't buy happiness! Then again, I bet having a luxurious lifestyle has its perks. This really swanky neighborhood, for starters.

Just when I was about to reach my destination, suddenly, a voice broke through my thoughts. "Welcome to our little piece of paradise!" It belonged to a silver-grey-haired older man wearing a suit uniform.

"Good afternoon, Fred!" I chirped.

Fred opened the door and ushered me inside the building, which looked even more impressive than its facade. There were marble walls everywhere and crystal chandeliers illuminating every room. The lobby looked more like a fancy hotel than an apartment building. Fred was probably on an afternoon break. Otherwise, you wouldn't see him outside of the building. During my first visit, he guided me around the hall while sharing stories about what he calls 'my hood.' Fred belonged to the 70's era and had great respect for the residents of New York, particularly the Upper East Siders.

Now he stopped mid-sentence, and with a mischievous glint in his eye, he said, "Do you want to know why so many people envy us rich folk? Come follow me." He always joked about being part of New York's rich and famous, and I couldn't help but laugh as we rode the elevator up to the 7th floor.

As we stepped out onto the observation deck, we were immediately greeted by a breathtaking view of Manhattan. The sun had just set, setting the city aglow with a golden-orange hue that stretched for miles everywhere.

"You know, Hope," Fred began, his voice filled with wisdom, "Money brings freedom, but not happiness. It can provide access to places that would otherwise be inaccessible, but only if you use it wisely. True joy comes from within, no matter your status in life."

I couldn't help but feel grateful for Fred's insight as we basked in the beauty of the sunset. Yet, despite our peaceful surroundings, my mind wandered to the people who often idolize and envy the wealthy. "Sometimes I wonder," I said, watching the city below us come alive with twinkling lights, "if these people deserve your admiration, Fred."

He took a deep breath when our conversation took a turn to the profound. "I just realized how fortunate these few are and why they deserve such admiration. I would like to believe that most of them, no matter their success, remain humble and appreciate where they came from while trying to make sure everyone around them is happy, too." Fred said as we walked back to the elevator. He pushed the 11th button for me as he returned to the lobby. "So, whenever someone asks what living among wealthy people was like, my answer was always the same — it's simply beautiful."

I smiled at Fred and kissed his cheek good-bye as I stepped onto Jenna's floor. Taking my phone out of my bag, I said, "Hey Siri, open Note. Write 'include Fred as a wizard character in the next book project.'"

———

Jenna answered on the first ring of her doorbell and opened the door to greet me, I couldn't help but notice her poised and elegant demeanor. At 52, she exuded a sense of confidence and grace that seemed to come effortlessly. Her auburn hair, with hints of silver, framed her face in soft waves, accentuating her high cheekbones and bright green eyes.

She was engaged in a conversation on her mobile phone, yet still managed to acknowledge me with a warm smile and welcoming nod and signaled me to proceed to her office. Her outfit was a perfect reflection of her stylish and sophisticated personality. She wore a tailored navy blazer over a crisp white blouse paired with well-fitting black trousers that fell above her black leather ankle boots. A delicate gold necklace adorned her neck, adding a touch of refinement to her ensemble. Despite being in the midst of a phone call, Jenna's presence commanded attention, making it clear that she was a woman who knew how to balance both work and style.

I trailed behind her down the hallway towards her office. I couldn't help but take in the surroundings. The room was tastefully decorated with a blend of modern and classic elements, creating an inviting atmosphere. A large, vibrant painting of a London cityscape dominated one wall, showcasing iconic landmarks like Big Ben and Tower Bridge.

As I was admiring the artwork, I was drawn to the striking 24 x 32-inch black and white photograph of Queen Elizabeth II's coronation. The image, encased in an intricately etched silver frame, hung proudly opposite her sleek, minimalist glass table. The British influence in Jenna's office was unmistakable — a subtle nod to her roots and proof of her love for her homeland's rich history and pop culture.

Jenna Huey was born in England and moved to America when she was in high school. She had been writing for thirty years, but unfortunately, not all her novels ended up on the bestseller list. However, her last two books finally received excellent reviews. She had wanted to start on her new novel for months, but something was missing until someone suggested she call in an expert to help jumpstart her story. That's how I came into the picture —a "creative genius" (as Charlie called it) specializing in creating and staging characters in stories.

"Perhaps I'm selling myself short," I murmured, as I reflected on my ability to create characters with depth and purpose during the writing of the story.

As I reminisced about the first project I worked on with Jenna, I couldn't help but recall how I immediately got to work crafting characters that would draw readers in and make them feel like they were part of the adventure. Jenna watched with wide-eyed wonder as I carefully created intricate backstories and personalities for each character, making sure every detail fit perfectly into place like pieces of a puzzle.

"You're good at it, Hope," she said admiringly. Jenna was thrilled to start working on her novel using the new characters I had created. In the past couple of weeks, she'd been busy plotting while waiting for my creations. Eventually, she started seeing her vision come together before her eyes.

"Creating characters is like staging an apartment for rent — you have to be creative enough so your reader falls in love," I said one day while we were discussing the personalities of each character. "You have to craft unique personalities, characteristics, and stories that will capture the reader's attention and make them relate with your characters. It's important to think about how a character would react in different situations and interact with the other characters to make them come alive on the page."

And now here I am again in her gorgeous office, waiting for her to finish her call. I studied the decor, which was far different from mine. Jenna had worked hard to create this luxurious atmosphere, which showed in every detail. In addition to the quintessential British mementos adorning her walls, she also showcased a curated collection of modern artworks, each piece thoughtfully selected to convey a distinct message. Positioned in a corner with a stunning cityscape vista, another circular glass table showcased a diverse assortment of accoutrements, reflecting her notable accomplishments and celebrating her success.

Unlike my humble writing nook, Jenna's office was meticulously designed and adorned with an impressive collection of trinkets from her world travels. An intricately carved wooden mask from Bali rested on one shelf, while a delicate Moroccan lantern cast a warm glow from a nearby windowsill. A small stack of colorful, handwoven textiles from her trip to Peru lay artfully arranged on a side table, each piece telling its own story.

The opulent displays were undeniable, and I couldn't help but feel her power radiating from every corner of the room. Jenna even confessed that she wished she could bottle up the sensation and sell it.

Just as I was getting lost in my thoughts, Jenna's voice snapped me back to reality, "Hey there! I'm writing your check now. It's Esperanza Williams, correct?" she asked, having just wrapped up her phone conversation.

"Yep!" I confirmed with a nod.

Jenna's eyes lit up, and she offered a warm smile. "You know, I love your name. Esperanza means hope. It's one of those things that stuck with me from my high school Spanish class." She paused for a moment as if savoring a distant memory. Her appreciation for the meaning behind my name added a personal touch to our interaction, making the atmosphere in the room feel even more welcoming.

"My dad came up with it," I said with a hint of bitterness. "I never get to use it except in banks and my passport."

"Were you able to see your dad after he left when you were a child? Where is he now?"

"I honestly don't remember his face at all," I confessed, "whenever I asked my mother about him, she would always bail out and change the subject."

My father abandoned me when I was just two years old. I had never seen him again. I didn't have any letters, pictures, or memories with him. He had entirely vanished from my life.

"Anyway, I've added a little extra, so treat yourself to some new clothes," Jenna said with a hint of motherly concern. "Don't waste that beauty and youth sitting in front of your computer writing. When you get to my age, you'll regret it."

I chuckled politely, "Thanks, Jenna. But as you know by now, clothes and I don't get along well." Before Jenna could reply, I pondered aloud, "Is there more to life than just paying the bills? Maybe I should consider moving to London and finding my own Prince Harry?"

Jenna laughed heartily, "Well, Esperanza, I haven't quite found my Prince Charming yet so I wouldn't hold my breath. But in all seriousness, life is what you make of it. You have the talent and the drive to succeed in anything you set your mind to. Just remember to enjoy the journey along the way."

I playfully pouted and quipped, "But, Jenna, where is my happily ever after?"

Jenna rolled her eyes. "Well, you'll need to be successful and a millionaire like Meghan Markle to hook up with a prince, too, my dear."

I let out a laugh, knowing that Jenna was right. But then she added something that genuinely shocked me. "But you know what, Esperanza? You are just as stunning as Meghan, with a huge heart to match. Who knows what opportunities may come knocking on your door?"

Jenna had always pushed me out of my comfort zone, and this time was no different. I glanced at her with a shy smile, and she seemed to understand what I felt —the uneasiness of being told you're attractive when you don't see yourself that way. Despite my reservations, Jenna kept pushing and encouraging me to try dating.

"I know it may feel uncomfortable at first, Esperanza, but trust me, there are plenty of eligible bachelors in town who would be lucky to have someone like you in their lives," she insisted with an arm around my shoulder.

I couldn't help but feel a pang of self-doubt. I've always considered myself quite ordinary, and I rarely wear makeup or put effort into dressing up. Nevertheless, Jenna's words lifted my spirits and gave me the confidence to try something new.

Despite my reluctance to date, deep inside I'm hoping to find my very own Prince Harry — someone who appreciated my unique looks and treated me like a queen every day. However, as of today, my fairy tale ending has yet to appear. Sometimes I wonder maybe my Prince

Charming hasn't even been born yet!

With a satisfied grin, Jenna sets down her pen and hands me the check. "Come on, let's celebrate our win today with some macarons at Ladurée!" she exclaimed, grabbing her coat and bag.

I couldn't help but feel grateful for Jenna's unwavering support and enthusiasm. Together, we strutted out of her impressive office, ready to indulge in sweet treats and continue chasing our dreams.

———

Jenna stopped at a clothing store window display as we strolled the chilly post afternoon. "Those will look good on you," she said. "At some point, you need to treat yourself to some nice clothes. Don't hide that slim figure with oversized coats or hoodies." She looked at me from my head to toe and shook her head sadly.

I smiled shyly at her before looking back at the beautiful dresses in the window. Could I ever afford something like that? With a deep breath, I replied, "Thanks, Jenna, but Salem and I will starve in the winter if I spend my check on those clothes!"

Jenna chuckled, hooked her arm through mine, and said, "Come on, let's just find you a young and attractive startup tech in Silicon Valley instead of those English royalties with their strict 'too-goody-you-can't-do-something-like-that' rules. I doubt there's still money in their hidden dungeons." We both laughed until our stomachs and lungs hurt.

We found the perfect spot at a cozy corner table in Ladurée, gazing across the bustling street. I caught my reflection in the window, still unsure of what could make me stand out from the crowd. Jenna always reminds me I am beautiful, but I couldn't shake the feeling that she was just being kind. Looking at my reflection, I took note of my long brown hair and the bangs that I consistently trimmed to prevent them from obscuring my brown eyes. I just knew I wasn't gorgeous.

Jenna's gentle voice interrupted my thoughts, "Esperanza, you remind me of myself when I was a struggling writer, full of ideals but lacking direction." I didn't respond. Jenna and I had a unique understanding; sometimes, silence said more than words ever could.

We sipped our coffee as we watched people hurry by, many carrying bags full of secrets and stories waiting to unfold. It seemed like everyone here had something that made them unique — except me. In this city of struggle and ambition, I was content to simply go along with whatever life sent my way.

Jenna broke the quiet with a serious question, "Don't you feel like there's more to life than this?" she gestured towards the bustling street outside before taking another sip from her cup. "I mean, don't get me wrong," she continued, "it's great that you're comfortable and happy, but wouldn't you like to do something more? Something bigger?"

I looked away quietly, still unsure of how to respond. "Maybe I'm just scared," I admitted slowly, "scared that if I try to reach too high, I'll fall even further down."

Jenna smiled as if she understood what it felt like to have big dreams only to have them shattered by fear or reality. "No matter what happens," she whispered, "keep moving forward because life has so much more in store for you than you can imagine." I felt a happiness warm me better than the coffee did. Jenna never failed to remind me that I shouldn't give up on my goals and that I deserved more than the rat race we were in.

Jenna finished the last sip of her coffee, her eyes sparkling excitedly. "Come on," she chirped, extending an arm towards me. "Let's go make some magic!"

As we stepped out into the bustling street, I felt a new sense of energy surging through me, fueled by our conversation, the moments of comfortable silence that spoke volumes.

It became clear that there were endless possibilities; all I had to do was take a step forward and embrace the unknown with open arms. Life could still hold so many surprises waiting for me just around the corner, and I was ready to discover every one of them.

3

Saturday.

The day I always spend at the park, running and feeding the ducks. It became a beloved ritual that helped me unwind and de-stress after a long week at work. But little did I know, today was more than just another routine day at the park.

This morning, I was determined to go running in Central Park, and it was already shaping up to be a great day. After slipping on my shoes and grabbing my water bottle, I set off with the crisp autumn air engulfing me.

Crossing the threshold into the park, I was fascinated by an array of golden-green leaves that had just begun to turn red and orange, an incredible hue against a blue sky. Now and then, a gust of wind swept through, carrying sweet aromas from nearby bakeries — the scent of warm croissants and freshly baked pies lingering in the air.

I spotted one shop with a sign that proudly proclaimed, Purple Apron.

This quaint little bakery on the corner of my street had been there for years. But recently, it had gotten an upgrade — a fresh coat of paint in white and purple! Passersby couldn't help but be drawn in by its colors and the smell of freshly-baked goodies. Inside, the bakery was just as wonderful. The wooden tables and chairs painted white matched the purple and white wallpaper stripes. There were delicious treats everywhere — cupcakes, cookies, muffins — you name it! Every single item was made from scratch by the baker herself, my friend Erin. Her signature cupcake, the classic vanilla topped with fluffy buttercream frosting and drizzled with chocolate ganache for good measure, is my favorite.

Every morning, the same excited customers queued up at the store's main entrance, eager to get their hands on the delicious treats. Little did they know I had my secret way in — a side door. What made it even more enjoyable was being greeted by Erin every time! She always appeared vibrant, cheerful, and perky, with her signature purple apron and hat creating a stunning contrast against the pristine whiteness of the kitchen. Today was no exception.

"Fresh coffee in the pot," Erin told me with a gentle smile. "And look here — there are even cupcakes!" I couldn't believe what my eyes were seeing! These heavenly treats smelled so irresistible that I had to take one, ready for my post-morning run snack. I quickly took a photo and shared it on my Instagram, basking in the delicious aroma that filled the room.

"Are you up for Mavi's yoga lesson next week?" Erin asked. "She met this new guru and insists we join this 'ten-days, no-talking meditation.'"

"Absolutely not! A full ten days of absolute silence?! We can barely manage a few minutes without speaking! I don't understand why she's so captivated by this extreme yoga masterclass. It's not like you'll acquire any supernatural powers by attending!" I stopped when I saw Erin's eyebrows raise higher than usual. I burst into laughter, and soon she joined in.

In spite of our playful teasing, both Erin and I recognized Mavi's unwavering determination this time around. My personal opinion took a backseat to offering support for our friend. However, I remained convinced that this silent meditation concept was absurd, and I had absolutely no intention of joining her! "Anyhoo, gotta go. Catch you later!" I said as I grabbed a chunk of bread, secretly hoping Erin wouldn't try to convince me to take up the challenge of Mavi's yoga master class.

As I began my jog down the winding trails that wore dappled sunlight, something caught my eye — ducks! I ran up to a pond full of adorable ducks playing with each other, quacking happily, and swimming in circles. They looked like they were having so much fun that I wanted to join in, too! After completing my run, I walked over to where the ducks gathered around some grassy patches and fed them small bits of breadcrumbs. They gobbled it all up!

"It is such an amazing day surrounded by nature's beauty, isn't it?"

I looked up to see a charming, sun-kissed blond-haired man. His British accent only added to his undeniable charm and appeal.

"Yeah, it's a gorgeous day!" I responded, tossing a handful of breadcrumbs. "And these adorable ducks just make it even better! You're absolutely right. It truly is an incredible day. Mother Nature has outdone herself today."

"How fortunate of them to meet a beautiful human being who shares food with them. My name is Henry," he said, extending his hand to me.

As I rubbed my right hand through my yoga pants and accepted his grasp, I was at a loss for words. His warm handshake was like an invitation to be friends forever. I nervously nodded before finally being able to say, "I'm Hope."

I couldn't help but chuckle nervously at his uncharacteristic flat tone, "You aren't from here. Your accent, you're not from the same side of the Atlantic as me." Without thinking, I blurted out, "Ah, Henry. Like Prince Harry..." My thoughts immediately darted back to the controversial memoir, and a mischievous twinkle sparkled in my eyes. "Is it true that he applied Elizabeth Arden lotion on his, you know, todger? When his south pole is on the fritz ..." I hesitated, feeling a twinge of embarrassment for posing such a bold question to a handsome stranger. Thankfully, I had managed to use the now-famous slang term for the private area instead of the more explicit word 'penis' that had almost slipped past my lips.

Henry laughed, "I don't know. I haven't read *The Spare*. Have you?" His eyes were laughing, too. He was adorable!

"Part of the occupational hazards," I replied, grinning.

"You get paid to read?" His tone was reminiscent of a young boy asking an innocent question.

"Mostly to read and write," I explained. "Sometimes, I'm asked to review books, develop characters in novels, or even ghostwrite for someone."

"So, you're like a writer for hire. Instead of an assassin for hire — who takes lives, you breathe new life into books," he quipped.

"You know, hearing you describe it that way — better than many of us who write for a living — makes me appreciate my job even more!" I exclaimed.

We both laughed at the playful banter that had unfolded between us.

Then I gazed at Henry. He had the perfect face — a chiseled jaw, blue eyes with specks of grey, and his long blond hair, which just grazed his shoulders, was tied in a perfect ponytail and glowed in the sunlight. His lean and toned body suggested he got in regular cardio, which explained his expensive athletic gear.

He looked back at me and smiled almost shyly before surprising me by asking, "Do you mind if I sit down with you?"

"Of course not! Please do!" I shifted sideways on the stone pavement to make room for him. "So, what's your story? Are you the new 007 assigned to spy on the CIA here?"

He chuckled. "I'm on a school break. I'll be off to med school in a few weeks."

"You seem quite young for medical school," I commented.

"I just turned 24 a couple of weeks ago. Not exactly young for someone who's about to go to a medical internship next year, but certainly too young for whatever British super spy stereotype you have in mind right now," he chuckled.

"How did you know what I was thinking? For the record, James Bond's age when he first started as 007 isn't explicitly mentioned in the original Ian Fleming novels," I challenged him.

"Ha! It's generally believed that Bond was in his early 30s when he began his career as a secret agent with the double-0 status," Henry insisted.

"His age has varied in different adaptations and iterations of the story over the years!" I wasn't about to back down from the conversation.

"Just look at the actors who've played Bond: Sean Connery, George Lazenby, Roger Moore, Timothy Dalton, Pierce Brosnan, and Daniel Craig. They weren't exactly twenty-somethings," he elaborated.

"Hmm... I see your point. Connery is my favorite Bond," I admitted.

"Mine too. He's not at the top of my list, though. Joseph Wiseman as *Dr. No* and Gert Frobe as *Goldfinger* are up there. I always root for the bad guys," he laughed.

"I second that! Loki ranks higher than Thor for me." I was amused by how similar Henry's and my preferences were. "Speaking of Loki, Tom Hiddleston is another Brit in Hollywood. Why do they always cast Brits to play American superheroes — Andrew Garfield and Tom Holland for Spider-Man, Christian Bale for Batman, and Henry Cavill as Superman?"

"Don't forget Daniel Day-Lewis as American President Abraham Lincoln in Steven Spielberg's film *Lincoln*," Henry added.

"Are we running out of hero material in Hollywood?" I asked. Henry laughed as if he was the only one who understood his private joke. When I probed further, he laughed more and shook his head as if telling me, *you'll find out soon.*

It turned out we had more than just duck-feeding and rooting for villains in common. I looked at Henry, his gaze was distant, seemingly lost in the tranquil ripples of the water, and his furrowed brow reflected the deep thoughts occupying his mind. Now and then, he would pause, absently watching a duck snatch a crumb before returning to his introspective state. The serene surroundings seemed to provide the perfect backdrop for Henry's quiet reflections as he sought solace in feeding the ducks.

"So, what brought you here?" I inquired.

"My dad has to work in the US from time to time, so he bought an apartment here," Henry said. "He was supposed to meet the real estate agent himself, but a pressing matter needs his immediate attention, so he sent me instead."

"Your dad sounds cool, Henry. Not all parents trust their children to handle significant financial transactions. My mom sometimes gets involved even in minor details like furniture purchases," I shared.

Henry smiled warmly, "He's the best father a son could ask for." I could sense the admiration in his voice as he spoke about his dad. "His work demands a lot of travel, and he was often absent, but he always made up for it during his breaks." His eyes sparkled, and he chuckled as if recalling a fond memory from the past. "One summer, when I was 12, my dad unexpectedly showed up at my summer camp. It turned into a bit of a disaster, as he unintentionally disrupted the entire afternoon's activities! Women and kids my age flocked to his side for attention."

"Your dad must be quite good-looking!" I blurted out.

"He truly is! If only I had inherited even a fraction of his striking features, I'd likely be faring much better," Henry remarked, casting a playful sideways glance my way, accompanied by a charming grin.

"Oh, please! That face of yours?" I gestured dramatically from his head to his feet, appraising him. "If you didn't inherit a substantial portion of your father's good looks, then he must be some sort of divine being!" I teased lightheartedly.

"If there is a god, my dad might just resemble one," he replied with a smile.

I found myself drawn to Henry; like me, he wasn't afraid to show vulnerability or conceal any flaws. Furthermore, it felt like we'd known each other for a lifetime as we spent the afternoon feeding ducks.

Henry smiled and tapped the edge of the stone pavement where we sat. He looked like he was carefully choosing his words before finally asking: "So, what's the story behind that gorgeous look of yours?" I grinned, raising one eyebrow. He was about to receive the long answer if he only knew it!

"You mean this 'mixed-race' look?" I asked with verve. Henry shifted in his position, suddenly agitated as he quickly replied, an edge crept into his voice. "No, no – I didn't mean it like that! That sounds a bit racist." He ended with a nervous chuckle.

"No worries," I giggled. "I'm used to it anyway." It was so easy to talk about everything with Henry, from his childhood and our career choices to where I'm from. He seemed genuinely interested in my culture.

I picked up a slice of bread, crumbled it into small pieces, and tossed them into the pond as the ducks eagerly wiggled their way to the crumbs. Turning to Henry, I shared that my mother had been a free spirit from New York. "One day, she embarked on a backpacking adventure with some strangers and met my dad in Manila, where he was attending an art exhibit. They fell in love and had me, even though my dad's family threatened to disinherit him if he married my mom."

Henry smiled and remarked, "Wow, that's a classic love story of choosing love over money."

"In the beginning, yes. My dad chose love over his inheritance. Unfortunately, he couldn't handle the hardships he faced in New York. So, one day, he packed his bags and returned to his family in Manila. That was the last time we ever saw him. After that, it was just Mom and me left together," I replied.

"I'm sorry to hear that, Hope," he said, patting my hand. I liked the warmth of his hand. "So, are you still living with your mom?"

"Oh, not anymore," I replied. "Mom married a tax lawyer and lives in California."

We swapped stories about our lives until we fed all the ducks, then he stood up and offered me his hand. I hastily swatted away the crumbs on my yoga pants and straightened up. Then, almost inaudibly, I asked, "So will I see you again?"

He shrugged. "I hope so. I'll be flying out for DC first thing tomorrow and then back to London soon after that." In a lighthearted yet dramatic tone, I smirked and said jokingly: "Same old me, though — Saturdays at duck ponds!"

As we said our goodbyes, Henry promised to keep in touch and that we'd meet again soon and I started the walk back home. However, it dawned on me that neither of us had exchanged mobile numbers or social media handles. I can't believe I had just spent an afternoon sharing my life with a handsome stranger I met in the park and then he vanished into thin air. I walked home feeling low and tried to put Henry out of my mind.

———

The constant buzzing from my iPhone was all too familiar when I arrived home. Jenna was bursting with excitement when I answered the call. "You'll never guess what just happened!" she exclaimed.

My curiosity was piqued. "What is it? Did you get a book deal? Are you going to be on *Oprah*?" I could barely contain my excitement, too, as I pressed my phone between my ear and shoulder while sorting through the mail.

"I received an email from my book agent in Los Angeles. A new producer wants to turn my novel *Back In Time* into a television series!"

"Wow!" I shrieked. Her hard work had paid off. This was a dream we both had and now it's coming true!

Back In Time had been gaining popularity, and I knew all too well just how powerful the story was. It was about an American soldier from the 1920s traveling through time to 2018 and falling in love with a woman he met in Seattle. Jenna's novel was about emotion — love and loss, heartache and joy. It tugged at your heartstrings and made you question how fate works.

My heart skipped a beat when Jenna told me the thrilling news. The novel she had worked so hard on will finally be made into a television series. I listened in rapt attention as she continued her non-stop chatter.

"This is a TV series and usually runs around fifteen episodes. I want you on my screenplay team, Esperanza," she said.

I couldn't help but feel a little overwhelmed as I absorbed the news. I knew the arduous task that lay ahead of me, but the thought of being involved in adapting a book for television was too thrilling to ignore.

While the prospect of collaborating with other writers excited me, I was nervous. Screenplay writing was unfamiliar territory for me, and I've always been more at ease working independently.

But then again, this was a lifetime opportunity that could take my writing career to the next level. Jenna quickly put my doubts to rest as she reassured me that we would work closely together to create something unique that people will remember for years.

"Don't worry, Esperanza. You're a very talented writer, and this will be your chance to showcase your talents on a much larger scale. And don't think for a second you're just a ghostwriter — your name will get out there too! *Back In Time* could be your big break."

Her words filled me with renewed excitement and confidence. She was right — this could be the stepping stone I needed to advance my career. I knew I would have to step out of my comfort zone and work with others, but the potential payoff was more than worth it.

"What if the producers don't go for me, though? I've never done anything for television or film or screenwriting."

"Of course, they'll go for you! That part's already taken care of," she said confidently. "I know you can bring something unique to the table. Plus, I made sure to ask that any work done by my writing team is credited and recognized — that should help preserve the story." Jenna coaxed me out of my anxiety. "You can do this, Esperanza —trust me. All your hard work and dedication are going to pay off!"

Jenna's unwavering confidence in me was genuinely heartening. As she spoke, I felt the weight of my anxiety slowly lifting. The prospect of having my name on a television series was beyond thrilling, and the fact that Jenna had made sure my contributions would be credited and recognized gave me a sense of reassurance that my work wouldn't go unnoticed.

"All right," I said, wholeheartedly embracing the opportunity. "I'm in. Let's do this!"

Jenna let out a chuckle, clearly pleased with my response. "That's the spirit," she said.

"Just give me two weeks to complete my other projects," I said. "That way, I can focus solely on working with you and writing the scripts for the entire season for the next six months."

"Two weeks sounds reasonable to me. Of course, I understand you still have other projects to take care of, so take your time with them. Our writing team must be focused and committed to carefully tackling each episode."

I let out a small sigh of relief. I knew the next six months would be challenging, but I was ready to put in the time and effort required to complete the job.

"I appreciate the opportunity, Jenna," I said gratefully. "I'm excited to see where this goes, and I'll do my best to give this project my all."

With that settled, I hung up the phone, excited and motivated. It would be difficult, but I was determined to make the most of this remarkable opportunity.   There was no turning back now — my journey as a television screenwriter had officially begun. I couldn't wait to delve into the world of television and unleash my creativity on a new platform. Things were looking up for me!

4

Jenna's apartment was transformed into a bustling hub of creativity, buzzing with energy as the writing team tackled each episode with fervor. The temporary Writers Room had everything we needed to work efficiently — from spacious workstations to comfortable seating and plenty of coffee to keep us going.

As lead writer, I knew the onus was on me to ensure the team delivered quality scripts each time. It was a big responsibility, but one that I relished. Then Jenna was appointed as one of the executive producers, underscoring the level of expectation that came with this project. She had to approve every final draft before we printed it for distribution, and I had to ensure that each episode's final draft was of the highest quality.

Since most of us were contract freelancers, we can work off-site with constant collaboration via Zoom or FaceTime. But we could still come together for occasional reviews and revisions in The Writers Room.

The news of a 16-episode season was nothing short of exhilarating. It was apparent that the producers of *Back In Time* had set their sights high and were willing to pull out all the stops to ensure the series was successful.

And, with the production just around the corner, they had already expressed interest in a second season and asked Jenna to start writing book two, a significant sign of faith in her writing skills and story-telling abilities. She was sure the series would succeed, but the interest in season two was still an unexpected surprise.

As Jenna's role in *Back In Time* expanded into TV production, I became the head of screenplay. I would oversee the entire writing process, from concept development to the final draft. With the workload about to increase exponentially, we knew we needed a formidable team to tackle the ambitious 16-episode season.

We began by hiring three staff writers who would focus on developing important story and character elements, bringing their unique perspectives and ideas to the table. Additionally, we brought in three copy editors whose job was to review and correct spelling, grammar, continuity, flow, and punctuation errors. We needed to have these professionals on board to ensure the finished product was of the highest quality.

We also had a set of seasoned episode writers who had experience with television series and could manage at least five episodes for the entire season. These writers would bring their flair and creativity to the story, helping to make the series even more dynamic and engaging.

With our team in place, we set to work, each dedicated to bringing our best efforts to the table. The next few weeks were nothing short of hectic —days and nights spent poring over scripts, editing, and revising until every detail was perfect.

"Robin Strong directing the entire 16-episode season? Incredible!" Exclaimed Patty, a recent NYU graduate who was a fan of our director. She'd been following Robin's medical drama, the highly successful *Heartbeat General: Life in the ER,* since its pilot episode.

Timmy chimed in. He was a Bronx native and aspiring novelist well-acquainted with film production. "His series is six years running —if anyone can do it, he can!"

We all shared Timmy's sentiment as we discussed the news of Robin taking on the project. He was renowned for his intimate understanding of story and character development, making him the ideal director for bringing Jenna's novel to life on screen.

"Wow, the producers certainly don't spare any expense," I said in awe as we discussed Robin's appointment.

"Except with us," Susie chimed in, her young blond features cast a look of skepticism. "We're at the bottom of the food chain, so expect them to squeeze the budget for our team."

"We all understand how hard it can be for smaller departments in filmmaking," I said. "But don't worry, Susie, we've got Jenna on our side." My smile widened as I thought about how much Jenna had done for *Back In Time* and how she could be relied upon to make sure everyone got their fair share no matter what.

I know there'll be more challenges ahead of us, but the important thing here is never to lose sight of the bigger picture. We were all driven by the same passion and dedication, determined to create a television series that will be regarded as a landmark in the industry.

The following week, Jenna confirmed that Robin Strong signed on to direct the whole season. Britanny Ginger will star opposite Richard Collins. Britanny was an acclaimed actress best known for her roles in heavy drama. She had also starred in many other high-profile films. Standing 5 feet 7 inches, she had an athletic figure with striking blond hair and piercing blue eyes. Her talent for capturing a wide range of emotions made her captivating. She fearlessly dives into each role, transforming into that character seamlessly and convincingly every time. With her natural charisma and beauty, there was no denying why she continues to be one of Hollywood's most sought-after stars.

Surprisingly, they got a British actor to play the male lead, who happened to be an American hero in the story. I remembered my conversation with Henry at the park when I found out who our lead actor was. Richard Collins was a very handsome British man with a chiseled jawline, blue-grey eyes, and dark hair combined to create a beautiful visage. He is physically fit and possessed a charm that draws people in. He was known for his captivating performances and devilish charm, earning him international recognition and acclaim. His powerful screen presence made him the perfect casting choice for any role requiring a character with intelligence, wit, charisma, and a bit of an edge. Whether playing a dashing hero or a mysterious antihero, he brought warmth and humanity to every character he plays.

Jenna had a particular vision for her story, but we still wanted to ensure it was entertaining enough for anyone who hadn't read her book. We were FaceTiming late into the night and emailing each other back and forth as we worked out our ideas. Our hard work paid off, though, as eventually, in a month, we managed to create a fantastic script that both adhered to Jenna's original vision and was entertaining for viewers of all backgrounds!

I couldn't have been any prouder of our team's efforts. The first drafts of our scripts had already exceeded all expectations — they were stunning, captivating works of art that genuinely embodied Jenna's novel in remarkable ways.

We were determined not to waste time, which meant strictly working on the settled deadlines. We spent countless hours discussing each scene, how it would play out on the screen, and how it fits within the storyline.

The following six weeks were intense as we finalized all the script details. The production management team made sure no stone was left unturned — they picked out costume designers, chose perfect locations, and researched possible actors to play each part. We prepared everything from planning to identifying and closing loopholes that might jeopardize the project.

Our team also had to ensure our story stayed true to the original book but with plenty of unexpected twists and turns. We brainstormed for hours about potential plot points and ideas for new scenes, ensuring that *Back In Time* would be a show like no other! To get there, we researched other similar shows and how they fared in reviews, ratings, and reception — comparing reviews and ratings of other performances to determine what elements made them stand out or fall short. We also looked into the public opinion of each show to gain even more insight and craft our script accordingly. With all this data finally at hand, we worked hard to hone in on the elements that would make our series unique.

After multiple drafts and late nights discussing potential edits or changes, the scripts for the first three episodes were complete! Now it's time for us to bring this brilliant vision alive on-screen.

5

Winter, New York City

It's finally happening!

The first week of December marked the beginning of an exciting new journey — the cast and production team will be coming together for the kick-off meeting at Rockefeller Plaza's Convene. We've all worked hard to ensure every detail, from scriptwriting to casting, was polished. It will be an epic moment for everyone involved, and we can't wait to see what magic will come out of it!

Jenna and I arrived at the party together. I had put in a little extra effort to look good, knowing that walking beside the always-fashionable Jenna had its downsides. I chose a stylish grey wool coat paired with black fitted pants and sleek black ankle boots. To complete the ensemble, I added a soft white cashmere scarf, a bold red clutch, and a classic silver watch that had been my mother's.

"You're looking sharp tonight," Jenna complimented me, offering a smile.

"Well, I don't want to be mistaken for your chaperone," I joked, enjoying the light-hearted banter. We both laughed, feeling the excitement of the night ahead.

Jenna and I separated at the party as she will have to mingle with the top executives and the stars. I settled in one corner of the bar, then saw Timmy across the room waving me to come over. I quickly gathered my drink and slid off the bar stool. In my haste, I stumbled over my feet and spilled my drink all over a man's immaculate white shirt.

Horrified, I apologized profusely, "Oh, my God! I'm so sorry!" I put down my drink, gathered tissue from the bar, and started wiping the liquid off the man's shirt.

I felt even more embarrassed as the man with his British accent started to reassure me. "Relax, it's not the end of the world yet." I looked up and saw Richard Collins! The leading man of our show! And I spilled my drink on him! How can I be so clumsy? How can a man be so beautiful? I was so embarrassed and wanted the earth to swallow me.

"I'm sorry. It's entirely my fault. I can reimburse you for the shirt," I blurted out, mortified. But as soon as the words left my mouth, I felt anxious. How could I replace such an expensive tailored shirt on my meager writing salary?

He waved his hand dismissively, offering a reassuring smile. "No need to worry about it, don't sweat the small stuff. I always carry an extra shirt in the car," he said. I watched him walk away, admiring how dashing he still looked despite the accident!

As soon as Richard was out of sight, Timmy and the gang gathered around me with suppressed smiles. I let out a sigh and managed a weak smile. "Let it go, guys," I said, trying to brush off the embarrassing incident.

But they weren't about to let it go so easily. They burst into hysterical laughter. I rolled my eyes but couldn't help but feel a little amused myself.

"So much for making a good first impression," I muttered.

Patty said, "Well, he is quite a looker, you have to admit," causing the group to laugh once again.

I couldn't help but blush a little at her comment, feeling embarrassed and appreciative of her honesty. But as the laughter gradually died, I realized that the day was one to remember despite the initial hiccup.

I wasn't particularly interested in the personal lives of Hollywood's who's who. While I did read some actors' and actresses' professional profiles, their private lives never caught my attention. When Richard Collins' name appeared on the casting list, I barely glanced at his dossier, even though most of the women on the production team had already memorized every detail about him. Perhaps it was because he seemed too old for my taste.

However, meeting him in person tonight changed my perspective. As the crowd gathered around the open bar, I discreetly slipped away, pulled out my phone, and quickly typed "Richard Collins" into the search bar.

A string of articles and reviews popped up, all singing the actor's praises. At 43 years old, he was considered a veteran in Europe and Hollywood, with a long list of films and TV shows under his belt. But what struck me the most was the overwhelming consensus that he had a certain charm and wit about him, as though he was always in on some clever joke that nobody else knew the punchline to.

I read that his British accent only added to his appeal, and women everywhere swooned when they heard him speak. In an industry that often valued youth and looks over talent, Richard Collins seemed one of the few who had managed to age like a fine wine, only growing more desirable with time.

Richard Collins began his career with minor roles in films, but it wasn't long before he made a name for himself as one of Britain's most sought-after stars. With every new project, Richard seemed to push the boundaries, taking on daring and challenging roles that showcased his versatility as an actor.

Whether it was an action film or a romantic comedy, Richard never shied away from trying something new. He brought a unique quality to every character he played, infusing his performances with charm, wit, and a magnetic screen presence.

As his career continued to skyrocket, Richard became a household name worldwide. Fans and critics alike clamored to see what new roles he would take on, eager to catch another glimpse into his life as an actor. And as I looked around the bustling room of Hollywood insiders, I realized that I was just one of many captivated by his talent and unique charm.

Despite his fame and success, Richard remained something of an enigma. He had steadfastly refused to join social media or share details about his personal life with the public. There were a handful of articles about his divorce fifteen years ago, but beyond that, his private life remained largely hidden from the world.

Yet, Richard was known in the film industry for being personable and professional. Every cast member and crew he worked with had nothing but kind words to say about him. He was a consummate professional, always well-prepared and willing to collaborate with others to achieve the best possible outcome for a film or show.

It seemed that Richard preferred to let his work speak for itself, to let the characters he played and the stories he told to be his legacy. And while I couldn't help but feel curious about the man behind the actor, I respected his desire for privacy and admired him all the more for his dedication to his craft.

Robin introduced the cast as I closed my phone and returned to the party. I admired Richard, now   changed into a new shirt. I was impressed by his sharp sense of style. He looked in my direction and gave me a playful wink as if to say, *'No harm done.'*

Despite feeling embarrassed, I couldn't help but appreciate his easygoing nature and ability to handle any situation gracefully. He exuded confidence and charm that only made him all the more intriguing to me.

I won't deny it. I was a little starstruck. As the night went on, I found myself stealing glances in his direction, wondering if I would have the nerve to talk with him. I suddenly remembered that I had my hands all over his chest the last time we talked. The thought made my heart race and my palms sweat; he was a famous actor, and I was just a writer.

―――

In Jenna's book, *Back in Time*, the story happened in Seattle, but the producers and the director agreed to change the location to New York. It was an economic decision since most of the cast and crew lived in the city.

As the shoot date drew near, the construction team began working tirelessly to build up the set piece by piece. Their days were long and filled with backbreaking work, but you'd never know; they were cheerful and dedicated, always willing to lend a hand or share a joke. Each person on the team had their specialty, whether it was painting, carpentry, or electrical work, and they worked in perfect harmony to bring the set to life.

Jenna and I went to an ocular visit to orient ourselves in filmmaking and production. The set was located in a warehouse in SoHo. It was more than 100,000 square feet bustling with activity.

"I can't believe we're actually doing this, Jenna!" I exclaimed with excitement.

"I know! I never imagined this would happen, not in a million years," she confessed, equally thrilled.

As we toured the set, the space was a whirlwind of activity, with the hammering and buzzing of power tools filling the air. Ladders and scaffolding were scattered throughout, and sawdust and paint chips mingled on the floor. But amidst the chaos, there was an unmistakable sense of purpose and pride in the team's work. They meticulously measured and re-measured each piece, making sure everything was in its proper place, and every detail was perfect.

"This is fantastic! The set is beginning to take shape!" I marveled at the extraordinary skills of the construction team.

"I can imagine how breathtaking these will look on camera, every bit as intricate and detailed as I envisioned it would be!" Jenna exclaimed as she gracefully danced across the wooden floor.

As production hurtled forward, we were pleasantly surprised at how the production team thoughtfully built offices for costume designers and writers, guaranteeing that every department had sufficient area and materials to operate effectively. Each office was equipped with advanced technology specifically tailored to foster innovation and teamwork.

Trailer parks for the actors were also set up, furnished with everything the cast needed for a comfortable stay. The designs for each trailer reflected the personality of its resident, giving the space a homey and personalized feel.

The care that went into creating these spaces was evident in every corner, from the soft lighting and comfortable seating to the carefully chosen artwork and decor. It was clear that the production team wanted to ensure everyone involved in the project had the best possible experience, and their efforts did not go unnoticed.

"I'm in love with Hollywood now!" I exclaimed, and Jenna hooked her arm around mine as we both danced with joy, realizing that our dreams were finally coming to life.

———

Today was table reading, also known as a read-through, a pre-production requirement for actors reading a script or screenplay in film or television.

I put in extra effort to make a good impression. It felt similar to dressing up carefully for the first day of school, just in case you encountered someone intriguing. Although I wasn't particularly fond of winter, it did provide me with an opportunity to wear my favorite knee boots. My fitted black pants were neatly tucked into my boots, accentuating my long legs. I chose to wear my finest Lauren white turtleneck top and allowed my hair to cascade freely under a vibrant red beanie.

The atmosphere was buzzing with festivity, as everyone eagerly anticipated working on this new television series. When Richard entered the room and removed his winter jacket, he revealed a navy blue knitted sweater and dark pants that perfectly complemented his physique. He flashed a smile while whispering something to Robin, prompting laughter from both men. To avoid drawing attention to myself, I discreetly hid behind Timmy and switched to my invisible mode. The last thing I wanted was to be thrust into the spotlight.

As the actors took their seats for the script reading, the air was filled with excitement and anticipation. The room buzzed with chatter as they caught up with each other and eagerly flipped through their scripts, ready to delve into the story.

The space was warm and cozy, with low lighting and plush chairs. The scent of fresh coffee and pastries gave the room a welcoming and intimate feel. A table at the front of the room was stacked high with snacks and beverages, and there was a sense of camaraderie as people mingled and shared stories.

"Alright, let's take a look at the script and see how it's shaping up," said Richard, which made everyone in the room chuckle.

Then Timmy exclaimed, "Oh my goodness! We've dedicated our lives to this project, and even had to give up sex to complete it." This statement was met with an even louder round of applause from the crowd.

As the script reading began, the actors settled into their roles, their voices rising and falling with the rhythm of the words. I can feel the magic in the room as the story comes to life. Each character leaped off the page and into our minds. The room was calm and focused, with everyone fully engrossed in the unfolding drama.

As Richard began to read aloud his part, the room fell silent, all eyes turning to him expectantly. To my surprise, his customary British accent was nowhere to be heard. Instead, he spoke in a flawless American accent, his voice clear and sure. At first, I thought it was a joke, a playful nod to the character he was playing. But as he continued to read, I realized that his accent was entirely genuine, a testament to his talent as an actor and his dedication to the craft.

Jenna whispered to me, "He's really, really good!"

I replied, "I couldn't agree more. He's fully immersed in his role, and his British accent is nowhere to be heard. I'm blown away."

His authenticity and mastery of the character he was portraying made the scene even more engrossing, leaving all of us in awe. It was clear that Richard had put an immense amount of effort into perfecting his role. It was fascinating to watch him inhabit his character so thoroughly and see how he seamlessly shifted between accents and personas. And though it was a small detail, it added an extra layer of depth and nuance to the character, making it all the more intriguing and memorable.

Even though I was on the writing team, I found myself drawn into the story's world, eager to see where it would go next and marveling at the skill and talent of the actors bringing it to life. And though I couldn't help but feel a little starstruck in Richard's presence, I also felt a newfound respect and admiration for the man behind the actor, who was serious about his craft and dedicated to bringing his characters to life in new and exciting ways.

Occasionally, there were breaks for laughter or discussion as people shared their thoughts on the story or asked questions about the characters. You could feel the festive atmosphere of a group of people who had come together to share the magic of storytelling. It was clear that everyone here was giving their all to make the project successful.

———

The production team had been in New York City for almost a week now, and they were beginning to feel the effects of winter. They'd arrived with their cameras, lights, and costumes expecting a glimpse of clear skies but instead dealt with snow and icy temperatures.

The first filming day didn't exactly go as planned — the sun was nowhere to be found. Every day became a fight against the elements, with the team pushing hard to set up shots and capture beautiful visuals despite the challenging weather conditions.

Robin called for an emergency meeting to address production issues and delays caused by the unpredictable weather. I attended the meeting as the writers' representative, joining a small group that consisted mostly of the filming team. To my surprise, Richard was there with Robin.

Paul, the gaffer responsible for designing and executing the lighting plan, explained the challenges they faced in producing quality scenes due to the constant cloud cover. "It's difficult to convey a cheerful atmosphere when everything around us is dreary and gray. And we're dealing with shorter daylight hours," he said.

"Can we shoot at night instead?" Richard suggested, capturing everyone's attention. "If the problem is creating a festive mood, we can utilize the holiday lights and decorations already in place. Street lamps and car headlights illuminate New York City."

"That's one of the options we wanted to discuss today. Thanks for pointing it out, Richard," Paul replied.

"Where's Olivia? We need to know the logistics of filming at night," Robin asked as he scanned the room.

"Right here!" A petite blond with thick glasses raised her hand. Olivia and her team were responsible for finding and securing suitable locations for filming and handling paperwork. "We'll obtain the necessary permits and coordinate logistics. We just need to add extra security and safety measures since people from all over the world are here to celebrate Christmas, especially New Year in NYC."

Robin gave his approval, "No problem, just get it done. Anyone from the scriptwriting team here?"

I raised my hand and said, "We'll revise the script, Robin, to accommodate the new setting." As I looked in Robin's direction, I couldn't help but unintentionally lock eyes with Richard, who was sitting beside him. He returned my gaze as if recalling our previous encounter.

That was my only contribution to the meeting. The remainder of the discussion focused on the production team's challenges, such as dealing with wind and snowfall while capturing breathtaking images without interruption. The meeting soon concluded, and Richard made a hasty exit. After the unfortunate disaster of our initial encounter, he seemed to have forgotten about me, which was fine. This was work, and that's how it should be.

As the weeks went on and the film began to take shape, it was evident that the care and attention put into creating a comfortable and functional working environment had paid off. The cast and crew were still as energetic and motivated as ever, their collective talent radiating in every film frame. Ultimately, this success resulted from the dedication and hard work of everyone involved: from the production team to the actors to even behind-the-scenes crew members who worked tirelessly to bring each moment of the project to life.

Thankfully, too, the acting team proved to be heaven-sent. Although I had braced myself for any difficult actors that may have been present, I was delighted to find them being supportive of one another and maintaining an amicable relationship with the production team. We all indulged in conversations about scenes on lunch or coffee breaks, building strong relationships between us — even Brittany, who had recently tied the knot with a Hollywood director. Despite being a high profile actress, she was down to earth and easy to work with.

"Hope, dear," Brittany said as she approached me. "Can we rework a couple of dialogues? I feel a tiny bit uncomfortable with some words."

I admired her willingness to work with me to make sure each line felt natural. "Sure thing," I replied. "Let me work on that, and I'll get back to you."

I glanced at Richard, who was busy reading the script. His eyes held a sadness as they scanned over each line of dialogue, and I couldn't help but notice his chiseled jawline and stunning cheekbones. I quickly reprimanded myself for letting my thoughts wander — there was no way someone like me could ever catch his eye and be on his level!

I walked over to Patty and Timmy and told them that Brittany had a few script changes. But they hardly heard me. They were observing Richard from a distance, noticing his aloofness. "He seemed so distant. While everyone else was busy chatting away or joking around, he was just focused on the script, going through line after line of dialogue," Patty said.

"Oh yeah, whenever someone asked him a question, he would answer as politely as possible, but just that," Timmy added, snapping his fingers to emphasize his point.

"Hey guys, leave him alone. Let's be considerate of his privacy. We should be making him feel at ease in our company, even if it means occasionally refraining from speaking around him," I reminded them, hoping to encourage sensitivity towards Richard's situation.

I took a deep breath, composed myself, and approached Richard. "Hello, do you need any help with the script? I'm available," I offered and winced at what I said. *I'm available.*

He glanced at me and grinned, "Ah, you must be the wonder girl in the script department."

"There are eight of us working 'round the clock," I said. I was wondering if he remembered me as the one who ruined his shirt.

Out of nowhere, Robin called him. Richard seemed to hesitate, but ultimately decided to flash me a grin, roll up his script, and make his way over to Robin.

It was soon obvious to the crew that Richard was holding something back. We didn't really understand why he was so reserved. Maybe he was shy or aloof? Many actors and actresses are like that. We didn't try to make him open up either; instead, we kept our distance and tried our best to make sure he felt comfortable with us. Even Brittany wasn't keen on meeting him around the set. However, she quickly warmed up to him once she saw his professionalism and dedication to his craft.

When the cameras started rolling, Richard became a different person whose personality matched perfectly with the character he was portraying! No matter what his role, Richard always managed to bring something new and unique to every scene — something irreplaceable. He may have been quiet outside of shooting hours, but when the cameras started rolling, he turned on his charm and it was like nothing else! It's no wonder women worldwide were going crazy for Richard — even I was taken aback by his natural talent and charisma. But outside of filming, he remained pretty private and reserved.

Meanwhile, I set to work on revising the script with new dialogues. An entirely new appreciation for the characters and their story flourished in me as I started to comprehend them more deeply. Every day on set was filled with joy and zeal — laughing at one another's jokes during shooting breaks, discussing personal anecdotes, and helping each other out when needed. The friendly atmosphere between us was unmistakable, resulting in solid bonds that made working much easier.

———

One night, while I was at Erin's bakery, munching on a vanilla cupcake while she closed up shop, she and I searched for Richard on the internet. "This guy of yours is too mysterious. Let's see if he has some dirt on him," Erin said.

"He's not my guy," I mumbled.

Several articles about his divorce from his ex-wife, a top model in Britain, and their son started appearing on the search engine. But none of the speculations have been confirmed from his side. Even more surprising was that there were no longer any reports about his love life after his marriage. There was occasional gossip of his alleged flings with different women who were said to have shared a passionate relationship with him, but there was no evidence, not even a paparazzi photo to prove he was with any woman.

"One report here said his ex-wife had wanted to move on with her life and pursue other goals. After much deliberation, they decided to get divorced despite having a son together who was said to be attending boarding school at the time," Erin was reading one of the tabloid pieces on her phone. The bakery was already closed, with just the two of us in the kitchen.

"Erin, he was married to a goddess!" I exclaimed, and Erin moved behind me to see what was on my screen.

Emilia Grant was acclaimed to be among the most beautiful women in the world, with perfect blond hair and deep blue eyes. Her body was shapely, with not an ounce of fat or any disproportioned features. She had the kind of beauty you don't see every day.

"Oh wow, I can only imagine!" Erin exclaimed. "Both of them together must have been a beautiful sight."

"She was always at some of the biggest fashion shows around Europe, which gave her a lot of exposure," I read aloud. "On top of that, she has a huge following on social media and is among the favorites of company endorsements and other brand campaigns."

"Here's one from a UK tabloid. It said Richard was attracted to Emilia for her beauty, fashion industry experience, and media presence. He knew she would be the perfect companion and a great asset to his career. Her cachet in the modeling world made Richard feel important and proud, and it was one of the things that drew him to her," Erin read a portion of the article on her phone.

One of the tabloid magazines revealed that Richard Collins grew up in London. He came from an affluent family. After university, he began working as a model and eventually met Emilia Grant at a fashion show. Despite being young, the two married when Emilia accidentally became pregnant. Ultimately, the marriage did not last and ended in divorce when their son was only eight. With his newfound freedom, Richard took on acting and quickly secured roles in period films where he played supporting characters. Eventually, he got a big break with a well-known drama which opened doors for him to audition for a wider variety of roles. He soon succeeded in multiple genres, becoming one of the most bankable actors in British and Hollywood films.

Erin and I continued to read articles about Richard. We read critics' reviews on his work and how he remained dedicated and focused on whichever role he took up — making it come alive with intense passion and emotion. Many articles noted that he was very private and guarded in his personal life, but when it came to acting, Richard never held back.

Suddenly, the kitchen's private door opened. It was Mavi, our yoga instructor from the 'hood. The three of us bonded over the years and often camped in Erin's kitchen on Saturday nights when the bakery was closed.

"What did I miss?" She asked while she handed us new pampering kits from her yoga studio. Tonight, it's a basket of foot lotion and massagers.

"She was stalking Richard Collins," Erin said while opening the peppermint foot lotion.

"Oh, my God!" Mavi squealed. "He is one of the most gorgeous Brits on the entire planet!"

Erin and I looked at each other. Mavi was the type of person who was not into Hollywood. She was a classicist, yet, she talked as if she already belonged to Richard's groupies or social media armies. We all started to laugh. Mavi usually wasn't one to get caught up in celebrity gossip, but even she couldn't deny the existence of Richard Collins. This man seemed to be everywhere — on TV, in magazines, and he had millions of fans hanging on his every word — the very few he utters anyway.

"So what's with Richard Collins?" Mavi asked.

Erin looked at me and asked? "You didn't tell her yet?"

"Tell me what?"

"Hope conveniently forgot to tell us that she is now writing scripts for a new TV series."

Mavi couldn't believe it. "Seriously?! This is your break, a big one at that! It seemed like Richard Collins wasn't the only one in the room attracted to something special! I am so happy that someone recognized your talent. You are about to take the world by storm, my dear friend."

Between Mavi and Erin, Mavi was the optimistic one. Often, I wanted to kill her, because she always saw the world full of unicorns and it got really annoying. Erin was more like me. We looked at it as a prelude to a disaster every time we received good news. But tonight, I'm glad for my friends' presence. We cheered as they gave me a congratulatory hug.

"So, which show are you working on?" Mavi asked.

"It's Jenna Huey's *Back In Time*,'" I replied. "The main character is Richard Collins — he plays opposite Britanny Ginger."

Mavi's eyes widened with surprise. "Jenna Huey's latest book? Wow, that's amazing!'

I nodded, my heart pounding with excitement, too. "Yes! And I'm writing the script for the entire first season with other writers. Can you believe it?"

Mavi beamed at me proudly. "Of course I can! You have an immense writing talent, and this is your chance to show it off!" She paused, her expression thoughtful. "What will Brittany Ginger be playing in the series?"

I smiled. "She's going to play Richard Collins' love interest." I could hardly contain my anticipation as I continued. "It's been a long time coming, but finally, the stars have aligned, and my writing career is taking off! ."

"Tell Mavi how you first met Richard Collins," Erin said with a cheeky grin.

"What happened?" asked Mavi.

"She dumped a rum cola on Richard's shirt!" Erin laughed so hard that Mavi and I soon joined in, too. "The worst part was that she volunteered to pay for his shirt, not knowing it was probably Dior!" That just made the whole situation even funnier.

"By the way, whatever happened to that handsome guy you met at the park, Harkin?" Mavi inquired.

"Oh, you mean Henry!" I replied with a somber expression, recounting the unfortunate circumstance where we parted ways without exchanging numbers. "We talked for hours, and yet we didn't exchange contact information."

"You really are a walking disaster when it comes to dating and finding a boyfriend, Hope!" Erin teased.

"I know! At this rate, I might end up single forever," I lamented.

"Hmm... my intuition tells me that you two will cross paths again soon," Mavi predicted.

"Let's see if our resident human magic crystal ball is right," Erin joked, prompting laughter from all of us as we playfully bantered with our lighthearted puns.

We talked about the show for a while longer, and it was clear that both of my friends were just as excited as I was. Eventually, we decided to call it a day and headed back home.

Walking on a cold winter night, I couldn't help but think of everything that had happened in the last few months. It felt so surreal to me — writing scripts for a TV series and having Richard Collins and Brittany

Ginger star in it! The dream was becoming a reality at last!

Back at home, I still had plenty of energy left. I switched on the smart TV and decided to watch a movie on Netflix. To my surprise, Richard was starring in a romantic comedy! Watching him on the big screen made me wonder what it would be like with him — is he a good lover? I quickly dismissed the thought. I was too plain and too young for him, or he was too old for me. So I let myself drift away in front of the screen while his character romanced some other lucky lady on-screen. That kept me going until the credits rolled at the end of that film.

Then as I started to fall asleep with Salem cuddled beside me, I whispered, "Don't worry, and he's way too far. He's just as good as a good night's dream." Salem just purred, agreeing with me.

6

The weather is still uncooperative the following week. A cold winter in New York, a few days after Christmas, covered the city in snow. The air had a chill that seeped through the bone. Even walking through Central Park was a challenge, with icy winds blowing against my face and snow crunching beneath my feet.

The holiday spirit, however, was alive and well. Strings of fairy lights adorned all the lamp posts, and I could see figures bundled up in their coats, heading toward Times Square for one last shopping spree before New Year's Eve arrived.

Filming during this season can be difficult as tourists flock to the city for the holidays. With the streets overflowing with people and extra security measures in place, finding a quiet spot to get some footage can be tricky. The production crew was also affected by the weather as camera equipment had to constantly be heated up or dried off from melting snow, and lights set up outdoors quickly became obscured by falling snowflakes or decreasing daylight.

Eventually, efforts paid off. What started as an unenviable task ended up being some of the most striking footage — scenes lit solely by lamp posts providing a visual feast that will leave audiences mesmerized when *Back in Time* is finally released months from now. In retrospect, it all seems like such a small sacrifice for something so grand. After all, who can put a price on art?

Watching daily shoots and observing what went on behind the scenes was a definite perk for us writers! We saw firsthand how our words were being brought to life onscreen. Today, we were filming a series of close-up scenes set in the 1920s, where Captain Jack, portrayed by Richard, falls in love with a young woman named Lilly, played by Brittany. I was thoroughly impressed by how Robin and the production team executed the scene without going to an actual location. The story was set against a backdrop of the sun dipping below the horizon, casting a warm golden glow over a picturesque meadow. There, beneath the shelter of an ancient oak tree, the two lovers would find themselves alone.

Richard and Brittany, dressed in their period costumes as Jack and Lilly, delivered their lines with conviction while standing before a green screen. This setup would later undergo extensive post-production work to add the appropriate background and atmosphere to the scene. I watched, captivated, as the entire sequence came to life before my eyes.

Jack, gazed deeply into Lilly's eyes, his own brimming with tender vulnerability. "Lilly," he began, "every moment I spend with you, my heart feels like it's going to burst with happiness. I've never felt this way about anyone before."

Lilly's cheeks flushed a delicate shade of pink as she shyly met his gaze. "Jack, I have to confess something, too. From the moment we first met, I knew there was something special between us. My heart races whenever I'm near you, and I can't help but lose myself in your eyes."

Jack took a step closer, gently taking her hands in his. "Lilly, I've been holding back these feelings for so long, but I can't keep them inside any longer. I love you. I love how you laugh, how your eyes light up when you're excited, and the kindness radiating from your soul."

Tears welled up in Lilly's eyes as she whispered, "Oh, Jack... I love you, too. Your strength, passion, and unwavering determination inspire me daily. You make me feel alive, and I can't imagine my life without you."

Their faces inched closer, their breaths mingling, Richard cradled Brittany's face in his hands. In that magical moment, their lips met in a tender, passionate kiss, sealing their love for one another under the supposed enchanting twilight sky.

Richard and Brittany were perfect for their parts. You could tell they have a natural chemistry that enhanced each scene with just a few changes in dialogue or improvisation.

It was inspiring to witness their ability to make something mundane into something extraordinary simply because of their talent and dedication. Seeing them create such memorable moments made us realize how important it is for every production team to have passionate people on board who are willing to go the extra mile for the project.

———

We had just finished one last discussion about the script when Robin announced that he'd like to treat everyone at the nearest pub as a reward for all our hard work. The entire cast and crew erupted into cheers — clearly, they were as excited by this idea as I was! We quickly wrapped up everything on set before heading off for some well-deserved refreshments.

Thank you, Universe, that I dressed up nicely today! My skinny jeans tucked perfectly inside my black knee boots. I bought this yellow turtle neck sweater that hugs my body perfectly last Sunday. Then I grabbed my oversized white-and-black checkered coat.

It was Tuesday and the pub was practically deserted save for us. They closed the pub so we can have more privacy and have an open bar. As soon as we arrived at the pub, drinks started flowing freely — although not quite as freely among some members of the crew who seemed rather strict regarding how much each person could have. They grumbled, "It's still a work day tomorrow!" It didn't matter; everyone had a great time catching up after such an intense few weeks of filming together. After several rounds of drinks, the stories began.

I watched on with delight from one of the bar stools, in awe at how special it felt being part of something so unique and exciting —no wonder people love Hollywood after experiencing days like these! I ordered a shot of tequila. "How's my new screenplay head," asked Jenna as she sat on an empty stool beside me. We haven't had the chance to talk face-to-face in the past few weeks.

"I'm beginning to enjoy it," I replied with my third shot.

"Have you dated someone from the crew?"

"I thought we agreed that we'll find a young startup dude from Silicon Valley?"

Before Jenna could start her argument with me, Robin came over and engaged her in some usual business discussion, and I was left alone, which I preferred. I was in no mood to talk. I just wanted a drink and observe the people around me.

Then someone made an unexpected suggestion — why don't we sing or play some tunes on the piano? The next thing I knew, the crowd broke into wild cheers. One guy from props and costumes took the microphone and made a boxing match-like announcement, "Ladies and gentlemen, let's give our hands...and our genitals to Hope Williams!" The crowd erupted with an even wilder cheer. Making an excuse was too late, so I decided to join in on the fun, too.

With alcohol coursing through my veins like firewater — not something I usually indulge in — I nervously made my way up to the stage, eyes darting around as if searching for escape routes in case things went wrong. I waved at Jenna, who couldn't hide her amusement and perhaps wondered what had happened to her super-shy friend. I sat behind the keys and began playing Sara Bareilles' "Manhattan."

I felt transported to another place as I lost myself in the song. The melody carried me away, and I became lost in its beautiful, haunting notes. But as I closed my eyes and let the music envelop me completely, I suddenly glanced up and saw Richard sitting directly across from me at another table.

Our gazes locked, and my heart skipped a beat. Richard was the last person I expected to see here, and I was surprised by how deeply his presence affected me. For a moment, I forgot all about the song and just stared at him, unable to look away.

And then, to my surprise, he didn't look away either. Our gazes remained locked, and I could feel a million different things racing through my mind. I'm shocked, confused, and intrigued all at once. What was he doing here? And why was he staring at me like that?

Despite my confusion, I continued to sing even more passionately than before. The lyrics spilled out of me as if the song was the only way I can convey everything I'm feeling. As I sang, I became acutely aware of the intensity of the moment — the charged energy between us, the way his eyes seemed to pierce through me, the way my heart was beating so hard in my chest.

When it was time for my final chorus, the crowd sang along while clapping enthusiastically in approval — something which would have never happened in my lifetime. Every moment spent practicing alone in my bedroom from a long-forgotten past had finally paid off. Sara Bareilles' "Manhattan" may have been written years ago, but this night it breathed new life...and into mine.

The sight of Richard staring back at me from across the room intensified the whirlwind of emotions already brewing inside my chest. The butterflies in my stomach took flight once more, and I can feel my cheeks flushed with heat.

But then, to my surprise, Richard gestured for me to join him at his table, a mischievous smirk playing on his lips. For a second, I hesitated, unsure if I was ready for whatever was about to happen. But something in his expression convinced me to take the risk. With a flutter in my heart, I walked towards him, ignoring the hustle and bustle of the other actors and production crew members milling about.

As I reached the table, I sat across from him, and I can't help but notice how confident and at ease he seemed.

"I think you owe me a new shirt," he said, and my heart sank. Of course, he remembered that embarrassing night when I spilled my drink all over him in a crowded bar. I felt a flush rise as memories of that disastrous encounter flooded my mind.

"But sitting with me tonight is a better compensation, I guess," he continued with a hint of a smile on his lips. I looked up at him, unsure if he was joking or serious, but the playful glint in his eyes gave me all the answers I needed.

Richard poured a glass of wine. One for him and one for me. We clinked glasses in a silent toast. The sound echoed in the moment's stillness, filling the space between us with anticipation.

All at once, I realized just how surreal this moment was. A few minutes ago, I got lost in my singing, and now I was here, sitting across from Richard, sharing a drink with him. It felt exhilarating and terrifying, like I was on the edge of a cliff, about to jump into the unknown.

"I didn't know writers could sing and play instruments beautifully," Richard remarked, surprise in his voice.

"Actors aren't the only ones who are good on stage," I replied with a smile, feeling a sense of pride as I remembered my performance earlier that night.

"Fair point," Richard said, taking a sip of his wine and glancing at me expectantly. I fumbled with my wine glass, unsure what to say or do. I wasn't much of a wine drinker, but I wanted to appear sophisticated and mature in front of Richard.

I took a deep breath and a big gulp of the wine, hoping it wouldn't make me look like a fool. Richard chuckled, clearly amused by my eagerness.

"How'd you like it?" he asked, and I could feel my cheeks turning red.

"Singing?"

"No, I mean the wine. And the singing, too." Richard can't hide his amusement from me.

I took a second sip and savored the taste. It wasn't as bad as I thought, but I was still out of my element. Richard could sense my discomfort and flashed me a mischievous smile, almost as if he was challenging me.

"It's all right," I said hesitantly, not wanting to admit that I wasn't exactly an experienced wine drinker.

He laughed heartily. "This is 1994 Bordeaux — it's supposed to impress you!' He leaned back in his chair as if daring me to disagree.

I blushed and looked at the wine to hide my burning face before responding. "Are you saying this wine tastes better than other wines?"

Richard nodded, took a sip from his glass, and explained, "1994 Bordeaux wine has a bold yet fruity flavor. On the nose are cassis and blackberry notes with hints of leather and tobacco. On the palate, it is full-bodied and smooth with a long finish that leaves notes of dark chocolate on the tongue."

Richard leaned forward as we sipped our wine and began to regale me with stories about different vintages and food pairings. I listened intently, impressed by his knowledge and experience in wine.

"Food and wine pairing is an art form. You must consider it carefully to achieve the best flavor combinations," he explained. "It's about selecting wines that bring out the subtle nuances of certain dishes or finding dishes that can enhance a particular wine's flavor profile. Certain regions and grape varieties have established through time classic pairings known as 'perfect matches' ——for example, Cabernet Sauvignon with steak or Chenin Blanc with oysters."

"I don't like oysters," I admitted, feeling embarrassed. "Everybody seems to like them, but it's an overpriced shellfish for me."

Richard chuckled at my confession and asked, "Have you tried it with the right wine?"

I shook my head, and I found eating oysters with wine absurd. "I don't think any wine could make me like oysters," I laughed.

Richard smiled, seeming to enjoy our banter. "Well, you never know until you try," he said, lifting his glass in a silent toast. "Who knows, maybe I'll find a wine that will change your mind."

"I still don't think I'll like it," I said.

He smiled reassuringly and said, "Trust me, it will be worth it." Richard recommended a dry and crisp Sauvignon Blanc to bring out the subtle flavors of the oyster and balance its texture. He asked the waiter to bring a tray of oysters and a pair of flutes. He requested the resident sommelier to select an excellent bottle of white wine to accompany our meal.

"I don't know if I can do this," I admitted nervously after the waiter left, feeling like a child coerced into eating vegetables.

His smile broadened, making him even more attractive. His perfect white teeth sparkled like newly polished pearls. I couldn't help but wonder how it would feel to have them pressed against my skin. *Get a grip, Hope! This isn't a date!* I scolded myself internally.

"Your team is doing a fantastic job. It's refreshing to work with such young talents," Richard remarked as he toyed with the stem of his wine glass. Once again, I found myself distracted by his long fingers… I shook off the thought.

The waiter returned with a tray lined with fresh oysters on ice and lemon wedges. Accompanying him was the sommelier, who carried three bottles of wine. He and Richard engaged in a conversation I couldn't quite decipher. The sommelier expertly uncorked a bottle, producing a satisfying pop.

Richard caught my attention and asked, "Will you let me?" I nodded, feeling a surge of warmth at the thought of him taking care of me this way. He poured the crisp white wine and carefully opened an oyster for me. "Open your mouth and close your eyes," he instructed, gently holding my chin as he placed the oyster in my mouth.

I took a tentative bite of the mollusk, feeling the salty brine wash over my tongue. And then, to my surprise, an explosion of flavor filled my mouth — sweet, delicate, and tangy all at once. I couldn't believe it. I was enjoying the taste of an oyster!

"Now, drink the wine," Richard said, his eyes sparkling.

I took a sip of the wine, feeling its crisp acidity balance out the rich flavor of the oyster. They were perfect partners in a dance of flavors and textures.

As I savored the taste of the oyster and wine, I felt a sense of wonder fill me. This experience was just one tiny moment in my life, but it felt like the whole world was opening up before me.

The combination of flavors was extraordinary. It was as if each sip added another layer of complexity to the experience, allowing me to savor every second I spent luxuriating in its flavor. The combination created an indescribable sensation that filled my stomach with warmth and happiness. Yes, that was how I would describe it. There's happiness in it! I opened my eyes and stared directly into his deep blue-grey eyes.

"The oyster offers salty and complex flavors balanced perfectly by the crispness of the white wine. Its acidity adds an extra layer to the texture, creating a perfect harmony of flavors in your mouth. The dryness of the Sauvignon Blanc complements the oyster's salty taste, with subtle hints of fruitiness and citrus." With Richard, describing oysters and wine was like looking at a Rembrandt painting. Beautiful!

"Thank you," I whispered.

"You're welcome, Hope."

I felt myself relaxing in his presence, enjoying the easy flow of conversation between us. Despite my earlier nerves, I was beginning to feel more confident and comfortable in Richard's company, and I wondered what the rest of the night had in store for us.

We continued to drink more wine as we discussed my background and experiences. I shared my passion for reading and collecting books. I also shared my plan to start a first-edition collection.

"What's your favorite classic?" he asked, leaning in with genuine interest. The warmth of his gaze was palpable on me, and I couldn't help but smile. "It's cliché, but there's no denying I'm a fan of *Pride and Prejudice*," I said. "I've read it a hundred times."

Richard nodded thoughtfully and smiled. "Ahh, an Austen fan." He remarked. "I played one of the film adaptations, not Mr. Darcy, though."

My mind started searching for scenes from Richard's films when my eyes lit up as recognition struck me, "Oh, you're that guy who played George Wickham! I remember now!" We lifted our glasses in a silent toast to celebrate the moment and the camaraderie between us.

When I asked about Richard's life, he hesitated before revealing that he was divorced long ago and how the split had affected his son, who now lives abroad, taking up his medical degree. Sadness colored his words, but there was something undeniably attractive about him. His face held an air of mystery while the richness of his voice reverberated through me whenever he spoke — not to mention that he smelled heavenly!

Time flew by without us noticing, and suddenly I realized that some of the cast and crew had already left, with Jenna nowhere in sight. Without a ride home, I wondered if I'd still be able to catch an Uber at this hour. To my surprise, Richard offered to take me home instead.

We stepped out into the chilly night air, so cold that I could see my breaths turn white as they escaped my lips. I had only brought my oversized coat, which was more for fashion than warmth. Richard must have noticed my discomfort and kindly removed his sweater, leaving him in a plain shirt underneath, and draped it over my shoulders. He made sure I was warm before walking to his car and bundled me in before inputting my address into his GPS. We set out on our journey home together, the darkness punctured by streetlights that made the night feel almost magical.

I could feel my eyelids growing heavier as I tried to stay awake.

Richard's sweater was now a blanket that enveloped me in warmth, its softness drawing me closer to sleep. As we drove, I listened to the sound of the engine humming quietly and felt the car judder slightly over bumps on the road. Suddenly, a thought occurred to me — I wondered where this experience would lead us next. Would this be a fleeting moment or something more? Would our paths cross again, or had fate brought us together only for one night? These questions lingered in my mind while an invisible force pulled at my heart.

At last, we stopped in front of my building. I opened my eyes slowly and saw Richard looking into my eyes. He leaned forward until our lips were just inches apart before he pressed his against mine. The kiss started gently but built quickly toward something more passionate than expected! I was surprised at first, but the sensation soon overwhelmed me, and I felt my cheeks redden with anticipation. Richard must have felt my heart, racing in response, beating like a drum in my chest as he deepened the kiss even further. Our hungry lips intertwined as we explored each other's mouths with growing passion, our bodies leaning into one another as if pulled by an invisible force.

I could feel the electricity coursing through me as Richard continued to kiss me, and my heart felt like it was going to burst. His lips were soft and inviting, his touch gentle yet firm. Our embrace only tightened when Richard's hands moved to the small of my back, sending sparks through every inch of me that it touched. His fingers began to trace lazy circles over my blouse as he kissed me deeper still — exploring every corner of my mouth with tenderness yet urgency at once. I ran my fingers through his hair. I had never wanted someone so badly as I wanted Richard at that moment. Suddenly, without warning, our kisses deepened, tongues intertwining feverishly until we were both out of breath and panting heavily against each other's faces. The sensation was intoxicating, and it felt like no time had passed before he finally pulled away. Our eyes met again, and we looked into each other's eyes with a newfound intensity that I hadn't felt before. Neither of us said a word for a moment, letting the silence linger between us as we savored the moment together.

Finally, Richard broke the silence with a whisper, "You better run inside while I still can control myself, Hope," he tilted my jaw and brushed my lips with his thumb. A big part of me wanted to tell him to take me to his place or get into my apartment and continue this magical dream, but I just closed my eyes, reminding myself to enjoy this moment without wishing for it to last any longer.

I reluctantly stepped out of the car, my gaze never leaving his. I wanted to reach out and return to him to keep us in that moment of bliss for a little longer, but I knew this was it for now. He looked back one last time before driving and disappearing into the darkness. A wave of sadness suddenly washed over me, realizing our moment had ended.

7

That kiss with Richard last night was both unexpected and mesmerizing. Every time I recalled it, a wave of electricity would run through my veins, reminiscent of the thrill I felt when his lips touched mine. My mind reminded me that Richard and I are professionals, and so far, he's treated me like any other production team member instead of someone he'd shared an intimate moment with. While I tried to keep myself busy to push away the memories of that night, it seemed my thoughts continually drifted back to him. Time seemed to be standing still, yet the words I sought remained out of my reach.

Before today I had never found writing so difficult. Something had changed since then, something fundamental. The creative passion which usually ignited my stories had become silent, weighed down by the implications of Richard's absence.

Desperate to escape the lingering thoughts of Richard, I found myself at Mavi's yoga studio. Although it wasn't my thing, I sought a much-needed distraction. The peaceful atmosphere and beautiful music helped me find an inner sense of serenity, letting go of all my thoughts and focusing on the moment. It felt like a tapestry of emotions intertwined through the movements and postures that taught me how to accept and embrace life's surprises. For those few precious hours, it seemed as if Richard had never even been part of my life.

Mavi's yoga studio was just two buildings away from mine. It offered a peaceful oasis on the rooftop of an old tenement building with a bright and rustic vibe that drew you in. Floor-to-ceiling windows looked out onto the bustling city below, creating a stunning backdrop for classes. The airy space was filled with soothing music and aromatherapy candles, providing an atmosphere of serenity and calm – making it ideal for practicing yoga. Its cozy cocoon-like ambiance and spectacular views made it an utterly unique experience.

Erin always said she can always find peace here, no matter how turbulent the rest of the world may be, and now I believe her. The instructors were all highly trained and offered gentle guidance that helped you feel connected to yourself while learning new poses. Besides yoga classes, there were workshops and talks on various topics ranging from mindfulness to nutrition and breathwork. Mavi's studio was a sanctuary away from the outside world that offered solace and support to its visitors.

Mavi had just finished her yoga classes and sat down beside me. "So, how's shooting going?"

"Everyone is busy with the deadlines and filming," I said.

Mavi nodded in understanding. "It's a lot of hard work, but it's always worth it in the end," she said. Her gaze drifted to the windows with their spectacular view of the city below as we shared a few moments of comfortable silence before I asked her about her yoga classes. She beamed enthusiastically as she described them — from the poses and movements that came almost effortlessly to her to the sense of peace and tranquility that filled the studio afterward. It was clear how much joy she found in teaching and practicing yoga.

She also talked about how yoga had changed her mindset and outlook on life, not only the physical benefit. It helped her become more mindful and present at the moment. She said, "It gave me a new perspective, letting me see beauty in the little things I would have normally overlooked."

She also spoke about how it made her more compassionate towards herself and others. She could recognize her flaws and mistakes through yoga without being overly critical or judgmental. And through this acceptance of self, she found that she could also accept others with open arms.

Yoga was like a journey for her — one that taught her to appreciate life more deeply each day, no matter its ups and downs.

Mavi turned to me, curiosity in her eyes. "So," she said with a mischievous grin. "Anyone special on the film crew you've been spending time with?"

I shook my head. "No," I said. "I haven't met anyone interesting enough to go out with yet." I fought the blush that threatened to spread across my cheeks and tried to keep my expression neutral, grateful that I didn't have to tell her about Richard.

Mavi laughed, and the mischievous glint in her eye only grew. "Oh, come on, surely there's someone you can talk about?"

My blush deepened as I shook my head again. "No, not yet. Everyone's been too busy with production to start a conversation, much less get to know each other better." I knew it would only become more complex if I told her about Richard now. So I said nothing and gave her a nonchalant shrug.

Mavi's tone was gentle, but I knew she could sense the turmoil in my mind. She had been my friend for years — she knew me too well. She said in a low voice. "Do you want to talk about it?"

I glanced away, biting my lip and shaking my head. I knew if I opened up to her, all the confusion from the past days would come spilling out, and I wasn't sure I could handle it. "Maybe some other time," I said after a moment.

Mavi nodded, understanding my hesitation. She reached out and squeezed my arm in a comforting gesture. "All right. I'm here for you whenever you need me," she said softly.

Her kindness was almost too much to bear, and I felt a knot of emotion well in my throat as I fought back the tears. I had never been able to hide anything from her before — she knew it all before I opened my mouth — and this situation was no different.

But I also knew that if I let myself open up to her, the floodgates of emotion would spill out into the open. She would listen without judgment and hold me while everything crashed around me. For now, though, I smiled sadly at her and remained silent.

Mavi sensed my discomfort and chose not to press the issue. She gave me an easy smile and a wink before changing the subject to the latest gossip in town.

———

I arrived at the set the next day, and to my surprise, there was a black-wrapped gift tied with a yellow ribbon. Attached to it was a simple folded note that said,

'Enjoy the first - RC.'

When I unwrapped it, I discovered that it was the first edition of Jane Austen's *Pride and Prejudice*, with its covers decorated with intricate designs and gold lettering. I was awestruck as I beheld the beautiful gift in my hands. These three volumes were highly sought-after collector's items. I carefully opened up the pages and discovered beautiful high-quality paper and wide margins for easy reading, decorated with delicate floral borders that enhanced its classic charm. It was a work of art that any reader or collector would treasure! The thoughtful gesture behind it was not simply an act of kindness or politeness. Richard had put so much thought and care into this gift, making sure it reached me, that it filled me with warmth and gratitude.

I knew there was no way I could thank Richard for the gift, as we hadn't exchanged phone numbers the night before. Moments later, Susie handed me the edited script for the second episode. After taking a close look and making some minor corrections of my own, I asked Patty to print off several sets of the new script and send them to the production team. But then I changed my mind and decided to distribute them myself. I would use this opportunity to thank Richard for the gift.

One thing I like about our setup, the Writers Room is conveniently close to the actors' lounge, where they often peruse scripts. Today was no exception, as Richard was studying his phone intently. My cheeks immediately flushed as I handed him his script for rehearsal. He looked up at me with his enchanting gaze, and a wave of electricity surged through me as he thanked me in his silky voice, reminiscent of the previous night.

"I can't thank you enough for the Austen collection," I murmured with a hint of shyness.

"It was my pleasure, Hope," he replied warmly. Then he turned to run lines with his fellow actors, leaving me with unexplained emotions.

As I fixed my gaze on Richard, a whirlwind of emotions washed over me, making my head spin. I couldn't stop wondering what had occurred between us that night. Would things between us remain strictly professional, or was there more to it? I let out a deep sigh trying to make sense of it all. It was hard to gauge his intentions: had he acted under the influence of alcohol, or was it something deeper? Being a big shot and me being a nobody, could it be that it was just a fluke? Or did the glimmer in his eyes hint at a different story altogether?

As I observed Richard on the set, I couldn't help but wonder about his relationship history. The rumor mill had it that he dated numerous stunning ladies over the years, but none seemed to stick around for long. Was he afraid of commitment, or was something else at play here? My mind spun with questions, trying to sort out the mystery of what lay behind that charming outward demeanor of his.

I studied Richard's body language for any signs that could provide insight into our situation. The broad smile he gave me when our eyes first met, and the way he lingered when taking his script from my hands only added to the feeling that there was something more significant between us. His body language seemed to echo an unspoken message that was impossible to ignore —this was not just a one-time kiss.

I had to remind myself firmly not to get swept away in this rollercoaster of emotions. *'Don't forget why you're here in the first place!'* I told myself. My dreams and ambitions extended far beyond a fleeting moment of romance and a one-night kiss. It was essential to stay focused and not let my emotions cloud my judgment.

I welcomed the solitude of my small office within the Writers Room, especially considering Jenna had gone out of her way to organize it for me. The space was intimate yet welcoming, pleasantly scented with coffee and books. The soft yellow walls generated an inviting atmosphere, and the minimalist décor embodied a sense of calmness, distancing me from the bustling world outside. My desk, in front of a massive window overlooking the lively street, was furnished with heavy vertical blinds that acted as a shield, blocking out light or distractions when necessary, especially when I needed to stay focused on my work.

My desk was empty except for my laptop, a writing pad, and coffee, which had long gone cold. It felt like an oasis of stillness compared to the chaotic outside world. Despite its emptiness, I could feel the creative energy radiating from it, almost as if it were beckoning me to stay focused on whatever task I had to accomplish. The looming deadline on my laptop's screen only heightened my sense of urgency. I kept on writing until I lost track of time. With the writers and film crews gone and only a few maintenance workers left, I was probably the last one still working. I gave myself a few more minutes to finish my writing before packing for the night. The silence in the room was almost eerie, but it was also calming.

Suddenly, a heavenly warmth filled the room. It was his cologne. His gentle hand on my shoulder caused me to shiver. I already knew who it was without even turning around. Richard. I looked up and I noticed he looked tired from the day's work. He leaned in and asked if he could look at what I had been working on.

Still unsure of what to do, I slowly turned the laptop so that he could see the screen better. He pulled up a seat next to me, his eyes scanning the page for some time before a warm smile spread across his face. Taking my hesitance as an invitation, he drew closer and started discussing his thoughts about what he had read.

"This is good," he said, his voice full of admiration. "Inspired you the previous night, huh?" I glanced back and saw Richard reading the love scene between the two characters. I felt my cheeks flush as he chuckled softly. Before I could react to this, his gaze suddenly intensified, and in a split second, our eyes connected — blue-grey eyes meeting brown.

In a shaky whisper, I begged him, "Please kiss me, Richard." Without a moment's hesitation, our lips met, and the pure intensity of that single moment caused time to stand still around us. Passion surged through our veins as all we could feel was pleasure. When at last our lips parted, neither of us spoke a word — the only thing left in the air was pure bliss.

Richard looked into my eyes with unspoken questions in them before he eventually asked, "What have you done to me, Hope?" I smiled knowingly and replied with a simple phrase that spoke volumes: "I've unlocked your heart's desire." We both knew exactly where we would go from here.

Without saying a word, I slowly got out of my chair, walked over to the door, and locked it. Then I walked across the room and settled onto Richard's lap. Our lips connected again, and I didn't care about anything else but us this time.

His kisses filled me with passion. His tongue explored every inch of my mouth while his hands moved lower, slipping beneath the fabric until they finally reached their desired destination — my breasts. Despite the thin material between us, my body trembled under his touch as he firmly secured his lips against mine and sent shivers of pleasure down my spine. I gasped at the overwhelming sensations coursing through my body as we continued kissing deeply. My heart raced faster than ever as he pulled away just enough to whisper sweet words into my ear between kisses. I had never felt anything quite like this before. His heart raced, too, as I touched him, the electricity between us almost palpable, and I trembled with anticipation. Nothing else mattered at that moment — no worries or cares could penetrate my mind when we were together like this.

Richard stood up and lifted me on top of the desk. I don't know how he put my laptop on my chair. He impatiently unbuttoned my blouse and kissed and caressed my body with his hands. I felt like I could melt into him. His delicate touch moved from my lips to my neck before lightly brushing against my breasts. He kissed them tenderly and lingered there for what felt like an eternity. His right hand moved lower towards the hem of my skirt, then slowly brought his fingers to the area between my legs.

I gasped at his boldness and found myself blushing even more as his fingers began exploring this unfamiliar territory with such skillful precision that it sent pleasurable sensations through every inch of my body. His lips replaced where his fingers once touched before finally returning to join mine in a passionate embrace that left us both breathless yet longing for more. Richard unzipped his pants and took my hands inside his bulge, and I almost cried, anticipating the pleasure to come. He was already hard. "Please let me have you, too," I begged him.

"We have more time for that," he promised. "I want to have you now!"

Richard ripped off my underwear and tossed them somewhere. He opened my legs further and slowly pushed himself inside me. He was huge so he was gentle toward me. He looked into my eyes as he moved gracefully and passionately — his every move was perfectly in sync with mine. It was as if an invisible force kept pulling us closer and closer until our bodies intertwined into one being of pure pleasure and bliss. We moved together like two parts of a single organism — a beam of energy connecting the two of us that nothing else could interrupt. As we reached new heights of ecstasy, all the desire I'd ever felt for him seemed to rush through me at once, and it filled up each crevice and corner until there was nowhere left for any other emotion to hide from its power.

Everything was in a beautiful blur. Everything around us melted away, and there was only our passion-filled embrace left in existence. Everything outside faded away until it felt like we were suspended in time — lost in each other's arms forever — making love passionately without end or pause until exhaustion finally overtook us.

8

The unexpected and passionate moment with Richard in my office changed everything. I never dreamed we would share such a profound physical connection. With one impulsive act, my previously ordinary life became incredibly complicated. What once seemed a simple project to write a script for a TV show had become more profound. As passionate feelings surged between us, our relationship crossed far beyond the accepted professional boundaries, and I was left unable to ignore that it was no longer just about work.

It seemed apparent that Richard was feeling awkward, too. Upon handing him the script for episode three, he wanted to rewrite some of the dialogue. This task had always been relatively seamless, but now, we were both struggling with our feelings. Everything felt different between us. Small gestures, such as a smile, seemed to hold a more significant meaning now, and every time we touched, it felt like there was a real spark. We became hyper-aware of each other's presence, and the subtle changes in our behavior only amplified this new intensity between us. Despite our attempts to maintain a professional demeanor and the desire to keep our relationship strictly work-based, it was clear that our connection was far too powerful for us to ignore.

As I worked alongside Brittany, I tried my best to stay focused on the task. However, my mind couldn't help but wander back to the unforgettable night with Richard. There was a stirring within me, an unexplainable feeling that kept me struggling to concentrate.

Without realizing it, I exclaimed, "What?!" causing Brittany to give me a questioning look.

"What's with 'what,' thing?" she asked curiously. I quickly apologized, admitting that my mind had been elsewhere.

Then I heard Richard cough lightly in the background, amusement barely concealed in his timid sound. "Oh, sorry, I was head-in-the clouds," I admitted sheepishly before focusing on Brittany's query again.

"As I was saying, wouldn't it be easier, and even more romantic, if I threw myself into Richard's arms and kissed him? Instead of me leaning my back against the car seat — just like what Rachel McAdams did with Ryan Gosling in *The Notebook*?" she asked with a triumphant grin.

I couldn't help but chuckle at her suggestion. "You want to copy Rachel McAdams' scene with Ryan Gosling in *The Notebook*?" I asked incredulously.

"Yeah, something like that," she replied. "What do you think?"

At first, I couldn't help but think that copying a scene from such a famous movie would make our project look like a cliché. However, I soon realized we could put our unique spin on it.

"Not my call, but I can rewrite the scene to make it happen," I replied to Brittany.

"Awesome! Let's talk to Richard," she exclaimed eagerly. "Hey, Collins, can you spare a few minutes? I'm discussing some changes with Hope about a few incredible modifications."

Richard rolled up his script and strode confidently towards us. His broad-shouldered frame, strong jawline, and piercing eyes — bluer now than the usual blue-grey — made my heart beat faster. The sun glinted off his dark hair as he moved closer. He was wearing a simple white shirt tucked into jeans that highlighted his muscular physique — I felt my cheeks flush in response.

As he drew nearer, I could feel the electric tension in the air between us. He gave me a wicked smile as he stopped in front of me. He knew how awkward this makes me feel. His eyebrows arched slightly as if silently telling me to calm down. My heart pounded anxiously against my chest — was this it? Was this finally going to be the moment where our relationship changed from friends to something more?

"I have an outrageous suggestion," Brittany said as we discussed the script. "What if I ran towards you instead of kissing you while your back was against the car seat?"

Richard seemed amused by this idea and joked, "You want to have sex on the grass instead? Do you think that's more romantic than doing it in a car seat?!"

Brittany responded teasingly, "Who wants to get it on inside a car? Too high school for me!"

"Huh?" Richard raised his eyebrows with a hint of suppressed laughter and stared expectantly at me. It was clear he wanted to hear my opinion on this unexpected request.

Before I could respond, Brittany enthusiastically butted in: "Of course! Hope deserves better than that from his man! Give her something romantic and beautiful for that first kiss — a love song, if you will!" She winked at me conspiratorially as if she knew what I was thinking.

Richard's mouth twisted into a smirk as he looked at me — no doubt wondering how on earth he was supposed to do that!

"Hope?" Richard wasn't letting the conversation go, and his fiery grin made it clear he was determined to find amusement. I cringed internally as I glared at him before I could form any complaints in my mind. That's when Richard burst out with loud laughter, and his playful nature didn't stop there. He tenderly touched my chin and tilted it so our eyes met before saying in a teasing tone, "You're so cute when you're mad."

Featherlight, Richard planted a tender kiss on my lips in front of Brittany, whose eyes widened in shock and mouth opened in disbelief.

My heart raced as I felt his lips brush against mine, though I was unsure of what was happening until a mix of embarrassment and joy turned my cheeks bright red. Before I could react further, the people around us erupted into thunderous cheers and frantic applause! Brittany brought both hands to her face, looking like she had just witnessed the most unimaginable event.

"So carry on, Brit. You want to alter the scene?" Richard chuckled with an amused tone. "You think a McAdams-Gosling kiss is going to boost the scene?"

"Oh, my God! So you two made out inside the car!" Brittany just laughed mischievously in response, and I felt my face heat up with embarrassment as everyone's eyes were transfixed on us. It was almost like time had stopped. I just knew this incident will become the subject of gossip countless times!

No! I thought to myself desperately, not like this! I couldn't let this moment become part of idle gossip —a screenwriter is sleeping with the lead star! This thing will put Richard and me in the spotlight, with constant stares, disapproval from coworkers, and the favorite joke during break time. Richard was oblivious to the trouble this will cause me, so it was up to me to take control of the scene and prove that our gesture meant something far more significant than any idle rumor. I grabbed tightly onto Richard's shirt and kissed him back angrily. I wanted my kiss to tell everyone watching, *'I decided this because I want it.'*

The crowd burst into cheers once more, and Brittany's voice playfully faded into the distance, saying, "You two, get a room, please." Richard's grin spread across his face in amusement before he wrapped his arms around my waist. I never thought this surprise moment would happen, so I was ecstatic that Richard showed his feelings in front of everyone!

I then watched in disbelief as the craziest of events unfolded before me. Robin warned Richard that he was violating workplace policy while the production crew kept up their crazy shenanigans. It seemed no one was taking Richard and me seriously.

Robin yelled, "Tell human resources that Collins is sexually harassing our writer. This surely kicks him out of this production." Richard just laughed along and shared a knowing smirk with me. His gaze never left mine, and I felt my heart swell with joy. At that moment, I believed nothing could tear us apart.

With relief, I remembered that Jenna wasn't here yet. I still had time to tell her when the right moment arrives. It was as if she heard my thoughts. I heard my phone buzzing in my pocket. Jenna. I took one deep breath and answered the call. Sure enough, she jumped straight into it as soon and didn't bother with pleasantries. She simply asked immediately, "You and Richard Collins...?!"

I paused for a moment, not sure how to respond. All I could muster was, "I don't know what to tell you yet."

"You've got A LOT of things to tell me, Esperanza!" she exclaimed.

As the news spread, the writing team exchanged whispers among themselves. Eventually, one of them, Susie, mustered the courage to ask if we were officially a couple. My cheeks flushed with embarrassment, and I hesitated to answer. Instead, I replied, "Let's focus on our work now, guys!" The room buzzed with intrigue as the newfound gossip added a spark to the workplace atmosphere.

Richard looked at me as if he felt sorry for whatever he had put me through. So the cat is out of the bag now. I couldn't help but wonder — were we officially a couple, or would this be nothing more than a fling between coworkers? I didn't want to put a label on it; I just wanted to enjoy the moment, whether it marked the start of something new or be simply a brief work romance.

———

Saturday. Running and duck feeding.

Thank God for weekends! I checked my bedside alarm clock and saw it was still too early to hit the pavement for my morning run. So, I decided to lie in bed for a few more minutes and try to shake off the lingering thoughts from the past few days.

At work, keeping up appearances around my colleagues was becoming increasingly difficult. I couldn't help but notice a change in their behavior toward me. The guys I used to hang out with after work or on weekend group outings had stopped inviting me. It seemed like everyone knew that Richard was more than just a co-star to me. Hollywood royalty that he was, no way anyone could compete with him for my attention.

I'm so glad we're all beating a filming deadline, so everybody, including myself and Richard, is in work mode. We kept our distance from one another while working, but sometimes our eyes met and held for what felt like an eternity before we looked away quickly.

With Richard filming at a different location, it's been a blessing for me as I can focus on rewriting and altering the script without distractions. Though the distance was a barrier, we still made an effort to stay in touch with each other. Richard would send me photo messages or an occasional emoji with no captions.

Today, he sent me a photo of a single tulip. As I lay in bed, I stared longingly at the picture he sent me. The flower was fragile yet resilient, reminding me of our relationship. Though we were apart, he was still trying to maintain our connection. It was a small yet significant gesture that made my day.

I was suddenly startled by Salem's screech at the front door. I turned to see what had caught his attention. It could have been anything — a rat or a stray dog that snuck into the building. I opened the door, and I couldn't believe what I saw. A bucket filled with vibrant white tulips sat at my doorstep as if placed there intentionally for me.

I wondered if my friend Charlie knew of some special occasion I had forgotten. The tulips were stunning — each stem was long and narrow, and their blooms were soft and velvety to the touch. They exuded a fragrant ambiance with every passing second.

Feeling curious and excited, I carefully collected the tulips in the bucket and saw a card attached to it. I wondered who could have left such a thoughtful surprise on my doorstep, and I couldn't help but feel a sense of anticipation as I opened the card.

'Dinner at my place.
Wear something nice.
Pick you up at 6.
—RC'

As soon as I got the bucket full of white tulips, I knew I had to make something beautiful out of them. I placed them carefully on my tiny dining table and focused on taking a close-crop shot that captured their vibrant beauty. As I sent the picture to Richard, I realized our conversation had gradually turned towards photo sharing.

For almost a week now, our communications have been basically muted. There were no voices, no texts — only photos and images that we shared back and forth. I was eagerly waiting for Richard's reply every time my phone buzzed. He had sent me a cropped view of Central Park, which I assumed was taken from his window-side spot.

It was no secret that I had a Saturday routine. I changed into my navy yoga pants, put on my old charcoal grey hoodie over my white tank top, and slipped on my trusty Nike running shoes. These were my usual go-to gear for the morning in the park. I looked at Richard's photo message again, I couldn't help but smile at how well he knew me. The exchange of subtle details about each other's lives gradually brought us closer.

I laced up my running shoes, ready to hit the pavement and tackle the three-mile mark. As I ran, my lungs started to burn and I pushed through the exhaustion, fueled by the satisfaction of reaching my fitness goal.

As I returned home, I passed by the nearby pond and couldn't resist stopping to feed the ducks. Little rewards like these made my morning runs all the more worthwhile.

Once back at my place, I took stock of the mess accumulated over the week and dragged everything to the laundry machine. I noticed a week-old pizza in the fridge and heated it in the microwave for a quick snack. My ears told me Salem was napping and I looked for him, and sure enough, his chest rose and fell like clockwork, signaling he was still sleeping peacefully.

I put fresh food on his dish in case he got hungry while I was gone. It was reassuring to know that even with the chaos of life, some things remained constant and predictable.

————

It was time for me to get dressed. I spent extra time washing and blow-drying my hair. Standing in my closet, I was unsure of what to wear. I tried on different outfits, but nothing seemed right. I finally settled on a pair of jeans and a turtleneck but changed my mind. He had written, *Wear something nice.*

Just then, my eyes landed on the only little black dress that I owned. It was simple yet elegant, with a subtle shimmer in the fabric that made it sparkle just enough when it caught the light. I slipped it on and wore it with a stunning pair of strappy heels adorned with tiny rhinestones. I bought these on impulse and have never worn them till tonight. To my surprise, they were incredibly comfortable despite their height!

I put on light makeup with almost nude lipstick and pinned my hair up in a messy bun at the last minute. I looked at myself in the mirror and felt satisfied. I didn't look so bad. I looked...decent.

On the dot, I went downstairs and decided to wait for Richard instead of letting him leave the car on the street and fetch me from my apartment. As I stepped out the front door, I heard a roar of an engine, and my date pulled up in front of the apartment complex. He got out of the car, already looking like the epitome of charm in his crisp navy suit, white shirt, and polished loafers. He smiled as if he could tell that I had gone through the extra effort to look nice for him as he opened the door and gestured for me to get inside. His blue-grey eyes fixed on me with admiration as he planted a gentle kiss on my lips before tucking a strand of loose hair behind my ear. "You look beautiful tonight."

He closed the passenger door and walked to the driver's seat. Our first kiss of the week reignited my confidence, reminded me why we were here tonight, and I quickly forgot about my pre-dinner jitters.

I was enveloped in luxurious comfort as I settled inside Richard's car. The plush leather seats wrapped me in comfort, and high technology gears gave the interior an air of modern sophistication. It was unlike any other car ride I'd taken before.

"I want you to meet someone," he said.

"So it isn't dinner for two, I guess."

"I hope you won't mind the extra company."

"What if I say I feel slightly disappointed because I can't have you alone?" I gave him a side glance and smiled.

"I feel the same way, too."

"I understand," I said with a smile, disappointed that I wouldn't have this night alone with him. He started the engine, and we began our drive, the anticipation of who we were going to meet adding an extra buzz to the air.

"He's someone important to me, and I wanted you to meet him," Richard said. I nodded, deeply curious about who this mystery person was.

I reached out and gently touched his free hand. He unexpectedly grabbed mine rather than releasing it. With a gentle yet deliberate motion, he brought my hand up to his lips. As he tenderly kissed each of my fingers, I was vividly reminded of how those same lips had once roamed every inch of my body, igniting a fire in places I never thought could bring such immense pleasure. At that moment, all thoughts vanished from my mind, and it seemed as if time itself had come to a standstill, allowing us to exist solely within the confines of our shared connection. As our hands parted, I felt a strange craving for something more. I looked up at Richard, who was now exiting the car and walking to my side to open the door for me. He tossed his keys to the valet, and we walked together toward Jenna's building.

"Do you live here?" I asked, curiosity rising inside me.

He gave me a small smile and replied, "Just recently."

We reached the lobby, and Fred opened the door for us instantly. "Good evening, Ms. Hope and Mr. Collins!" Fred spoke formally, but I could tell he was thrilled behind that poker face.

"Hello, Fred! It's good to see you," I said with a smile and caught Richard's curious expression, likely confused about the connection between his doorman and me. I explained, "Jenna lives on the eleventh floor."

Richard's lips parted in slight surprise, a bemused expression dawning across his face as he remarked, "Ah… I see."

We stepped into the elevator, and Richard pushed the little 'P' button. He lives in a penthouse! I felt slightly nervous about meeting Richard's other guest for dinner, but this feeling quickly dissipated when we entered Richard's sophisticated home. It was decorated with mahogany furniture and pieces of impressive artwork. At the same time, the warm light from the fireplace created a subtle glow. I spotted a delicate watercolor painting hanging above a mahogany armchair in one corner. To my right was an oil painting depicting a countryside village, while to my left was a vibrant abstract piece that seemed to dance with color. Each artwork was picked and brought together to create a beautiful display. Book collections were arranged neatly in different sizes and shapes along the walls. Some seemed generations old, while others were new and glossy hardcovers of the latest bestsellers. I could tell that much care had been taken in curating these collections, as they added an intellectual touch to the room while still complementing its cozy atmosphere.

I noticed a blond man at the corner of my eye who gave me a warm welcome and then shifted his attention to Richard with a mischievous grin.

"So this is your date," he said. "It's nice to meet you… again, finally."
His voice was familiar, and I suddenly realized I had met him at
Central Park while we were feeding ducks!

"Henry!" I said, surprised. He grinned at me as he extended his hand
in greeting. His blond hair and good looks made him stand out even in
this room full of art and book collections adorning the walls and
corners.

Richard looked bemused between us, and I smiled cheekily in
response. "So you two have already met?" he asked in disbelief.

"We met a few months ago, feeding ducks at Central Park. Then we
never saw each other again," I laughed.   He shook his head in
amusement. "You are full of surprises today," he remarked before
pouring drinks for us. He offered one glass to Henry and one to me, a
twinkle in his eye as we both grasped our glasses.

I reached out to touch his face, and he replied by lightly pressing his
lips against my hand. His touch was warm and gentle, like a distant
memory, and it felt increasingly familiar between us as time passed.
Then he gestured towards his son, who stood alongside him. "Hope,
I'd like to introduce you to my son Henry, formally."

Henry and his father shared many similarities. Even though their hair
was different, their family resemblance could not be mistaken when
they smiled or laughed.

Henry grinned at me, his face full of warmth. "I'm so glad to see you
again, Hope," he said. "I forgot to get your phone number before we
left Central Park. I tried looking for you on Instagram, but it wasn't
easy — you don't have many selfies there, just cats, flower shots, and
heart-melted ducks!"

He glanced at his father. "I can't believe you're the girl my dad wants
me to meet. Have you been able to keep it under wraps? The press
doesn't know yet?"

Before Richard could reply, I let out a laugh. "We're just enjoying whatever we got right now; this hardly qualifies as dating or anything."

Richard cleared his throat and gestured to the dining room. "Let's deal with 'whatever' later. First, let's hit the dinner table before the food gets cold," he said.

We headed into the dining room, set with a delightful array of dishes. Perfectly roasted vegetables accompanied the salmon fillet, and Richard offered generous refills from his extensive wine cellar collection throughout the meal.

He asked Henry how life was going in med school. Henry replied with a brief update of recent events, both good and bad, then followed it up with an assurance that he was doing fine. Richard nodded in agreement before continuing the conversation with another topic.

I watched father and son banter away, intently listening to the exchange between them while giving occasional comments of encouragement or appreciation. I was content to be there with them, happy to observe this light-hearted exchange.

The dark chocolate cake garnished with fresh strawberries served as a delightful finale to our meal. Afterward, the three of us settled comfortably in the living room. As we sank into the plush cushions of the sofa, Henry inquired, "Hope, what type of music are you into?" His father tended the fireplace nearby. The orange flames flickered and danced, creating a warm and inviting atmosphere.

"I'm old school, actually," I replied with a smile. "I like Peggy Lee and Nina Simone. But I like new stuff, too—Billie Eilish and Dua Lipa."

"And where do you hang out these days?" he continued, curious to know some of New York City's favorite spots.

"There's this bar around the 'hood that plays all kinds of music," I said enthusiastically.

Henry perked up. "What do you guys do when you go there?"

"We usually just sit at the bar and talk," I replied. "Sometimes we'll play pool or shoot a game of darts, but mostly it's about catching up with friends and meeting new people. The music they play is always top-notch."

He nodded as Richard and I sunk further into the couch cushions, enjoying the warmth of the fire while Nina Simone crooned from the old record player in the corner.

Richard shifted and paused momentarily, holding the bottle over his already half-filled stemware — smirk curving into an exaggerated pearly grin — before carelessly inquiring, "Henry, may I have my girl back?" His grey eyes glinted with playfulness.

He got up and carefully placed the needle on one of Nina's records at just the right spot. He then walked back over to me and offered his hand to help me off of our cozy little nook on the couch. Once standing, he pulled me close into a slow dance and we moved together in time, with Nina's beautiful voice echoing throughout the living room.

I saw Henry look at his father, a smile on his face. He simply wanted happiness for Richard, and so did I. The warmth of the fire and the melody of Nina Simone were the perfect backdrop for our intimate moments.

As we danced, no worries or cares existed outside that very second in space and time. We embraced each other tightly. Finally, Richard released my waist, only for us to collapse onto the sofa, laughing giddily at what had become our private concert hall. On impulse, I picked up my phone, intending to capture the moment with a photo for my Instagram, as I often did. But then I remembered how fiercely private Richard was and how he preferred to stay out of the social media spotlight.

"You know, I'm still amazed by how people share every aspect of their lives on the internet for the world to see," Richard commented, peering over my shoulder. The warmth of his breath tickled the back of my neck, sending shivers down my spine.

"It's not all about selfies, though. Some of us use it as a platform to showcase our photography skills," I said, opening my Instagram account to reveal an array of snapshots featuring Salem, ducks on the pond, vibrant flowers, scrumptious cupcakes, and everything in between – except selfies.

"You've got quite a following. Are these people genuinely interested in seeing these kinds of photos?" he asked, intrigued by the role social media played in the lives of celebrities and ordinary people like me.

As Richard and I continued browsing through my Instagram feed, Henry stealthily captured a photo of us. Grinning mischievously, he teased, "Dad, how would you feel about sending the press into a frenzy?"

"Don't you even think about it!" I exclaimed, lunging across Henry's arm to snatch his phone away. In the commotion, I hadn't even noticed Richard reaching for mine. His arms enveloped me like a protective cocoon, and he planted a soft kiss on the back of my neck, causing me to erupt in a fit of giggle. "Hey!" I gasped, feigning surprise just as Richard snapped a photo! To my astonishment, he uploaded the picture to my Instagram account with the caption:

I hacked Hope's account — # RichardCollins

My jaw dropped in shock, and Henry's eyes widened in disbelief. "What have you done!?" I cried out theatrically. Almost immediately, my phone began vibrating with a flood of notifications. Richard had used the very hashtag his fans employed whenever they shared news or photos of him. Within moments, his ever-vigilant fans who seemed to camp out on Instagram, Facebook, and Twitter around the clock had spotted our photo. It didn't take long for them to cross-post it on various social media platforms, spreading the image of our intimate moment like wildfire across the internet.

I turned to face him, speechless for once — all I could see was his dazzling white smile lighting up the room.

Henry innocently asked, "Should I start calling you Mom now?" I immediately threw the pillows across him and yelled, "Don't you dare!"

Richard laughed while he held me tight from behind, "That's the second time you said that, darling!" I couldn't help but feel overwhelmed as I listened to Richard's heartfelt words of endearment, his affection for me seemingly blossoming out of nowhere. Our whirlwind romance felt akin to boarding a bullet train and suddenly arriving at our destination in the blink of an eye. Although we had made love only once, our interactions and tender gestures seemed to indicate a long-lasting affair. As much as I reveled in the depth of our connection, I couldn't help but feel a twinge of concern for the potential impact on our careers, particularly Richard's. Undoubtedly, I gladly gave him a brief kiss on the mouth in front of his son, who is closer to my age than his. "Are you that scared to look at your phone?" Gently, he nibbled my ear.

Henry was looking at his phone and said, "Close to five thousand likes and probably hundreds of comments in replies in less than five minutes!"

"Richard, you just put a target on my back! Imagine millions of women around the world hating me now," I wailed.

Before he could answer me, his mobile phone buzzed. He looked at who it was and let me go, "It's Peter."

I mouthed, "Who's Peter?" to Henry.

"His agent. England is probably on the brink of catastrophe now," he laughed.

"That means trouble, right?"

"Not something he and Peter can't handle."

"That was reckless of him."

"I never saw my dad so happy until tonight, Hope," Henry said. His voice carried a hint of awe, like he couldn't believe it was true. I smiled despite the sudden onslaught of emotions that threatened to overwhelm me.

"He makes me happy, too, Henry," I said softly.

He patted my shoulder and gave me an encouraging smile. He pressed a brief kiss on my cheek and smiled one last time before he turned to leave. "Just take one step at a time. I better go. You two might need some privacy," he said with a wink before picking up his glass of wine and walking toward his father, who was wrapping up his conversation with Pete. He grasped Richard's shoulder lightly and muttered something under his breath. Richard pulled his son toward him. I can't believe what just happened — meeting Henry again, the Instagram-official announcement, the warmth Henry radiated, especially tonight when Richard looked happier than ever.

Richard sat down beside me, ever graceful and confident. I sighed deeply in confusion, "So, what kind of trouble are we in?"

He touched the side of my face and gave me that contagious smile I could never resist. "It's nothing hostile or catastrophic Peter can't handle; just a statement that I would like to preserve my right to privacy. He is more concerned about how you'd cope. This isn't your world. The British tabloids are a nasty business, and they can write anything." His fingertips flickered across my skin while he gushed in embarrassment. "That was carelessness on my part. I'm sorry, my darling."

I lay my head across his chest and closed my eyes. He grabbed my hand and affectionately kissed the tip of each finger. At this moment, I felt so secure. We spent hours afterward conversing about everything under the sun while Nina Simone's voice played softly in the background. Tonight was so perfect, and I didn't want this to end. I will deal with my phone tomorrow. Tonight, it was just Richard and me.

9

Today was a circus. Veronica knocked on my door, holding several folded tabloids with a bouquet of flowers from their flower shop. "My dad said you needed company." She sat on the small chair and spread the papers on my table, including her iPad. "By the way, those tabloids are from Dad. He practically wants to buy every copy on the newsstand. I was under the impression that print media had died out a long time ago."

It was almost noon. I overslept after Richard drove me home. "What do you wanna read first? The good stuff or the bad stuff?" She asked.

"The bad stuff, I guess," I replied, feeling apprehensive. She nodded and selected one of the tabloids on my table, revealing a headline: *'Richard Collins Dating His Screenwriter!'*

One article said, *'Jenna Huey's writer writing a love story with Richard Collins.'* I took one of the newspapers from her hands, not wanting to know what I'd find inside but knowing I had to face it eventually. I opened it instantly and saw *'Young Writer Hit Jackpot: Sleeping with Richard Collins!'* How did they know that?

My phone lit up with notifications from several people, including Henry and my mother. I quickly unlocked it to see what was happening. As I scrolled through the barrage of messages and notifications on my Instagram, a sinking feeling began to take root in the pit of my stomach. People were discussing Richard and the dramatic revelation from the previous night. Some comments featured good-natured humor, but others were painfully cruel. I was called ugly, fat, and mongrel—a derogatory term referencing my biracial heritage. Some even likened our relationship to Disney's *Beauty and the Beast*, with me cast as the Beast and Richard as Beauty. The onslaught of opinions left me feeling exposed and vulnerable, questioning the consequences of our public announcement.

It didn't help that Veronica kept asking questions about Richard and me. She told me that her father's floral shop had been unexpectedly busy today — she was almost sure it had something to do with the events of last night. "Some of them were asking if you actually live in this building and if Richard Collins is a frequent visitor," she said. It seemed like things had spiraled out of our control. Suddenly, we found ourselves in the spotlight with rumors circulating about us and no way to escape it any time soon!

I attempted to recount the recklessness of our actions that night, but she deftly changed the subject, diverting our conversation toward the news articles instead. We both quietly read through the stories, trying to make sense of the circus that had erupted from last night's events.

"People are talking," Veronica said softly, looking at the newsprint. "They're saying a lot of things."

I closed my eyes, trying to process all the information from every direction. It had been such a fun evening — how had things gone so wrong so quickly?

Veronica looked at me with deep concern in her eyes. "Will you be all right, Hope?" she asked quietly.

I sighed, my gaze shifting towards Salem, who was meowing as if telling me I should have known better than to date a celebrity. "I guess I will be," I said softly. "I'm not used to being at the center of the universe like this. All my life, I was so invisible, and no one even noticed my existence."

Veronica nodded with understanding and then gave me a small but reassuring smile. "Everything will be okay," she whispered, her words stopped me from crumbling under the pressure of this unexpected fame.

Veronica finally broke the sad silence and talked about how we could handle the situation diplomatically. I sat quietly listening — trying to take in everything she had to say as best as possible.

Veronica sat back in her chair thoughtfully. "Look, this might not be ideal for you," she started. "But it's not all bad either. You're still dating the most gorgeous and famous guy in the world!"

I nodded but didn't say anything. I was still overwhelmed by the sudden turn of events. Veronica must have seen my confusion because she patted my arm and gave me a knowing smile before she got up to leave, advising me to take some time to think things through.

Before she left, she turned around again and told me I could call her anytime if I needed any advice or help to handle the media circus. I was finally alone with my thoughts. I looked around at the room full of tabloids and thought about Richard's fame and how suddenly I found myself in an unfamiliar world of celebrity gossip and public scrutiny.

———

I opened my computer and stared at the blank screen with a sigh. I knew I couldn't leave the house with the media circus outside, so I had no choice but to find solace in writing. Even in moments of emotional turmoil, I could always draw strength from diving into my own stories and creating characters.

I started typing away furiously — letting my mind get lost in these imaginary worlds far from my reality. As the words flowed from my fingertips, I felt myself begin to relax and find peace once more as the story unfolded before me. Everything else seemed to blur into insignificance as I created beautiful yet complicated characters who would soon embark on a journey for their destinies.

I had been writing for hours. The words had come easily — lost in my creative world a million miles away from reality, when I heard a knock at the door. I opened it to find Charlie standing there with a steaming hot bowl of Vietnamese noodle soup. He must have known I couldn't leave the house because of the media circus outside. Grateful for his kindness, I exclaimed, "Thank you, Charlie. I'm sorry for the mess."

"No trouble at all. What's important is that you're okay," he said with a smile before leaving. "Eat that before it gets cold." His thoughtfulness made everything feel a little better — even in the middle of the chaos that engulfed me, I was glad people like Charlie and Veronica still cared about my well-being. As for Richard, he seemed to have vanished without a trace, leaving me with a sense of abandonment just when trouble reared its head. Not a single message or phone call came my way — it was as if he had gone completely radio silent.

The hot Vietnamese noodle soup was a savory delight — fresh herbs and spices flavors danced on my tongue with every sip. As I savored each spoonful, I felt l the tension melting away, and a sense of calm washed over me.

After eating, I quickly took a shower and changed into a comfortable white tank top and pink underwear bottom before returning to work. I turned on the heater. With renewed energy, thanks to Charlie's food, I started to write again. At this moment, I felt a sense of freedom unlike any other. I felt liberated from the restrictions of the physical world and could express my innermost thoughts and feelings in words. Everything contained inside me had suddenly released onto the page. This was how I found strength — by writing my story one word at a time and freeing myself from the constraints of reality.

There was a knock on my door. Probably Veronica or Charlie checking on me again. To my surprise, Richard stood outside my door. I almost couldn't believe it was him. His light blue shirt and navy-blue jacket made him look even more handsome than I remembered. His laugh as I threw myself into his arms made me feel even more alive — it was like all the emotions I had been trying to keep away came flooding back with a vengeance. We stayed that way for what felt like an eternity — then he whispered in my ear, "I guess this means you miss me."

Richard knew exactly how to snap me back to reality, and he did just that as he gently nudged me away, saying, "We really should get inside quickly. Your panties are cute, and I do like them, but you shouldn't let all of New York City see them." A knowing smile played on his lips as he took in my scantily clad state, while he himself stood there impeccably dressed. At that moment, I felt embarrassed and exposed, but I also felt a wave of comfort knowing that Richard was here looking out for me. I felt so safe and so taken care of, as nothing else mattered.

"You're here," I whispered, barely able to contain my excitement as I pulled him inside and closed the door.

"I should've been here earlier, but Peter and I discussed the next steps," Richard replied, looking at me with a mischievous twinkle in his eye. "In particular, how on earth am I dating someone who is almost half my age!"

"Oh yeah, I'm dating an old man," I said, my face flushing as I shifted my weight from one foot to the other. " A dirty old man."

"Hmmm, dirty old man," he said with a chuckle. He looked at me, took a deep breath, and crushed his mouth on mine. His lips were tender yet passionate, and I melted into him. The warmth of his mouth sent a rush through my body, and I wanted to stay in this moment forever, away from the world and all of its worries. His kiss was intense yet gentle, like a storm cloud raging on with no end in sight as it caressed my entire being. My heart beat faster as he pulled away and looked deeply into my eyes. It felt like an eternity had stopped, and we were the only two people in the universe that existed at that moment.

He pulled away, and I felt my heart skip a beat. Then he flashed me his infamous mischievous grin and said, "That's how dirty old men show their love."

I couldn't help but laugh and feel the butterflies in my stomach flutter. I looked into his eyes and replied, "Maybe I should start calling you 'Dirty Richard' from now on."

He chuckled once more, shaking his head slowly as though he found it hard to believe me. Yet, I could sense that he secretly loved it. "My darling," he said, "we have much to discuss, such as how the producers feel that people would focus on us rather than on me and Britanny. Additionally, we need to address the onslaught you're facing due to your bi-racial background and your security concerns."

I went up on my tippy-toes and touched his lips again with mine. "We can talk while we kiss and touch, right?" I helped remove his jacket.

Richard smiled and replied, "We most definitely can." His eyes twinkled with mischief, and I couldn't help but feel even more attracted to him. With a gentle touch of his hands, he began tracing circles on my back while I unbuttoned his shirt. He then took my face and kissed me again, this time almost desperately, as if he never wanted to let go.

A momentary wave of reality rippled through me as I hesitated and thought about the smallness of my apartment and if Richard would even fit into my small bed. Richard pushed me gently against the wall, our lips still locked in an electrifying kiss. His embrace was firm yet gentle, and I felt completely safe in his arms. As he kissed me passionately, I felt a wave of warmth wash over me, enveloping my body in a comforting blanket of security. The intensity of emotion and desire between us was overwhelming, and our connection grew stronger with each moment we shared in this kiss, only broken by a few moments to catch our breath before starting all over again.

Richard's murmurs were like an intoxicating drug that fueled my desire. His breath was warm on my skin as he moved his hands across my body, whispering in my ear, "You smell delicious." Those words sent electrical currents down my spine, and I felt completely alive. Every inch of me felt energized and ignited by his touch, every nerve ending thrumming with pleasure. "I don't think we'll reach the bedroom, darling."

His words sent an intense wave of excitement coursing through my veins. My breathing quickened, and I could feel heat radiating from my body. "I want to see you naked. I want to make love to you," I said softly, removing his shirt and unbuttoning his jeans as he reached below my top and grabbed my breast. His fingers delicately rolled around my nipples, already erect from the mere anticipation of his touch. We were so close that our hearts were thumping in sync, the electricity between us so strong. Everything around us ceased to exist. All that mattered was the passion sparking between us. Every movement and every caress seemed charged with electricity as we explored one another's bodies. This moment was pure bliss.

We explored every curve of each other's bodies with hungry kisses and gentle touches. His fingers gently danced across my back, tracing the contours of my spine before trailing down to my hips. I gasped in pleasure as his fingertips moved lower until they found the softness between my thighs. "Oh, Richard, please."

"Please what, darling?" Richard continued to tease me with his finger. "Tell me what you want." He looked into my eyes as his fingers stopped playing between my legs.

"Don't stop. I want you!" I cried. Then I felt Richard's fingers glide inside me while his other hand pulled my tank top aside as he sucked my left nipple. Those fingers rapidly moved inside me, sending waves of pleasure through my body. His expert touch drew out a response from deep within me. "Please, don't stop!" I begged him. His mouth and tongue explored my breast as his fingers played inside me with an intensity that made me dizzy, leaving no doubt about the connection we shared at this moment. My hands eagerly followed his lead, exploring the curves of his body while savoring its warmth and perfect shape. We were an ideal harmony of desire and exploration, our movements fueled by passion and love. Richard's hands played inside me, increasing the pressure, slowly but surely leading me to a blissful climax. The intensity of the moment was palpable, and it only grew. He let go of my nipples bruised with his kisses and looked at me as he commanded that I open my eyes. "I want to see them as you reach your peak." When I did, his gaze met mine, dark with passion and love, urging me to let go.

"Oh, Richard, this is too much," I cried, and I was about to close my eyes. But he tilted my head up. "Look at me, darling, let it go, and don't hold back." He held my gaze. He expertly explored the depths of my desire. Finally, I reached a level of pleasure so intense that fireworks seemed to explode inside me. With each wave of pleasure, my connection with Richard intensified, and I caught a euphoric state that seemed to last for an eternity.

He looked at me with utmost satisfaction, "Desire suits you," and kissed me again with hunger.

Richard swept me up in his arms and carried me toward my bedroom. I felt wrapped up in a cocoon of emotion and desire with each step. I don't know how we got to my bedroom. He slowly helped me onto my bed, his hands trailing across my body in a way that made my breath catch in anticipation. Richard slowly undressed me, making sure to savor every moment. As I lay there, exposed and vulnerable, I felt nothing but a pure desire for the man standing before me. I wanted to make love to Richard's body. His jeans were quickly discarded, and I raised my head to look at him in all his glory. I looked up into his eyes, seeing an intensity of emotion that took my breath away as he finally laid down on top of me. My hands ran along his body, exploring every inch of him with a passionate intensity. As I pushed him onto his back, I kissed his chest and felt the heat radiating at each touch. Finally, my eagerness drove me down further until I reached the most intimate part of him. I felt my heart racing as my hands connected with this part of his body.

Every nerve in me seemed to fire at once as I explored him, tracing lines of pleasure over his skin. Hot shivers raced through me at each caress, and every breath felt like pure bliss. Nothing had ever felt so ideal before that moment, as if nothing else mattered but the two of us together. Richard's body was like a perfect landscape, sculpted and smooth with subtle curves in all the right places. His chest rose and fell with each breath, emphasizing his strength and power. Everywhere I looked, his body entranced me more, beauty and power stirring up a fire deep inside that could not be tamed. As I ran my hands over his chest and stomach, I felt a surge of electricity that made it hard to keep my eyes off him. Every fiber of my being seemed to be drawn towards him as if he was an irresistible force of nature that I couldn't help but be attracted to. No matter how hard I tried, I could not resist the captivating allure of his body.

I took the lead, guiding him inside me. His body trembled beneath my touch, and I felt his strength and power radiating off him. With every movement, pleasure coursed through my veins like an electric current. Sensations of pleasure released throughout my body as I moved on top of Richard, our connection growing deeper. With each movement, the intensity only increased, pushing us higher and higher until every fiber of our beings was electrified. There were moments when the sensation was almost too much to bear, and I clung to him for support. As we approached the peak of our pleasure, Richard let out a cry that seemed to reverberate through my entire being. He called my name — filled with intensity and desire that I had never experienced before, and it sent us both tumbling over the edge as we reached our ultimate pleasure. Waves of blissful sensations cascaded over us like a waterfall until we were spent and left gasping for breath.

———

I felt so safe and secure in Richard's embrace. His strong arms held me close, and I could feel his warm breath on my neck as we lay still. His feet dangled over the edge of the bed, but nothing mattered except that moment when we were together. The sensation of his hand tracing small circles on my back sent shivers down my spine, and I was content to just listen to the sound of his heart beating beneath my ear. Even though my bed was too small for us both, it was perfect at that moment.

I looked up into Richard's eyes, trying to read his mind. "You said you wanted to discuss something important with me," I said.

His hand stopped its gentle circles and rested lightly on my back as he answered my question with a low chuckle. "Yes, there is something I wanted to talk about," he said softly.

A slight spark of anticipation lit in the air, and I waited with bated breath for what he had to say next. Richard's face had a gentle warmth, even in the room's dim light. His eyes hinted at mischief, with lips curved into a slight smile. The light stubble on his cheeks framed his strong jawline, and overall he presented an air of calm confidence. "Peter, my agent in London, thinks it's the best option for us to be honest and let the public know what's going on," Richard said, studying my eyes for my reaction. His expression was serious yet compassionate as he explained how coming out in the open would help us protect our privacy better than staying hidden. "The press has been speculating and making up their own stories, so we must show them our version of the truth and control how they perceive us."

"You mean to say we should tell them we're dating," I asked.

"Not just telling them, darling, we'll show them," he answered, smiling.

"I'm Richard Collins' girlfriend," I whispered.

Richard smiled warmly at me, nodding in agreement. "Yes," he said confidently. "We should show them that we're together and happy." He looked into my eyes reassuringly and took my hand in his own. I could feel the strength of his grip, and it made me realize just how much he truly cared for me. "We'll tell them, 'I'm Richard Collins's girlfriend,'" he said with emphasis and a teasing smile. I felt my heart flutter as Richard kissed me and laughed.

"Or Hope Williams' boyfriend," I said with a smile, glad he was embracing the idea of our relationship being out in the open.

His laughter made my chest swell with warmth, and I could feel we were becoming closer and more connected each day. "My feminist girlfriend," he teased, still smirking as his arms wrapped securely around me.

I felt embarrassed by my words and tried to protest, but Richard just gave me a knowing look. "Oh, no, I have to upgrade my wardrobe!" I said.

"I like you just the way you are," Richard said reassuringly. He gestured towards his crumpled pants on the floor, grabbed his wallet, and handed me his credit card. "But if it matters to you, you'll need this," he said.

I shook my head and answered firmly, "No, Richard. I don't want your money – I can buy myself clothes and still have savings anyway."

He smiled, enveloped me in a hug, planted a kiss on my forehead, and looked at me with a mischievous smile. "Darling, your writing salary can't buy a decent designer dress or a bag," he teased.

Pretending to be offended, I playfully punched his upper arm, only to hurt myself in the process. "Ouch! That's so rude!" I exclaimed, though I knew there was truth in his words. Richard took my hand and tenderly kissed my knuckles, chuckling at his candid remark.

Before I could argue with him, my eyes fell on the credit card in my hand, and I noticed that it bore my name! Surprised, I looked up at him and asked, "How'd you do it, and when?"

He smiled back at me and answered, "This morning, I requested the bank to give you an extension to my account, and they sent it a few hours after."

"But I can't accept it, Richard!" I said firmly.

He smiled and replied, "Just keep it for now, and you can use it whenever you need it. Let's not argue about this. Did you know you look so cute when angry and upset?" He joked before leaning in to kiss me. His kiss lingered on my lips. I wanted to protest further and tell him this wasn't necessary, but I knew it was useless. He had already made up his mind, and there was no changing it.

Sighing, I accepted the card and thanked him for his generosity. We both knew it was a big move on his part, but he didn't think twice before doing it, just as he hadn't thought twice about coming out publicly to protect me. All of this showed how much he cared for me, making my heart swell with love for him.

"And there's another thing, darling," he quickly added. My curiosity was piqued, and I asked, "What is it?"

He smiled and said, "We're taking a mid-season break in four weeks. Do you have anything planned for those two weeks?"

"None at all," I replied, adding, "I might do some serious writing."

He probed further with a smile, asking, "Can you do that somewhere?"

My heart skipped a beat as I asked nervously, "Somewhere like where?"

His grin widened as he said, "I would like to take you with me to Paris."

My jaw dropped in shock, and all I could manage was a simple yet excited breath, "Paris?!"

He chuckled and said, "You don't like Paris."

I propped myself up on my elbow so I was looking down at him and replied with a mischievous smirk, "I don't know. I haven't been to Paris." His eyes twinkled as he asked, "That's settled then. Make sure to reserve March's second and third weeks on your calendar."

My excitement was uncontainable, and before I knew it, I had blurted out excitedly, "We can leave tomorrow or now!" A broad grin spread across his face, and I followed it up with a passionate kiss.

———

As the first light of dawn crept into my room on Monday morning, I woke up to find Richard peacefully sleeping beside me. Gently, I traced my fingers along his jawline, marveling at how familiar my touch already seemed to him as a smile graced his slumbering face. Careful not to disturb him, I slipped out of bed and tiptoed around the room in search of my shirt. Among the crumpled clothes strewn across the floor, I spotted it and then retrieved a fresh pair of underwear from one of my drawers.

Peering out the window, I noticed the crisp chill of the morning air. Grateful for the warmth the perfectly functioning heater provided, I continued to navigate the room barefoot. Entering the kitchen, I finally located my phone, which had remained untouched since Richard's unexpected arrival at my doorstep yesterday. With a sense of anticipation, I prepared myself to check the messages accumulated during our time together.

Until now, I couldn't shake the lingering terror that gripped me whenever I thought about opening my Instagram account. The onslaught of negative comments and backlash I had seen in the tabloids continued to haunt me. I knew that eventually, I would have to confront my fears and face whatever remarks awaited me. But for now, the mere thought of it seemed overwhelming, a challenge that would require every ounce of courage I could muster. Deciding to face it head-on, just like ripping off a Band-Aid from a wound, I took a deep breath and opened my Instagram.

A wave of notifications was popping up with every second. Likes flooded my post at an unimaginable rate. My heart raced as I scrolled down the thread, eyes scanning each comment for any sign of hostility. In the end, however, it turned out to be quite the opposite — what awaited me was a wave of love and support from people all around the world who shared in our joy...or, more accurately, Richard's.

I never imagined that my relationship with Richard would spark so much conversation. The sudden surge in followers overwhelmed me — many of them were fans of Richard who had no access to his private life before, and they could finally see into our lives together. Although the massive reaction initially took me aback, the comments flooding in showed me that people were genuinely happy for us both — that gave me a feeling of warmth.

I looked closely at the beautiful candid shot of us both. We were laughing and enjoying ourselves, with my back warmly cradled against Richard's chest as he held the phone before us to take the picture. The image was filled with joy and good vibes, encapsulating our wonderful moment. I felt undeniably happy and content just looking at it — a perfect snapshot that captured that night. The warm light from the fireplace danced on his features, and his smile was so genuine — it made me feel like I could reach out and touch it. Although I looked good in it, too, I couldn't help but feel like I was too plain-looking in comparison. It doesn't matter if it seemed like I was being photographed next to a god. I could feel the warmth radiating from both of us — it was as if nothing else mattered except for that moment.

Then it hit me, I found myself falling even more deeply in love with him — hopelessly, madly in love. His infectious laughter, generous heart, and ever-present smile reminded me why he captured my heart in the first place. There was no denying that Richard is the one who has my heart wholly and completely.

Something caught my eye as I was scrolling through the replies on my Instagram post. It was Henry calling for a FaceTime session. I quickly accepted the call and greeted him with a warm smile. "How's my evil stepmother?" Henry joked, eliciting a laugh from me.

"Don't you dare call me that," I replied.

"Seriously, how are you coping with this circus?" He asked.

"You can't even begin to imagine, Henry. I've been cooped up in my apartment the entire weekend. There were paparazzi lurking around my neighborhood, just waiting for a glimpse of your father or me with him. I never knew until now how much my life could change just by dating a celebrity. I'm really starting to miss my privacy and the freedom to stroll around without attracting attention," I whispered.

"Welcome to my world," he said with a chuckle. "Just put your head down, don't smile or wave. You'll get used to it — it's the price of dating my father."

"Henry," I asked quietly, "Am I doing the right thing?"

He looked at me with sincerity in his eyes and said, "Hope, I truly believe he's serious about you. My dad has never invited any woman into his home before. And from what I can see, it's clear that you feel deeply for him as well. In the grand scheme of things, that's all that really matters." His reassuring words washed over me like a soothing balm, and I couldn't help but smile in response.

We chatted about his day and everything that had been going on in his life since we last talked. Even though it had only been a few days since we had a conversation, it felt like a lifetime had passed in between. The time flew by as we shared stories and laughed at each other's jokes — just like old times.

The sound of Richard's footsteps echoed through my small kitchen as he joined me. With a warm smile, he greeted "Good morning," and pressed a swift, tender kiss upon my lips. His gaze then shifted to the Nespresso machine, his expression betraying a hint of disapproval. Just last night, Richard had made a bold attempt to persuade me to move to his place, citing the limited space of my bed as one of the reasons. Despite his efforts, I couldn't shake off the nagging concern that we might be spotted by prying paparazzi if we were seen leaving my apartment together. In the end, it was decided that he would stay over at my place, putting to rest any worries about unwanted attention.

"I just talked to Henry," I said. I felt slightly embarrassed for not being able to offer him anything for breakfast — given that my fridge contained week-old pizza and leftover cat food. I asked him instead if he wanted coffee.

"It could have been easier if we were at my place. There's someone who makes breakfast," Richard said with a smile as I placed another pod in the Nespresso machine.

"It's tempting, but who will look after Salem?" I asked, and right on cue, my cat appeared from the kitchen window, walking around Richard's feet and murmuring. I bet he was saying something about how Richard had ruined his peaceful life.

"I don't think he likes me," Richard said with a laugh as my cat started screeching.

"He'll get used to you," I promised. "I'll ask my neighbor Charlie to look after him when I go over to your place. My bed is too small for us and looks pretty uncomfortable for you, too."

I handed him his cup of coffee, and he asked me about Henry. I ran through the conversation I'd had with his son and then told him my plans for the day. Suddenly, my phone rang. "It's my mother. I've been ignoring her messages since yesterday," I informed Richard.

"You should answer her call. She must be worried about you," Richard said, gently kissing my hand.

With a deep breath, I closed my eyes, opened FaceTime, and returned my mother's call. She answered on the first ring, exclaiming, "I've been calling you nonstop, worried sick, and I have no idea what's going on with you over there!"

"I'm sorry, Mom. I just haven't felt like talking to anyone."

"I thought you were only writing the script, but now the whole world is saying you're sleeping with the lead actor!" I glanced apologetically at Richard, who adjusted his chair and moved behind me.

He looked at the screen and addressed my mother directly, "Hello, I'd like to properly introduce myself. I'm Richard Collins. I wish we could have met under better circumstances."

"So do I! Look, you've ruined my daughter's life!" my mother exclaimed.

"Mom! This isn't Richard's fault. Can we stop this blame game? I'm fine. I'm happy right now." I gestured toward Richard beside me, "This is my mother, Debbie," then turned back to the phone screen, "Mom, this is Richard." This wasn't how I had envisioned introducing him to my mother.

"Hello, Debbie. I am truly sorry for the situation Hope has found herself in. There's no excuse for it. My communications and PR team are working tirelessly to rectify this," he assured my mother.

"They're saying horrible things about my daughter. She's not like that," she protested.

"I know, and I promise you, I will fix this," Richard said, his reassuring tone seeming to put my mom at ease. He explained his plans to control the narrative and advised her to avoid the internet and tabloid publications.

My mother and I continued our conversation, discussing my situation further. I tried to calm her down and assured her that everything was fine on my end. After we ended the call, I rested my head on Richard's shoulder, and we remained like that for a while.

Eventually, I reminded him that we needed to get ready for work. Richard said he would drop me off at the set while he needed to swing by his place to change and get ready for filming.

"I will take a quick shower and change in fifteen minutes max," I said. I saw Richard's devilish twinkle in his eye, as though he had something else in mind — however, I quickly cut him off and said, "Nope, my bathroom is too small! Besides, I need to be at work on time." And before scuttling off, I quickly kissed him on the mouth.

10

All work this week was filming in the studio set within the city. Richard dropped me off discreetly at the back entrance, avoiding any predatory paparazzi. When I arrived at the studio, the crew still treated me as they always had — nobody asked about Richard and me. I kept myself busy while on set by fine-tuning the advanced script for the next episodes. There were several notes from Jenna that I needed to work on.

By noon, I closed my laptop and watched Robin work with a couple of scenes — it was marvelous to see the story and script we had worked on come alive. From my vantage point in the far-end corner of the room, I observed Richard as he was carefully groomed and dusted in his chair, engrossed in reading his script before the cameras began to roll. Unaware of my presence, he prepared for the upcoming scene where Captain Jack would catch sight of his beloved Lilly for the first time.

The entire filmmaking process still amazed me as I watched the crew meticulously set up the stage. As the lighting technicians expertly illuminated the scene from various angles, both Richard and Brittany set aside their scripts and took their designated positions. Robin approached them with an air of authority. He offered detailed guidance on the scene's tones and the desired dramatic execution. Richard and Brittany attentively listened and nodded in agreement, absorbing Robin's directions. Retreating to his position behind one of the cameras, Robin settled in as the two actors, now fully immersed in their roles, stood poised to breathe life into the enthralling narrative that awaited them

Robin was an experienced director with a passion for storytelling. He was well-equipped to handle any situation on set, from adjusting lighting to fine-tuning dialogue between actors. He was known to strive for perfection in every detail, no matter how small, often going out of his way to ensure that any scene filmed lived up to his high standards. He also encouraged collaboration between the actors and crew, creating an atmosphere of trust and openness where everyone felt comfortable expressing their creative input. Hence, the constant revisions of the scripts to accommodate the actors' ideas and feedback.

The film industry sometimes undervalued the vital contributions of the lighting and audio teams, who diligently worked behind the scenes to enhance every shot's impact. But not for Robin, who recognized them as the backbone of filmmaking. These professionals were responsible for establishing the mood in each movie or television scene. Their mission was to provide flawless lighting that accentuated each actor and their surroundings, effectively capturing the scene's emotions. Moreover, the team carefully considered camera angles to ensure they captured every essential aspect of the film. Everyone worked in sync, focusing on perfecting this particular scene, as it was the story's turning point.

Robin was also known for his dedication to coaching the actors on their performance, helping them unleash their character's unique personalities through dialogue delivery and expression. He shouted to someone to adjust the lights. It was fascinating as the crew set up critical lights to illuminate the actors and their surroundings properly. They then changed the intensity and direction of these lights until they achieved the desired effect. Someone used a huge bounce board to add texture and mood to the environment.

The cameras were rolling on Richard. I couldn't help but be mesmerized by how handsome he was. When Brittany entered the room, Richard acted surprised, like he was finding his one true love for the first time. The camera quickly panned in to capture his expression and the range of emotions that crossed over his face: surprise, confusion, joy, and a hint of something else. His body seemed to tense as he watched her walk closer — all the while, the camera focused on him, documenting every second of this scene with an intensity that pulled viewers in and held them there until the very end.

Then Robin shouted, "Cut!" He called Richard's attention. "Collins," he said, "I want to see the look of love on your face as you see her," pointing at Brittany. Richard nodded and tried to focus on the reshoot. He took a deep breath and allowed himself to be filled with emotion as he stared into Brittany's eyes — the camera capturing every passing moment with perfect clarity.

Robin still couldn't get the expression he desired for that scene. He shouted, "This is the most important scene, Collins!" Richard closed his eyes and concentrated on another take, but Robin saw me standing in the corner. "Hey you, come over!" I looked around and hoped he was talking to someone else, but his directive was focused solely on me — there was no mistaking it. "Yes, you, Williams!" my heart sank as I walked over to him. He placed me behind the camera and then shouted at Richard again. "Don't look at Brittany! Look behind the camera and concentrate on Williams!"

I took a deep breath and held it as Richard slowly turned his head in my direction — our eyes locked for what felt like an eternity before time seemed to stand still. Our emotions intertwined into one perfect moment captured by the camera's lens. And then, like that, Richard's genuine and natural act was captured in time, frozen in place.

"Well done!" Robin shouted, a satisfied smile crossing his face. Richard looked at me and blew me a kiss, my cheeks turning pink with embarrassment at the sudden attention — but also feeling a warmth inside that was as comforting as it was thrilling. I could feel my heart racing from the excitement of being part of something so special.

———

As I was turning off my computer and getting ready to go home, there was a light tap on the door. It was Richard, still wearing his 1920s costume. He stepped inside and gave me a long kiss — one I never seemed tired of. When he pulled away, he handed me a set of keys with labels attached. "My housekeeper Leticia usually leaves after dinner, so you'll be on your own for a while," he said. "I need to shoot some interviews with Stephen Colbert. I will be late, but I'll do my best to finish everything early."

"Richard, I can stay at my place. We don't need to do this," I protested.

"I want to sleep comfortably tonight. I love your place, but your bed can't fit us," he said with a smile.

"Okay, I'll take Uber in a while to get a couple of things from my place," I replied.

"No, Jeffrey will take you there and bring you to my place."

"Who's Jeffrey?" I asked, confusion creasing my brows.

"I hired a security personnel to drive and shadow you whenever I'm at work," he answered.

"Richard, this is too much. I'm independent! I'm used to walking, taking a subway or Uber," I argued stubbornly.

He sighed and looked into my eyes. "Those were before you started going out with me. It's for my peace of mind, knowing you'll be safe. Please, darling." He flashed me a charming smile before exiting the room, and my heart raced. I sighed and looked at him — my life will never be the same again...

———

Jeffrey was bulky, looking like a bar bouncer in a suit. He opened the back seat door for me and silently walked to the driver's side. Despite my lack of directions, he stopped at my apartment building and opened the door for me when we arrived.

I quickly packed some clothes for work and toiletries before pouring food into Salem's dish. He was still sleeping, so I turned on the kitchen light as if that would make up for leaving him behind. "I will be back tomorrow," I whispered. I couldn't shake the guilt as I returned to Jeffrey's car, heading towards Richard's place.

I said a quick "hi" to Fred as he opened the door for me, with Jeffrey tagging along with my bag. We entered Richard's apartment, and Leticia graciously took my bags and placed them in the walk-in closet in the master bedroom.

Richard's bedroom had a spectacular view of Central Park as the sun was on the brink of setting. The bed was huge, with white bedding that seemed to glimmer in the fading light. The room was decorated with fine furniture and luxurious rugs, creating a peaceful and welcoming atmosphere. The walls were in a deep navy blue that accentuated the large framed painting mounted directly across from the bed. White curtains hung from the windows, and books were placed throughout the room. Richard was a reader, just like me. And I can't help but smile at the thought of finding a man who reads.

I followed Leticia through the hallway, admiring the navy blue walls and bookshelves as we passed. I arrived in the kitchen, where Leticia had already begun to prepare dinner. "Madam Hope," she said with a smile, "I will be leaving shortly, so can I get you anything before then?"

I returned her smile warmly and replied, "Please call me Hope, Leticia. I don't feel old enough to be called Madam yet." I looked around the kitchen and asked if she could show me which foods were out and how to reheat them when Richard came home.

She showed me a few dishes she had prepared and then explained how to use the oven to reheat them. She pointed out which buttons to press and briefly described the temperature settings. Finally, Leticia gave me tips on when a dish was ready and when to reheat it just in time for Richard's arrival.

After Leticia left, I changed into my comfortable oversize white T-shirt, which had a vast pipe printed on the front, almost covering the entire front side, and paired it with black bikini briefs. I wore my oversized black-framed glasses, which is what I use when reading and working at home, and found myself drawn to Richard's book collection. While browsing, I stumbled upon a first edition of *The Count of Monte Cristo*. Overwhelmed with excitement, I seized the book and retreated to the living room couch. Nestling into its cushions, I opened the book and began reading, eagerly anticipating Richard's return.

The elegant red hardcover, embellished with gold lettering on the cover and spine, signified the treasure nestled in my hands. For a moment, I was captivated by its physical beauty alone, momentarily forgetting the reason I cherished this classic. Flipping through the pages, I realized that this edition was unlike any I had seen before. It included an errata sheet addressing any discrepancies within the printed material, as well as illustrations by French artist Alfred Nanteuil and the complete original text by Alexandre Dumas.

"Oh, Richard! You own the finest edition of one of literature's most extraordinary stories!" I exclaimed to myself. The first edition of *Pride and Prejudice* he had gifted me originated from this very collection. This revelation unveiled another charming aspect of Richard — not only was I dating one of Hollywood's most desirable men, but he also had a passion for reading!

Clutching the book close to my chest, I inhaled its intoxicating scent of aged paper and weathered leather. This corner of Richard's home truly served as a sanctuary for readers. Taking a deep breath, I reopened the book and immersed myself in the tragic love story of Edmund Dantes and Mercedes, which had been my favorite classic since junior high school. Each time I revisited its pages, I found myself utterly absorbed by the narrative.

Dantes' arduous journey through life's complexities, fueled by his unwavering desire to reunite with his beloved Mercedes, struck a chord within me. The early chapters, brimming with raw emotion, drew me deeper into the story, creating an immersive experience that left me craving more. Completely engrossed in the heart-wrenching tale, I lost all sense of my surroundings, feeling as though I had become part of Edmund's world.

My emotional investment in the characters' fates grew stronger. Tears welled up in my eyes as Mercedes grappled with the harrowing reality of Edmund's unjust imprisonment. Her pain and desperation were so strong as she clung to the hope of receiving news from her one true love, praying for his eventual return. This timeless classic, steeped in tragedy and love, had once again captured my heart and held me captive within its pages.

As exhaustion eventually took over and I drifted to sleep, all I could think about were the bittersweet feelings of love and despair that this novel brought me.

I was jolted awake from my slumber by a familiar scent that wafted through the room. At that moment, I knew Richard had come home. True enough, there he stood, looking dapper in his navy blue suit and perfectly fitting light blue shirt. With a gentle kiss, he breathed, "It's nice to come back home and find you sleeping in my living room."

His words warmed my heart and sent chills down my spine simultaneously. No matter how long time had passed since we last saw each other, his presence still felt like coming home. Richard wrapped his arms around me and tenderly kissed me. Taking off my glasses, he placed them on top of the book I had been reading before helping me up from the couch.

"Have you eaten?" I asked, and he replied no, so I said that we can reheat the food Leticia had left earlier. Suddenly, I remembered that I wasn't dressed for dinner and felt slightly embarrassed.

Richard chuckled as he looked at my oversized shirt and black underwear. "You're perfect for dinner," he said.

Leticia had prepared a classic roast beef with truffle mashed potatoes and roasted asparagus on the side. It was already arranged on individual plates, so I popped them in the oven to reheat. I followed her instructions as best I could, hoping I hadn't forgotten anything crucial. Meanwhile, Richard selected a bottle of wine from his extensive collection to enjoy together. Soon enough, our dinner was ready to be enjoyed.

"How was your interview?" I asked Richard.

He shrugged wearily and said, "It went well, I think. Shot and locked, they will air on the weekend." I could already tell how exhausted he was, so I reached up to touch his face, hoping to somehow get rid of his exhaustion. He responded by kissing my hand tenderly. "I'm glad you're here, darling," he said with a small smile.

We enjoyed a few more glasses of wine before Richard looked at me and said, "I think we need to talk about something minor we overlooked in the past few days." I cocked my head to the side in confusion, trying to figure out what we might have missed. His lips curled into a mischievous smile as he said, "We were making love without protection."

My cheeks flushed slightly in embarrassment, but Richard immediately said he was clean and hadn't been sexually active for months. I said I hadn't slept with anyone for years, which made him smile even wider.

We then agreed that we should find a discreet gynecologist to get some birth control for me and that we both need to be extra careful in the meantime. He touched my lips gently before saying, "Let's just leave all of these here for now. You're tired, and I need to take you to bed."

After brushing my teeth, I slipped into the comfortable warmth of the bed, and Richard took a few minutes to finish up in the bathroom. He joined me on the bed, wearing nothing but his underwear, and I snuggled up against him. His embrace was comforting as sleep soon overtook both of us.

———

My iPhone buzzed, telling me it was already seven in the morning. It was Jenna calling me. "Hi there," I said, a little groggy from being woken up so early.

"And if my guess is right, we're in the same building," she said. Richard was still sound asleep beside me, his arms protectively draped around my waist as I adjusted my position without waking him up.

"Why are you calling this early?" I asked her.

"I think we can work here today," she replied, emphasizing the word 'work' and hinting that I'd need to fill her in on what had happened between Richard and me recently. "Don't worry, though; your man is busy today with Robin's advance filming before we all go on a two-week break."

"Okay," I murmured before saying goodbye and ending the call.

I gazed lovingly at the man beside me. Richard had solid and masculine features that were noticeable even when softened in sleep. He had a square jawline and arched eyebrows, his high cheekbones framed by thick brown hair. His lips were full and soft. His blue-grey eyes may be closed now but when he was awake, they always shone with warmth and love. I traced Richard's cheekbones gently before finally settling on his mouth, which curved softly into a smile even while he was asleep. Placing a feather-light kiss upon his lips, I hoped not to wake him up. But he stirred and opened his eyes, those mesmerizing blue-grey eyes looking deep into mine. Suddenly, his lips were upon mine before he rolled me onto him in a passionate embrace, cradling me with one arm as the other caressed my back.

Richard's phone began to ring, and no matter how much he tried to ignore it, the sound wouldn't stop. His groan showed irritation as he finally picked up the call.

"Yes, Peter," his voice had a hint of annoyance.

Slipping out of bed, I gave Richard privacy to take his call. As I approached the kitchen, I noticed his coffee machine was much more advanced than my Nespresso back home. So I decided to leave the coffee machine to Richard. I took out some eggs, milk, and butter from the fridge. I aimed to make fluffy scrambled eggs that would pair nicely with a freshly reheated croissant from the oven.

As I scoured the fridge for jam, I felt two warm arms wrap around me from behind and a soft kiss on my neck. "I can get used to seeing you in my kitchen," he murmured into my neck as his head rested there. "I love having you here and playing house with me," he added before closing the fridge and bending me over the kitchen counter. He hurriedly removed my underwear, parted my legs, and took me from behind without any warning. Richard gently bit me on the neck as if marking his territory. His kisses and movement were making my head spin. Our desire was so intense that he made love to me quickly, without hesitation. He began to move faster but passionately, pushing us higher and higher until we reached a euphoric state.

"That was quite the speedy quickie," I said jokingly, feeling Richard's soft chuckle against my neck. He bent down and helped me with my underwear as I giggled. We settled at the kitchen counter for breakfast, and I told Richard that Jenna and I would be taking our work over to her apartment on the 7th floor instead of heading to the set.

"Darling, I hope you don't mind that I asked Jeffrey to have your neighbor Charlie check up on Salem," Richard said as he savored his scrambled eggs.

I smiled reassuringly. "Not at all, though I'm sure Salem is still out having fun. When he gets hungry enough, he'll make his way over to Charlie's."

"I just don't want Salem to hate me for taking you away," Richard said with a hint of playful concern. "By the way, Leticia usually handles the menu, but if you want something special, don't hesitate to let her know." Richard paused briefly before adding, "Oh, keep your phone handy. I have someone who will be in touch about your wardrobe."

I let out a laugh. "Richard, I can handle shopping for myself, you know. But thank you for the offer."

In response, he rolled his eyes, exclaiming, "Trust me, you'll need something more appropriate than that oversized T-shirt for tonight. We're having dinner with Peter, after all."

I laughed and teased, "What's wrong? I thought this T-shirt was a fashion statement!" Richard smiled and shook his head, clearly not convinced.

"Hey, that's for my eyes only!" Richard warned playfully, then quickly added, "I'm off for a quick shower." He shot me an inviting grin before walking toward his bedroom to get ready.

I laughed. "As tempting as that sounds, if we shower together, we'll never make it on time." With that, he gave me a quick kiss goodbye and disappeared into his room.

———

I was completely stunned when I stepped into Jenna's apartment, laptop in hand. Racks of clothes filled the space around me, flanked by two personal shoppers standing nearby. In the far corner, a series of printed photos caught my eye. Upon closer inspection, I realized that they were all pictures of me!

My suspicions were confirmed as Jenna emerged from one of the bedrooms, warmly welcoming me. She explained that she had brought the clothes so I could look perfect when I was with Richard. "I just want you to stand out and look amazing among all the other people we'll be seeing," she added, trying to convince me.

As my eyes nervously traveled around the room, I whispered to Jenna. "I... I can't afford all of this," I said softly.

Jenna smiled reassuringly. "Don't worry. It's all taken care of," she said.

Feeling confused and embarrassed, I protested, "But I can't let you pay for all of this, Jenna."

Jenna's following words made my heart sink. "Richard talked to me about helping you with your wardrobe. All of this is on him," she said softly, putting an arm around me for comfort. The realization hit me like a ton of bricks. Why was he spending so much money on my clothes? I felt my cheeks burn with frustration, and tears threatened to the brim in my eyes. "He would do anything for me, wouldn't he," I muttered bitterly, turning away from Jenna.

She gave me a sympathetic look. "Esperanza, you're dating the most handsome man in Hollywood and the top male British celebrity. We both know that Richard adores you no matter what — whether you're bundled in a flour sack or with designer clothes." Her words were kind but couldn't erase the confusion I felt about the situation.

"Thanks, Jenna," I said, trying to smile despite my unease about Richard's lavish gift.

Then, she handed me a big box of lingerie and smiled. "These are from me," she said, her voice brightening. "You have no idea what kind of publicity you and Richard have created for my book and TV series, even before it airs."

Her generous gift touched me, and I thanked Jenna for her thoughtfulness. She smiled warmly and hugged me, saying she was glad that I liked it. "There's a golden yellow necktie in there that matches one of the black, sexy sets," she added, a mischievous twinkle in her eye. "You could channel your inner Julia Roberts from *Pretty Woman*."

I laughed so hard at her comment and gave her a tight embrace. It felt good to laugh and appreciate the humor in the situation. Jenna's warmth and kindness were a bright spot amid my confusion and apprehension about the expensive gift from Richard.

Tears of frustration welled in my eyes. I understood that Richard and Jenna had good intentions, investing their money and time to help me appear more presentable. Yet, I couldn't shake the feeling of being a mere pet project, akin to how the wealthy pampered their pets. Sensing my emotional state, Jenna handed me a tissue and reassured me, "Whatever is playing on your mind right now, it's not what you think. Richard doesn't want you to be in a situation where the press writes compromising stories about you. You need to be ready at all times, including your appearance and demeanor." Her comforting presence calming me down. "Now," she said with a determined grin, "let's make you look fabulous!"

With that, she started combing through the racks of clothes and choosing the best pieces for me to try on. I felt renewed excitement as I began browsing through the selections, my confidence growing with each new outfit. As I tried them on in front of the full-length mirror, I saw a transformed version of myself – someone whose inner beauty shone even brighter on the outside.

In no time at all, my wardrobe was prepped and ready for any occasion that might arise. I was grateful for the kindness and generosity of both Richard and Jenna, and I knew that I was fortunate to have such wonderful people in my life.

Jenna suggested I pick some shoes for my new wardrobe, and I eagerly agreed. We combed through the shoe section, trying on ankle boots, high heels, flat sandals, and block-heeled mules until we found the perfect pairs. Each was more stylish than the last, and I couldn't believe how comfortable they were.

Soon after, I browsed through an array of designer bags, trying on each in front of the full-length mirror. Looking at myself in the reflection, I couldn't help but feel amazed at how much my wardrobe had transformed. The ordinary clothes of days past had been replaced with exquisite gowns and fine jewelry, ready for any formal occasion. With my newly revamped wardrobe, I felt ready to take on the world with a renewed sense of confidence — and to turn heads wherever I went.

My iPhone rang, and it was Richard on the screen. "How's your morning going?" he asked with amusement.

"Richard, you don't have to do all this for me," I said, but he just chuckled.

"Think of it this way — we need to look good in front of those stolen shots from the paparazzi," he replied.

"I don't know how I'm supposed to store these clothes in my closet," I sighed.

"Hmmmmm…half of the closets in our room are yours. If it's not enough, you can put them in one of the guestrooms — except the one Henry is using," he suggested.

"I can't! I have my own home, after all," I protested half-heartedly. Richard just laughed and told me that if I ever needed extra space, he'd be more than happy to renovate one of the guestrooms and turn it into a full closet.

"We'll discuss that some other time. In the meantime, we need to help your neighbor Charlie get his business back on track. The press has been camping outside of your building and disrupting everything. I've asked Jeffrey to pick up Salem, and Leticia has already prepared something for Salem's essentials. You'll go back to your apartment when the tide is low."

Despite the morning's chaos, a smile crept onto my face as I thought of reuniting with my beloved cat Salem. While separated only for a day, I couldn't wait to spend some much-needed quality time together. I was so grateful that Richard remembered to check on him while I dealt with everything else this morning.

"I will be late since we're filming a couple of scenes," he said before we hung up, "so don't wait for me." With a few more reassuring words from him, our call ended.

The personal shoppers packed all the items in boxes and placed the dresses in gown bags before they proceeded to Richard's apartment in the penthouse. I stayed behind to update Jenna on what had happened the past few days.

"He may not be a prince, Esperanza, but he treats you like a true princess," she said with a smile. "And don't forget, he's incredibly fortunate to have you in his life." I embraced Jenna, and despite the uncertainties swirling around me, her words provided comfort. We continued our conversation for a while longer before I made my way back to Richard's place. The anticipation of seeing him later that night filled my heart with warmth. As I rode the elevator up to his floor, I experienced a fleeting moment of tranquility amidst the chaos.

———

As I lounged on my favorite reading couch, I checked the time and sighed, anticipating Richard's arrival. I smoothed out the black lace underwear bottoms, the only piece of clothing I was wearing, and straightened the yellow necktie Jenna had gifted me, adding a playful touch to my serious reading glasses. I fixed my hair in a messy bun. It felt like I looked exactly like a scholar from a porno film!

As soon as I opened *Tales of Victorian Life and Struggle,* a collection of Charles Dickens's works, I was in another world, my reality fading away with each turn of the page. I didn't hear Richard arrive, so when I felt his hands on top of my tights and looked up into his eyes filled with desire — they were greyer now than blue — I was surprised.

"Did I enter the wrong house?" he joked, but before I could reply, he had joined me on the couch and begun kissing me passionately and deeply. Every time we were together, I felt my heart racing like it was trying to tell me something important.

In a sudden, electrifying moment, he reached for my hand and took it in his own. A jolt of sensation surged through my body, making my heart race. To my surprise, he scooped me into his arms and carried me toward his bed, leaving me breathless and eager for more.

He laid me down gently on the sheets and then leaned over so that our lips could meet in a passionate kiss. Richard kissed me tenderly for what seemed like an eternity until I felt myself melting into him completely. His hands moved slowly across my body as if exploring every inch of it for the first time. His hands cupped my breasts and pinched my nipples before he kissed them and rolled his tongue around them, causing waves of pleasure to ripple through my veins until desire consumed every part of me.

He stood up without leaving my gaze and removed his clothes. His body was beautiful. I couldn't take my eyes off him. When he joined me, he parted my legs and traced his fingers across my inner thighs. He swept my lace underwear to one side; his fingers brought me to a new level of pleasure. I felt myself losing control of the fiery passion consuming us both. "Oh, Richard!" I cried.

He looked at me, his dark eyes clouded with desire. His fingers created magic, hypnotizing my body, "You're so beautiful," he whispered. Our kisses were intense and filled with an insatiable hunger, igniting electricity with every touch. The desire between us built with great intensity, and the world outside faded away with Richard's presence. His touch consumed my thoughts, leaving no room for anything else.

I held his face with both hands and begged him to take me. "Richard, please take me now!" I hungrily kissed his mouth and bit his lower lip to show him how much I wanted him. With one swift move, Richard replaced his fingers with his manhood. His movements were hard and fast until nothing was left to give, but our bodies intertwined in pure blissful exhaustion.

As we lay there afterward, our bodies still entangled, I knew that this moment would stay with me forever as a pure, unadulterated expression of our love.

"I love coming home to this," he said, holding me close with a smile, his fingers tracing circles on my back that sent shivers down my spine.

"I'll have you know that dressing up was worth every penny," I joked, teasing him.

"Well, then, I'll have to keep splurging on you," he laughed, his eyes sparkling affectionately. "By the way, did you pack for our trip? " he reminded me.

"Almost. The personal shoppers you sent took care of half the job," I replied. "I still need to pick up a couple of things from my apartment."

"You'll love the shops in Paris," he smiled at me. Propping myself up on my elbow, I stared down at him. "Richard, as you know, shopping and I don't exactly get along. This whole idea of dressing up is making me uneasy."

"I know. I like your natural style, especially when it involves minimal clothing," he chuckled. "But we're now walking PR for *Back In Time*. The producers are pleased with the publicity this entire situation is generating."

As his lean frame drew closer to mine, I felt a magnetic pull that held my gaze captive. His eyes had an intense, almost hypnotic depth, as if he could see right through me. At that moment, time slowed to a crawl. Our lips met, and I felt his strong arms envelop me in a warm, tender embrace. He brushed his fingers over my yellow necktie, his gaze lingering on me as if I were the only thing that mattered in the world.

"You make anything look stunning," he breathed, his voice thick with admiration. "But you look incredibly sexy in that necktie, darling."

Our intimate moment was cut short by the insistent ringing of his mobile phone, which he had forgotten in the living room. "I'm sorry," he said, reluctantly pulling away. "I better get that."

As he left the room, my thoughts were a jumble of anticipation for our upcoming trip, an almost unbearable desire for him, and the memory of his intense stare just moments before.

11

Spring, Paris

Flying first class was a new experience for me. I had experienced nothing beyond priority seating in the economy class. At best, it had given me additional legroom and entryway proximity, and even that made me feel like royalty. Still, I couldn't help but wonder what luxury treatment awaited in the first-class cabin, with its expansive seats, gourmet cuisine, and unmatched luxury.

Richard's celebrity status and money allowed us to bypass the usual long waits and security checks at immigration and customs. It was like being in a protected sphere of privilege, shielded from the crowds of people outside. I didn't know what to expect from our travels, but with Richard by my side and the feeling of exclusive treatment, I felt like I could be ready for anything.

As we settled into our first-class seats onboard the flight from New York to Paris, the comfort and sophistication on display were superb. The private enclosures provided complete privacy, and the adjustable firmness and incline settings of the roomy seats allowed for maximum relaxation. The gourmet meals prepared by award-winning chefs were delicious, and the top-shelf beverages were served to us personally by dedicated flight attendants. The range of entertainment options, including high-definition visuals on large screens and noise-canceling headphones, only added to our unforgettable travel experience.

"I can't believe how incredible this is," I whispered to Richard, awed by the luxurious surroundings.

He squeezed my hand, a warm smile spreading across his features. "I'd trade these seats for any economy couch just to be with you."

"No way! This is amazing!" I laughed, my eyes alight with joy. As I looked at Richard, he caught my gaze and brushed a soft kiss on the back of my hand. "Did I tell you I love you?" he asked gently.

Tears welled up in my eyes as his words sank in. Even though I knew how he felt, there was something special about hearing him express it out loud. Smiling softly, I replied, "No, you haven't. But I love you, too."

His eyes sparkled, reflecting a blend of relief and joy upon hearing those words. Gently, he grasped my hands in his, drawing me nearer. Gradually leaning in, he cradled my face with both hands and delicately brushed his lips against mine. As we separated, he traced the outline of my lips with his thumb – a gesture he often made when words failed him. Then, in a hushed tone, he murmured, "At last, I've found you."

During the flight, Richard and I happily lost ourselves in our books, taking advantage of the attentive flight attendants, who were another reason to appreciate our first-class experience. As the hours passed, I eventually drifted into a peaceful sleep, nestled comfortably against Richard's chest.

The gentle bump of touchdown at Charles de Gaulle International Airport woke me up, its sprawling expanse of terminals and runways stretching out before us. The airport's bustling crowds and modern architecture nestled harmoniously with the landscape, and it was easy to see why travelers were captivated by its beauty. Excitement bubbled inside me — the flight from New York had been smooth, and now we were on the brink of a new adventure, just the two of us. As we made our way through the airport, I couldn't help but feel giddy with anticipation.

As we stepped outside the airport, a car was waiting to whisk us away to our hotel. Driving through the bustling streets of Paris, I caught glimpses of the city's romantic charm and felt excitement at exploring it further. Our destination came into view, and my heart skipped a beat.

Richard and I went to the Ritz Paris, feeling like Hollywood royalty, I mean, me, as Richard was used to it be treated as VIP. Our driver navigated the city streets with ease as we soaked up the sights and sounds of this romantic destination. When we arrived at the exquisite hotel, I felt awe at its grandeur — from the gorgeously landscaped gardens to the classic design and modern amenities.

Our hotel suite was lavish, with modern furnishings and a wealth of amenities. The large windows gave us a stunning view of the Eiffel Tower while natural light streamed in from the French balconies. We found plush bedding, fine linens, and plenty of space to relax and enjoy our stay in our room. There was also a luxurious bathroom where we could soak in a hot tub or take a refreshing steam shower. With its high ceilings, sparkling chandeliers, and state-of-the-art entertainment system, it was clear that this was no ordinary suite.

Twilight had arrived, and the sky was a stunning blend of pinks and greys illuminated by the city's twinkling lights. Richard asked me if I wanted to get dressed for dinner downstairs or have a room service meal. I saw an opportunity to make an impression, so I chose the former. I decided on a little Dior black dress and black and beige Jimmy Choo shoes for the evening. I styled my hair into an effortlessly messy bun, with makeup that added a subtle yet glamorous touch. I couldn't help but admire my reflection in the mirror – I never looked so good! Richard emerged from the bathroom, looking dashing in his perfectly tailored formal dinner jacket. I couldn't resist the urge to smooth out his collar and compliment him, so I said, "You look so dazzling, my love."

Richard smiled and nibbled my left ear before saying, "I think something is missing with your dress." In a surprise move, he produced a black rectangular box. When I opened it, there was an elegant set of diamond earrings and a matching necklace. They were absolutely stunning! For a moment, I was speechless — this set was the most beautiful gift I had ever received.

"They're beautiful!" I exclaimed, putting my arms around Richard.

He kissed my neck and said, "You can always return the favor after our dinner." His kiss was passionate, and he gently bit my lower lip. The desire in his eyes was undeniable. But he said we'd have more time for that later, then proceeded to put the necklace on me as I put the earrings on both ears. Looking at us in the mirror, I realized how perfect we looked together. I had never felt so different from weeks ago — tonight, I finally matched Richard's charm and elegance. He kissed the side of my neck and sucked on it softly, leaving behind a delicate mark that would be visible tomorrow morning. At that moment, I knew without a doubt that I was deeply in love with him. We admired each other in the shimmering light of dusk before heading downstairs for a memorable evening.

Richard took me to L'Espadon with the perfect table for two in an intimate corner space with plush seating and a cityscape view. The warm lighting and soft music and a singer crooning her version of Ingrid Michelson's "Keep Breathing" created a truly romantic atmosphere. We started with a glass of champagne and then indulged in an exquisite multi-course meal. We savored every bite while enjoying our conversation that seemed like it would never end. It was the perfect night at the perfect place.

As we sat at the table, Richard filled me in on his latest project and the exciting opportunities it could bring. "Peter is working on a new endorsement deal for global retail. It might involve filming and shooting some ads in Asia and parts of Europe," he said.

"That sounds amazing! Though I'll miss you when you're gone," I admitted, pouting.

Richard leaned towards me, his eyes full of warmth. "I could take you with me," he offered, a smile spreading across his face.

"I have a job and responsibilities. I can't be Richard Collins's groupie," I joked, though the thought of being with him was tempting.

He laughed and took my hand, bringing it to his lips for a soft, intimate kiss. "Hmmm... let's see what comes of it," he said, a hint of promise in his eyes as he locked his gaze on mine.

Richard and I were savoring the last bites of our desserts and finishing our coffee when we were rudely interrupted. A tall blond woman in a tailored black dress approached our table.

"Richard, love! It's so good to see you!" she chirped, ignoring me as she greeted him.

"Emilia," Richard said dryly, gripping my hand under the table. He remained seated, making no motion to greet his ex-wife or stand up for her. She introduced her date, a tall Eastern European man in a navy blue pinstripe suit.

"Michael Runn, this is Richard, my hus–" she said, introducing the man beside her. Before she could finish her sentence, Richard interjected with a stern "ex-husband." His cold tone effectively put a damper on her enthusiasm, leaving an uncomfortable silence lingering in the air.

Despite her haughty demeanor, Emilia was undeniably gorgeous, her blond hair cascading down her shoulders in soft waves, her blue eyes still beaming despite the tension in the air.

"Love, I had dinner with Mama two days ago," she said, this time looking directly at me. "His mother," she added to remind us they were family. "She was planning new artwork acquisitions from contemporary artists and asked if I had the time to accompany her. And why is Henry planning to transfer to America?"

"You can talk to my mother, Emilia. But when it comes to Henry, stay out of it," Richard's voice was stern. Richard's typically warm and kind personality had vanished, replaced with short, abrasive words that lacked his usual charm. It was startling to see how much Emilia could cause him to lose his usually composed facade, revealing a side of him hidden from view.

"Pleasure meeting you both," Michael declared, instantly lightening the tense atmosphere between Richard and Emilia. I saw her shoot me a look of disdain as they left. Richard tenderly reached out and cupped my face when they were out of sight. His fingers ran softly across my lips, his expression becoming increasingly affectionate and passionate — it was almost like he wanted to kiss me right there.

As Richard and I headed off to our room, my mind was boiling with questions — why had she made him so uneasy? I looked up at him and saw his features had softened somewhat, still unreadable but no longer showing any signs of tension. We arrived at our room, and he brought me close in a gentle embrace. He lightly kissed my forehead and said softly, "It's going to be alright." As we went inside, my heart brimmed with an even more complex mix of emotions — feeling confident and bewildered by Richard's peculiar behavior.

Finally, seeing Emilia stirred strange emotions in me, likely driven by jealousy of her beauty. I wanted to eliminate those feelings of insecurity and kissed Richard aggressively, hungrily pressing my lips against his. I bit his lower lip slightly. Richard seemed to love this newfound side of me, embracing me tightly. His tongue probed inside my mouth, and he took control of the kiss. He tasted like wine and desire, and another shot of lust poured into my bloodstream.

I immediately took off his jacket and unbuttoned his shirt. I ran my nails across his chest. I left his mouth and traced kisses across his chest while unbuckling his pants. He was hungry for it, and so was I. In one swift movement, his pants and boxers were around his thighs. I ran my tongue across his already-hardened nipples. Richard let out a groan and grabbed my hair gently. I bit and sucked at his left nipple, then I went down to my knees and kissed his erection hungrily. He tucked some loose strands of hair behind my ears before he dropped his head back.

Richard closed his eyes. This wasn't the sweet side of me, this was the aggressive me, and I could tell he loved it. I looked at him, and his eyes were intense and passionate. He stepped out of his pants and underwear. I explored the rest of his body with my hands, tracing the contours of his thighs and muscles as he moved with me in perfect harmony. Richard pulled himself out from my mouth and carried me swiftly into the bedroom.

He laid me on the bed, held my wrists above my head, and kissed me. Deeply. Our tongues entwined with an ever-increasing hunger. He hiked the hem of my black dress around my waist, grabbed my black lace underwear, and tossed it. He took me without warning, and my head spun with desire. This time it was more urgent, his breaths quickening. His movements matched mine. His touch felt like velvet on my skin as we moved together, each caress more compelling than the last. His breath was hot against my neck as he whispered words of love and devotion into my ear. I felt completely enveloped in bliss and contentment as our connection deepened with each movement. There was nothing else but him and me at that moment.

————

Enjoying the morning in Paris, we explored some of its most iconic landmarks — from the grand Eiffel Tower to the ancient Notre Dame Cathedral. We eventually found a quaint little café on a cobblestone street, where we soaked up the atmosphere and tried local delicacies. It had a cozy vibe with muted paint colors adorning its walls and rustic wooden furniture throughout — one look was enough to make us feel at home. The café had outdoor seating with umbrellas and indoor areas bustling with people enjoying drinks or light snacks while admiring their gorgeous surroundings. The sweet aroma of freshly roasted coffee beans and pastries filled the air, creating an inviting ambiance.

Suddenly, a paparazzi took our photo — it annoyed Richard, but he kept his composure and smiled at me as he wrapped his arm around my shoulder. "It's alright, don't worry about it," he said gently. He was determined to prove that, despite their intrusive presence, we remained happily in love, offering them the perfect story to write. Richard skillfully controlled the narrative, ensuring that his actions portrayed the most favorable depiction of our relationship for everyone to witness.

As we sat in the cozy café, I couldn't help but notice that the attention of the patrons had gradually shifted toward Richard. People seemed to have recognized him and were eager to take selfies with him. Sensing my discomfort, Richard tenderly cupped my face and whispered reassuringly, "Darling, allow me to handle this situation. It's best if we limit your public exposure for now. These photographs could end up anywhere — or worse, in the hands of tabloid journalists."

I understood his concern and replied, "Go on, make their day."

With a gentle kiss on my forehead, Richard stood up and graciously attended to his fans. As I observed him from a distance, a swell of pride and happiness washed over me. He effortlessly charmed each person with thoughtful responses and courteous gestures, sharing laughter and heartwarming moments with them. It was no wonder that people adored him; Richard genuinely appreciated those who had played a part in shaping him into the remarkable individual he is today.

Finally, the selfies were done and we finished our coffee in peace, enjoying the moment together. I couldn't help but admire his composure in such a situation. "Thank you for not letting them take away our moment," I said, kissing him on the cheek.

"So, where do we go next? Let me guess, library, museum, or bookstores?" he asked.

"I want to meet Da Vinci and Leonardo," I said excitedly.

"Meet Da Vinci and Leonardo?" Richard asked, his eyes sparkling with amusement. My cheeks reddened as I explained how much I admired their creations and was captivated by the prospect of seeing the actual paintings, rather than the common replicas or reproductions. He grinned and agreed that it was an excellent idea.

Walking through the bustling streets of Paris, Richard and I headed toward the world-famous Louvre. As we got closer, I felt a flutter of excitement in my chest that only increased as we stepped through its grand entrance. We admired the architecture, sculptures, and other artwork from various eras and genres. Although initially overwhelming, Richard was patient and encouraging, helping me understand each piece more deeply. My admiration for him grew with every step. Soon enough, we were both lost in our little world, marveling at the art around us.

One of the most captivating artworks that Richard and I encountered was a massive painting by Leonardo da Vinci. "The *Virgin and Child with Saint Anne* depicts Mary holding Jesus while flanked by his grandmother, Saint Anne," explained Richard as we both admired the art piece. Painted with incredible detail, one can make out the golden hues of Mary's hair or the soft tones of her blue eyes. Even more impressive is that each figure in the painting conveyed deep emotion, making it seem almost alive. Observing this classic work of art up close and personal was truly mesmerizing!

As we studied the incredible collections in the Louvre, I quickly realized that Richard was an expert tour guide. His knowledge and passion for art and history were evident in every step we took. His enthusiasm was infectious, and his guidance was invaluable. He helped me see things from a new perspective and discover hidden treasures I had otherwise overlooked. But it wasn't just the paintings and sculptures that Richard appreciated. He also loved literature, often quoting passages he admired as we walked through some of the most famous works of all time. This newfound side of Richard truly opened my eyes to his depth of knowledge and character, and those around him rarely see it.

Richard often wrapped his arm around me as we walked through the various art galleries and whispered stories that he had learned in my ear. I was content with being in his embrace, feeling safe and loved.

There was a moment when I couldn't help but wonder why his phone, which typically buzzed incessantly with messages from friends and work, had remained silent. I asked him about the unusual tranquility. Richard pulled me close, his eyes filled with affection, and explained, "I turned it off. I don't want any interruptions or distractions right now. This moment is exclusively for us."

As he tenderly kissed me, my heart swelled with happiness. I couldn't help but smile, appreciating the realization that this was an experience solely for Richard and me — a rare respite from the perpetual demands of work and the outside world. We were enveloped in an atmosphere of love and beauty, creating memories that would be etched in our hearts for a lifetime.

After spending an entire day exploring the wonder-filled halls of the Louvre, Richard and I found ourselves both exhausted and exhilarated. The aroma of freshly prepared food wafted through the air, drawing us towards a charming restaurant with an inviting atmosphere and a mouthwatering menu. I entrusted Richard with the task of selecting our dishes.

Once he had made his choices, I gently took his right hand and placed it on my cheek, feeling the warmth of his touch against my skin. As he tenderly caressed my face with his thumb, he observed, "Books and art really do bring you joy."

I kissed his thumb and replied, "It's the writer in me, Richard. Paris' vibrant art scene creates an environment that nurtures creativity that fuels the imagination of writers like me to draw upon!"

Richard nodded knowingly, adding, "Indeed, Paris has been home to some of the most influential writers in history, such as Victor Hugo, Marcel Proust, Ernest Hemingway..."

Unable to contain my enthusiasm, I interjected, "And Gertrude Stein!"

Smiling, he continued, "Did you know that Paris is also renowned for its numerous independent bookstores? I think I should take you to Shakespeare and Company and Librairie Galignani tomorrow." He handed me a glass of wine as he spoke.

Overwhelmed with excitement, I threw my arms around his neck and kissed him. "I would absolutely love that!" Richard chuckled and tucked a stray strand of hair behind my ear, responding softly, "I know."

As we enjoyed our meal, we recounted the day's highlights and experiences, eager to share every memory. The conversation was filled with passion and joy, igniting new insights and reflections within us. When we finally returned to our hotel suite, we were still eagerly reliving our cultural excursion, but our exhaustion was overwhelming.

I stepped into the hot, fragrant water of the hotel tub, soothing my weary muscles. Lavender bubbles danced in the warm steamy liquid surrounding me, and a pleasant fragrance filled the room. Through a window overlooking the city skyline, I could make out stars twinkling in the night sky and a crescent moon smiling down at me. It was a beautiful sight that brought me much-needed peace and relaxation after our long day of adventure.

Richard soon joined me in the tub, bringing a bottle of chilled champagne and two crystal glasses. I leaned back and nestled my head onto his chest and enjoyed the bubbly beverage together.

"Thank you for bringing me here, Richard," I tilted my head to kiss his mouth.

"Hmmmmm...the pleasure is all mine. I haven't enjoyed Paris as much as today," his warm breath fanned the back of my ears.

"This is now my favorite city, aside from New York."

"We can get an apartment here, and you can spend a couple of months here, then a couple of months in New York. Paris is a good place to write, it provides a wellspring of inspiration."

"I know, but that is too much and too sudden. I mean it when I say I still like my independence. I love being with you here, but my life is in New York." I took his free hand and placed it on my cheeks, as I always do when my words were not enough to express my feelings.

"I can picture you, much like Gertrude Stein, who was known to write in the cozy confines of her own home at Rue de Fleurus — which is, by the way, just a 25-minute walk from this hotel. She would often sit in a large armchair with a writing pad on her lap, composing her thoughts. Stein hosted her renowned literary salon at her residence, attracting numerous avant-garde artists and writers of her time," Richard shared.

I leaned back to gaze up at him, my eyes widening as I processed the information. "I must say, I'm quite impressed, Richard! First, you prove to be an excellent gallery tour guide, and now this?" My admiration was evident in my voice.

"Well, my darling, I'm not just a pretty face," he teased playfully.

"Lucky me! Not only am I dating the sexiest man alive, but he's also well-read!"

Richard chuckled, his eyes sparkling with amusement. "Flattery will get you everywhere, my darling. But in all seriousness, I'm fortunate to have such a talented and beautiful writer by my side."

Shifting to a more serious tone, he continued, "You know, I can't envision you anywhere but here. This city would undoubtedly transform your writing. You'd fall in love with the Parisian café culture. I can easily see you spending hours at your favorite haunts, sipping coffee or wine, penning your latest manuscript."

"That's true," I said thoughtfully. "This place does have a special aura about it — one that inspires me. It's like being filled with new ideas, new perspectives, and even words that come more easily."

He smiled knowingly and kissed my forehead tenderly before we settled back into a comfortable silence. We stayed there for ages. "We'll work out something after the filming. We have to arrange this long-distance affair," he chuckled.

We talked softly while sipping our champagne, luxuriating in the warmth of the water as I nestled my head deeper into his chest. He stroked my hair gently, his fingers dancing through the strands and tracing patterns on my scalp. Before long, I found my eyelids drooping as sleep slowly crept in.

———

I woke up the following day in our bed, all cozy and bundled up in sheets. I was surprised, remembering that I had fallen asleep in the tub.

Richard kissed my nose and said, "Good morning, beautiful."

When I asked how he got me there, he chuckled and said he just pulled me out of the tub while I slept like a baby. He handed me a cup of freshly brewed coffee and said, "I ordered breakfast. I didn't know what you wanted, so I got a little of everything."

As I took a sip of the steaming cup, pleased by its flavor, I could see Richard watching me fondly. The warmth emanating inside my chest was overwhelming, and my smile reflected it to him.

"Thank you," I said quietly, setting the cup on the bedside table.

Richard had ordered various breakfast items from room service, including freshly made pancakes with maple syrup, bacon, scrambled eggs, assorted pastries, and a bowl of fresh fruit. He also had put in an order for orange juice, coffee, and tea. Every item was carefully arranged on the tray.

I ate happily, savoring every bite as Richard watched me with a smile. After I finished my last bite, he reached over and tucked a stray lock of hair behind my ear before planting a soft kiss on my lips. I closed my eyes with pleasure, feeling the warmth radiating inside me.

I looked at the most beautiful man who captured my heart. Richard had an athletic physique with broad shoulders and a toned chest. His deeply tanned complexion gave him an air of mystery, while his dark blue-grey eyes sparkled with mischief. His dark hair was slightly messy and brushed back from his forehead, giving him a sexy bedhead look. He wore fitted jeans, a white shirt that hugged his frame, and a tailored navy blue blazer.

"Why are you fully dressed like that while I'm still naked?" I asked, my face turning pink with embarrassment. Richard smirked, his eyes lingering on my body as if admiring the view.

"I could say the same thing about you," he said in a husky voice as his gaze swept over me. "I thought you wanted to explore the city," he said, his smirk widening as if he knew something I didn't. His eyes glinted with amusement, and he couldn't resist running his hand through his hair. He stepped closer to me, an irresistible heat radiating from him. "Let's go out and have some fun."

"Let me get dressed," I said and I left our bed. As I dressed, a cloud of worry hung over me. Though I was ready for another day of adventure, I had a persistent feeling that I'd forgotten something but couldn't figure out what it was. No matter how hard I thought, the answer eluded me.

"What's wrong?" Richard asked, his voice laced with concern. I shook my head and stepped out of the bathroom, arms crossed over my chest.

"I don't know," I said slowly. "Something is bugging me, but I can't figure it out."

Richard laughed and put his arms around me in a comforting hug. "It's probably just vacation jitters," he reassured me. I felt safe and secure in his embrace for a moment — until suddenly, it clicked! My body clock reminded me that my period was two weeks late!

"Oh, my God!" My eyes grew wide as the realization hit me full force. Richard seemed worried now and pulled away slightly to look at me. "What is it?"

"I think I missed my period," I said nervously, cheeks growing hot. "It was supposed to come two weeks ago. And I am never late."

Richard's eyes narrowed as he calculated the number of days. Then his expression softened, and he suggested, "Why don't I call the hotel concierge so they can get you a test kit from the pharmacy?"

My head was spinning with all the possibilities and what-ifs, but I nodded and let Richard hold me while he picked up the phone to speak with the concierge. He gave instructions on what to send us. When he hung up the phone, I feared what the future holds.

"I'm sorry," I said, unable to contain my emotions. Richard held me close and said softly, "Everything will be alright." Even though I doubted he could promise that, the warmth of his embrace was reassuring.

A few minutes later, there was a knock at the door. Richard settled me on the bed before getting up to answer it. When he returned from the door, he had a box of pregnancy test kits. "Would you like me to help you with that?" he asked, concerned.

I shook my head and replied, "I will be fine." Taking the box from his hands, I went into the bathroom to take the tests.

Carefully following the instructions on the pregnancy test, my heart pounding as I waited for the results, two lines appeared. Positive. Pregnant. I slid down the bathroom wall in tears, unable to tell if I was happy or scared. Richard suddenly opened the door and knelt beside me, his face etched with concern. Gently tilting my chin to look into my eyes, he took the test kit from my trembling hands and murmured, "Oh, my darling." He embraced me tightly as I continued to sob uncontrollably. We stayed like that for a few moments until my tears disappeared.

He scooped me into his arms and carried me to the couch next to our bed. The silence in the room was almost deafening as he stared into my eyes with a concerned expression; then, he asked me the question I had been dreading: "Are you happy? Do you want to keep it?"

My tears fell again as I nodded. Richard then ran his fingers softly along my jawline, looking intensely into my eyes. "We're going to be parents, Hope," he whispered with a gentle smile. Richard's expression was one of love, understanding, and a hint of excitement. His eyes were warm and tender as he looked into mine, and his lips tugged into a reassuring smile.

"It's okay to be scared, Hope," Richard said with an understanding nod. He then placed his hand on my still-flat abdomen and looked up at me with a look that radiated nothing but love. "From now on, it's the three of us," he whispered.

I felt Richard's love for me intensify at that moment, and I wanted to express my love for him in every way I could. We kissed passionately, and our bodies intertwined as we moved together. Our lovemaking was gentle yet passionate, each movement an expression of our mutual admiration and desire for one another. It was intimate, tender, and full of emotion — an unspoken connection between us.

We stayed in the hotel suite that day, embracing this new milestone. Richard was more than happy to comply with whatever I wanted, and we discussed the steps I should take to have a healthy pregnancy. First, we talked about the need to see a gynecologist to plan for a healthy pregnancy. With my new situation, Richard insisted I stay at his penthouse when we returned to New York. However, it pained me to leave my apartment. I also can't imagine how Salem would react to leaving behind the life he was used to — Charlie, his daily prowls, and all the other cats in the neighborhood. Richard argued fiercely for my safety and the progress of my pregnancy, leaving me no choice but to concede.

"Richard, I need to finish this season of work. I can't leave it behind," I said firmly.

"Of course, this will never hinder your plans and your career. But Jeffrey will be shadowing you around the clock — and that's non-negotiable," he said in an equally firm tone.

"You're overreacting!" I argued.

"There are two lives at stake here, yours and my child's." The look on Richard's face and the tone of his voice sent a clear message that any further argument was pointless. Jeffrey would be shadowing me full-time for the safety of myself and our unborn child.

My FaceTime buzzed. It was my mother.

"How's Paris, sweetheart?" Her green eyes sparkled with excitement when she saw me and Richard sitting behind me.

"Hello, Debbie," he said casually.

Mom looked at me and seemed to sense something slightly off. "Did I catch you at the wrong time?"

"Mom, no. Everything is fine," I said, but Richard's kiss on the back of my neck and tender touch on my abdomen gave me away. He had figured out that I wanted to have a moment alone with Mom to tell her the news.

Mom looked at me intently, her gaze full of questions. "What's wrong, sweetheart?"

I took a deep breath, my eyes locked on Richard's as he gave me an encouraging nod. "Mom...we're expecting a baby," I finally shared, my voice quivering with emotion.

My mother's eyes widened in surprise, and soon tears flowed down her cheeks. "Oh, my dear! How are you feeling? Have you seen a doctor yet? I have so many questions!"

"Mom, I understand there's a lot to process. Richard and I need some time to come to terms with this news and make plans," I gently reassured her.

Her voice trembled as she replied, "I was so concerned about you weeks ago when those tabloids targeted you, and your peace and privacy were shattered. I couldn't be there for you. And now, I just can't help it — you are still my baby."

"Let's focus on the joy this brings, Mom. I've never felt more content. I know we'll face challenges, but with you and Richard by my side, I'm confident we'll be fine."

We laughed and cried together, finding joy in this shared moment of revelation. We talked endlessly, discussing names, nursery themes, and what life would be like with a baby. My mother was full of advice and wisdom and included Richard in the conversation whenever possible. Mom promised to be in New York when we got back, eager to help set up the nursery and give us any moral support we needed throughout our journey into parenthood.

As I hung up the call, I looked over at Richard, who was just about to wrap up his own phone conversation and sit beside me. On the screen, I could see Henry grinning mischievously as he cheekily greeted me, "Hello, Mommy dearest!"

I playfully retorted, "Don't you dare call me 'Mommy dearest'! I'm only three years older than you, remember?" Richard chuckled softly and planted a gentle kiss on my shoulder.

Henry's expression shifted to a more serious tone as he said, "Congratulations! Dad told me about your pregnancy."

"Thanks, Henry," I replied, taking a deep breath. "It feels overwhelming — there's so much to process. But your dad and I are beyond excited. This is such a new and incredible experience for us."

Henry chuckled warmly. "I'm happy for you both! Just make sure you take extra special care of yourself, okay?" Richard nodded in agreement and moved closer, taking my hand into his as he smiled lovingly.

I looked at Richard with a deep appreciation for his understanding and patience. We kissed gently before I turned to face Henry again on the screen. "Henry, I know you are caught off guard, too," I said, trying to explain casually. "You've been your dad's only child for twenty-four years, and now you're going to have a sibling."

But as always, Henry was full of positivity. "I'm so excited to meet my little brother or sister!" he beamed enthusiastically. "On the brighter side, there will be someone else that Dad will focus on, not just me." We all laughed together, appreciating this new life ahead of us. My feelings were a mixture of joy and excitement to anxiety and fear, but Richard's touch reminded me that I was not alone.

Henry cleared his throat, breaking the momentary silence and returning us to reality. "I know there's a lot to take in at the moment," he said, "but make sure to visit a gynecologist and get checked up as soon as possible."

Richard and I exchanged warm smiles before saying our goodbyes. As Henry's image gradually disappeared from the screen, I felt reassured, knowing that we had him on our side. I couldn't imagine navigating the complexities of interacting with Richard's children — in this case, I'm glad I was just dealing with one — while going through this new phase in my life.

The momentary silence felt blissful, a reminder of what lay ahead: an emotional rollercoaster as we journeyed together through parenthood.

12

We discovered a beautiful, romantic park not too far from our hotel. Captivated by its charm, we escaped the hustle and bustle of the city and ventured into this idyllic oasis. Time seemed to stand still as we wandered amidst carefully manicured gardens, taking in breathtaking views of monuments and landmarks that created a stunning backdrop. The gentle breeze cooled us off on an otherwise hot day while the sweet smell of blooming flowers filled the air, creating a truly peaceful atmosphere that invigorated us with life and love.

The park was full of old-style gazebos, lush gardens, and sculptures that brought us back to an era of forgotten times. The fountain in the center was incredibly captivating with its intricate details and mesmerizing cascades. We found a shady bench and sat down to soak in the beauty of the world around us. The sight of children playing nearby brought smiles to our faces as we observed their carefree antics. At that moment, it truly dawned on me that I would soon become a mother. Within the next few years, Richard and I would find ourselves sitting on a park bench, watching our own children run and play. Any lingering doubts I had about this pregnancy were swiftly replaced by the anticipation of a thrilling future, one that I couldn't wait to experience.

Springtime in Paris is a magical experience. Flowers of every color imaginable burst through the ground, flooding the streets with pastels and vibrant hues. Butterflies fluttered through the air, their wings twinkling in the sunlight like glimmering jewels. The air was heavy with fragrant blossoms that danced on the breeze, creating a dreamy atmosphere that made it hard to believe we were still in this world.

The sun shined brightly against Richard's handsome face, illuminating his features in a way that made my heart skip a beat. His smile lit up the world as his eyes sparkled like stars in the night sky. He was charming, and I couldn't help but feel so lucky.

I quickly snapped a photo of Richard, wanting to preserve the moment. Even in a picture, his beauty shone brighter than ever, so I promptly put away the image, not wanting to share it with anyone just yet. But soon enough, my heart won over my rational side, and I opened my Instagram app. With a few clicks of the button, the picture appeared on the screen — breathtaking. Before hitting the post, I added a caption that simply said, *'Hello, handsome'* along with a heart icon.

Richard ran his nose up the back of my neck, sending a shiver down my spine. He whispered, "You're getting comfortable with us, right?" I giggled and smiled shyly.

I told him that all I ever wanted was to keep him for myself, to enjoy our moments without any of the prying eyes or cameras constantly invading our privacy.

"I know how you feel," he said. "Peter wants me to be more sociable and be seen by the people because they want to see every part of me. But that's my boundary; no social media, no constant photos of my private moments. Eventually, people get used to it."

When I asked if he ever got tired of all those things, he smiled and said, "One day, I'd like to take a break from acting and modeling. Directing and producing quality films is what I dream of doing." He spoke with such passion that it made me realize how determined he was.

I caressed his jawline with my fingers, a silent gesture that showed my agreement. He then joked, "And that's the reason why I'm dating a writer! A screenwriter!" We both started laughing as he mockingly pretended to be hurt when I punched his chest.

We sat in the park for hours, admiring its beauty until nightfall, when the deepening darkness finally hid its beauty from our eyes.

———

The following day, Richard and I embarked on a scenic drive to the Domaine Guy Allion vineyard just outside Paris. We left the tranquil streets of Paris at daybreak. Richard donned a classic combination of jeans and a white and black striped top, while I opted for a vibrant yellow dress with a short hemline. We both grabbed our sunglasses to shield our eyes from the radiant sunlight illuminating the countryside. Richard then lowered the convertible top, affording me an unencumbered view of the vineyard's undulating hills adorned with seemingly endless rows of grapevines. We eventually parked the car at the side of the road to bask in the beauty of the sunrise.

Stepping out of the vehicle, I wrapped my arms around Richard's waist as he placed his arms around my shoulders. Together, we witnessed a breathtaking sight as the sun rose, painting the sky with a glistening golden hue that cast a warm light over the sprawling grapevines. "Oh, Richard! It's stunning!" I exclaimed.

Looking into my eyes, Richard said, "To me, that's how beautiful you are, my darling. You are my very own sunshine," before kissing my lips tenderly.

After savoring a few moments in each other's arms, we resumed our journey toward the Domaine Guy Allion vineyard. The drive was both soothing and energizing as we passed through quaint towns, verdant countryside, and scenic hills. The morning sun cascaded a gorgeous radiance over the idyllic landscape. As we neared the vineyard, we could already sense the striking blend of history and tradition infused with a contemporary touch in the air. The vineyard's sprawling grapevines stretched across the horizon, creating an awe-inspiring sight.

We finally arrived at our destination. Domaine Guy Allion vineyard was established in 1965 and was renowned as one of the oldest vineyards in the region. The vineyard boasted an exquisite terrace, offering breathtaking vistas of its verdant grapevines and rolling hills. We took a guided tour and got a fascinating explanation of the various grape varietals. Richard tasted several delightful wines made from a blend of indigenous grape varieties such as Chardonnay, Merlot, and Pinot.

As for me, following my early pregnancy diagnosis, I refrained from partaking in wine tasting. Nonetheless, Richard made sure I savored the flavors, offering the glass to smell each variety or occasionally sharing a kiss, allowing me to taste the wine vicariously through him.

Once Richard completed the wine-tasting experience, we indulged in a delicious meal at the Domaine Guy Allion's restaurant. The menu boasted a diverse range of traditional French cuisine crafted using high-quality local ingredients. It featured many dishes ranging from freshly-caught seafood to classic French fares such as Coq Au Vin and Ratatouille.

Richard opted for a selection of exquisite wines sourced directly from the estate winery to pair with his meal. As for me, I requested for fresh-squeezed lemonade made from freshly-picked lemons from their private orchard. The serene outdoor seating area provided the perfect ambiance for us to relish our meals amidst the stunning backdrop of the sprawling vineyard.

Exploring the vineyard often requires various modes of transportation, particularly if you wish to have a more immersive experience in the winemaking process. One of the tour guides suggested we rent their bicycles, enabling us to maneuver around the estate quickly while taking in all the magnificent sights along the way.

"I would love to ride a bicycle again!" I exclaimed excitedly.

"Actually, mama, you cannot," Richard interjected firmly, citing my pregnancy.

"I apologize, sir," the tour guide said apologetically in perfect English.

"Alternatively, we can provide horse-drawn carriages to venture deeper into the property, where you can interact with the animals that coexist harmoniously with the environment."

So that's how we toured through the vineyard. We began exploring the serene atmosphere — glimpses of vibrant sunlight filtered through the grapevines, giving the landscape a dream-like quality.

We wound through the rolling hills, surrounded by lush grape vines and breathtaking scenery. It created an inviting backdrop as we observed the workers tending to the vineyards with great care. As we continued, grazing sheep provided us with pleasant company until we reached the far side of the property, where rows of ripening grapes lined up against each other perfectly.

We settled onto a weathered but comfortable wooden bench in the open air. The sun was steadily setting, gilding the sky with vibrant shades of pink and orange. Richard and I reclined on the bench, stretching our legs and enjoying a quiet moment in each other's company. I placed my head on his chest while he gently wrapped his arms around me as he enjoyed the remaining bottle of wine, gazing at the final rays of the sun as it dipped below the horizon.

13

During my first visit to the gynecologist, I was nervous and excited. I felt as if all eyes in the room were fixed on us as Richard completed the necessary paperwork. While one of the nurses assisted me with preparation for the ultrasound scan, I noticed a glimmer of recognition in her eyes as she looked at Richard — no doubt he had graced the covers of many magazines and newspapers across Europe.

The gynecologist was a striking French woman who resembled a fashion model more than a medical practitioner. As I lay on a small medical bed, she greeted us in her native French while Richard responded fluently.

Surprised, I blurted, "You speak French?"

"Oui, ma chérie," Richard replied as he leaned in to kiss me.

"Hello, Hope. I'm Doctor Sylvie," she introduced herself. "How are you feeling today?" She spoke in English, realizing I didn't understand French.

"Oh, hi! I'm feeling a bit tired after a non-stop tour, but otherwise, okay," I replied, grateful for her consideration.

"That's quite normal during pregnancy. Make sure you take some time for yourself to rest and recharge after a long day," she advised, her reassuring demeanor putting me at ease. "Let's start by checking your vitals."

Dr. Sylvie meticulously checked my blood pressure, temperature, and pulse rate. "Everything seems to be in order. Now, let's determine how far along you are in your pregnancy. For accurate detection, I'll be using a transvaginal scan. You may experience a bit of discomfort during the process. I'm going to recline the bed, okay?"

She carefully picked up a wand-shaped transducer and explained its purpose. "The ultrasound waves emitted by this device will generate images of your pelvic organs, allowing us to examine your uterus, ovaries, cervix, and other pelvic structures more closely and accurately."

My eyes widened in surprise, and I hesitantly asked, "Are you going to put that inside me?"

Richard, unable to contain himself, suppressed a laugh while continuing to hold my hand for support.

"You can handle this perfectly," Dr. Sylvie reassured me with a gentle smile. As she carefully inserted the scanner into my vagina, I took a deep breath and gripped Richard's hand tightly. After a brief moment, her expert eyes found what she was looking for — the image of our baby on the screen.

It was just a blob at that point but seeing this small life growing inside me was a surreal experience, and I felt a wave of emotions overwhelm me.

Richard and I gazed at the screen in awe, transfixed by the flicker of our baby's heartbeat. "The heartbeat is robust at five weeks," Doctor Sylvie explained, her voice steady and reassuring.

At that moment, I knew this little life would change everything for us.

Richard's eyes were on the flickering image of our baby on the screen, and I could see the awe and wonder radiating from his expression and how much this moment meant to him.

"Hello, little one," Richard whispered, his voice tender and full of emotion. He held my hand tightly, and I felt an overwhelming sense of love and warmth from his touch. At that moment, I saw a new side of Richard — a gentle and caring side that only added to my admiration for him.

Sitting in the doctor's office, we could not get over watching that wonderful flickering image move on the screen. I felt a sense of peace and comfort knowing we were together. Richard's gaze never left the screen, and I could see the love and devotion in his eyes. I knew he was going to be an amazing father to our baby.

I couldn't help but think about the challenges that lay ahead. Pregnancy and parenthood would bring their fair share of ups and downs and countless moments of uncertainty and doubt. But at this moment, we were simply two people brought together by the miracle of life growing inside me.

Excitement and joy filled me at the thought of embarking on this new journey with Richard. I had never felt more sure of anything in my life than what I am experiencing now.

His expression was full of joy and wonder — mirrored in my own. I felt a mixture of emotions wash over me. I was anxious yet fascinated, excited yet terrified. It was overwhelming, and I could hear my heartbeat in my ears as I watched the image of our baby flickering on the screen. I couldn't help but feel a strong connection to this little life growing inside me. Tears welled up in my eyes as I stared at the screen, and Richard cupped my face and kissed me tenderly yet passionately.

"I love you, Hope Williams. Will you marry me?" Richard's declaration took my breath away. My heart was pounding in my chest as his words sank in. He loved me and wanted to spend the rest of his life with me. Everything else seemed to fade away at that moment as we looked into each other's eyes.

He continued, "I don't have any ring with me right now, but I couldn't wait to ask you." I could see his genuine love shining in his eyes and knew his words were true. He didn't need a grand gesture or a sparkly ring to express his love. It was enough that he was here, asking me to be his partner for life.

Tears streamed down my face as I spoke, "Yes, Richard, I will marry you." I could feel his strong arms wrap around me in a tight embrace, and I knew that our future together would be full of love, laughter, and endless adventures.

As he pulled away, his eyes were beaming with love, and I knew we were bound for an incredible journey together. We didn't need anything grand to celebrate this moment; we had each other, which was enough. The love we shared was all the sparkle and magic we needed.

Dr. Sylvie's reaction was priceless as she witnessed Richard's proposal. She seemed fascinated by the unexpected turn of events and the love that was visibly present between Richard and me.

"I think congratulations are in order," she said with a smile, clearly touched by the moment. "I have never seen a proposal quite like this one before."

She congratulated us both, wishing us a lifetime of happiness together. Her good wishes filled me with joy and excitement for what was to come. It felt hopeful that the world would shower our life together with happiness, and I couldn't wait to embark on this new journey with Richard by my side.

Dr. Sylvie provided me with detailed and helpful recommendations for my prenatal care. She advised me to eat a healthy and balanced diet with plenty of fruits, vegetables, lean proteins, and whole grains while avoiding foods high in sugar, salt, and fat. She also stressed the importance of getting enough rest, taking prenatal vitamins, and doing light exercises like walking, yoga, or swimming. Dr. Sylvie also warned me to avoid harmful substances like alcohol and tobacco, which can harm the baby's growth and development. Finally, she recommended scheduling regular prenatal checkups to monitor my health and the baby's.

"Since you will be in New York most of the time, let me know where we can forward your initial medical evaluation," Doctor Sylvie said, handing me her card. "We're looking at third week to October or first week of November for your due date, and I'll continue to see you whenever you're in Paris."

As we walked out of the clinic holding hands, we both glowed with happiness. I was elated to be starting a new chapter in my life, and I knew that everything was possible with Richard by my side. We were blurring the boundaries between us until there was nothing else in the world but us and our passion.

———

We had a quick lunch at a nearby café and then took a stroll to the Van Cleef & Arpels store at 12 Place Vendôme. We walked into the store, and Richard asked me to try on a few rings to get an idea of my style. He picked out a ring that caught both our eyes — it featured a striking diamond center stone surrounded by a halo of smaller diamonds, all set in 18K white gold. When I tried it on, the sparkle was so bright I was mesmerized! We knew this was the perfect ring for us. Richard couldn't stop smiling as he watched me admire my new ring.

As I saw the price tag, my eyes widened, and I started to protest, "Richard, this is way too much! I'm okay with any ring or even one from a cereal box!" But Richard just kissed my hand and smiled. "You deserve a beautiful one, mama," he said sweetly. His words made my heart swell with love as tears welled up in my eyes.

The jeweler informed us that adjusting the ring was unnecessary since it fits my finger perfectly. Richard slipped it on and kissed me passionately. Then, he tenderly placed his hand across my abdomen, a symbolic gesture, as if sharing the joy and promise of our future with our baby. It was a wonderful, powerful moment.

I stood in our hotel suite, admiring my beautiful ring with the Eiffel Tower in the background. I couldn't help but take a photo to capture the beauty of it. It had been weeks since Richard and I made things official, and I hadn't posted anything on social media since he hijacked

151

my Instagram account to hint that we were dating...except the one from the park. So, when I finally posted the photo with no caption, the notifications started pouring in almost instantly. Brittany Ginger was the first one to comment, "Oh, my God! You guys are engaged?!" I couldn't help but smile — with this post, our news was out!

Richard walked out of the bathroom and put his arms around me, kissing my neck. "Hmmmm... I like that smile. What's this all about?"

I showed him my Instagram post and explained what had happened. "I think I accidentally announced our engagement," I said.

He laughed. "Now that the whole world knows about my future Mrs. Collins, I guess I'll have to call Peter to send a statement formally." He winked at me, excited that our news was finally out for the world to see!

My FaceTime rang, and when I clicked the green button, there was Henry's smiling face. "Hello, Mommy dearest!" he chirped.

"Hey there," I replied with a smile. "Since I'm going to be your evil stepmother, I'm going to make your life miserable the moment I say 'I do'!" We both laughed, but it meant a lot to me that he called me before his dad.

"How's little bean?" he asked, referring to my pregnancy.

I couldn't help but beam when I replied. "We heard the heartbeat for the first time today, Henry. It was so magical."

The moment seemed to linger between us, and suddenly, I felt a wave of love wash over me. Henry would be my stepson, but I knew that no matter our relationship, he is, first and foremost, my friend, and I would love him unconditionally. I touched the screen as if touching his face. We both smiled at each other in understanding, and I couldn't help but feel like this crazy family of ours was starting right.

Richard suddenly embraced me from behind, a broad smile on his face. "You're going to be a big brother!" he announced proudly. "She said yes, too," holding up my finger with the ring on it to the screen. I turned and kissed him lightly on the cheek.

"I'm happy for you both," Henry said. His eyes were shining with genuine joy. "Dad," he continued, turning his gaze to his father, then to me, "I'm glad you're happy. It's been a long time."

He smiled back at his son before replying softly, "I know." His eyes flickered between us, both in understanding and contentment.

After talking to Henry, I put down my phone and put my head on Richard's chest. He held me for a moment, his strong arms comforting me as we shared a silent understanding. I looked into his eyes and asked softly, "Will it hurt the baby if we make love now?"

Richard smiled, swept me into his arms, and lay me in our bed. His touch was gentle yet passionate. His lips slowly moved closer to mine as our eyes locked in a gaze of pure adoration. Every inch between us felt like an eternity, yet it all passed instantly. The warmth of his body enveloped me, and I closed my eyes, finally allowing the happiness from this moment to take over.

We made love with a newfound intensity that seemed to rise above time and space. It felt like we were merging souls, becoming one with each other and unifying in a way that only two people deeply in love can understand. With every touch and kiss, I could feel my tenderness for him growing even more, and I grasped onto him tight.

14

And just like that, our amazing two weeks in Paris ended and we were home in New York. Upon opening the door to Richard's apartment, Salem leaped out to greet me as if he'd missed me terribly while I was away. His purring and licking were so comforting that it felt like no time had passed since I left home.

"Oh, there you are!" I exclaimed, delighted to see him. I scooped him up in my arms and lovingly scratched his neck just the way he adored.

Planting a kiss on Salem's furry head, I teased, "I hope you didn't give Leticia too much of a headache." In response, he purred even louder and affectionately licked my face, almost as if he were grooming me.

Salem suddenly became aware of Richard's presence after a few blissful moments of our reunion. He let out a loud hiss before darting down the hallway, leaving us both laughing at the unexpected turn of events.

"When are we going to be friends, Salem?" Richard jokingly called out as he watched the cat disappear down the hallway.

We soon heard a familiar voice, "Congratulations, Señor Richard and Madam Hope, on your engagement." Leticia greeted us with a smile. Despite my insistence that she call me Hope, she still called me "Madam" fondly. She carried our luggage inside, and Richard thanked her for her help.

Just then, both of our phones began to ring simultaneously. My furrowed brow didn't escape Richard's attention — the intrusive sounds were a stark reminder that we were returning to our regular routine. Sensing my unease, Richard smiled reassuringly before kissing my forehead tenderly. As he answered his call, I couldn't help but feel a sense of calm wash over me, his warm touch grounding me in the midst of our bustling lives.

My mother's voice came through on the other line of my call, and she seemed very excited to hear from me. "Honey, I've been calling you! "

"Hi, Mom. I intentionally turned off my phone because we were flying. We just got home."

"Are you sure about getting married to Richard?"

I told her that we weren't in a rush and that we were just enjoying the moment. Richard hugged me close and whispered in my ear, "We'll take all the time we need," before turning back to finish his phone call. There was something so comforting in how he said it — like everything would be alright and that this was only a beginning for us.

"Honey, what's your plan in the next three weeks?" my mother asked. I was confused and asked her what she meant. She reminded me it was my birthday, and I nearly forgot about it.

"I don't have a plan, Mom," I told her. "I just want to stay home and finish some work before we resume filming next week in Amsterdam."

She agreed and told me that Steve, my stepdad, was also sending his love. We talked briefly about the pregnancy until Richard appeared behind me, putting his hand on my abdomen and kissing the back of my neck.

I said goodbye to Mom and promised to see her in California. Richard held me close as we hung up the phone.

"That's Henry on the line. He's visiting New York the next few weeks. I will have him booked at The Mark."

I turned around to face Richard. "And why are you putting Henry in a hotel?" I put both my hands on my hips.

"Darling, that's his idea," Richard explained. "He doesn't want to be intrusive as this is your home now."

"This is Henry's home, too!" I shouted, mad at him for the first time. As he tried to appease me, I dialed Henry's FaceTime. As soon as he appeared on screen, I yelled, "You are not going to stay at The Mark! Don't you dare talk me out of this! I'm pregnant, and this is upsetting me!"

Both Richard and Henry smiled at my use of the pregnancy card. "Yes, ma'am," Henry replied humbly.

I pressed the red button in satisfaction, and Richard hugged me with a smile on his face after seeing me angry for the first time.

———

Time seemed to fly by in the blink of an eye. Over the course of four weeks, I found myself balancing doctor's appointments, writing, and adapting to a new environment. I instinctively reached over to Richard's side of the bed, only to find it empty. I buried my face into his pillow, inhaling his familiar scent. He was likely out for a morning run in the park or immersed in a script in his study.

I rose from the bed, still clad in my oversized T-shirt and underwear, feeling the weight of my eleventh week of pregnancy. As I gazed out the window, taking in the bustling city life below, I couldn't help but feel a pang of nostalgia for my old neighborhood, Veronica's spontaneous late-night visits, and Charlie's delectable cooking. In the early days of autumn, I had often wondered what life would be like on the Upper East Side. Now, here I was, acclimating to the luxuries of a housekeeper, chauffeur, and doorman greeting me each time I entered the lobby.

As winter's icy grip began to recede, spring ushered in a renewed sense of life throughout New York City. The once-barren trees lining the streets sprouted delicate buds that soon transformed into a lush canopy of green leaves. Cherry blossoms, magnolias, and dogwoods bloomed, adorning the cityscape in gentle hues of pink and white, while daffodils, tulips, and crocuses awakened from their slumber to add vibrant splashes of color to parks and gardens.

The air came alive with the sweet fragrance of blossoming flowers, accompanied by the gentle hum of bees and the melodic chorus of birdsong. As the days grew longer and warmer, New Yorkers eagerly shed their heavy winter coats, embracing the mild temperatures with open arms. Sidewalk cafés and rooftop bars buzzed with activity as locals and tourists alike ventured outdoors to bask in the sunshine and savor the city's renewed energy.

I closed my eyes, attempting to imprint the city's stunning beauty into the depths of my memory. Suddenly, strong arms enveloped me as Richard whispered tenderly into my ear, "Happy birthday, darling." I spun around, stood on my tiptoes, and pressed my lips against the most handsome man before me. He was already dressed for work, sporting his customary light blue shirt and well-fitted jeans.

"Hmmmm, you look and smell absolutely divine," he teased, a playful glint in his eyes. "I'm sure even a lead actor can afford to be late for filming once in a while." He began to trail kisses along my throat while his hands slipped beneath my shirt, seeking the warmth of my breasts. I knew all too well where this would lead, but I couldn't let him be late for work. Richard was known for setting an example on set by always arriving ahead of schedule.

With a passionate kiss, I gently extricated myself from his embrace. "As much as I'd love to spend the entire day tangled up with you in bed, I don't want you to be late," I told him, my voice laced with affection.

He leaned in, pinched my nipple, and whispered, "Tonight, my darling." His eyes burned with desire, nearly causing me to surrender to my own longing. Instead, I walked him to the door, where my gaze fell upon the exquisite flowers adorning our living room. I decided to check the cards attached to them later, just before heading off to work.

Once Jeffrey had driven Richard to the filming location, he dropped me off at the studio, I returned to the Writers Room, where my days were filled with refining scripts and performing edits. Jenna and our team devoted the entire afternoon to story conferences, particularly because we were preparing to move to Amsterdam for the next phase of filming.

My phone buzzed — it was Richard. "Hey, just wanted to check if you made it to the studio. I'm about to ask Jeffrey to pick up Henry from the airport."

"Oh, is that today?" I replied, realization dawning. "I must have forgotten. I should go with Jeffrey."

"You don't need to do that. Jeffrey can handle it," Richard reassured me.

"Your son is visiting, and I could use some fresh air too, so don't worry about it."

"Alright, just be careful," he said before ending the call.

I called Jeffrey, asking him to meet me in the parking lot. Then, I knocked on Jenna's office door to let her know I was leaving to fetch Henry. Jenna raised an eyebrow, to which I responded with a grin: "Mommy duty." We laughed at this, but reality kicked in as I thought about the traffic; would we make it in time? Thankfully, despite the rush hour gridlock, we were able to collect Henry on time.

I turned to face Henry in the back seat and smiled. "Welcome to New York City!" I said, giddy with anticipation.

Henry grinned back at me. "Thanks," he replied. "It's been a while since I've been here."

"So, how long you're staying?" I asked.

"I'm not sure yet, probably three weeks," he replied. "How is little bean?"

"The baby is doing really well," I replied with a smile. "Seven months to go, and he can't wait to meet everyone!"

Henry chuckled. "You're glowing. Pregnancy suits you."

I laughed. "Tell me that again when I'm bloated and can no longer see my feet!"

———

We finally reached home. "Hi, Fred!" I greeted my favorite doorman. Fred smiled back and was about to say something but changed his mind when Henry started chatting on his phone.

We stepped out of the elevator, and darkness filled the room — strange, considering Leticia had likely forgotten to turn on the lights. Suddenly, the room filled with light as everyone shouted "Happy birthday!" in unison.

Richard enveloped me in a warm embrace and kissed me deeply. "Happy birthday, darling," he said. His embrace and kiss were the perfect punctuation for this wonderful surprise. I looked around at all my friends and my mom!

I was overwhelmed by the sight of everyone gathering to celebrate my birthday. It was with indescribable happiness, and as my friend Erin showed me the cake she made for me, I was overjoyed! Erin had outdone herself. She had baked a two-tier cake with a typewriter design on the top layer. Erin brought the vintage typewriter to life with details such as candied keys and an edible paper roll. She had even made edible typewriter ribbon out of fondant. It was truly stunning, and I could not believe she had gone to such lengths for my special day. "Oh, Erin! This is lovely!" I hugged her. "Happy birthday, my dear friend," she hugged me back.

Someone handed me a champagne glass which Richard took. "I'd like to toast to my lovely fiancée," he said, his gaze locked on mine. "Despite being hard-headed, she made me fall in love with her." There were oohs and aahs from the crowd.

"It's her birthday," Richard continued, his voice growing softer. "But she's the one who gave me the greatest gift in advance." He put his hand on my tummy with a gentle touch and said, "We're having a baby!"

There were joyous cheers and clapping after Richard lifted his champagne glass to me. His heartfelt words made my heart melt. His loving words made my heart soar. Tears of happiness streamed down my face, and Jenna's warm hug was the perfect way to mark this memorable occasion. "I'm going to be the godmother, whether you two like it or not," she announced, looking at Richard, then she kissed both my cheeks. Richard laughed in agreement.

———

I awoke to an empty bed, the clock reading 7 am. I usually roam around the house with just a shirt and underwear. Then I remembered Henry was here, so I hurriedly dressed in comfortable yoga pants and a crop top, glancing at my reflection before heading to the dining room. I looked at myself in the mirror. My tummy is still flat, but I already feel a little bump forming.

I went to the dining room. Richard and Henry were already there with a middle-aged guy in a suit. All men stood up when they saw me; Richard pulled a chair for me and kissed me. "'Glad you're awake, darling. Hope, this is Rafael. His firm manages my legal and financial matters. Rafael, my fiancée, Hope."

"Pleasure to meet you, Hope," he said as he extended his hand.

"Likewise," I said as I grasped his hand.

Leticia had laid out a spread of delicious food — sunny-side-up eggs and bacon and toast with orange juice — that made me realize just how hungry I was! The men had already finished breakfast and were discussing some important matters over coffee.

"Don't let me disrupt your meeting, gentlemen," I said as I feasted on my plate.

"Darling, Rafael and I were discussing some changes in my finances, but before that, I want to give your birthday present first," Richard said as he handed me a sealed document in a brown envelope.

Confused but curious, I opened it to find documents about the property ownership of this Park Avenue apartment. My eyes widened at the prospect of owning this lavish place.

Raphael explained that the documents required my signature for each page before he could log them. "Richard, I can't accept this!" My eyes looked around at what I was about to own.

"Darling, I want to give you and my child a decent place to live," Richard said. "If you're worried about Henry, he'll have the London flat. Then I'll let you look for a house in London."

"Richard, can we have this conversation some other time? This is stressing me out," I said. Though I knew my protest was futile, I still tried to talk my way out of it.

Henry looked at his father and said, "She's using the pregnancy card."

Richard chuckled and took both my hands in his. With a playful smirk, he said, "Nice try, darling, but you can't use that one now."

Despite feeling overwhelmed by his generosity, I insisted, "Okay, but on one condition," I said.

"Anything," Richard said.

I looked at Henry, "I want you to stay here whenever you're in New York, and I don't want to hear you're checking in at a nearby hotel!"

"Yes, ma'am! So can I bring my girls here?" Henry teased.

"No! Don't you dare!" I exclaimed.

Henry grumbled good-naturedly while Richard chuckled and warned his son, "Don't push your luck."

Henry replied, "Maybe I will try some other time." And they both laughed over the private joke shared between father and son.

As I signed each page, Raphael discussed a new will with Richard. He explained that the current will didn't accurately reflect recent changes and needed to ensure everything was clear and precise. He outlined the different clauses of the new will while Richard and Henry listened attentively.

Raphael meticulously pointed out crucial aspects, such as financial investments and endowments. "Any disputes or conflicts would be handled fairly and amicably among family members, both now and in the future, he explained. Additionally, he outlined potential inheritance rights for those who had recently joined the family, like me.

"If this is a prenuptial agreement, I can assure you there will be no objection from my side..." Richard cut me off before I could continue.

"No, darling, quite the opposite," he clarified.

"Richard, I want nothing from you — just you. This gift is already more than enough." I gestured towards the house he was giving me, emphasizing its grandeur.

"I know," he touched my face as he looked into my eyes. "My priority is ensuring that you and our child are protected and well taken care of if I'm gone, or something happens to me. The same goes for Henry," he said, glancing at his son, who nodded in agreement.

"Hope, you don't need to sign any of these documents, except for the transfer of title for this property's ownership. Since Richard is our firm's client, it's our duty to provide him with the best legal advice, including suggesting a prenuptial agreement with you, which he refused," Raphael elaborated.

"Oh, Richard..." I wrapped my arms around his neck, touched by his constant care and concern. It felt like it was just the two of us in the world for a brief moment, and nothing else mattered.

After signing all the documents, Raphael gathered all the papers, left a couple of copies for Richard to review, and left.

I was about to finish my orange juice when I started feeling strange. My stomach churned, and before I knew it, I rushed to the bathroom, slumping onto the toilet to vomit. Richard knocked on the door, but I shouted, "Go away! I don't want you to see me like this."

But he insisted that I let him in, then I heard him instruct Leticia. Before I knew it, Leticia had opened the door. He came in and sat beside me, gently wiping the sweat from my forehead. My stomach felt uneasy, and I was nauseated and struggling to keep anything down. He gathered my hair away from my face and said softly, "I've got you."

"Dad, let me take a look at her," Henry said and Richard stepped aside to make way for Henry. Kneeling on the floor, Henry took my wrist to measure my pulse and looked into my eyes with a small flashlight. His expert hands and steady gaze made me feel reassured. "You're experiencing a wave of morning sickness," Henry said soothingly. "Just keep yourself hydrated; this rough patch will soon pass." He looked to his father, reminding him to visit my gynecologist as soon as possible.

"Thanks, Henry," Richard said, cradling my head on his chest.

"I'm not qualified yet to look at her," Henry admitted. "So it will put all of us more at ease when you guys visit her doctor or at least call her."

Richard and I nodded in agreement. He swept me in his arms, carried me to the bed, and laid me down gently. Fishing for his phone in his pocket, he said, "I will call and cancel filming today."

"No," I protested, trying to sit up in bed. "You can't cancel every schedule because of my morning sickness. Besides, I will have this every morning for the next few weeks!" Richard was scheduled for a two-day filming in Madison County before we moved to film in Amsterdam. He was leaving today.

"But I can't leave you like this," he said, concern etched in his expression.

"Leticia is here, and I've got you on speed dial." I cupped his face and kissed him tenderly, adding, "Besides, as soon as I feel better, I need to go to work today." Richard was about to protest again, but I silenced him with my finger across his lips this time.

"I will return tonight," he said.

"That's a long drive and unreasonable. I am going to be fine, don't worry about me here," I reassured him with a smile. "This is an opportunity for us to miss each other. Besides, I haven't tried doing a strip tease on FaceTime yet!"

"Arghhh, get a room, guys," Henry rolled his eyes and chuckled as Richard and I erupted into laughter.

"You're in our room, Henry!" I blurted out, unable to contain my amusement. We laughed as Henry excused himself from the room and left us alone.

———

My desk was full of script notes to work on, and Jenna stuck to her traditional ways — marking up drafts with a bright red pen.

That was one of the things Robin liked about this team — scripts come with open-ended revision changes as we moved along. We also considered the input from actors who would deliver the lines, all while ensuring that the story remained faithful to its source material.

Jenna entered the office with determination, her printed copies and Post-It notes in her hand. She explained that we also needed to work on precise instructions for stunts and special effects.

I nodded, putting on my glasses and arranging the printed copies, annotations, and Post-It marks. This was no small task, as we had to be sure that actors understood the action steps to execute them accurately and precisely.

Jenna placed a copy of a UK tabloid atop the pile of printed scripts. "Have you read this?" she asked, an edge in her voice.

My eyes widened when I saw the picture of Emilia Grant on the front page. "Richard has strict instructions that no tabloid is allowed in the house — they're off limits. So to answer your questions, I haven't seen any of those."

"Well, the bitch is peddling fake news, and the UK press is having a field day out of it," she said with a frown. I didn't know how to respond. All I knew was that we had a job to do and needed to get started immediately.

But I read the story out of curiosity — and it sickened me. Emilia gave an exclusive interview about bumping into Richard again in Paris and invited her for a drink. Unfortunately, she was with someone that night. Emilia concluded she and Richard ended up having an intimate dinner in the countryside instead. To make matters worse, she implied that Richard was seeking her friendship again — a blatant lie.

"This isn't true! I was there! Richard practically pushed her away!" I exclaimed, my fists clenched in frustration.

"Apparently, she's implying it's the other way around," Jenna hissed. We both knew this was bad news: not only did it paint the wrong picture of what actually happened, but it could also damage Richard's reputation unfairly.

I got Richard on speed dial, and he answered after one ring. "Did you see the headline on the Daily Mail?" I asked without any preamble or greeting.

"What did I tell you about not reading any tabloids?" he replied, a hint of irritation in his voice.

"Your ex is peddling fake news about you and her," I continued, hastily explaining the situation. "We must think of something fast to keep this mess from spiraling out of control."

"Darling, we won't do such a thing," he said firmly. "I don't even want to acknowledge it in the first place."

I knew I was pushing my luck here, but I couldn't help myself. "It's easy for you to say that because you're Richard Collins."

He chuckled ruefully. "Hey, listen, to make everything easier, just don't read anything printed on paper or posted online." I sighed, all my annoyance coming back again. Then he tried to tease me, "Hmmm... I think we have to deal with more than just morning sickness. Your mood swings as well!"

I kept quiet this time, knowing it was the only way to cope with my annoyance. He tried to make me feel better, but it didn't work this time. "We'll talk more about this when I get home," he said soothingly. "I love you."

"Okay," I said quickly before hanging up, with no 'I love you too' or endearment.

I looked at Jenna in frustration as soon as I put my phone down, "My life could have been a lot easier if I had fallen in love with a non-celebrity!"

She laughed. "Probably more boring, too. But not as handsome as Richard, so it's probably for the best." She gave me an encouraging smile. "You'll get used to it, dear."

Jenna and I worked quickly but also with meticulous care. We both knew there was no way we could take this task lightly. We talked through our progress together, debating various solutions and approaches.

"I think we should look into this option," Jenna said thoughtfully.

I nodded in agreement. "Yes, it could help us out."

We spent the next few hours poring over all the details, ensuring everything was perfect before we finished. As we finalized each step, a sense of accomplishment swelled within us.

Finally, we were done. I looked at my watch and saw that I still had some time. Right on cue, Jeffrey knocked on the door and gathered my computer bag and paperwork. I was taking home a few things, as tomorrow was Saturday. Picking up my phone, I saw several missed calls from Richard, and it rang again just as I was about to leave the office.

I answered it on the third ring. "Hope Williams, why were my calls being ignored?" he asked.

I sighed internally, holding back my irritation at today's news and Richard's decision to ignore it. "I'm working. I put my phone on Do Not Disturb mode," I snapped, unable to hide my emotions any longer.

"I'm worried when you don't pick up your phone," his voice sounded tired, as if he was attempting to make a meaningful conversation despite our current state of affairs.

"Look, if you can't reach me, then you know you can always ask Jeffrey or Leticia; they've been guarding and shadowing me 24/7."

"Hey, do you want me to go home tonight?" he asked cautiously.

I paused for a moment before answering him; there was so much going on in my mind right now that I could hardly keep track of anything besides the pregnancy-induced mood swings that had begun to take over me lately. "No! Look, I have a lot on my plate right now. Robin wants adjustments and revisions made for the filming next week," I said firmly but patiently.

Richard was quiet momentarily before saying, "Okay, just rest for tonight then. I'll be home tomorrow." We were both silent until finally, after taking a deep breath, I said, "Alright, gotta go then, see you tomorrow," before hanging up.

———

"Where are you going?" Henry asked, lounging in the living room as I prepared for my Saturday morning run.

"It's Saturday — I want to clear my head," I replied, adjusting my ponytail in the hallway mirror. I made sure I looked presentable in case any paparazzi lurked around the park benches. The black shorts and pink tank top made me look more like a teenager.

"Wait for me — I'll just grab my running gear!" He jumped up and ran off to his room.

"Henry! Not you, too!" I protested. "I'm perfectly capable of taking care of myself!"

He rolled his eyes but said simply, "I know, but I'm still joining you." Then he disappeared into his room.

Henry and I ran along Central Park, taking in the sights of New York City as we went. We passed people strolling with their dogs and tourists snapping photos of the iconic Bethesda Fountain. The morning light cast a soft glow on the trees, making them seem almost ethereal.

The air was crisp and clean, and as we continued to run, I felt my worries melt away with every step. Now and then, Henry would give me a playful nudge or a nod of encouragement when I was starting to lag. We both laughed, enjoying each other's company while breathing in the freshness of the early morning air.

I don't know if it's just my pregnancy jitters, but I felt like my third sense was activated. I had been glancing over at the two Asian men running behind us for a while now. Something about them seemed vaguely familiar.

Henry noticed my discomfort and asked, "Is everything okay?"

"Yeah," I replied. "I just have this feeling that someone has been following me the past couple of days."

"Are you sure?" Henry asked, looking around warily. "Do you want me to approach them?"

"No, Henry," I said, squeezing his arm gently. "It's probably just my imagination. I'm not used to your dad's overprotectiveness."

"That, I can't help you," he laughed. "But I can't blame my father. He just wants to protect you and little bean."

"Do you want to grab the best cupcake in NYC?" I asked Henry, excited to change the topic. "I've wanted to drop by my friend Erin's bakery—they have the most amazing cupcakes!"

"Come on!" Henry said, licking his lips. "I'm craving sweets anyway."

So we walked a couple of blocks to The Purple Apron, and Henry was surprised to see people lining up in front of the store. "Don't worry," I said with a smile. "I know a secret entrance."

Erin greeted us with her cheerful smile as she was busily working in the kitchen. "It's so good to see you!" She hugged me warmly and then turned to Henry with a friendly nod. "Hello, Henry! You can pick anything you want from that corner—there are fresh-baked treats over there," she said enthusiastically. "And you can get a nice cup of coffee from that side."

Then she turned her attention back to me and smiled again. "As for you, there's some fresh milk in the fridge. Are you taking your vitamins? Are you eating at all?" Erin asked, pinching my upper arms. "You're still too thin!"

"I'm eating plenty," I said, between bites of dark chocolate cupcakes with butter frosting. "We have a full-time housekeeper who's feeding me non-stop. Gone are the days of cold leftover pizza for me." I turned to Henry and pouted as he sipped his coffee.

"Sorry, but you can't talk me out of giving you one either," he said with raised eyebrows.

"Collins men sure do love to be controlling!" I told Erin.

"By the way," Erin said, sliding two tabloids toward us. "Have you read this? It's all about Emilia Grant's so-called date with Richard in Paris."

"Jenna showed me a copy of it yesterday. It's all lies!" I told Erin, explaining my argument with Richard and his stance on not commenting or correcting his ex-wife.

Henry took a glance at the papers before shaking his head. "Don't believe anything printed on UK tabloids—they make big money off spinning lies and sensational stories." He explained why his father never made any statement when rumors were circulating about him. "His best answer is no answer at all."

"I'm still mad at your Dad," I said, dipping my fingers into the chocolate frosting from my second cupcake.

"Oh, is that why the phones stay so quiet at home? How 'bout the FaceTime stripping?" He chuckled.

"Trouble in paradise already?" Erin gave Henry a wink. "Knowing this girl, this will give your father a week's worth of cold shoulders."

"It's a good thing I'm leaving in two days," he said.

"You're leaving already?" I asked, feeling an unfamiliar pang of sadness.

"I have to, but I will drop by now and then," Henry replied with a small smile. I went to him and put my chin on top of his head. I would miss my soon-to-be stepson more than I had imagined.

Erin and I caught up with news from the neighborhood while Henry took a bakery tour. Then, it was time to say our goodbyes. The morning air was crisp but warm, sunlight streaming down from the sky above us. I smiled as I looked around, feeling a sense of peace.

When we reached home, we stood in comfortable silence for a few moments before Henry eventually spoke, his voice full of emotion. "I'm really going to miss you," he said softly.

My heart felt heavy at his words. I smiled sadly at him and said, "Me, too." We hugged each other tightly before I finally let go.

After dinner, I settled back down to work on the script. But as I did, Leticia's voice came from the kitchen. She had fixed a warm meal and tried convincing me to eat more to stay healthy for the baby. I smiled fondly at her efforts and ate as fast as possible. There was still too much to do.

Suddenly, I heard the door open and close. Henry must have gone out with his friends.

I finished my work and decided it was time for bed. It had been an exhausting day, and my body felt heavy with weariness. With one last look around, I snuggled into bed, allowing sleep to take over quickly.

I felt a weight shift on the side of our bed. Richard had returned home. He kissed the back of my ears softly and whispered, "I'm home, darling." Despite my anger at him for coming home so late, I couldn't help but feel relief from his presence. I pretended to be asleep. He tried to wake me up, running his hands across my abdomen as if saying hello to our baby inside my tummy. He then slid them up my breast, sending a wave of shivers through my body. Even though I wanted to pretend I was still asleep, my body's response betrayed me, and I couldn't keep my eyes closed any longer. My nipples stood erect, and he pinched both, and I almost cried with pleasure, but I didn't want to address the issue just yet, so I ignored him and my desire. So Richard kissed the back of my neck again before finally getting out of bed. I heard him opening a bottle of wine in the kitchen and talking to someone on the phone. Despite the emotions that raced through me, I closed my eyes and eventually fell back into a deep slumber.

When I opened my eyes, the morning light was streaming through the window, and I noticed that Richard was no longer in our bed. He had left, but his presence still lingered. I put my head on his pillows and breathed in the comforting scent filling the room. I missed him so much, despite the unresolved issue with Emilia.

I got out of bed, brushed my teeth, and quickly put on a pair of cut-off denim shorts and a white tank top before tying my hair in a ponytail. I walked barefoot to the kitchen to look for my phone and found Richard with Peter and Henry in the dining room, surrounded by tabloids. His smile burst to life without warning when he saw me standing there.

When I looked at those pages, my eyes widened as I realized they were all pictures of me and Richard. There was one photo where we shared a romantic kiss in a cafe, another of me dancing joyfully in our favorite park with the sun shining down on my face, and one of us leaving Van Cleef & Arpels. The headlines screamed, *'Richard Collins is engaged to Hope Williams.'*

I put both hands on my face and glanced up at Richard, who was already beside me. He said, "You're welcome." Without hesitation, I threw myself into his arms, and he caught me happily as he kissed me passionately in front of Henry and Peter.

"Don't tell me that's a signal that I must leave now. I worked the entire night until the wee hours to ensure these would be out today." Peter said jokingly.

"Hello, Peter!" I said sweetly with a hint of playful teasing. "So you're the guy who kept him up all night?"

Henry couldn't help but chuckle at the situation while Peter simply rolled his eyes. "Your guy isn't himself when you're not around!" He joked before heading back to work with an amused wave of goodbye from him and Henry.

"Guess I'd better do my exit, too." He quickly kissed me on the cheek and said, "I told you." Then he stood up and exited the room, pausing to give me a wink before leaving.

After the two left, I turned my attention to Richard and asked, "What changed your mind?"

He touched my lips with his thumb and said, "I know how stubborn you are, and until you get what you want, you will treat me like a stranger." I punched his chest, only to end up hurting my hands instead. With a slight smirk, he added jokingly, "Kidding aside, I think this announcement will speed up the process of you marrying me."

"Why are you in such a hurry?" I asked in surprise. "I'm already yours!" I caught his right hand and placed it on my breast, silently reminding him of last night's intimate moment. His eyes held a passionate intensity, lighting up with emotion as he looked at me. His gaze was intense yet gentle at the same time. It felt like time stood still while his gaze lingered on mine. At that moment, nothing else mattered. He pushed the left side of my tank top to expose my left breast and pinched my nipple to remind me about last night before he ran his tongue around and sucked it gently. I cried with pleasure, but then I remembered, "Leticia!" He let go of my nipple to remind me it was Sunday, so no housekeeper or anyone who was working for us.

Richard swept me off my feet, but instead of putting me on the bed, he carried me to the bathroom and slowly undressed me as he took off his clothes, too. The warm water sprayed on my body as his hands busily explored my every curve. He was stopping at parts that gave me pleasure. He stopped at my abdomen, "Your baby bump is noticeable now. This makes you sexier." His hands continued downward until they reached between my legs, and I closed my eyes. "Your temperature in here is warmer, and you are more tender." He put his fingers inside me, and my feelings went out of control.

"Oh, I can't wait anymore! Please take me now," I begged. "I'm more than ready." Richard scooped me up in his strong arms, cradling me against his chest as if I weighed nothing, and put my legs around his waist. He guided himself inside me, and I moved in the direction he wanted me to. Under the warm shower, he made love to me tenderly and passionately, showering my body with gentle caresses and whispers of love. His hands moved around my body expertly until I was lost in blissful pleasure.

15

Spring, Amsterdam

As our plane descended over Amsterdam, I could see the city's iconic canals and houses stretching before us. The view was breathtaking, and I felt a sense of excitement and anticipation building inside me. We landed at Amsterdam's Schiphol airport, and I couldn't help but notice how clean and organized everything was. The *Back In Time* local crew arranged our transport to the studio set. We stepped outside into the crisp spring air, and I could feel the energy of this vibrant city.

As we made our way to the van, I noticed the bicycles. Amsterdam is one of the most bike-friendly cities in the world, and it showed. Everywhere I looked, people were on bikes, from schoolchildren to businesspeople in suits. I took snapshots from my iPhone, "These are fascinating!" I blurt out with excitement.

"Welcome to Amsterdam, darling!" Richard kissed me carelessly, not minding the paparazzi anymore.

The van was comfortable, and we settled in for the ride. "I couldn't wait to see this incredible city!" I leaned my head on Richard's chest.

When we arrived at our destination to film the 1920-themed episodes, the spectacular studio set took my breath away! This was no ordinary series episode. The attention to detail was incredible, and the production crew had outdone themselves this time. But what made my day was when I discovered that Richard and I would spend the next

174

two weeks together in the same trailer van. We had worked together before, but never like this.

As Richard and I approached the trailer van parked on the studio lot, we could see it was really small. The door was on one end, and a couple of small windows were on the other. But I was delighted that the van was much more spacious inside than it looked from the outside. The sleeping area was around one-third of the truck and was comfortable and cozy, with soft bedding and pillows.

The seating area was in the middle of the van, with a couch and two armchairs. There was even a small coffee table and a rug on the floor for added comfort. There was a small kitchenette equipped with a fridge, a microwave, a sink, and some basic cooking utensils and tableware. The bathroom was compact but clean, with all the necessities, including a toilet, a sink, and a shower.

"I've never lived in a trailer van," I exclaimed excitedly, looking at Richard.

"You've never been a celebrity groupie before?" he asked playfully.

I looked at him seriously and asked, "Did you bring any groupies into your trailer van before?"

"Darling, that was before you came into the picture." He smiled and kissed me, anticipating the trouble coming his way.

I touched my tummy and talked to it, "Little bean, let's put an end to your daddy's groupie adventures." Richard laughed and put his hands on top of mine.

"Yes, Mama, that's a promise," he said with a grin.

We both knew that our lives were about to change forever, and the arrival of our little one was going to be a new chapter for both of us. The spring weather in Amsterdam was just perfect, and the view from our trailer was spectacular. I could see the city stretching before us, with its canals, bridges, and quaint houses. Sharing this moment with Richard in the cozy trailer van made it all the more special.

As we were settling in, we were interrupted by a knock at the door. Richard went to answer it, and I followed him, curious to see who was outside.

"Hi, Mr. Collins. I'm Luigia. I'm your personal assistant here," said a petite young girl, who I assumed was an intern.

Richard extended his hand and introduced us, "This is Hope Williams, by the way." I waved and smiled at her.

"Nice to meet you both," Luigia said with a smile. "Would you guys like a tour now? I can show you where the pantry is, the dressing room, and the writers' nook for Ms. Williams."

We gladly accepted the offer and followed Luigia out of the trailer van. As we walked around the studio lot, I couldn't help but feel excited about all the possibilities that lay ahead of us in Amsterdam.

Luigia led us to the pantry area, a spacious room with shelves, baskets, and compartments. There were shelves stacked with snacks, fruits, and bottled water. Different types of chips, cookies, energy bars, and nuts were perfect for snacking in between breaks.

She began to explain the schedule of meals for the cast and crew, and I counted the minutes before our first meal. The aroma of freshly brewed coffee filled the air as she poured us each a cup from a nearby coffee maker. I accepted the cup but toyed with it instead. Coffee has to park for now during my pregnancy.

"As you can see, we have a range of product options to keep everyone fueled throughout the day," Luigia said, pointing to the shelves. "Breakfast, lunch, and dinner are usually served at these times, so you don't have to worry about going hungry."

I smiled at her, impressed by her attention to detail. From the pantry arrangement to the meal schedules, they planned this area accordingly to ensure the cast and crew were well-fed and energized. Richard nodded in agreement, and he could see the excitement in my eyes.

After we toured the pantry, she led us to the dressing rooms, which were spacious and well-lit, with mirrors, shelves, and clothing racks lined up along the walls. Luigia pointed to the clothing racks, "These are your costumes for the next two weeks, Mr. Collins. Your outfits are organized and labeled in each wardrobe."

As I walked to one of the racks, I saw his name on a tag next to a row of period costumes and shoes. I couldn't help but feel thrilled at the prospect of him transforming into a character from the past.

She then showed us the prop room, a treasure trove of vintage items like hats, books, and typewriters. The attention to detail was incredible, and I knew immediately that this TV series would be special. "In this room, you'll be able to familiarize yourselves with the props you'll be using for each scene," Luigia said as she led us around the room. "Just make sure to return each item after using them, and we'll keep the room organized and ready for you."

Richard seemed equally impressed, and I could see the gears turning in his head. He was a creative type, and I knew the props and costumes would inspire him to bring his best to the role. As we left the dressing rooms and prop room, I couldn't help but feel excited about filming the period drama episodes.

Luigia led us to the writer's nook, a private area where the writing team could work on our scripts. The cozy space had plenty of comfortable chairs, tables, and couches to accommodate up to ten people. The walls were covered with whiteboard notes and inspirational quotes, giving the room an organized yet creative vibe. I could already imagine my group brainstorming ideas around the table while we sipped coffee — in my case, hot chocolate — from nearby mugs.

"Here is where your team can work on their scripts without distractions," she said as she pointed towards two large monitors at the end of a long table. "We can also project images or videos here for reference."

We hopped into the golf cart again, and Luigia drove us back to our trailer. On the way, she asked if we planned to have time to explore the city before filming starts which is the day after tomorrow.

Richard said he'd love to look around, and I agreed it would be great to get a feel for where we'd spend the next few weeks. Luigia nodded and smiled, "I'm sure you two will have no problem finding something fun to do here."

As we reached our trailer, I sincerely thanked Luigia for her extraordinary hospitality. Her exceptional service ranged from giving us guided tours of the set to providing necessary resources. As we said farewell, she handed Richard her card, "Mr. Collins, here's my number. Please feel free to call or message me at any time. I'm here to serve you throughout your stay." Luigia departed in her golf cart, leaving us tired yet thrilled with the experience.

———

The next day, Richard and I ventured out to explore Amsterdam. We took in the sights, from the cobblestone streets to the canals that stretched across the city. We strolled around De Wallen, admiring the Dutch architecture and colorful tulips busting out of window boxes on narrow terraces.

Richard and I were enjoying our day in Amsterdam when we noticed the constant greetings from people who wanted to take pictures with him. Locals seemed to recognize him wherever he went and enjoyed a selfie.

At first, it was fun for him to oblige — but before we knew it, there were paparazzi around. There were flashes of light everywhere I looked as photographers tried to capture candid shots of Richard. We had no choice but to smile and joke our way through the commotion as quickly as possible.

He always held me in his arms, constantly keeping me safe and within reach. "I know it wasn't exactly what either of us had in mind when we set out on our adventure, darling," he said.

"It's okay, part and parcel of being with a celebrity," I replied with a smile. He looked relieved as he kissed my forehead and held me tighter against him. We both knew this was the best way to ensure we didn't get separated during all that commotion.

After dealing with relentless paparazzi and locals, we grabbed lunch at a small café near the Anne Frank House, taking in the view from a nearby bridge before heading deeper into the city. We stopped by Dam Square, admiring its regal beauty, and visited some of Amsterdam's museums. But it wasn't until we arrived at Vondelpark that we looked up in awe. The enormous green park was full of people playing sports or tucking into picnics under tall oaks — it was breathtaking!

We finished our journey with a canoe ride through one of Amsterdam's many canals, marveling at how efficiently those little boats could navigate such winding routes beneath low-hanging trees and quaint houses. It was a great way to finish off our day exploring this beautiful city!

————

Like any first day in a new film location, there was an atmosphere of festivity and reduced stress. I handed out thick folders filled with episode outlines, character bios, and other documents related to the production. I skimmed through it several times to ensure no detail was left out. Today was a bit different as we'll be meeting the primary producer in person for the first time.

Jenna and I sat in the far corner of the table while the director and principal cast were seated in the middle.

"You mean to say this guy bought the license to produce your book into a TV series, and you haven't met him yet?" I asked Jenna, curious about their relationship so far.

"Nope," Jenna replied. "I heard he's super rich — he owns malls in Asia and Europe — but it's his first time producing a film or TV series."

"What made him venture into film producing?" I asked her.

"I have no idea, dear," she said with a shrug. We both looked up as we heard a commotion coming from outside. Suddenly, the conference room doors opened wide to reveal our mysterious producer. Every eye was on him as he strode into the room with confidence and gravity befitting his status. The once casual conversation ebbed away as every team member stood up in reverence for him — the man behind this ambitious project that had brought us together today.

Standing 5 feet and 11 inches tall, Oliver Ortega is an Asian man with an average build, dark hair, and black eyes. His reputation preceded him as someone with a strong work ethic and an outgoing personality. According to his bio, he loved to explore the world and often took the road less traveled. His ambition led him to explore many different countries and cultures, giving him a unique perspective on the world. Yumi, his most trusted assistant, accompanied him on his travels. She was a beautiful Singapore national with a rumored interest in women instead of men.

When Oliver Ortega entered the conference room, Robin warmly welcomed him and his assistant, "Welcome to the Amsterdam team, Oliver!" Richard and Brittany extended their hands in greeting while Robin pointed over to Jenna, "Over there is Jenna, the author, and her team." It was time for Oliver to meet the rest of the people that would be working on this ambitious project with him.

Before Jenna could even walk to where Oliver and Yumi were, they both approached her. "Pleasure to meet the woman behind the story," Oliver said, his English perfect as he grasped Jenna's hand.

"Oh, this is our head screenwriter, Hope Williams," Jenna introduced me. Oliver stepped forward and clasped my hand while Yumi stepped backward instead of extending her hand like the rest. She bowed a bit — an Asian way of showing respect — and I was puzzled by her gesture.

Oliver broke my thoughts and said, "It's finally good to meet you, Hope."

"Thank you. It's a pleasure meeting you as well," was all I can say. There was something in his eyes that spoke something to me. It was clear he'd been looking forward to meeting the entire team.

"Thank you, everyone," Oliver said as he addressed the group. "I look forward to meeting all of you. As you know, it's my first time producing a TV series. And as everyone knows, I'm just a real estate guy." Everyone in the room laughed at the joke before Oliver continued. "I hope Jenna here will write the book sequel as soon as possible so we can plan for the next season."

The unexpected announcement surprised all of us, especially Jenna, who couldn't help but cover her mouth and giggle with excitement. The crowd around us cheered wildly in response. With that, he waved goodbye and looked at me again with a nod in my direction before exiting.

Jenna whispered to me when Oliver left, "His hands lingered on you, and the Ice Queen gave you special treatment - what gives?"

I smiled at Jenna knowingly. "Both probably know I'm pregnant and their lucky star. You know how Asians believe in those."

"Not possible," she said with a shake of her head. "No one knows you're pregnant yet. Maybe he likes you. Take note; he's way richer than Richard." We both giggled at that last comment.

"Hey, I heard that!" Richard suddenly stood behind us, adding jokingly, "You better watch your back, Jenna!"

"Oh yeah?" she challenged him, her voice taking an edge. "Well, I could always make your dialogue ugly in the screenplay or...I can kill off your character in the middle of the series."

Richard looked at me with a mock-shocked expression before gesturing for me to speak up. "Tell her, darling," he prompted playfully.

I couldn't help but giggle as I turned back to Jenna and declared, "I can't, Jenna, he's my baby daddy!"

"You traitor!" she exclaimed before we all laughed.

As I cuddled in Richard's arms that night, my thoughts drifted back to the strange meeting that day with Oliver Ortega. "There's something strange about him," I said out loud.

"Who?" Richard asked sleepily.

"Oliver," I replied. "There's something about him that I can't quite put my finger on."

Richard stirred beside me and nodded with understanding. "I was also surprised by how Yumi treated you." He suggested thoughtfully. "Yeah, maybe he likes you," he said hesitantly, my thoughts racing. "But over my dead body!" He added firmly, laughing at the idea as

Richard tickled me playfully.

———

I can't believe we're doing it! Today, we were filming the 1920s era. Richard was directing this particular episode. It was his debut in TV directing. I felt simultaneously nervous and excited since I wrote the screenplay for this. The costumes, in particular, were fantastic! The detail and craftsmanship were astonishing. They all helped bring the character to life and transport the audience *Back In Time*.

Brittany's dress was an actual work of art, made of silk fabric with a beautiful art deco print in shades of green and gold, perfectly complementing the era's vintage style. The dress featured a dropped waist, the signature style of the 1920s, and a midi-length skirt that flowed gracefully around her ankles. The dress's bodice was lightly adorned with delicate white beading and trimmed with a scalloped edge, giving it an air of elegance that befits the character she embodied. In addition to the dress, Brittany wore a black headband decorated with a subtle feather design, adding to the ensemble's overall glamorous look. Her hairstyle was in a sleek bob with well-defined finger waves — perfectly capturing the essence of the golden age of Hollywood.

Richard looked so handsome in an elegant, light grey, double-breasted suit. The jacket featured peak lapels, a breast pocket, and flap pockets, all of which perfectly evoke the fashion of that era. He paired the coat with a waistcoat in the same shade that fits him exceptionally well. Underneath, he wore a light-colored shirt and a classic tie with a subtle pattern that accentuated the suit perfectly. The trousers were slightly tapered and reached just before the ankle, which exposed his black Oxford shoes. With the slicked-back hairstyle, Richard screamed 1920s sophistication.

"He looks like a natural fit for the drama era," Luigia commented as we stood far from the set.

"Richard is so natural," I replied, beaming with pride.

My heart fluttered when I saw Richard's face light up as I approached him from afar. We were on a midday break, and Richard stood across the set, gazing in my direction. At first, he looked focused and determined, but as soon as he saw me, his lips slowly curled into a warm and joyful smile. It was a smile that made my heart skip a beat, and it was clear that he was genuinely happy to see me.

As he started walking towards me, his smile widened and grew even more infectious. I couldn't help but feel a giddy warmth inside me as I made my way over to him. It was a beautiful moment, and it felt like we were the only two people in the world as we slowly closed the distance between us.

"I feel so giddy the entire time," I said with a laugh, "but I'm so proud of you, my love." I tiptoed and kissed him lightly on the mouth.

Richard kissed me back tenderly and put his hand on my abdomen. "Hmmm... See that, little bean? Your mama will be a natural stage mom — she'll always be there cheering for you during football practice," he said with a wink.

Despite the chaos and activity around us on the set, Richard's smile when he saw me was one of the day's most heartwarming and genuine moments. It was a moment that made all my hard work and effort into this show worth it.

Richard was an incredibly talented actor. Today, he showcased why he landed this role. He completely embodied his character and delivered his dialogue beautifully. Britanny, playing his love interest, also did an excellent job. Together, they captured every emotion within their scene perfectly, making it feel like we were in the original book.

The set, lighting, and camera work were all perfect — everything combined to make it seem like we were *Back In Time* — to 1920s America. It was incredible how every effort came together to make the scene feel alive and real.

There were also some funny moments on set. Brittany had to learn how to ride vintage bicycles for one of the scenes, and let's just say it was a bit of a learning curve! She had a few mishaps, but we all laughed them off and kept going. It had been a long, tiring day of filming, but seeing everything come together made it all worth the effort.

I couldn't wait for our viewers to see how this episode turned out. This was undoubtedly my best experience in filming so far! Not only because Richard was directing it, but more importantly because the local crew was absolutely fantastic. They worked so hard to ensure that each scene came to life exactly as we envisioned.

It had been a long day of filming, but despite the exhaustion, everyone was in great spirits. From the early morning hours until sunset, Richard and Brittany had been hard at work delivering their lines accurately. The local crew was also fantastic. They planned every detail before executing the filming for the day.

The sun was setting as we finished, and I couldn't help but feel proud of what we had achieved throughout the day. Every ounce of hard work and effort that had gone into making this episode indeed showed in the results. Even when the going got tough, everyone rallied together to make sure everything went smoothly, and it paid off! I can't wait for our viewers to see it — I'm sure they will love it just as much as we do!

16

Peter had arranged a business meeting between Richard and Oliver in Restaurant C, located on the Prinsengracht of Amsterdam. This luxurious restaurant was known for its stunning views, creative menu, and fresh local ingredients. When I found out that Oliver himself had requested this particular event with the intention of me attending as Richard's plus-one, I couldn't help but tease my fiancé with a playful comment.

"He really likes me," I said with a grin. Before I could react, Richard was suddenly behind me as I put on my earrings, and he nipped my ear. "Over my dead body," he replied teasingly.

"My baby bump is now finally noticeable," I said, beaming.

"Hmmm... that just makes you even sexier, mama," Richard replied warmly.

I looked at myself in the mirror. My yellow Dior dress was the perfect mix of elegance and fun. The lightweight fabric felt like a dream against my skin, while the cap sleeves and ruffled bust added a touch of playfulness. The wrap-around skirt hugged my curves in all the right places and flowed gracefully to the floor. The bright, sunny yellow complemented my complexion with little gem embellishments that sparkled in the light.

"You look beautiful, darling," Richard said with a smile.

"Thanks," I replied shyly. I stood there momentarily, basking in the joy of the new yellow dress. Although unfamiliar and slightly uncomfortable, it made me feel graceful and elegant — something my old jeans and hoodie couldn't do. Then I turned around to kiss him.

We arrived ten minutes early yet Peter was already there, ready to give Richard a background on what the meeting was for. Oliver needed a global celebrity endorser for Oliver's, his mall franchise located in Asia and Europe that was developing one of the largest franchises in North America. Things were going as smoothly as expected until Richard's mother and ex-wife suddenly appeared uninvited.

Richard couldn't believe his eyes when he saw his mother and Emilia standing there. "What are you doing here, Mother?" he asked in a voice that sent an icy chill running down my spine.

"We're looking at some artwork to bring to the London gallery," she replied coldly, her gaze darting between Richard and Peter as if daring them to challenge her presence.

Richard then turned to me, introducing us. "Mother, this is Hope Williams," he said with a slight tremor in his voice. "Hope, this is my mother, Catherine Collins."

I smiled warmly at Richard's mother and Emilia, trying to put them both at ease. They seemed surprised by my presence, but I pushed aside any awkwardness with a friendly hello. I knew this was a big step for me, and I wanted to ensure it went as smoothly as possible.

Richard informed his mother that we were in a business meeting and he'd see her in the morning. I touched his hand, "It's okay," I said softly. "Let them join us."

Emilia looked at Richard's mother before turning her gaze back to me with an expression that seemed equal parts anger and disbelief. "We don't need your approval, do we, mama?" she asked pointedly.

I was taken aback by Emilia's rudeness but I quickly composed myself and replied calmly but firmly, "Well, Emilia...today I do have a say." With that declaration, I gestured for the waiter hovering nearby to

come closer, adding two more sets of cutlery and glasses to our table —
as well as extra bottles of wine and whatever food preferences my
guests might have had in mind for their meal tonight.

Before any more unwanted exchanges happened, Oliver and Yumi
arrived. Richard introduced his mother and Emilia, shaking both their
hands in greeting. Then Oliver took my hand and said, "It's good to
see you again, Hope." I was seated between Richard and Yumi.

Upon hearing Oliver's name, Emilia didn't waste time talking about
her modeling gigs in Asia. "Richard and I used to travel and work at
some modeling agencies in Singapore, didn't we, Richard?" She
glanced over at him with a twinkle of mischief in her eye before
turning back to Oliver. "If you need an English model, you can contact
me directly, there's no need to go my agent. Do you need someone to
work on your fashion shows?" She asked as she handed him her
business card.

Yumi accepted the card that was offered to Oliver and quickly changed
the topic, putting Emilia's question hanging in the air, and asked me if
I'd been to any South East Asian countries. "I was in Bali once, but that
was long ago," I said.

Richard held my hand, grateful for me playing hostess for tonight's
dinner.

Oliver asked, "I heard you two are engaged. When is the wedding, if
you don't mind me asking?"

"I can marry her any time, any day, at any place," Richard said proudly.
"But she's holding out because of work."

"I hope it isn't because of me," Oliver said kindly.

"Oh no!" I said quickly. "There are pressing issues that Richard and I
need to settle first, such as our living arrangements. As you know, we
live on separate continents."

Before I could continue, Richard chose this moment to announce my
pregnancy. "I just hope we do it soon before the baby comes out," he

said with a smirk.

Yumi hugged me and exclaimed, "Oh my God! Congratulations!" Emilia smiled knowingly, not letting her surprise show.

"This calls for an impromptu celebration," Oliver said and gestured for the waiter to bring us a bottle of champagne to toast the joyous news.

Catherine asked her son, "Have you finalized your prenuptial agreement yet, Richard?" She looked at Oliver and spoke about the importance of a prenuptial agreement to protect Richard's wealth since I had no assets.

"Mother, this is a private matter," Richard said sternly.

"Richard, it is best that everyone knows about this. You've worked hard for all of this, and I must also safeguard Henry's interests." Initially, Richard kept his cool, but then the conversation gradually devolved into an argument between him and his mother regarding financial security. His anger toward her intensified by the minute while I remained silent, trying my best to stay composed throughout the ordeal.

"Even Oliver probably agrees with me. He, too, needs to protect his assets from anyone, and he can tell you how important it is, right, Oliver?" Catherine asked.

"Mother!" Richard said, losing his cool. I grabbed his hand, placing it on my stomach as a silent request for him to remain calm. Oliver saw my gesture and spoke in a more controlled manner. "I agree with you, Catherine." He said calmly, "Both need a prenuptial agreement to protect their financial interests."

His mother gloated in victory, and Richard's jaw clenched in annoyance at her attitude. "If Richard has to protect his financial interests," Oliver said, "Hope has to do so, too." I was puzzled by this statement since I had no savings, property, or value worth protecting.

Oliver took over, looking directly at me as he spoke, "Hope is worth more than a hundred billion dollars in stock values."

"We're not counting yet on the properties she will soon own," Yumi added.

"I'm sorry, but I think you've mistaken me for someone else. I don't have anything valuable to declare," I said, laughing.

"Oliver?" Yumi looked at her employer.

"I know this is not the best time, and it is not how I planned it. Hope will soon inherit Ortega's Global Holdings. She is my sole heir." Then he looked at me directly, "You are my daughter."

Yumi added, in a gentle and understanding voice, she said, "I'm sorry, Hope. He should have told you this sooner. We were all looking for the perfect time. But yes, Oliver is your father. And you're about to become part of one of the wealthiest families in the world."

Their words left me spinning, my stomach turned upside down, and I held onto Richard as I felt myself losing consciousness before everything went black...

————

As I slowly opened my eyes. The comforting sight of Richard's smiling face gazing down at me was all I needed. "Hi there," he said, and relief flooded me to see him there.

Looking around the pink room, I realized I was still wearing my yellow dress from earlier, but someone removed my shoes. Everything was surreal, and I was overwhelmed by confusion.

"Where am I?" I asked Richard, my mind still foggy.

"You're in a hospital," he answered, and there was an edge of fear to his voice that I couldn't ignore. "You scared the hell out of me."

My heart skipped a beat as I took in his words, and my mind raced to try and catch up with what was happening. "What the hell is going on?" I demanded, my voice cracking with fear. "How's our baby?"

"Your consciousness shut down to protect you from too much stress," he explained, tracing the contours of my face with his thumb. "You and the baby are fine." A wave of relief washed over me as those words sank in; that moment had been my biggest concern.

As the reality of the situation sunk in further, my head started to clear, and my thoughts turned to Richard. "What's going on?" I asked him again, my heart racing with fear. His eyes were like dark pools of emotion as he took my hands in his own, squeezing them lightly before answering.

He took a deep breath before answering, "Oliver is outside. He needs to talk to you privately if you feel comfortable enough." His expression was unreadable as he continued, "But don't feel like you have to do anything you don't want to do — not today or ever."

I nodded and took a bracing breath. Richard's strength gave me courage as he held my hands in his own. We stayed like this until his gaze softened into a reassuring smile. It was all I needed, and everything would be alright, no matter what awaited me outside.

"Will you stay with me? I want to know the truth, Richard. Why he left me and my mother? But I can't do it alone . . . please stay," I implored him, gripping his arms as if my life depended on it.

A determined look crossed his face as he replied: "Let me handle Oliver. But I'll ask him to leave if I see that you're under too much stress." His voice was firm and reassuring, and I felt a wave of relief wash over me at having his strength by my side. I nodded, and Richard kissed my hands as he left to talk to Oliver.

When they both entered the room, Oliver looked much older than I'd seen him just a few hours ago. He shuffled to the chair beside my bed while Richard sat on the bed next to me.

"How are you feeling," Oliver asked me, his voice cracking with emotion. "I'm so sorry. I didn't mean for any of this to happen. I wanted it to be perfect, but no one should ever talk down to you like that," he continued, glanced at Richard, and said, "That is for your mother."

My eyes glistened as I struggled to hold back tears. "I want to hear the truth — all of it. The good and the bad," I said, my voice shaking with emotion. "You owe me this much after twenty-five years of being away from me."

Oliver opened a black leather box in front of me. Inside were letters addressed to me marked 'returned,' along with photos spanning my life from toddlerhood to the present day. Most were candid shots as if someone had been watching and capturing moments without my knowledge.

"I never missed anything when you were growing up," Oliver said softly, his eyes full of regret. "But I just couldn't bear being near you."

"Start from the beginning, where you so conveniently left me and my mother," I said calmly, though there was a hint of anger in my voice.

"It wasn't an easy decision, Hope," Oliver replied quietly. He explained that his father had been terminally ill then, and they needed him to take over their family business for it not to be turned over to the state in his absence. He didn't want to leave us behind but had no choice. The company was too important, and he felt obligated to keep it going until his father died. "My intentions were never to hurt you and your mother. I loved her, I never loved any woman, but my responsibilities as the heir of the family business took precedence. To do what was best for everyone involved, I had to leave you and your mother temporarily, but your mother was stubborn, and she made me choose between you and my family back home."

He knew he would miss out on moments with me growing up, and it pained him that he couldn't be present in my life. Nevertheless, Oliver felt obligated to pass down his father's legacy and ensure the future of their business before attempting to reconcile with us.

"Your mother filed a restraining order so I couldn't come near you," he continued. "So I put people around you to ensure you were protected."

"Two men are following me, Asian-looking men. Are they yours?" I asked.

"Those are Arthur and Chen," said Oliver. "They've been shadowing you since you were in university. There was a separate group working on that when you were younger."

"And Charlie?" I asked again.

"Charlie used to work for me in Vietnam," he replied. "When I found out he was staying in New York illegally, I talked to him and arranged to legalize his paperwork and bring his family over with him. In exchange, they look after you."

"I hope he isn't nice to me because you're paying them," I said.

"Absolutely not, Hope," Oliver reassured me without hesitation. "Charlie is genuinely a good person. It's true that I provided him with seed money for his business, but he has since repaid me in full."

"So, his kindness towards me isn't influenced by any financial obligation?" I asked, seeking further confirmation.

"No, not at all," Oliver affirmed. "Charlie values friendship and sincerity over material possessions. You can trust that his actions are genuine and not motivated by financial ties."

I was relieved that Charlie cared about me and wasn't doing it for the money. I couldn't bear the thought that people around me looked after or cared for me because my father paid them.

"And Richard?" I asked again.

"Darling, there's no arrangement between me and Oliver," Richard protested.

"I need to know everything!" I cried out as Richard held me close.

"Richard is right," Oliver conceded. "When I learned that you were working with Jenna Huey and she took care of you, Yumi suggested we produce a film adaptation from one of her books. It's my small way of repaying her kindness towards you. Getting Richard to lead is not part of the plan — that was Robin's decision."

Oliver continued, "When I found out that you two were engaged, I wanted to get to know him better, so I asked Yumi to get him involved as one of the corporate endorsers."

The tears started streaming down my cheeks. "You should have fought for me," I said softly.

Oliver smiled, understanding in his gaze. "Your mother, despite our issues, raised you well. I couldn't have done a better job. I dedicated my life watching you from a distance, never got married nor sired children from other women. I only have you, Hope."

The tears continued to stream down my cheeks as I looked at them both, Richard, who was offering me comfort, and Oliver, who had devoted his life to protecting me from afar. I tried to find my voice again and finally said, "If you cared about me so much, why weren't you ever there for me?"

Oliver sighed deeply. "Hope, your mother was a stubborn woman. After my decision, she didn't want anything to do with me and did everything she could to keep me away from both of you. After a while, I stopped fighting with her, knowing it wasn't in your best interest to uproot you from the home you knew." He paused before adding softly: "But that never meant that I stopped caring about and loving you."

I looked up at Oliver then, trying to reconcile the man before me with the one absent for so many years. He smiled down at me tenderly and caressed my face lovingly.

I nodded, understanding what he was saying. I knew it would take me time to process all this, but I also wanted him to see that he didn't need to keep his distance —I still appreciated his looking out for me.

"You're the only one left for me," he said, reaching out and taking my hand. A tenderness in his touch spoke of his deep love and devotion to me. "I hope one day, when you've forgiven me, you'll let me be your father again. I will trade anything for that day to come."

He stood up then and gently kissed the top of my hand before patting the black box. "I will leave these with you," he said softly before turning and walking away. I watched as Oliver slowly disappeared into the night, wishing more than anything that one day soon, we could put this all behind us and have a fresh chance at rebuilding our relationship.

17

Yumi showed up at our hotel the next day. Richard was supposed to take me to a tulip park, but he had to reshoot some scenes. With only two days left of our stay in Amsterdam, I decided to take the tour alone.

"Thank goodness I caught you!" Yumi exclaimed as she opened the backseat door of a luxury car and stepped out. Chen and Arthur were already sitting in the front seats. She was wearing a glamorous casual dress instead of her usual business suit. "I heard your date bailed out because of prior commitments, so I'm taking his place."

"Do you have time today?" I asked as I slid beside her.

"Your father's schedule is not as busy as it usually is, so it worked out perfectly," she said with a smile.

I then couldn't resist asking what she does for him exactly. "I'm his second eye and ensure all his bases are covered," she answered confidently.

"So where does he usually live? I mean, like girlfriends or something..." I asked, curious if there was someone special in his life.

"He's not into that," she said with a smile, and I could sense the respect in her voice. "He has worked hard to build his business and hasn't had time for relationships. But when he gets home, he always looks at photos or videos of you taken by some of his people during the day."

Yumi then explained that my father has never really left my side, even though he stays in the background and shadows. She told me about how she was with him during my graduation from university. They were in the backseats, and he was very proud when he saw my photo flashed on the screen and I stepped up on stage.

I felt a lump in my throat form when I thought of the countless memorable moments my father could have shared with me yet chose to remain in the background. Growing up, I always longed for him to be present at events like birthdays, graduations, and other important milestones. The idea of him staying in the shadows to avoid causing further pain to my mother and to me seemed illogical. He could have fought for a relationship with me. He could have exercised his rights as my father and actively participated in my life.

"Why didn't he try?" I asked Yumi. "Why did he choose to remain distant when he could have been there for me, supporting and guiding me through all those important moments?" It was a question that would continue to haunt me, a reminder of the fatherly love and presence I had missed out on despite his existence in the periphery of my life.

She took a deep breath and said, "I don't have any answer to that question, Hope."

"There's so much 'could have been,' Yumi. I can't process all of these yet."

"I understand. So does your father. That's why he's giving you space until now." Yumi suddenly smiled and said, "So much for these sad talks! Let's see the beauty of Amsterdam while it is still in Spring."

We started at Vondelpark, a peaceful haven filled with lush greenery and stunning tulip beds. We then moved on to Hortus Botanicus, the oldest botanical garden in the Netherlands and home to thousands of colorful tulips. Finally, we ended up at Amstelpark, surrounded by magnificent rows of blooms in all shapes and sizes.

Yumi was right. During the springtime, tulips bloom in abundance throughout Amsterdam, painting the landscape with their vibrant hues. This is the home to some of the world's oldest tulip gardens, where visitors can stroll through rows of carefully cultivated blooms.

As we walked down the pathways lined with multicolored tulips, Yumi explained its long and illustrious history in Amsterdam. "The tulip was introduced to the city by a 16th-century botanist sent to Constantinople on orders of Emperor Charles V. But it wasn't until the Dutch Golden Age or 17th century that tulips became a major part of the culture and heritage. During this era, attending tulip auctions was considered fashionable. Thankfully, they preserved this tradition, and visitors can still experience such events at tulip markets around the city."

Gazing in awe at the spectacle of vibrant tulips in full bloom, I couldn't help but appreciate the beauty of the flowers. No wonder this country treasured them. Beyond their breathtaking appearance, the flowers' intricate petals and distinctive shapes fascinated me. "They've always been my favorite," I remarked to Yumi. "I'm captivated by their beauty, from their vibrant hues and delicate petals to the unique formations of each bloom. Every time I come across one, I'm awed by its intricate design and delicate elegance." The memory of Richard sending me my first tulip to symbolize his love made them even more special — a moment that is etched forever in my memory.

"Too bad we missed the Tulip Festival and Bloemencorso Bollenstreek," Yumi said, then quickly added, "Let's grab some lunch!" As we walked away from the flower gardens, I could not help but feel a bittersweet sense of leaving behind such beauty.

Yumi got us a great table at Restaurant de Kas, the restaurant renowned for its authentic Dutch cuisine made from fresh seasonal ingredients sourced directly from its garden. Taking in the delightful aromas of home-cooked dishes, the charming atmosphere, and the cozy seating, I wanted nothing else but to stay here for the rest of the day.

Yumi suggested I try their signature dish Stamppot while she went with the Hutspot, a thick beef stew. "My girlfriend and I used to dine here. It's our favorite place," Yumi said as she looked at me, saw my expression, and laughed. "You think I am sleeping with your father?"

I couldn't help but laugh, too. "Oh, no. Although it's completely none of my business," I replied jokingly. "Where is he staying here?"

"Same as yours. He occupied a suite at the Waldorf Astoria and converted it to a conference room," she said before adding, "You know that he will drop everything just to see you, especially now," Yumi said encouragingly.

"It's too soon, Yumi," I said.

18

Upon my return to the hotel, there was still no sign of Richard, no calls or messages. It appeared that he was still engrossed in his filming. My visit to the garden had stirred something inside me, igniting a passionate urge to put something special down on paper.

The exquisite beauty of the flowers with their intricate petals moved me deeply, and I felt an overwhelming sense of inspiration wash over me. I couldn't help but think that they had been presented to me to awaken my creative spirit, urging me to pick up my pen and give life to something truly magical.

I had drafted several stories before but never got around to finishing them. But this time, it felt different; I knew I wanted to finish what I started. So, after taking a quick shower, I changed into one of Richard's shirts, which always made me comfortable. I opened my laptop and began typing away at the keyboard without thinking about titles or outlines.

The story flowed out of me as though it had been waiting within, searching for an outlet through which to be released. Each chapter felt like an extension of myself, every word drawn from a place deep within my soul. I knew I couldn't express these in any other way but through the written word. It was as though every person in the garden was a part of my tale, speaking back to me from the pages and propelling the story forward with every second spent amongst the tulips.

———

As night fell over Amsterdam and the world outside my window darkened, I was finally satisfied with what I had written thus far. I felt a sense of accomplishment as I looked over the three chapters filled with love and hope for my characters. I knew there were still untold adventures awaiting them in the future, and maybe even some for me as well.

I turned off my laptop, and there he was, standing in the doorway with a tired look on his face. He had been filming all day, but when our eyes met, I saw something sparkle in his gaze.

As he approached, I could feel the anticipation building inside me; it felt like every nerve in my body was alive with desire. Our eyes locked as he closed the gap between us, our lips meeting in a passionate moment that seemed to last an eternity. As I moved closer, Richard grabbed the back of my head and pulled me tighter against him while deepening our kiss until we were lost in each other's arms. "I miss you, darling," he murmured between kisses.

Richard knew how vulnerable I had been feeling lately, so he never pushed for anything more than what I wanted to give him at that moment — love and comfort from someone who understood how difficult this situation was for me. I looked into his tired eyes. I knew instantly his day didn't end well. Today, he needed me more than I needed him. So I went up on my toes and kissed him without holding back. Then he pulled from the kiss and looked at me hungrily. He cupped my breast and said, "You're so sexy in my shirt, don't you know that?" I wore nothing under his shirt except my black panties.

With trembling hands, I slowly unbuttoned my shirt as I stepped back toward the bedroom door. But before I could get too far away from him, Richard caught my hand and whispered, "Don't! Let me do that." His voice sent shivers down my spine as he gently guided my hands back onto his chest and started undoing his buttons with them instead.

As our fingers intertwined around each button of his shirt, an intense passion began radiating between us like waves of electricity. Richard slowly undressed while holding on tightly to my hand until he was totally naked — no more barriers or inhibitions standing in the way. The last rays of light were fading away as I watched Richard move gracefully through the room. His toned muscles, his legs, and his chest — everything about him captivated me. He had a way of making my heart race with just one look, and I knew exactly what he wanted from me.

He turned me around and kissed the back of my neck. His hands were on my breasts, tenderly caressing them at first, but then his touch became rough. His left hand remained there while his left hand traveled between my legs. I cried out his name! That was the signal Richard was waiting for, and he entered me from behind. The passion between us felt like an electric current running through our bodies, and it seemed like nothing could come between us now — not even time or distance. Our lips met again, and I could feel the passionate intensity surging between us. His hands were firm on my waist, holding me in place as he tenderly caressed me as our tongues explored each other hungrily.

When we finally broke apart, there was a smile on both our faces that said it all — we would never tire of this moment together or get bored seeing each other's bodies over and over again no matter how many times it happened because for us passion always burned bright like fire!

19

Summer, Los Angeles

As Richard and I arrived in dreamy Los Angeles to film the remaining episodes of *Back In Time*, the world seemed to bathe in a golden glow. Even though we were tired from the long flight, the energy of the bustling airport kept us going. We headed straight to Rent A Car after reaching the bustling Tom Bradley airport. Despite both of us sporting dark shades, people were already starting to recognize Richard. We received many selfie requests — I mean, just Richard. Fans flocked around Richard, eager to catch a glimpse of the star.

People cheered and clapped as Richard walked by, offering encouraging words and well-wishes for the upcoming season of the popular show. As we made our way to the exit, we couldn't help but feel slightly overwhelmed by the sudden frenzy of attention. But Richard handled it all with grace, taking time to interact with every one of them.

In the car, Richard let out a deep sigh of frustration as we maneuvered through the congested Los Angeles traffic. "It would have been so much easier if we had hired a limo service," he grumbled.

I couldn't help but chuckle at his comment, knowing that navigating the car-centric city was no joke. "Richard, this is California. Everything around here is car-dependent," I quipped. "And besides, it's refreshing to enjoy our own company without the constant presence of a bodyguard or housekeeper."

My summer dress felt like a second skin in the oppressive heat, causing me to fidget uncomfortably in my seat. My nineteenth-week pregnant belly was still barely a bump, but it was on full display, and I couldn't help but feel a mixture of delight and trepidation about the impending changes that awaited us.

As I glanced down at my growing belly, I couldn't help but feel a pang of sadness at how my body was transforming. "My jeans don't fit me anymore," I admitted ruefully, my hand resting protectively over my stomach.

Richard's warm eyes met mine. His expression was sympathetic. "You should get fitted for a new dress for The Emmy Awards," he suggested.

I hesitated, feeling self-conscious about my changing body. "Can I have a raincheck on that?" I replied. "I'm pregnant, Richard. I will probably just look like a fat chick beside you."

Richard shook his head, taking my hand and pulling me closer. "Who told you that?" he asked, his breath caressing my skin. "You're the most beautiful pregnant woman I've ever seen."

His words calmed me, and I couldn't help but release an exasperated giggle at his comment. His love and affection gave me the reassurance I needed, even as my body transformed.

As we continued our journey, I couldn't help but ponder the changes that were yet to come with our baby's arrival. The future seemed both exciting and a little daunting. Turning to Richard with a smile, I asked: "Do you ever think about what our lives will be like once the baby arrives?"

His eyes lit up, and his smile widened as he enthusiastically responded. "Of course I do," he said. "I can't wait to be a dad again."

Our conversation flowed freely, our minds wandering through many topics as we traversed the busy streets of Los Angeles. Despite my concerns, I knew Richard and I had this: we would face everything that came our way head-on.

We finally made it to Malibu, which would be our home for the next month as filming took place. Even with the air conditioning blasting in our car, the sweltering heat of summer in Los Angeles was almost overwhelming. It felt like we were driving inside an oven!

But as we made our way through the winding roads of Malibu, lined with palm trees and overlooking the Pacific Ocean, I couldn't help but feel a sense of awe. Something about this city instantly made you fall in love with it.

The vibrant pop culture and cuisine of Los Angeles is still what drew people in. From the incredible Mexican food to the chic cafés and trendy juice bars, there was no shortage of delicious options to explore. And, of course, the art scene in LA was legendary, with museums and galleries showcasing some of the most cutting-edge artists and exhibits. In fact, I couldn't wait to visit The Broad during my free time.

But for me, the real draw of California was Malibu and its wide and sandy beaches. We were lucky enough to stay in a luxurious house on the beachfront, with panoramic views of the ocean stretching out before us. I can't wait to wake up to the sound of the waves crashing against the shore every morning.

As Richard pushed open the front door of the beach house, my eyes widened in surprise. The space was even more beautiful than I'd imagined, with soaring ceilings, floor-to-ceiling windows, and picture-perfect views of the sparkling ocean beyond. The living room was spacious yet cozy, with plush white sofas and rustic wood accents giving the space a comfortable yet luxurious feel. I could see the ocean waves breaking on the shore through the expansive windows while a delicate sea breeze wafted through the house. It was a perfect escape from the hustle and bustle of the city, and I knew we were in for a fantastic month living here.

My eyes widened with surprise and amazement. "This is heaven!" I exclaimed, barely able to contain my excitement. I put both hands over my mouth to suppress a loud shout of joy, but the grin on my face gave it all away.

Richard chuckled at my enthusiasm, clearly amused at seeing me act like a schoolgirl in a candy store. But I couldn't help it — the house was simply incredible.

As I walked into the living room, the views of the ocean beyond took my breath away. I threw myself at Richard, hugging him tightly. "I can't believe we get to stay here," I said, still in awe of the beauty around us.

He wrapped his arms around me, his eyes filled with the same appreciation and joy. "I'm just happy that we get to spend this time together before I have to head back to London for another filming," he said, his voice tinged with sadness.

I felt a pang of regret at the thought of Richard leaving, but I knew it was inevitable. We had discussed his demanding schedule on numerous occasions, and as much as I wanted to go to London with him, I just couldn't leave New York and abandon my ongoing commitments.

"I wish I could come with you," I said, my voice filled with longing. "However, post-production might still require our assistance, and our department may be needed for marketing efforts. Moreover, we have to start working on the scripts for Season 2, which will demand a lot of time and attention. And, of course, my book remains my top priority at the moment."

"I understand," Richard said. "It's just that I'll miss you terribly while I'm away. But I know how important your work is to you, and I would never want to stand in the way of your success and fulfillment. We'll just have to figure out flying across the continent on weekends or during a filming break."

I smiled, grateful for Richard's understanding and support.

That night, Richard and I sat outside on the deck, bundled in blankets and staring at the glittering stars above us. As we curled up together in a cozy embrace on the plush white sofas, the sound of the ocean waves crashing below us provided a calming rhythm, lulling us into a state of peace. Wrapped up in Richard's arms, I felt more intimate with him than I ever had before — even more than making love.

Richard's tone was gentle and his concern palpable as he leaned in to ask, "Did your father talk to you yet?"

I couldn't meet his gaze as I shook my head, feeling a knot form in my stomach. "I haven't given it much thought yet. First, I need to confront my mother," I said with conviction. "Keeping this secret from me isn't fair, not to her or me, or even to my father."

Looking at him, I could see the concern on his face, and I felt guilty that my situation could potentially jeopardize his contract with my father. "I'm sorry, I jeopardized your contract with my father," I said softly. "Did he talk to you?"

Richard's expression was calm as he took my hand, his eyes unwavering. "Not directly, no," Richard replied. "But I know your father cares for you deeply, and he's giving you space. He's also respecting our relationship by letting everything go through Peter, just like I asked him to." His voice was with conviction and reassurance.

Hearing his words, a wave of gratitude washed over me. I knew that Richard's unwavering support would help make this journey easier. "I know he does," I said with a small smile. "It's just that I'm not quite ready yet."

Richard nodded, his understanding clear. "Take all the time you need," he said, his voice gentle. "We'll face whatever comes our way together, no matter what."

That was what I loved most about Richard. He was always there for me and made me feel I was not alone.

We sat there in the quiet moment, lost in our thoughts. But even as the uncertainty and fear threatened to overwhelm me, I knew I had Richard by my side. We talked for hours, our conversation weaving in and out of various topics ranging from our plans for the future to our fondest childhood memories. It was a beautiful moment of connection, a chance to simply be together and bask in the joy of each other's company.

As the night went on, the stars slowly disappeared, replaced by the soft hues of dawn. But we stayed there, wrapped up in each other's arms, no longer shivering from the cool night air but warmed by the love we shared.

———

The Emmy Awards arrived earlier this year, and Richard was among the actors nominated for a supporting role in his sixteenth-century drama series. The event was nearing, and Yumi arranged my fitting at Vera Wang on Rodeo Drive. Just like in fairytales, your fairy godmothers could transform you into a magical creature. In my case, they turned a pregnant duck into a glamorous swan. My long, backless dress was jet black, and the elegant silhouette flattered my twentieth-week pregnancy. Jenna had arranged for one of her contacts, who specialized in celebrity makeovers, to take care of my hair and makeup.

Today, two stylists were working their magic on me. My hair was styled in an intricate high bun, elegantly swept away from my face. The makeup artist highlighted my best features, with a soft pink glow on my cheeks, and accentuated my eyes with mascara. I adorned my neck with two thin, sparkling diamond chains that caught the light and reflected their sheer beauty. The perfect accessory to complete my look was a pair of diamond earrings, adding that final glamour for a magical evening.

When Richard emerged from our room, he took my breath away. His black tie suit clung to his body perfectly, accentuating every muscle and showing off how handsome he was. His look was complete with a pair of polished patent leather shoes and a crisp white pocket square tucked neatly into his pocket. He stood tall and proud, with a magnetic aura that drew all eyes.

As Richard crossed the room, his eyes fixed on me, I felt my heartbeat quicken. His gaze softened as he reached out to touch my chin, and with a gentle kiss, he whispered, "Darling, you look beautiful."

His words stirred something inside me, and I couldn't help but feel a blush rising to my cheeks. Richard made me feel like the most important person in the world, his loving presence filling the room with warmth and love.

With a smile, I reached up to softly touch his face. "And you look handsome, my love," I replied, my heart overflowing with love and adoration.

At that moment, time stood still, and there was no one else in the world but Richard and I.

I felt a knot in my stomach as Richard and I drove closer to the Microsoft Theater in Los Angeles. My nerves were high, and I found it hard to breathe. But with each passing minute, Richard squeezed my hand a little tighter, reminding me everything would be alright. He was the light that shone through my insecurities, the rock that kept me grounded when life seemed too overwhelming. No matter what happened, one thing was for sure. I had Richard by my side.

When our car stopped at the red carpet entrance, I felt my heart pounding. Richard got out of the car and offered his hand to me. Taking a deep breath, I held onto his arm tightly and whispered, "Don't let me fall." He smiled reassuringly and gazed into my eyes as if he could see straight into my soul. His touch reassured me that everything would be alright. We stepped out onto the red carpet, arm in arm, ready to take on this night together.

As we walked along the red carpet, I felt blinding lights hit us as photographers aimed their cameras in our direction. Reporters on the side were shouting questions at Richard and filling the air with excitement. With every step we took, flashes of light illuminated the night and captured our every move. The atmosphere was electric, and I looked around in awe at all the glamorous celebrities. It felt surreal that I was here.

As we approached the official photo wall, Richard and I stood together, our eyes locked in a moment of pure happiness. We posed for the cameras, our faces beaming with joy and love.

At that moment, the unbreakable connection between us was undeniable. It was evident to all who watched that we were destined to be together, our love radiating through every smile and touch.

Despite the flurry of activity around us, we were lost in our world, immersed in the beauty of the moment. Flashes of light filled the air, and as everyone watched, we happily embraced, enveloped in our own love bubble.

As we walked away from the photo wall, hand in hand, I felt a sense of contentment and happiness wash over me.

One of the reporters asked Richard what made his nomination different tonight. He turned to me with a smile and replied, "It's a good performance, and I enjoyed it. What makes it extra special tonight is my date."

With those words, Richard leaned in and kissed me, eliciting loud cheers and applause from the crowd. For a brief moment, everything else faded away as we savored this perfect moment together.

I couldn't help but feel immense joy at being able to share this experience with Richard. We shared a look of understanding before continuing with the evening, proud to have shared this moment with everyone.

We made our way inside the theater. We joined a crowd of talented people who had been part of Richard's latest TV series. Everyone was beaming with pride and admiration, welcoming us warmly as they chatted and shared stories when they were filming the show. The atmosphere in the theater grew even more jubilant. It was fascinating to be part of such a celebration.

When they announced the nominees for Best Supporting Actor, I could feel my heart pounding in anticipation. When they read Richard's name along with the other five contenders, he turned back to me with a proud smile, and I kissed him.

The presenter then called Richard's name again as the winner of the prestigious award, and he stood up, looked into my eyes, and planted a passionate kiss on my lips before walking up to the stage to accept it. The audience erupted, and I felt immense pride watching Richard receive the award that was well deserved.

He had worked so hard for this moment, and now it had finally happened — it was truly amazing! Everyone applauded him when he received his award and gave an emotional speech about how much this recognition meant to him. He thanked everyone, from the production team to the director and producers.

"Of course, I should thank my lucky stars, this year is extraordinary. I finally got my first Emmy. I am engaged to the most beautiful pregnant woman in this room," his eyes focused on mine as he spoke. My heart swelled with pride as tears filled my eyes. Never in a million years did I think I would make it here and with one of Hollywood's most celebrated stars.

Richard came back to me, beaming with happiness and love in his eyes, and whispered, "You are everything." We embraced each other tightly under those bright lights until they dimmed away again into darkness.

———

After the Emmys, Richard's show producers invited all its attendees to an exclusive after-party at The Belasco, a luxurious venue near Microsoft Theater. They transformed it into a glittering wonderland, with string lights illuminating the space and music inviting everyone to dance their cares away.

The guests enjoyed the lavish spread of delicious food and drinks, including decadent desserts and free-flowing champagne. Everywhere one looked, celebrities were milling around, talking about the Emmy winners and celebrating in style.

The air in The Belasco was nothing short of electric, and the celebratory mood was just palpable. Everyone was so animated, gleefully chatting, taking selfies, and sharing congratulatory messages with Richard on his historic Emmy win. Richard stayed by my side throughout the evening, his arm wrapped loosely around my waist as we move through the stars gathered to toast his victory.

My feet were getting tired from all the standing and walking, and as soon as Richard noticed, he offered to escort me out of the party. We said our goodbyes to the other guests and made our way out of The Belasco quietly slipping away into the night.

———

I was exhausted. Filming the remaining episodes of our TV series, not to mention all the rewriting and editing of scripts I must do, had taken its toll on me. My morning sickness made it worse, and I wasn't fun to work with anymore.

Richard had to bear with my mood swings, too. As the lead actor, he bore an enormous burden on his shoulders. During these moments when my hormones were all over the place, I couldn't help but feel guilty for unloading on him even more with my issues.

So weekends come around like a blessing from above — days when we took a break from filming and we can spend some quality time together. On those days, I got busy working on my first novel while

Richard reviewed new contracts and studied scripts.

Henry was spending the weekend with us as part of his summer stopover. The two of them headed out into the ocean together, leaving me in peace to work on my laptop. I took a moment to watch them from afar, admiring the bond between father and son — something that I'm grateful to be able to share. Before I turned back to my work, I touched my stomach gently, "Soon, little one, you'll be joining your father and brother out there."

I was so focused on my writing that I didn't notice Richard and Henry on the deck until their voices distracted me. They stood in their swimming trunks, their towels around their shoulders as water dripped off them. The sun began to set, casting a pinkish hue across the sky. They both entered the house with Henry going to the kitchen to get some steak for grilling on the deck and ice-cold beer. I missed having drinks, but my pregnancy prevented me from having a refreshing sip.

Richard leaned down and kissed me tenderly. He was holding a bottle of beer with a mischievous grin. "This is the only thing you can have now," he said, then drank from the bottle and winked. I laughed and kissed him just to taste the beer on his lips.

Henry came into the room and settled himself into one of the chairs. "So, how's the book coming along?"

"If all goes according to plan, it should be ready by the beginning of autumn," I replied confidently.

"And when are you due to give birth again?"

"End of autumn," I said with a smile.

"You'd better be a boy, little bean," Henry said, talking to my tummy with an amused smile. "One girl is enough in the family. Too many hormones and mood swings," he rolled his eyes so far back his head, making fun of me.

I threw a pillow at him and shot him a mock exasperated look. "Why haven't I started making your life miserable yet, you know, being your evil stepmother?" I joked.

But he just grinned back at me knowingly. "You can't because I'm still your favorite, and you will always consider me your firstborn," he replied earnestly. What he said moved me and I felt my eyes prickle. Despite the three-year age gap between us, he already treated me as his mother.

We went out to the deck and spent the outdoor barbeque in pure bliss. Richard cooked up some steak and hotdogs on the grill, and Henry laid out an assortment of cold drinks for both of them to enjoy. We all sat around the deck, listening to the sound of the surf and watching as the sun slowly set, painting the sky with its mesmerizing hues of crimson, orange, and pink.

At nightfall, the stars twinkled above us like diamonds against dark velvet—it felt like we were floating in a faraway galaxy. Henry selected some mellow songs from his Spotify playlist and paired them with a Bluetooth speaker. Michael Buble's "Home" started to fill the night air. Richard gathered me in his arms and we swayed to the rhythm under a sky blanketed with stars. His hands were carefully placed on my waist while his chin rested atop my head. We swayed and glided together with the gentle melody, feeling every beat that seemed to echo within our hearts. The moment felt eternal, like time had stopped, and all that was left was us. Even after the song had come to an end, neither of us wanted the moment to end. We stayed there, holding each under the starlight.

As the night wore on, Henry had dozed off on the couch, a bottle of beer still in his hand. I grabbed a blanket from the living room and draped it over him. Richard and I watched him for a moment, and I whispered how lucky his mother must be to have him. Richard held me closer, his eyes sparkling as he said, "You're his mother now, too." I gently kissed Henry's forehead, careful not to stir him from his slumber.

Richard and I settled back onto the couch. Despite the warm night, the air from the water across the deck was chilly, so we curled up together under the blanket. We talked and laughed until well past midnight, watching shooting stars and making wishes that in my heart had already come true.

———

I watched Richard finish his last scene, and the crew applauded him. It seemed like only yesterday when we started this journey together, yet at the same time, it felt like a lifetime ago. I'll never forget this day as we wrapped filming. We had been working on it for months, creating something unique and special that we could cherish long after we left the set. Everyone had become like family during those months, quarreling over scripts and ideas but ultimately finding common ground in our shared passion to make something great. We had made so many memories on set — some happy, some sad — but now it was time to say goodbye.

Brittany burst into tears. She hugged me tightly and thanked me for listening to all her suggestions throughout the project. "You were always so patient with me," she said through tears. "And I enjoyed working with you more than anyone else." With a final squeeze, she put one hand on my slightly rounded stomach — a reminder of the unexpected joy coming soon! Brittany looked at me with love and told me not to be a stranger: "Give us updates about our little bean!" she said with a laugh as she wiped away her tears. And just like that, she was gone.

Jenna looked at me with understanding, as if she knew this was difficult for me. I had grown up here, fallen in love here, and became the best version of myself through all the experiences. She put her arms around me as my tears started flowing uncontrollably. *Back In Time* was my love story, marking an important milestone in my life.

"Hey, we will be writing season two soon, Esperanza. Thank you for working with me on this. This would've been different without you," She kissed me on both cheeks before quickly leaving, as if trying to avoid the sad and drawn-out goodbyes that would otherwise have followed.

I stepped out of the studio and into the warm summer sun. It was a bittersweet feeling. Looking around, I saw all the other sets being dismantled, props packed away, and lighting equipment rolled up. The wardrobe team stood off to the side, waving me goodbye with bright smiles — they knew how much this meant to me.

Tears started welling up in my eyes, and I couldn't help but smile back at them. I can't thank them enough for helping make this project possible. As if they could sense what was going through my mind, one of them blew me a kiss from across the lot. And at that moment, I felt so loved, like all of these strangers had come together over months to create something beautiful — something that would hopefully stay with people for years to come.

Moments like this remind me why we do what we do: To bring joy and inspiration into our audiences' lives by telling stories that matter most to us.

The memories of all the laughter, conversations, and joyous occasions I'd experienced in this place flooded my mind. All the happiness, excitement, and growth I had experienced here throughout those months filled me with emotion. Despite the sadness of leaving, I was grateful for all that this place had given me — a newfound sense of independence, strength, and self-confidence to help me face whatever came next.

Richard turned to me with a bittersweet smile and said, "Well, I guess this is it." He reached out and took my hands in his own, squeezing them gently.

20

As our time in California came to a close, I knew that I couldn't keep running away forever. It was time to face my parents, confront the truth, and finally put this weight hanging over me for so long to rest. I'll admit it, I had been dreading this moment for what felt like an eternity. The thought of confronting my parents at once and finally allowing them to come clean about the truth filled me with an indescribable sense of dread. I had been dodging my mother's invitation to visit them in Sta Monica for weeks. But as our time here drew close, I couldn't ignore it anymore.

One evening, while Richard and I were lounging in our room, he suggested inviting them over for dinner while we were still here in Malibu before he went back to filming in London, and while I started pitching my book to some agents in New York. My heart raced at the thought of confronting them. Despite my reservations, I knew that Richard was right: it was time to face my fears head-on.

"Have you ever experienced celebrating the Fourth of July here in America?" I asked Richard while munching on fresh strawberries drizzled with condensed milk, a combination he found odd. Strawberries and cream, yes, but condensed milk is not always available in the supermarket. This unique treat came from my mother, who had learned it from my father. She said it was one of the Filipino traits I'd kept with me.

"That's something to look forward to. Why don't we invite your parents on that day? Perhaps the occasion could help soften the blow of any unpleasant discussions we might have," he suggested.

After much internal debate, I finally mustered up the courage to call my mother and father separately to set up a meeting. My heart pounded as I nervously dialed their numbers, unsure of what kind of response I would get.

To my relief, both of my parents agreed to meet with me without hesitation, though my mother had no idea that I was also inviting my father. As we spoke on the phone, I tried to maintain a calm and confident tone, but my mind raced with a thousand different scenarios and potential outcomes.

Reflecting on the past, I realized I wasn't entirely sure what I expected from this meeting. Perhaps I was hoping for some kind of reconciliation or closure among us all. Or maybe I just wanted to finally lay all the cards on the table and address the elephant in the room — why they had lied to me all these years. Growing up, I saw my mother struggling to make ends meet by juggling two or three jobs. Our apartment, while cozy, was far from grand. Considering my father's access to billions of dollars in funds, we could have at least lived a more comfortable life, if not in luxury.

It puzzled me that they chose to keep this secret from me for so long, especially when it could have significantly improved our living situation. Was there a hidden reason behind their decision, or were they simply trying to protect me from something? These questions swirled around in my mind as I prepared to confront them, hoping that our upcoming meeting would provide the answers I so desperately sought.

As I hung up the phone, I was filled with a mixture of relief and fear. What would the future hold for us after this meeting? Only time will tell.

As the days leading up to the dinner dwindled, my anxiety grew. I spent countless hours worrying about what to say to my parents and how to come to terms with whatever versions of their truth that had been troubling me for so long. The truth terrifies me. The thought of opening up to them was equally daunting.

To make matters worse, I'm a terrible cook — or worse, I can't cook at all. The idea of preparing an elaborate dinner for my parents was daunting, to say the least. But Richard had a stroke of genius and hired a restaurant chef to take care of everything. As we waited for my parents to arrive, Richard held me close, his hand gently rubbing my stomach. His warmth and affection calmed me down whenever my anxiety threatened to surface.

And then, finally, they were here. My mother arrived a bit earlier with my stepfather by her side. She looked elegant in a silk blouse, and my stepfather was sporting his signature fedora. As soon as she walked in the door, my mother embraced me warmly and kissed my cheeks. I couldn't help but feel a sense of relief wash over me — despite my nerves, seeing my mother's smile and feeling her embrace was one of the best feelings in the world. "Oh, sweetheart, you look wonderful," she said.

My mother greeted Richard and congratulated him on his Emmy before adding, "I've bought and collected all magazines and tabloids with you two on it!"

"Thank you, Debbie," Richard said politely. "Care for a drink, Steve?" Richard asked, holding out a glass of red wine.

"Thank you kindly," Steve replied, accepting the glass with a smile. "And what a lovely place you have here! Is this your home?"

Richard chuckled. "Actually, no. One of the realtors loaned us this place for the summer, hoping he could convince us to buy it. But we'll be heading back to London soon enough."

Mom asked me if I had started decorating the nursery. The question caught me off guard. I hesitated for a moment, unsure of how to respond. "To be honest, Mom, we haven't started decorating yet. We've been so busy with everything else that it just hasn't been a priority."

My stepfather jumped in. "Are you two planning on living in London or New York?" he asked Richard.

Richard chuckled. "That's a tricky question, Steve. Of course, I want Hope to give birth and settle in London, but her life is in New York. And as someone who travels around constantly because of filming, it wouldn't be fair to ask her to uproot her life and move to a place she's unfamiliar with."

I couldn't help but feel a sense of gratitude and admiration for Richard. He was always so considerate when it came to my wants and needs. As the conversation flowed on, we discussed the possibility of splitting our time between London and New York or finding a compromise that would make everyone happy.

Suddenly, the doorbell rang, signaling my father's arrival. As he entered the room, I couldn't help but notice the commanding presence he had. Though slightly shorter than Richard, he carried himself with confidence and authority that seemed to fill the room. His eyes twinkled mischievously as he surveyed the scene, his broad smile lighting up his face as he saw me and my mother. His eyes took in my mother's confusion and Richard's welcoming smile. In his hands, he carried a bottle of wine and a bouquet. He handed both to Richard. "You've got a refined taste in wine, Oliver," Richard greeted him warmly as he looked at the label.

But as my mother looked from my father to Richard and me, confusion etched across her features. "Mom, calm down," I said gently, reassuringly touching her arm. "I can explain everything. But first, I want both of you to listen to me — just this once."

Despite my earlier doubts and fears about this dinner, seeing my father in the flesh made me feel a sense of calm wash over me. While he had never been a steady presence in my life or a rock I could lean on when things got tough, today, I felt secure.

As he approached my mother, his movements were swift and confident. He offered his hand and said, "Hello, Debbie. It's good to see you."

My eyes welled up with tears, and Mom knew that her next move would determine whether those tears would fall. She accepted my dad's hand and replied, "It's good to see you, too, Oliver. This is my husband, Steve." My stepfather extended his hand as well, which my father accepted graciously.

"Pleasure to meet you, Steve. I'm Oliver Ortega."

In an attempt to break the awkwardness and tension in the room, Richard suggested that we all head to the dining room. Richard took the lead, charming my parents with his wit and easy charm. As we sat down to dinner, the delicious smells wafted through the air. He held my hand on the table as soon as we were seated, giving me an encouraging squeeze that filled me with calming reassurance.

Clearing his throat, he announced, "As you can see, Hope is pregnant, and we're trying to keep her from getting too upset or stressed." I looked at my mother, my eyes begging her to understand what I had gone through. But before I could say anything, my father interrupted.

"Let's not talk about the past," he said firmly. "I respect your mother's decision, and I don't want ever to question it. We all have our reasons for why we do something. Right now, I want to be part of your life, if you allow me, as we move forward." His words were heartfelt, and he truly wanted nothing more than to be part of this new chapter in my life. I couldn't help but feel a warmth radiating from him as he spoke. It was clear that his love was unconditional and would never waver.

A hushed silence fell over the room as I surveyed the dinner table. Everyone was anticipating my response to my father's words. Would I be angry and resentful or understanding and accepting? Richard squeezed my hand reassuringly, and I knew that whatever decision I made, he'd be there for me no matter what.

"For years, I've played this scenario repeatedly in my head. That one day, you'd find me, and you'd take me home. My responses varied. When I was a kid, I would have surely wrapped my arms around you, and I will be happy the rest of my life. But during my teenage years, I became more cynical, and I would have resented you and told you to go to hell," I chuckled, even as tears streamed down my face.

My dad started to reach for my hand but hesitated, allowing me space to process my emotions. I continued, "As a young adult, I didn't care anymore if you showed up or not. But now that I'm about to become a parent myself, I suddenly realize the value of family. I don't want my child to grow up without knowing his or her grandparents."

"I'm sorry, Hope. If I could turn back time and do things differently, I would." His words were measured, but I could sense the regret in each syllable. For someone who was always in control of every situation, apologizing in front of others must have been incredibly difficult. "But if there's one thing I would give anything for, even everything I have, it's to have a life with you in it."

"Mommy?" Tears began to well up in my eyes.

My mother smiled warmly, her eyes shining with excitement. "We're all so eager to meet our grandchild!" she said.

My father chimed in, blurting out, "I hope he's going to be a healthy boy!"

Surprised and slightly annoyed, I turned to him. "Why does everyone keep assuming our baby will be a boy? Even Henry!"

Richard chuckled and replied, "Darling, if our child takes after you, it might be safer if the baby is a boy!" His words were teasing but affectionate. It was clear that no matter what gender our child was, we'd all be overjoyed and proud parents, nevertheless.

I took a deep breath and calmly replied, "I'm glad everyone here is so excited to meet our baby. Whether it's a boy or a girl makes no difference to me. All I care about is that she is healthy and happy."

"Richard," my father began, turning to him with a smile. "I hope you don't mind. We set up trust funds for all of the Ortegas as soon as they were born. Just our little way of ensuring their financial security."

"Thank you, Oliver. I genuinely appreciate your offer. As you can see, both Hope and our baby are financially secure. In fact, it's the first thing I arranged with my legal team the moment we found out she was pregnant," Richard replied gratefully, then quickly added so as not to offend my father, "However, your grandchild would certainly enjoy occasional trips to Tokyo Disneyland and private tours of African Jungle Safari with you."

My heart calmed in my chest seeing my parents, including my stepfather and Richard laughing and joking with each other. Surprisingly, things weren't quite as awkward as I expected — no exchanging of hurtful words or raising voices among the three throughout dinner.

The Fourth of July celebrations started, as the night sky transformed into a mesmerizing canvas of color and light. We all gathered our drinks and went to the veranda overlooking the ocean. Spectacular fireworks burst forth in a dazzling array of hues, casting brilliant streaks across the velvety darkness. I looked at Richard, it was the first time he celebrated the Fourth of July. Each explosion illuminated his captivated face. He touched my face and kissed me passionately. The fireworks danced in the background, intertwined in a breathtaking choreography.

After a couple of glasses of wine, my parents said their goodbyes and made their way out the door. Richard and I were left alone at last, and we sat on one of the couches in the living room with a deep sigh of relief.

"We have a house in Chelsea, which, by the way, you need to see so you can plan where to put the nursery and meet with some interior design firms in London to help you decorate it," Richard said. I was nestled in his arms, my head resting comfortably on his chest.

"I haven't thought about that. In fact, I haven't even started planning where to put the nursery in the penthouse or my apartment on 89th," I admitted.

Richard chuckled at the idea of setting up a nursery in my tiny apartment. "What are you going to do with the lease on your old apartment?" he asked.

"I haven't thought about that yet. I'm still paying for it, and I don't have any plans to let it go just yet," I replied.

"You need to start moving some of your things into our home," Richard emphasized 'our home,' highlighting that our futures were truly intertwined now. "I don't know where to begin with all those things. My priority right now is the nursery. Or should I say, nurseries!" I touched my stomach and said, "Little bean, you are the luckiest baby in the world, having two nurseries in two different countries!" We both laughed, and I felt relaxed. The heavy burden had been lifted from my shoulders after meeting with my parents.

Finally, after what seemed like an eternity of talking and planning, we decided to turn in for the evening. As I closed my eyes to sleep that night, I knew everything would be all right.

21

When we returned to New York, Richard flew out to London the next day, leaving a huge void in the penthouse. Even with Leticia's regular cleaning and cooking schedule and Jeffrey resuming his duties as driver-slash-bodyguard, it was still far too quiet.

I spent my days buried in my manuscript — editing, rewriting, and refining lines until I felt satisfied with the final draft. Now all that remained was to pitch it to various agents, which filled me with excitement and anxiety at once.

I was proud of this novel, *Fleeting Embers* — a heart-wrenching tale of love, loss, and the fleeting nature of happiness. Set against the backdrop of a quaint, picturesque town, the story follows the lives of two young souls, Sarah and Martin, who find solace in each other's company amidst the turmoil of their own personal struggles.

From the moment they meet, Sarah and Martin are drawn to each other, sharing an undeniable connection that transcends the boundaries of their circumstances. As their love blossoms, they realize their time together is fleeting, for Sarah has been diagnosed with terminal cancer. In the face of this devastating revelation, the couple vows to make the most of their remaining days together, creating unforgettable memories and cherishing every moment.

As their journey unfolds, Sarah and Martin navigate the complexities of young love, finding joy in simple pleasures and forging a bond that defies the odds. With each passing day, Sarah's condition worsens, and the inevitability of their impending separation looms ever closer.

Fleeting Embers is a poignant reminder of the fragile beauty of life and the profound impact that love can have on our hearts. Through Sarah and Martin's story, readers will experience the full spectrum of human emotion, from the exhilaration of new love to the depths of despair accompanying loss. I was so proud of this novel!

Then, reality hit me during pitching. They were not interested in my novel. No one seemed to recognize me as the screenwriter for an upcoming TV series; instead, I was now more commonly known as Richard Collins' fiancée. Most literary agents showed interest the moment they recognized my name, but when I began pitching my book, they countered by suggesting I write a memoir rather than fiction. Being with a celebrity had its downsides, too, with some agents treating me far more strictly than they would any other aspiring author. They judged me based on my association with Richard, rather than on my writing abilities.

I had hoped that *Back In Time* would be the breakthrough I needed to gain recognition as an independent writer. But it seemed they were only interested in publishing stories about Richard. Whenever I pitched my book, I couldn't help but overhear whispers in the backroom about how much help I must have received from him along the way. It was disheartening to know that no matter how hard I worked, people still assumed my success was due to someone else's influence rather than my own skills.

The harsh reality began to sink in: my dream of publishing meaningful material instead of a gossip-laden memoir – which I would never do – was staring me right in the face. This feeling of disappointment was only heightened by the loneliness I felt without Richard by my side. Despite our best efforts, our differing time zones meant we had almost no contact with each other. I missed the way he used to encourage me at every step, with a gentle squeeze of my hand or a reassuring smile.

In an effort to distract myself from these disheartening thoughts, I immersed myself in tasks from the marketing department and delved into Richard's extensive book collection at home. I even joined Erin for a private baking lesson – anything that could help me pass the time and ease the longing I felt for Richard. Above all, I knew I needed to determine how to get my book published successfully.

As I kneaded the dough for a chicken pie in Erin's bakery, we talked about how drastically my life had changed in the past few months.

"Don't you think it would have been easier if you had fallen for Henry instead of Richard?" she asked, raising her eyebrows.

"Ugh, he's too young for me!" I exclaimed, wiping my nose with a flour-covered hand.

"Three years doesn't make him too young for you," she retorted.

"Erin, it's strange, but now he feels more like a son to me," I sighed. "Honestly, Henry is a great catch. He's a wonderful person and quite handsome, too. His future girlfriend will be incredibly lucky."

"You could be that girl," Erin persisted.

"Erin! I'm in love with Richard, and I can't imagine being in love with anyone else. Sometimes, though, I wish he wasn't a famous celebrity."

"Well, you'll just have to get used to being the wife of a star!"

"I'm not his wife yet," I reminded her. Internally, I felt an odd mix between nervousness and excitement as we discussed our plans together — or lack thereof. It wasn't like Richard hadn't asked me. He had proposed months ago and presented me with a beautiful engagement ring which made all doubt evaporate after seeing it glimmering on my finger. Still, something held me back.

"When are you two getting married?" Erin asked, bringing me out of my reverie and back to reality where things weren't so easy anymore; not with everything else that weighed in on our decision-making process.

I looked at my engagement ring, covered with flour. "Richard was waiting for me, and I don't know why I'm taking so long," I said.

"Are you having second thoughts? Especially now that you are the sole heir of your father's empire." she said.

That, too, added one more layer of complexity to our relationship. But this is not entirely why I was reluctant to marry Richard. Our whirlwind romance meant there were still many things I had yet to learn about him. At this point, all I could see was his good side and his mother's rudeness toward me. As if reading my mind, Erin asked me, "How's your future mother-in-law? How has she treated you since finding out you aren't poor after all?"

"I've no idea. I passed out when my father broke the news to me, and I haven't seen her since," I replied seriously, but then we both broke into a fit of laughter at the thought of it all.

"But I won't deprive my child of his name, and a family to support and love him. That's what I can promise you," I told Erin.

She looked at me seriously, "As long as you're happy." She paused before continuing, "You deserve to follow your heart, and if that means marrying Richard, then so be it." Her words brought me peace and comfort, and I knew she was right — ultimately, it was only my decision to make.

———

I was at Mavi's yoga class for expectant mothers and decided it would be the ideal way to keep myself busy. Suddenly, my phone rang — it was one of the agents from Astral Ink Publishing House with good news. They had read my manuscript and were willing to publish it with just a few minor reworks by their in-house editor. I was overjoyed and wanted to share the news with Richard — if only he weren't so far away in London!

It was already past midnight there, but still, I speed-dialed his number, and he answered on the second ring.

"Hello, beautiful," he greeted me. Hearing him on the other line still gave me butterflies in my stomach.

"I got in, Richard!" I shouted. "Astral Ink will publish my book!"

"That's brilliant! I never doubted you and your work," he said warmly. "That was fast! Congratulations, my darling." He didn't know that this was the only one who had accepted my manuscript; the others had countered with offers to publish our love story. Those details, however, were something I'd save for another day.

"How's work? Is the new movie exciting?" I asked him next, eager to hear more about his creative projects.

"It's okay," he replied, "but I'm missing you terribly."

"So am I," I said softly. "It gets lonely and frustrating waking up in an empty bed."

"Five more days, and I'll hop on the first flight to New York," he said with a hopeful smile. Then suddenly, Salem hopped onto my lap and screeched at Richard on my phone screen, who said. "Salem, get off her, you little critter!" He meowed one more time before beginning to groom himself on my lap.

I laughed and looked at Richard through the phone screen. "When are you two going to be friends?" I teased.

"Darling, I get the feeling he's jealous of me," Richard chuckled. I loved hearing his laugh; it was like a balm for my soul. I could see longing in his eyes, too. We both knew how hard this long distance between us was. We talked a bit longer before finally saying goodbye so that Richard could sleep — his film call time was early morning tomorrow, after all — and then reluctantly hung up our phones as I got back into position for the yoga class.

My body was still toned, thanks to my regular running and yoga. The only giveaway that I was pregnant was the slight bump on my stomach. I remember the first time Mavi welcomed me into her class and carefully selected the poses I could do — she knew exactly what a pregnant woman needed! When I arrived at the class, all eyes were on me — amused to see Richard's girlfriend in a hole-in-the-wall yoga place in an NYC 'hood. But they welcomed me warmly and gave me an understanding smile as Mavi introduced me to everyone else in the room.

The calming environment and soothing voice of our instructor set the tone for a peaceful yoga session. As I inhaled and stretched my arms high, I felt the tension slowly melt away from my body. I could feel every cell of my being responding to the gentle movements, my breathing becoming deep and rhythmic, and my nerves began to relax.

The other women in the class seemed to have an innate understanding of the physical discomfort and emotional stress that pregnancy brings. It felt like I was part of a supportive community. Though we were all strangers, the fact that we shared the experience of being expectant mothers created an unspoken bond that permeated the class.

As I exhaled and moved into the next pose, I realized I had found a place of peace and solace where I could leave behind the outside world and connect with my mind, body, and baby. It was a moment of clarity and realization, and I was grateful for this opportunity to take care of myself and my growing baby in this way.

I slumped on the mattress, wiping my sweat, when Mavi joined me. "How's your long-distance love affair?" she asked as we shared a pot of her own brew — a combination of chamomile flowers, ginger root, dried orange, and hibiscus flowers — which always had a calming effect on me.

"I miss him so much, and I can't stand being in the house without him," I said sadly.

"Are you still keeping your apartment at 89th ?" she asked, looking at me intently.

"Yes, my stuff is still there," I replied. "I'm not sure what to do with it yet."

"I heard your father's been eyeing that building apartment," she said, ever watchful of how the news might affect me.

I sighed heavily. "I've no idea. As much as possible, I'm staying away from Dad's business and finances. Same with Richard's... I still want to do things on my own," I admitted reluctantly. The funny thing is, though — now that all our bills are taken care of and Richard's team in London managed the salaries for household staff — I still missed working on my budget. "I'm not used to having someone pay for everything for me! So I'm just glad I'm still in charge of paying for my old apartment."

Mavi smiled sympathetically before continuing. "Speaking of money, if you're missing Richard so badly that five days feels like an eternity, why don't you get the first flight to London tomorrow? It's just another seven-hour flight!"

Surprised at her suggestion, I grinned back at her cheekily before replying: "Mavi, I just can't show up there; I don't know where he lives and might get lost in London!"

"Call Henry," she winked at me while nodding her head in encouragement. "Why don't you surprise him on the film set?" Why not?! At this point, nothing was holding me back... except waiting yet another day!

I called Henry when Salem and I got home, but he wasn't picking up, so I hung up and fixed myself a sandwich. When Leticia saw me, she grabbed my hand and seated me at the counter.

"Madam, just let me know what you want to eat. It will give me joy to provide a service to you. Let me take care of you," she said kindly as she began arranging cold ham, cheese, and dressing on the freshly sliced bread. Then she lovingly poured warm pumpkin soup into a bowl to go with it.

"Thank you, Leticia. I didn't realize how hungry I was until I smelled that soup," I said as I took a spoonful of the warm liquid.

"You should eat more; you're too skinny," she said as she watched me with concern. Halfway through my meal, my phone suddenly rang — it was Henry!

"Sorry, I just woke up. Is anything wrong?" I heard a hint of concern in his voice.

"No, silly," I said with a laugh. "I'm planning to take the first flight to London tomorrow, or if I can get the last flight out tonight so I can be there early morning. I want to surprise your father, so don't tell him."

"Okay, let me know your flight details, and I'll pick you up at the airport. And I'll inform the housekeeper that you're coming over — dad's away on location shoot so he won't know." Henry said reassuringly.

"I'll let you know in an hour. Let me check what flights are available," I replied.

"Hope, no coach please. Get a first-class seat! You're an Ortega now, soon-to-be Collins," he teased .

"Yes, boss!" I laughed in response. "Thank you for checking in on me!" And with that, we hung up.

22

Summer, London

I stepped off the flight from New York, relieved to be on solid ground again. I wore my comfortable black yoga pants and a white tank top underneath a thin, oversized grey cardigan. My black Prada flats were the only thing preventing me from ultimately looking comfortable. After hustling through immigration and luggage pickup, I emerged into the bright morning Britain sunshine.

I quickly spotted Henry in the crowd, his blond hair tied neatly in a ponytail. When he saw me, his face lit up. I rushed over to him and gave him a quick hug. "It's good to see you, Henry!"

He hugged me and said, "It's good to see you and little bean." He patted my stomach affectionately; I was already three months pregnant and soon to be four. Henry then noticed my single luggage bag beside me and raised an eyebrow in surprise. "Is that all you have?"

I nodded, explaining that I hadn't wanted to lug around too much extra weight while pregnant. "I'm not used to seeing Hollywood stars with a single luggage," Henry joked.

I laughed, "I'm not part of Hollywood, Henry — just your dad!"

Henry laughed and shook his head fondly before taking my bag and heading for the exit.

As Henry drove to Richard's flat in Chelsea, I was captivated by the city's magnificent architecture and stunning landmarks like the Tower of London, Big Ben, and Westminster Abbey. "It's beautiful, Henry!" I said as I marveled at the vibrant parks and lush green gardens that lined the roads before eventually finding myself in the exclusive neighborhood of Chelsea. I enjoyed passing by luxe theaters, upmarket boutiques, and modern galleries before finally arriving at Richard's sophisticated abode.

"Chelsea is known for its cosmopolitan feel, not just beautiful parks but chic boutiques as well." He took a glance in my direction, amused by my reaction.

Upon arriving at Richard's London flat, I was immediately struck by its beauty. The serene, calming blue walls with crisp white trim framing the doorways and windows created a soothing atmosphere. There was a comfortable white sofa before a cozy fireplace, flanked by two armchairs upholstered in chic navy and white stripe prints.

I quickly realized that Richard's London flat was much smaller than our apartment in New York, but it had a cozy charm that made it feel like home. The wooden floor gleamed in the light that streamed through the windows and shone on the little kitchenette with its fridge, microwave, and all the necessary cutlery and crockery tucked neatly in nearby cupboards. Beyond this were two doors leading to two other rooms, which I would explore later when I settled in.

A woman in her fifties emerged from one of the doors. Henry quickly introduced us, "Elena, this is Hope. Please bring her things to Dad's room and fix something for her to eat."

"I'm fine. I ate airline food," I said. "I just need to hydrate, I guess." Elena nodded and took my bags before disappearing.

"So shall we surprise your dad at the set?" I asked Henry with a smile.

"Try to catch your breath first," Henry laughed as he uncapped the water bottle, which he passed to me.

After finishing my drink, I eagerly exclaimed, "Alright, let's go!"

Henry simply shook his head and ushered me out of the house.

The drive from Chelsea to Notting Hill, where Richard was filming his movie, was nothing short of scenic and enjoyable. As Henry drove along the iconic streets of London, I took in the views of its classic red buses, splendid architecture, and lively marketplaces. When we finally reached our destination, teeming with film crews and various movie sets, I couldn't help but admire its charming townhouses with their bright colors and detailed designs.

"Where's Hugh Grant's Travel bookstore and the blue door?" I excitedly asked Henry, referencing the famous scene from *Notting Hill*. He looked at me momentarily as if my brain had dropped onto another planet before realizing what I meant. He chuckled and shook his head as he pointed out the place in the distance.

We parked across the street, on one of the side lots where the filming occurred. As I stepped out of the car, I rested my arm against the car door and caught a glimpse of Richard from a distance. He was wearing jeans and a light blue T-shirt while filming with an actress, and their faces were just inches away as if they were about to kiss. Despite knowing that it was all part of his acting job, I couldn't help but avert my eyes, not wanting to witness him sharing such an intimate moment with someone else.

Henry cleared his throat. "I thought you were getting used to it," he said, a hint of sadness in his voice.

"There's no getting used to it," I replied, feeling my heart sinking.

Just then, Richard turned around and caught sight of me. His eyes widened, and his mouth curled into a smile as he quickly said something to the crew before making a beeline toward me. As soon as he reached my side, he kissed me passionately, the familiar warmth and love emanating from him stealing away all those sad feelings I had just moments ago.

"I can't believe you're here!" Richard said excitedly, his hands framing my face as if he wanted to commit every detail of me to memory.

"Five days seem like such a long time now," I pouted, gazing into his eyes lovingly. He threw his head back and laughed before tenderly touching my stomach as if wanting our child to know that their parents were together again .

Just then, someone called for him to return to work. "I'll be right back, darling," he said lovingly before turning around to hug his son. "Take care of your mother," he said as he ran back to resume filming.

"Mom, I'm hungry!" Henry said mockingly. I punched his upper arm and winced as my knuckles connected with solid muscle. "You can't just stand here and stare at him all day," he teased. "There's a coffee shop a couple of blocks away. Care to walk?"

I glanced at Richard before I looped my arm with Henry's, and we began walking together.

The modest coffee shop had an air of old-world charm about it. Warm wooden tables and chairs welcomed patrons, along with the smell of freshly ground coffee beans. The counter was decked out in quartz and marble while art prints from local artists lined up the walls. A wide selection of homemade pastries, cakes, and bags of locally roasted coffee beans were available to entice customers. It was a cozy spot that made me feel right at home.

We each ordered separate plates of crispy strips of bacon with scrambled eggs and roasted tomatoes on the side. Henry got a fresh pot of coffee while I settled for tea, as pregnancy prohibited me from indulging in too much caffeine.

"I think you need to get ready to meet my grandparents while you're here," Henry said.

"I met your grandmother in Amsterdam with your mother. It wasn't a pleasant experience," I said as I took a mouthful bite of bacon and roasted tomatoes.

"I heard about that. Those two are thick as thieves, you know," he replied with a wry smile. "There are some unpleasant surprises you'll discover, too. This is when you must focus on Dad's feelings for you."

His cryptic message worried me and I could feel my anxiety rising. "There are so many things I still don't know about your father," I mumbled, almost to myself.

"You'll find out most of them here," he said somberly. His tone warned me that something was about to happen.

I touched Henry's hand on the table and thanked him for always being on my side. Quickly, I changed the subject and asked him if there was a girlfriend that I should meet during my stay.

"Sadly, none," he said with a rueful smile. "Dad and I have the same taste in women, which is rare. He got one of them in New York."

My heart sank a little at his words, although it did cross my mind how handsome Henry was when we met that day in the park with the ducks. But Richard had captured my heart since we first met, and nothing could change that.

We continued talking, catching up on things like his school and my book that was soon to be published. Time flew by as we enjoyed our conversation until Richard suddenly showed up. Richard's face lit up when he saw me, "There you are!"

He rushed over and embraced me, not caring that his son was watching. He kissed me passionately and whispered, "I've missed you. I finished my parts, and they've allowed me to take you home." His love for me was evident, and his affection was unconditional. I felt the same way about him.

"I think I need to head back to my place and get ready for my classes," Henry said.

"Wait, you dropped school today just to fetch me? You should have said something," I protested.

"Relax, my classes aren't due in four hours." He put several bills on the table and kissed me on the forehead. "I'll see you tomorrow," he said, hugging his father.

"Thank you, Henry, for taking care of her," Richard said as he hugged him back.

———

When we arrived at Richard's place, his mother was waiting in the living room.

"What are you doing here, Mother?" he asked coldly.

"Elena called me because Hope is here, and no one discussed that with her since her employment was solely to serve you in the house. You should have given some consideration, Richard," she said.

"I think she'd be better off working with you than with me," he replied. He then summoned Elena, who looked between Richard and Catherine nervously.

"Elena, you can pack your things now and move to my mother or anywhere else you wish to work. The office will send your salary into your account first thing in the morning," he said firmly.

Elena protested, but Richard dismissed her. I was tongue-tied the whole time. Catherine looked at me with disdain, "You haven't been here for a day, and you've already caused chaos in our home, Hope."

"Mother! This is my home and Hope's. You should mind your household," Richard yelled.

I could sense the tension in the room as Richard and his mother faced off. Catherine mentioning my name had only added to the strain.

I touched his arm to try to calm him down. He looked at me, his eyes full of sadness. He grabbed my hand and kissed it. I held his face and whispered, "It's okay."

"You're being unreasonable, Richard! The reason I am here is to clean up your mess again. How many times do I have to do that? Does Hope know about your past?" Catherine was furious.

Richard's mother stood her ground, her voice carrying a hint of reproach. I could tell there was more to the story but I didn't want to pry. Instead, I stood awkwardly in the doorway, unsure what to do or say.

"Mother, please leave. Don't make me ask you a second time," Richard said sternly. I could sense the anger and terror in his voice. I grabbed his hand and placed it on my stomach. It was my way of reminding him that this whole incident was upsetting both me and our unborn baby. Catherine looked at me with dislike and stormed out of the room.

Richard gathered me in his arms as if wanting to shield me from all the unpleasantness. I touched his face, "I'm sorry for just showing up here like this. I hate that I had to come between you and your mother. She's right. I should have given you more consideration before doing this."

"Darling, showing up here today is one of the best things that's happened to me since leaving New York. My relationship with my mother has always been so complicated," he explained as he gathered my hands and kissed them, then releasing them to kiss my mouth passionately. I could feel the need in Richard's kisses as if he was trying to erase some bad memories.

I closed my eyes and felt the warmth of his embrace. I wanted to stay here forever, at this moment, but he pulled away eventually. His blue-grey eyes stared into mine, "Never apologize for being here. You make me happy."

He kissed me tenderly and I felt my heart swell with love. He scooped me up in his arms and carried me to the bedroom, never breaking the kiss. I felt Richard's hands exploring my body, caressing me lovingly as our passionate kiss deepened. His touch was gentle yet full of desire as he removed my clothing piece by piece before laying me down on the bed with such admiration and care. He traced his fingertips down my spine, onto my hips, and finally between my legs.

"Richard..." I moved my hips to meet his. His hands were gentle and loving. I could feel the tenderness in each caress.

"You're so beautiful," he looked into my eyes; his eyes were full of desire. His fingers moved harder as he claimed my right nipple in his mouth. I cried out loud, this combination drives me crazy, and he knew it. He knew my body and how it responds to his hands and mouth. Finally, he let go of my breast and kissed me passionately, and I felt a deep connection that went beyond anything physical. Everywhere he touched, I felt alive, and for a moment, I forgot everything but him.

As he moved to hover over me, I held my breath, anticipating what would come next. Richard opened my legs further and entered me slowly and carefully.

I found immense comfort in knowing that Richard was cautious not to hurt me and that he treated me with exceptional love and care because of my pregnancy. As he wrapped his arms around me, I felt safe and protected. His movements were graceful, as if he was attuned to every beat of my heart, which raced with excitement as he made love to me like never before. Every touch felt magical, and every moment precious. It was as though we were two entwined souls, experiencing an inexplicable connection beyond anything we had ever felt before.

Richard lovingly folded me in his arms after making love to me. We stayed completely wrapped up in each other for quite a while, neither of us wanting to break the spell. Our hearts beat in sync, and I felt secure in his arms. Richard ran his hands through my hair and kissed my forehead, whispering how much he loved me.

The night was peaceful and calm, contrasting with our passion only moments before. I felt content as it kept any lingering worries or anxieties at bay, and with his gentle embrace, I finally drifted off to sleep.

23

It's good that Richard was filming nearby, which means we get to spend the night at home together. He offered to cancel his schedule so he could take me sightseeing in London, but I convinced him to go on with his regular work week as I wanted to explore the city alone.

London was one of the most fascinating cities in the world and a book lovers' haven for its vast collections and selection of books from different bookstores. I could barely contain my excitement when I heard about this in university since I am a huge book enthusiast. Eagerly, I made plans to discover all the hidden gems London has to offer by scouring through the shelves of old-fashioned independent bookshops and uncovering incredible stories in them.

As a first-time visitor to London, I was overwhelmed by the sheer magnitude of the city. Everywhere I looked, something new and exciting was waiting to be discovered. I put a hold on exploring the historical sights of Westminster Abbey and Buckingham Palace since I was not a fan of the Royal Family and their history of slavery. Instead, I chose to take a stroll along the River Thames.

Strolling along the banks of the River Thames was a captivating experience. The gentle chime of bells from boats ringing in the distance and the smell of salty air were soothing to my confused mind. Richard in New York seemed different from Richard in London. His harsh demeanor towards his mother was unmistakable, yet he remained protective of me. Both Henry and Catherine had hinted at something unpleasant that might surface during my stay. What secrets might I uncover about Richard? What was he not telling me? I had fallen in love with Richard so quickly that I neglected to get to know him truly.

The sun broke through the clouds to reveal stunning views of London's skyline along with its signature landmarks while shimmering reflections on the surface of the river were breathtaking. It was like stepping into a fairytale – it was magical and calming. At that moment, I was captivated, and my worries about Richard faded away.

After a long, exhausting walk, I needed a bite to eat. Luckily, I stumbled upon a café in the banks of the River Thames. It was decorated with natural, earthy tones, creating a warm and laidback atmosphere. I sat at a single table with two comfortable chairs, feeling slightly overwhelmed by the wide selection of options. After a few moments of indecision, I soon settled on sourdough bread with poached eggs, avocados and bacon, and a cup of steaming hot tea. The smell of freshly baked cakes and pastries filled the air, tempting me to try something sweet. As soon as the food arrived, I ate with gusto — I didn't realize how hungry I was. As I was enjoying my tea and a gluten-free cannoli which I ordered at the last minute, I sensed someone standing behind me.

Someone cleared his throat. I turned around, and a man with gentle features and deep wrinkles extended his hand to me. "You must be Hope Williams," he said softly. His bright blue eyes twinkled mischievously as he introduced himself as George Collins. Richard's father! His appearance suggested that he was a man with a wealth of stories and life lessons to share. Although I had never met him until now, his warm smile gave the impression that we had known each other for ages. "Mind if I join you?" he asked with a friendly smile.

"Of course," I replied, offering him the empty chair beside me. Feeling a little embarrassed, I quickly wiped my hand with a napkin before offering it to him. "Call me Hope," I said.

The waitress came by to fill George's cup with freshly brewed coffee. "You shouldn't be roaming around on your own," he said with a smile as he took a sip from his cup.

I smiled back at him, feeling slightly embarrassed yet comfortable in his presence. "I don't mind at all," I told him. "I love touring by myself. I'm kind of an introvert, you know."

His gaze shifted to my stomach. "How far along are you now with the pregnancy," he asked.

"I'm on my twenty-second week. It's getting visible," I said shyly.

"You look younger than Richard — more like Henry's age," George said.

"I don't know how to answer that," I replied. I still felt taken aback whenever people mentioned our age difference. After all, Hollywood is filled with couples who have significant age gaps between them.

"No, no — don't mind me," he quickly added. "I'm used to speaking bluntly based on what I observe. I'm sorry to hear about what happened with Catherine yesterday," George said, shaking his head. "It's probably hard for her to accept someone else in the picture."

"It's all new to me," I replied. "In America, parents usually expect their children to be independent and make their own decisions. I'm still learning how things work over here and adjusting as needed. But I'm used to being in control of my own life."

"It's the same here; kids move out at a young age. Richard is an only child, and Catherine is used to having control over his affairs. It's not just Richard, though; she tries to control mine and sometimes even Henry's," George explained. "I heard you and Henry are getting along well. That's more important than worrying about old people like me and Catherine."

"No, George," I replied firmly. "You're both important to me. That's why I wanted to get to know you and Catherine. I just want her to like me," I expressed sincerely. He nodded appreciatively before gently tapping my hand in a comforting gesture. "What matters is that you understand Richard and his past. It wasn't an easy journey for him."

My mind was swimming with questions as he spoke, wondering why this was the second time I had heard such unsettling things about Richard's past. He was obviously not telling me something important.

As if reading my mind, George asked: "Has Richard shared his past life with you?"

"Not really," I said hesitantly. "I never asked... it doesn't matter to me." Even as the words left my mouth, I knew they weren't entirely true. But I didn't want to push Richard into sharing something he wasn't comfortable talking about yet.

"Will my grandchild be born English or American?" George asked, his eyes twinkling with anticipation.

"We haven't discussed the details yet," I replied. "But, since my doctor is in New York, we'll likely have the baby there. But he will definitely get plenty of holidays over here to spend time with his grandparents. I can guarantee that."

"Thank you, Hope," he said, smiling warmly at me. "I just want my son to be happy finally. Why don't the two of you come to dinner at our place tomorrow? Henry will be there, too."

"I'd love that!" I exclaimed happily.

His face lit up. "That's wonderful," he said and clapped his hands. "So I'll leave you to explore the city for now," George said as he stood up. He leaned forward and kissed me on both cheeks. His newspaper was tucked neatly inside his sleeves. With a smile and a wave, he was out of the door and gone instantly, leaving me with a heart full of warmth and anticipation for dinner tomorrow.

When I returned to Richard's flat, I suddenly missed Leticia. She was our reliable housekeeper in New York and always made sure we had everything we needed, from freshly prepared meals to a spotless home. With Richard's housekeeper's departure yesterday, I knew I would need to rely on the skills Erin had taught me in her kitchen to make dinner for us tonight.

The aroma of garlic and herbs filled the kitchen as I stirred the pot of boiling pasta. Taking a few moments to chop up some fresh tomatoes, peppers, and onions, I added them to a hot pan with oil and spices. As the vegetables cooked, I stirred the pasta occasionally until it was al dente. I remembered all the lessons I had learned in Erin's kitchen. From peeling and chopping vegetables to perfectly seasoning a dish — all the skills were coming back to me as I prepared dinner.

The vegetables quickly sizzled in the hot pan while I stirred the bubbling pasta. Finally, after adding some freshly chopped herbs and grated cheese, I was ready to plate .

While I was wiping the sauce from the pasta bowl, a familiar voice filled the kitchen. It was Richard! "The kitchen smells good! Did someone enchant this place?" he asked with a smile as he stepped into the room.

"There you are! Take a seat at the table," I replied before quickly giving him a quick kiss.

"This deserves a perfect wine," he said as he turned to go to his wine cellar in the basement. But before heading down, he changed his mind and looked at me with love in his eyes. "I forgot I'm now living with a pregnant and beautiful woman."

"Go, get the wine. I can take a sip. My doctor said I can occasionally in small amounts," I convinced him.

He smiled briefly before responding. "I'm already liking your gynecologist!" With that, he stepped out to get the bottle of wine.

I carefully placed the two steaming bowls of pasta on the table and watched as Richard uncorked the bottle of wine. He brought two glasses before pouring the dark red liquid into them.

"Hmmm....you can cook, darling," he said in between a mouthful of pasta, a look of pure satisfaction on his face.

"One of the perks of having a friend who runs a bakery and went to culinary school in France," I said proudly. "Oh, before I forget, I bumped into George earlier today," I told Richard, excitedly recounting my encounter with his father and his invitation to dinner tomorrow. "I already confirmed, so don't back out!"

Richard took a deep breath before responding. "You don't have to like them."

"Richard, I want to try. Please let me do it," I pleaded. I held his hand, and he squeezed mine back. I looked into Richard's eyes, unable to contain the emotions swelling up inside me.

"Richard," I said, my voice trembling with emotion. "I know it may seem sudden, but I want us to get married soon. I want us to be together forever."

He stared back at me in silence for what felt like an eternity. Then he slowly reached out and took my hands in his, squeezing them gently as a tear trickled down his cheek.

"Yes," he whispered, his voice breaking slightly with emotion. "Yes, of course I'll marry you." He kneeled in front of me and tugged me close, and before I could say anything else, he was leaning in and kissing me passionately. Everywhere his lips touched, it felt like it was alive with electricity as if the universe had been waiting for this moment. We stayed like that for what felt like an eternity until Richard finally pulled away and smiled at me tenderly.

"Finally," he said softly. Richard placed his hand on my stomach, and suddenly we both felt a gentle flutter — it was the baby quickening, our first real connection. Tears welled in my eyes as I realized our child had been with us all along, waiting for us to decide to tie the knot and finally become a family. It felt like our precious little one had known that we were ready and was welcoming us into this new stage of life. "I love you, Hope Williams," Richard's eyes were full of wonder and shining with tears. He claimed my mouth again for a passionate kiss.

We talked into the night, discussing every aspect of the wedding. Our ideas seemed to differ vastly —I wanted a quick, straightforward ceremony in city hall with no fanfare or white dress walking down the aisle. In contrast, Richard wanted an intimate but grand ceremony to celebrate our union. We debated and argued until he finally leaned forward and kissed me gently on the head.

I smiled at him and snuggled deeper into his arms, overcome by exhaustion. Before long, my eyes began to close, and I drifted off, safe in his embrace, even though we were still lounging on the couch in the living room.

———

I dressed carefully for dinner, choosing a deep royal blue dress with a soft, flowing skirt. I clasped the diamond earrings and matching necklace Richard gave me in Paris around my neck, their sparkle adding to the ensemble. I applied light makeup to enhance my features and pulled my hair back into an elegant bun, emphasizing my slender neck.

Richard looked dashing as usual —he had chosen a pair of charcoal grey tailored pants with a light blue shirt that fit him perfectly. We were quite the couple tonight, perfectly matched in our attire.

George welcomed us into their beautiful home with open arms, planting a kiss on each of my cheeks and exclaiming, "You look beautiful, my dear!" He then pulled his son in for an embrace. Before Richard could relax, his father told him his mother had invited Emilia tonight.

Richard's face turned furious, but I touched his face gently and whispered, "It's alright, my love."

George was full of warmth and hospitality as he guided me through the house, pointing out the different family photographs lining the walls. Catherine and Emilia unexpectedly joined us and shared stories from Richard's previous marriage and Henry's childhood growing up around London.

It was an awkward situation for everyone, but Richard stayed close to my side as I stepped forward to offer my hand to Catherine and said, "Thank you for having us tonight."

Suddenly, Henry arrived and walked toward me with his usual cheery greeting, "Hello, mummy dearest!" He kissed me on the cheek and placed his hand on my stomach, saying, "Hello to you, too, little bean." My baby quickened in response, and Henry and I exchanged a surprised look.

"He recognizes his brother's voice," said Richard as he pulled me close.

Henry laughed in awe, exclaiming, "Oh my God! He knows me!"

Richard smiled proudly, responding, "Of course!" At that moment, the world seemed to revolve around us —Richard, me, Henry, and our precious little bean.

We soon heard the pop of a champagne bottle, and George cheerfully exclaimed, "This calls for a celebration!"

Catherine's voice was sharp and cold as she said, "Henry, you're supposed to greet your grandparents and your mother."

Henry obliged, walking to his grandfather and embracing him before turning to his grandmother. He kissed both of them on the cheek and said softly, "Hello, granny...and mother." Then he walked back to his father and me, accepting a flute of champagne from George. He looked around the room and grinned, "So, are we having a double celebration tonight? Little bean's arrival and, of course, your wedding in a few weeks?" I looked in surprise at Richard as Henry said cheekily, "I'm my father's best man, so I was the first to know the news!"

George clapped his hands together in delight. "This day is perfect!" he exclaimed.

After a few minutes of chattering and excitement, we went to the dining room. The room was grandly decorated, with a long, elegantly set table surrounded by high-backed chairs. Twinkling chandeliers hung from the ceiling, casting a warm, golden light over everything. The table had been set with silver platters filled to the brim with an abundance of delicious food, making it impossible for us to resist. Delicate flower arrangements of freshly-picked spring blooms adorned the elegant setting, adding their sweet fragrance to the already perfect environment.

George sat at the head of the table with his wife on the left side, Emilia and Henry beside her, and Richard on the left side with me. Henry requested to move his plate beside his father and me.

Emilia protested, "Henry, don't make last-minute changes."

"It's no big deal, Mother. They just need to move my plate. I need to catch up with Hope," Henry insisted.

George smiled at Henry's request and said, "Of course, this is no trouble, Emilia. No trouble at all." He gestured to the servants to move Henry's plate as requested. Then everyone settled in for dinner. Richard smiled warmly at me and said, "You two seem to be getting along nicely." I blushed and quickly looked away. Henry grinned cheekily and gave me a wink.

An awkward silence fell in the room, and I could feel the tension in the air. George cleared his throat and tried to lighten the mood by asking Richard and me about our plans for the future. Richard shared that we were still working on the details, but he was hopeful it would be in New York.

"Have you worked on your pre-nuptial agreement?" Catherine asked.

"Mother...." Richard's jaw clenched tightly as he resisted saying anything, so I held his hand to remind him to remain civil.

"Richard, your mother is protecting our son's interest," Emilia's voice echoed around the room.

Richard's face turned to stone and he slammed his fists onto the table. "This is none of your business, Emilia," he spat out. His mother tried to intervene, but he was beyond reasoning. "I paid our divorce settlement in full! You squandered it away, and I can't allow you to touch Henry's money."

Emilia remained quiet, seemingly taken aback by the outburst.

Catherine stepped in then, her voice soft yet firm as she said, "Richard, I invited her here so we can settle this once and for all."

Richard's face hardened as he spoke again. "Here's my plan, and it's already been executed by my legal team," he said coldly. "Half of my assets will go to Hope, and the remaining half will be divided equally among my children, including Henry. Do you want to contest that, Mother? You can get a lawyer and see which court will allow you to meddle with my finances."

His mother protested immediately. "You're insane, Richard! That's unfair for—!"

Henry cut her off before she could finish her sentence. "Granny, it is fair," he said calmly. "My dad already sent me to the finest schools, and I can carve my future from that."

Richard nodded in approval, then turned back towards his mother. He seemed to wait for her response, but all she did was glare at him with a mixture of anger and disbelief in her eyes.

"You fucking murderer!" Emilia's eyes are glaring furiously. Then she looked at me. "He didn't tell you how he killed my baby?"

Richard looked at Emilia and said, "Get the fuck out of here before I kill you myself."

I froze, feeling a chill go down my spine. This was the side of Richard I have yet to discover. I looked at Henry, "Please take me home."

Richard seemed to sense my distress and snapped back to his old self in an instant. "I'm sorry, darling," he said softly, putting his arms around me tightly as if seeking solace in my embrace.

Richard turned to his father and said, "We'd better be going." Without glancing back, he grabbed me in his arms and walked out of the room and out of the house.

24

The tension in the air was oppressive. Richard seemed distant and distracted. As we drove further away from the house, I felt something inside me slipping away with each passing moment we spent in silence.

We drove home in silence, neither wanting to break the stillness. I didn't want to ask Richard the question that was on my mind for fear of what I might find out or hear. Every time he looked at me, the sunshine had gone and was replaced by dark clouds forming in his eyes. His jaw clenched, a sign that he was suppressing something.

Whenever Richard and I returned from a gathering or dinner, we would always spend fun moments talking non-stop in the bathroom as we stripped off our clothes, cleaned ourselves up, and changed into our sleeping clothes. But tonight, I cleaned my makeup and changed into my night dress without any company. When I emerged from the bathroom, Richard sat quietly on a couch near our bed, still wearing his dinner clothes. When he saw me, he stood up immediately and tucked me into bed before kissing my forehead. He left the bedroom silently after that.

I couldn't sleep. My eyes were fixed on the ceiling as I thought about Richard and what Emilia said. I had been with him for months, yet I still didn't know much about him. Now his ex-wife had accused him of murdering their child. It made me feel sick just thinking about it. How could she even say such a thing unless it were true? And why hadn't Richard ever told me anything himself?

With Richard's silence, my mind wandered to all kinds of dark places —what if he wasn't who I thought he was? What did Emilia mean when she called him a murderer? Was that an exaggeration, or did it literally mean he killed a child?

The thought of it sent shivers down my spine, and tears started streaming down my face as I buried my face in the pillows in silence. It felt like no matter how hard I tried to push these thoughts away from me, they kept coming back stronger than before. All I wanted was for Richard to tell me everything so we could move past this together, but until then, nothing seemed certain.

When I woke up in the morning, my heart sank when I saw Richard's side of the bed was empty. A note on his pillow told me he didn't wake me up because of an early call time. Even though I knew he had to work, it felt like a punch in the gut that he had chosen to leave without saying goodbye.

I couldn't help but feel like things between us were slipping away with each step he took further from me. No matter how much I wished things could stay the same, there was no denying that something had changed and couldn't be undone.

Today, I decided to stay home and take care of some overdue work. When I opened my laptop, my cramped mailbox was full of unread messages from the last few days. The post-production team had finished their final cut for each episode. The marketing team had pitched several posters and trailers along with PR guidelines and a release schedule. *Back In Time* series would be airing at the beginning of fall.

My agent was happy to tell me that the editorial team was satisfied with my manuscript, so he attached their version for my review. He noted that the revisions were minor and hoped I wouldn't mind making them. Now it was time to discuss with creatives the design of my book cover. This is happening, finally! I touched my stomach and whispered, "Little bean, Mommy is finally becoming a published author."

I replied to a few emails, and my stomach soon reminded me it was time for breakfast. I haven't eaten anything since last night. I went to the kitchen and discovered that our fridge contained all my favorite food, like milk, eggs, and orange juice. It never failed to amaze me, Richard's thoughtfulness. Despite being in London, he ensured I still got my favorite American breakfast. I took out slices of bread and put them into the toaster before grabbing jars of peanut butter and jelly. After pouring orange juice into a glass and placing the hot toast on a plate, I carried it to the kitchen counter.

I have loved eating peanut butter directly from the jar since childhood, and this morning was no different.

I was startled by the ring of my phone. It was Yumi on the other line.

"Are you in England? Did you just dodge Arthur and Chen?" She asked, referring to my father's twin goons.

"I thought they already stopped doing that," I said, annoyed that they were still tailing me.

"Your father won't stop protecting you, especially now that you are officially the sole heir," Yumi said cautiously.

"Let's not talk about that right now. I can't process that yet." I replied. "So what made you call?"

"Where in this hellhole are you right now? I'm sending Arthur and Chen over," she continued.

"Please, give me some space on this trip. I want it to be as normal as possible. When I'm not with Richard or Henry, I never stray from the city limits."

"I don't make the rules here, Hope, and I understand Oliver perfectly," she said softly. "Now more than ever, he is more protective of you and was furious when he found out you left New York alone."

"Let me talk to him," I pleaded.

"Okay, since I can't t get any information from you." She replied with a hint of amusement in her voice.

"Where are you now? And, Dad?" I asked.

"I'm in Singapore and your father is in DC right now. You can reach his mobile number."

We talked for a bit longer before Yumi and I ended our conversation. I took a deep breath and closed my eyes as I leaned against the kitchen counter.

I glanced at the clock and saw that it was already nine o'clock in the morning. London is five hours ahead of Washington, so it was still quite early to make a call. However, I wouldn't be surprised if Dad were awake at four o'clock in the morning.

I busied myself with answering several work emails, and before I knew it, lunchtime had arrived. I quickly whipped up an omelet with cheese and a side of cherry tomatoes. I didn't have much of an appetite, but I reminded myself that I needed to eat, especially since I was pregnant.

Jenna had sent over a couple of pages for me to edit for her new book. I considered using Richard's office as a workspace, but after what happened last night, I didn't want to be reminded of him. Instead, I opted to work at the kitchen table.

I was so engrossed in my work that I nearly forgot to call my father. Even after I learned how powerful my father was, I had never called in a favor. But I had no one else to turn to who could look at my problem objectively. I knew he could help me get the information I needed if not already in his possession.

So I started dialing my father's mobile number, feeling butterflies in my stomach as the call connected, and after a few rings, a woman answered the phone.

"This is Oliver Ortega's office. May I help you?" She said.

I had thought this was his direct number to call him. "May I speak to him?" I asked.

"I'm sorry, but Mr. Ortega is in a boardroom meeting right now," the woman replied. "May I know who is calling, please?"

"I'm sorry. I'll call back some other time," I said hastily. "This is Hope Williams."

"My apologies, Miss Hope, I didn't recognize your number," she said kindly. "All calls, including Mr. Ortega's personal line, were forwarded to me during an important meeting." She added before continuing with a polite offer: "Let me connect him to you."

"No need to disturb him," I said quickly, not wanting to impose on his time. "I will call again."

But she persisted, saying that he'd be furious if he missed a call from me and put the line on hold while she tried calling him back —which thankfully worked, and a few seconds later, he answered with familiarity in his voice: "Hope? Where are you?"

I told him I was in London and explained what led me here. After a long pause, he finally said, "Something is bothering you. Otherwise, you wouldn't make this call."

"Dad, I need your help," I said, feeling guilty about betraying Richard by asking my father to do this. I told my dad about the information I needed on Richard's background, and despite being a public figure, that information either was sealed or erased from the internet.

"I already have that information," he replied, confirming my suspicions. "Would you like me to tell you the summary, or would you like me to send you the full report?" he asked.

"Just tell me what I need to know," I said firmly.

He then filled me in with all the missing details, leaving me shocked at how thorough his resources were. Before Richard had filed for divorce, Emilia was pregnant with their second child. The hospital records showed that she suffered a miscarriage after falling down the stairs, leading to Richard having therapy sessions three years later. Emilia fought him hard for the divorce, and the court took her side eventually, leading to an out-of-court settlement where Richard paid Emilia a large amount of money as part of the divorce settlement.

"You finally discovered those while you were there, I supposed," he said.

"Why had he kept those from me?" I cried.

"I don't know his reasons. Men are sometimes complicated. We're not that good at expressing our thoughts and feelings. Look at how I handled things with your mother," he said.

"Dad, what should I do?" I asked.

"Ask him. Listen and try to go beyond reasoning."

After we finished talking, we said our goodbyes and hung up, but before he ended the conversation, I pleaded with my father not to send Arthur and Chen.

"That's a lot to ask, Hope," he said.

"Dad, trust me on this. I just want to enjoy this little bit of freedom."

"You won't even know they're there like it was years ago," he replied.

"That was different then, but now that I know about them, I feel like someone is always watching over me, and I want to feel normal like I used to. Please . . ."

"Okay, but don't make me regret this," he said reluctantly.

Then we said goodbye one more time and ended our call.

So Emilia was right. She was pregnant with their second child. Could Richard have had something to do with her miscarriage? Was that the reason he had been going through so many therapies? Guilt? My heart couldn't process these revelations. I silently wept. Finding out Richard's secrets was like a gut punch to me. It felt like someone had reached into my chest and ripped away a part of my heart. I couldn't believe what I discovered. I was full of conflicting emotions: sadness, anger, betrayal, and confusion. The more I uncovered, the deeper the wounds feel.

The sad truth was no matter what Richard had done in his past, I couldn't make myself hate him. His actions may have been wrong, but my heart was still full of love for him. Nothing could change that. All that mattered was our bond and the moments we had shared. I know that in the end, that's what will stay with me forever.

I felt an emptiness as I looked out the window. The sun was setting, and soon Richard will be home. What will I do? Should I confront him? Suddenly, my phone chimed with a notification from Richard. A wave of emotions ran through me as I opened the message. His message felt distant and impersonal, and I knew he was still struggling. He doesn't want me to wait for him tonight and will be home late. Just like that, no "I love you."

———

I woke up to the sound of the bedroom door creaking open. I glanced at the bedside clock. It was two o'clock in the morning.

Richard walked over to my side of the bed and kissed me on the forehead. "Go back to sleep," he whispered. Despite his words, his scent still lingered with alcohol — a sign that he had been drowning his sorrows in heavy drink. I urged myself to sit up. As Richard moved away from me, I grabbed his hand tightly, refusing to let him go. I want my Richard back, so I have to do what I know the best I can do. I put my mouth on his, desperate for a kiss. Richard responded coldly and tried to unwind my arms around his neck. I was close to tears.

I breathed deeply and asked him desperately, "You won't touch me again?" His fingers nervously ran through his hair as he tried to put into words what he felt inside. Our eyes locked for a moment before he pulled away from me. That was the last straw of my patience. I stood up from the bed and cried out, "Why are you shutting me out, Richard?"

He pleaded with me to go back to sleep, but I could no longer let this go on. I shouted, "I don't care what happened to you or your other child with Emilia!"

"But I do, Hope! I do!" He shouted back.

This was the first time Richard and I had ever raised our voices at each other. He slowly looked away, his sadness visible as he silently struggled with his emotions. He started to reach for me but changed his mind and left the room swiftly without looking back.

The pain of watching Richard walk out of the room was unbearable. His coldness felt like a punch to my heart, and I could feel the tears stinging my eyes as he stepped away from me. My desperate attempts at reaching out to him were all in vain. I felt helpless, alone, and utterly broken inside. I wanted nothing more than for us both to find our way back to each other and have things go back to how they used to be, but it seemed like an impossible feat at that moment.

Waking up the next day without him was more painful than anticipated. There were no messages or even a trace of his presence on our bed — it felt like a I had just woken up from a nightmare. Even his grey jacket, neatly folded on the couch in his study, was a reminder of how he had left me without a word. My heart ached as I gathered the coat in my arms and breathed in his scent, tears streaming down my face as reality sunk in.

The tears and the pain came flooding back as I dialed Henry's number. I knew it was selfish of me to call him after witnessing his parents' outburst during the dinner with his grandparents, but I was in a foreign land and had no one else to talk to. Things would have been easier if this had happened in New York, but London was too far away from home.

Henry picked up on the third ring, "Hey, everything all right?" I couldn't speak at first, just crying into the phone as he listened. "Do you want me to come over? I just have one more class to finish," he offered gently.

"No, Henry," I managed through my sobs, "I just need to let this out. I'm okay."

"Are you sure?" There was concern in his voice. Despite my insistence that I was okay, Henry continued to ask if I needed anything. I could hear the worry in his voice. "Granny and my mother wouldn't come near you or the house," he explained to me. "Dad got a restraining order from the court. Even Grandpa can't call you. He was furious. I've never seen my father so angry in years."

I felt a wave of guilt wash over me as he spoke. "I'm so sorry, Henry. I shouldn't have come here," I said, wiping away some of my tears.

"Granny shouldn't have invited my mother," he said sadly. I hated all of them for putting Henry in the middle of this ugly war between his parents, and it was clear that it had taken its toll on him.

Someone called out to Henry in the background, and I quickly told him that I was okay and that we would talk soon. He promised he's going to call me after his class. We got off the phone, and even though our conversation had done little to improve the situation, I felt comforted.

Hugging Richard's coat closer to me, his presence still lingered in my thoughts as I curled onto the floor, finally allowing my tears to overwhelm me. The events from the past days washed over me like a wave. Tears streamed down my face, and I couldn't stop them if I tried. It was like a dam had burst, and all the emotions I had held back for so long came out in a flood.

The pain of the situation was almost too much to bear. With each passing second, it felt like the weight on my chest grew heavier, constricting my breath and making it impossible to stifle the sobs that wracked my body. I cried out Richard's name in anguish, the sound painfully raw and unfiltered.

It was like every tiny shard of hope I had clung to had shattered into a million pieces, leaving me feeling lost and alone. As the tears continued to flow, I only wanted Richard to hold me, to tell me that everything would be okay. But even as I called out his name, I knew he was slowly fading away from me.

That's how Richard found me when he entered the room. He ran towards me and gathered me into his strong arms. "I'm sorry, darling," he said as he held me tightly, not wanting to let me go.

"Richard, I can't! I can't bear it. It hurts so much," I cried in anguish. I clung to him tightly, not wanting to let him go. We were on the floor with my arms wound around his neck, my face buried in his chest as my tears soaked his shirt. I felt my heart tear in two as he held me. It was like a physical pain that ripped through me, and I couldn't control the sobs wracking my body. If only I could turn back time to before this awful mess had started. But it was too late now, and all that remained was Richard's arms around me, providing me with some small measure of comfort.

Amid my pain, having him by my side made it all a little bit easier. For a few moments, it felt as if I didn't have to bear the burden alone. As my tears poured uncontrollably down my face, he silently sat with me, a companion whose presence alone gave me strength when mine had run out. He stayed by my side until I had shed every last tear.

Richard broke our silence, his voice gentle and full of compassion. "My darling, I'm going to put you on the couch. The floor is too cold," he said. I tightened my hold around him, not wanting to let go.

"Don't leave me," I begged with my eyes. He smiled reassuringly at me before picking me up and carrying me to the couch. Sitting down facing me, he lightly traced his fingers over my face, wiping away tears before kissing my mouth passionately. Richard's kiss was electric, sending a shock wave throughout my body. His lips were gentle yet firm as they moved against mine, conveying a quiet yet powerful sentiment of love and compassion. Our tongues intertwined in an intimate dance as I felt his hands pressing me closer to him.

The kiss felt like it would never end, each passing moment filled with an outpouring of emotions and meaning that could never have been expressed through mere words alone. When we finally parted our lips, I remained awash with an undeniable warmth radiating from the exact spot we locked lips.

Richard looked into my eyes, and his voice filled with sadness as he began his tale.

"I owe you this. As much as I buried them where I can no longer unearth them, you should hear it from me."

He paused for a moment to take a deep breath before beginning. Slowly and carefully, he revealed the story of his struggles and pain, the fears and doubts that had been hidden away for so long — all the courageous acts he had taken to try and overcome them.

"I met Emilia when I started my modeling career," he said. "She was beautiful and fun, and we got along fine. She's older than me and more experienced. Being young, everything was new territory: drugs, sex, and being constantly drunk. I did love her, I think," then he looked at me, "but not the kind of love I have for you."

He told me about Emilia getting pregnant and their sudden marriage, "I wanted my child to have a name and a decent home. Emilia hated the changes in her body. Her modeling job was put on hold, and it was all that mattered to her. I thought having me and Henry would change her priorities, but I was wrong. The more her pregnancy became visible, the more she partied and drank. I couldn't restrain her. When Henry was born, she refused to breastfeed him. She insisted that it would ruin her body. I arranged a full-time nanny for Henry because Emilia returned to work as soon as her body recovered from giving birth. She starved herself nearly to death just to comply with weight requirements. She accepted shows in Milan and other countries. She traveled the whole time and missed Henry's milestones." Richard paused, stood up, poured himself a drink, and sat again beside me.

"When Henry was three years old," he continued, "Emilia started doing drugs regularly, and often she was stoned. So I moved Henry to my parents' house because I didn't want him to see his mother like that. Then I started working in TV and movies. Emilia hated me even more. She started sleeping with other models, men, and even women."

Richard paused, then he continued again. "One day, as she was visiting Henry with my parents, she announced she was pregnant. I wasn't surprised, but claiming it as mine was something I couldn't stand, especially when my parents were thrilled with the news. I never corrected that misconception and lies. I don't want to ruin Henry's relationship with his mother." I held Richard's hands and touched his face. I wanted to comfort him from that nightmare.

I could feel my heart breaking for him as he spoke, but I knew he needed to open up and heal. I remained silent, listening until he had finished telling his story. When he fell silent again, I held him close in a comforting embrace and understood why he had never wanted to share this with anyone. Richard tucked the hair that fell on my cheeks behind my ears. Then he closed his eyes to continue. I knew the next would have been more difficult for him, so I held his hands and never let them go.

"I was filming *Echoed* at that time. The tabloid was running stories about Hilary Prost, who played my love interest in the film, and me. One night when I came home, Emilia was furious. She threatened to get rid of her pregnancy, and I said I didn't care. We fought a very ugly one. She was hitting me physically, whatever she could hold on to at that time. I ran to the stairs, wanting so much to get out of the house, but she followed me, grabbed my arms, and I pushed her back, not realizing we were on the stairs, and she slipped." Tears fell down Richard's face.

As I wrapped my arms tightly around him, I knew his nightmare was like a demon never leaving his side. I felt him squeeze me back, his grip tightening around me. I could feel the pain he carried, the nightmares that haunted him and never let him be.

"I killed her baby, Hope." His voice was painful, and as he finished speaking, I held him close in a comforting embrace, understanding why he had kept hidden such painful memories for so long.

"No, my love. That was an accident." I was angry at Emilia for putting Richard and Henry through so much pain. Her life was miserable, full of hate, and she wanted Richard to go down with her. "I hate her, Richard, for doing this to you and Henry."

I held him closer, feeling his pain and wanting desperately to take it away. I looked into his eyes, wanting him to know he wasn't alone in this moment. I kissed him deeply, passionately conveying all my love and support for him.

I knew I couldn't erase his nightmare completely, but for just this moment, I can take his pain away. I gently ran my hands over Richard's body, tracing the curves of his muscles, exploring and caressing him tenderly. I made love to him slowly and passionately, wanting him to feel that even in this moment he was safe, desired, and fully loved. The sensual pleasure filled our souls with joy and comforted us both in the knowledge that our love could overcome anything we faced. All of his pain melted away until it was just us two who existed in the world.

25

It was the last day of Richard's filming, and tomorrow we'll fly back to New York. So I took the time to explore the city. London's bookstores were a delight to explore. From the cozy, family-run stores tucked away in back alleys to the vast, bustling chain stores that dominated the high street, each had its unique atmosphere and selection of books.

As I strolled down the street, I stopped at a particular bookstore nestled among the other shops and restaurants. The store windows displayed colorful arrays of books that promised a fascinating selection within. My heart skipped as I stepped inside and explored the shelves filled with everything from beloved classics to hot new releases. The rows of carefully chosen titles sang out to me, beckoning me closer and inviting me into their pages. There was something special about this place, and I felt my excitement growing as I browsed its collection.

After browsing for hours, I finally bought several books I will bring home with me. As I stepped out of the store, suddenly, a car pulled up nearby. Before I knew it, two masked men leaped out of the vehicle and dragged me into the backseat. I fought as hard as possible, but it was useless — they were far too strong.

My heart was pounding in fear as the car flew through the streets. Then, just as suddenly as it began, all went quiet. The men had knocked me unconscious with a swift punch to the face and an injection to the neck.

When I awoke, things looked even worse than before. I was bound up tightly, and an old barn's musty, decaying walls surrounded me. Three men from Eastern Europe stood around me, each with a menacing grin spread across his face. Their satisfaction at my regaining consciousness was palpable.

"What do you want from me?" I asked weakly, my voice trembling with fear.

"Ah," one of them said mockingly. "The princess has finally found her tongue." He paused for a moment before continuing. "You have something that our boss wants — if you don't give it to us soon, things won't end well for you."

I tried to take in my surroundings, but it was difficult with my wrists and ankles bound so tightly. I swallowed hard. My heart raced as my mind filled with fear — the kind that leaves you unable to think straight. I knew I was trapped and had no way out of this situation. All I could do was sit there, bound and helpless.

The three men watched me expectantly, and my fear grew stronger as I saw the malicious intent in their eyes. Every sound seemed amplified around me, each little noise confirming they were out to get me. The only thing keeping me together was my determination not to let them take what they wanted, whatever it was.

I saw the door slowly creaking open out of the corner of my eye. I whipped around to find a tall, slender blond woman entering the room. It was Emilia!

She looked around the dingy barn contemptuously before fixing her gaze on me. Her eyes were hard, and I held her gaze determinedly despite being unable to move my arms or legs.

Without warning, she strode over to the three Eastern European men and started shouting in a foreign language. She seemed to have authority over them as they all cowered beneath her presence. After a few moments of heated debate, she turned towards me, fury still burning in her eyes.

Her lips twisted into a bitter smile. "Don't worry. Everything will be alright," she said. "Richard will never know my part in this, and it's all that matters. Tomorrow, you'll be on your way to a brothel in some third-world country where Richard can't find you. I'm not selling you to the highest bidder — just the lowest one. You will be nothing but just a piece of stale meat."

I clenched my fists as rage welled up inside me. "Richard will never forgive you!" I shouted.

"He won't have to," Emilia replied confidently. "I'll be there to console him when he's nursing his wounds, and before long, he'll forget that you ever existed. That's how I get my family back."

My anger faded as I realized what she was saying — she had no intention of stealing her family back, no matter what I may or may not have done; she wanted them back without breaking any laws — something that only time could bring her.

"I didn't steal your family, Emilia," I said quietly. "You left them."

Suddenly, Emilia's gaze dropped to my hand, and she spotted the engagement ring on my finger. Instantly, her expression changed — her eyes widened with rage, and her lips twisted into a snarl. Before I knew it, she was trying to pull the ring off my finger. I fought back with all my strength, clinging to the symbol that connected me to Richard. But Emilia was far too strong for me — with one quick movement, she broke my finger and yanked the ring from me, causing me to scream in pain.

One of the men said something to Emilia, and she nodded, taking a syringe full of drugs from him. Then she turned to me and looked me straight in the eyes with an evil glint. "No," she said. "Not yet. I want her to feel the real pain."

I could barely find my voice, but I managed to whisper, "My baby. Please, Emilia, I'm begging you — spare my baby."

Emilia's expression immediately changed, and she coldly replied, "Oh no, my dear! That one has to go. It's not good for your next job." She eyed the syringe on top of the table near her. "That will help you induce that pregnancy instantly. Just how I lost my pregnancy."

Panic and fear washed over me on her plan to hurt my baby. "Emilia, I am begging you, don't hurt my baby. I will do anything!" I cried desperately.

"There's nothing I want you to do. I just need you gone!" At her words, a wave of despair and hopelessness washed over me. No one had told me about this kind of pain — not my mom or Richard. Tears streamed down my face as I tried to pull myself together in an attempt to keep from crumbling apart.

The men around me watched in silence, their faces devoid of compassion. None of them had any intention of helping me. I pleaded with them, too, but they just stood there like statues, ignoring my cries and pleas.

Emilia remained expressionless, her stare fixed on me as I begged for mercy. That's when I realized that she wouldn't change her mind. And with that understanding came a deep sorrow that sank into my bones, bringing tears to my eyes again.

Two men held me steady as I fought back, then I felt the needle injected into my upper arm. Then I was so caught up in pleading with Emilia that it took me a few seconds to realize someone had struck me across the face. My left eye shot with pain and another blow followed, and suddenly my nose broke. Some stripped me of my clothes, leaving me with just my underwear. All around me, the men watched as if this was nothing more than a show, their faces still lacking any ounce of compassion.

My body went numb from the shock and horror of what was happening. Blood started flowing down my face, and I realized that I had lost hope — there was no way to save me and my baby now. Tears rolled down my cheeks as I sat there, bound and helpless. All hope was fading fast, and I was only too aware of the precious life Richard and I had created that may be lost forever.

My thoughts drifted to my mom and how worried she must be. Surely, she knew something was wrong by now. Richard, too — he must be going crazy searching for me. My life was just one fleeting moment, and I was happy with the last few months, the best I have had. Now, I may not be able to see the light of day. I may never get to see his smile, smell his scent, or hear his voice as he whispers how much he loves me and our unborn baby. My baby! I could feel its presence inside me, yet helpless to protect him from the darkness surrounding me. How could I have been so stupid to put myself in this situation?

A life filled with moments of pure bliss and happiness flashed before my eyes. So many beautiful memories that we had shared, lying in each other's arms, talking until the dawn of a new day. Richard's laugh echoed in my ears like a distant memory as I remembered how he had looked at me with love in his eyes — would I ever get to see his beautiful face again? It was a painful thought, and I sobbed, knowing the future held uncertainty. It all felt so real, yet here I was, caught up in a nightmare I may never wake from. I closed my eyes tightly and tried not to think of what might come next.

I was suddenly jolted back to reality by a cold splash of water hitting my face. It stung fiercely, especially against the open wounds that had already formed. My eyes snapped open, and dread filled my body at the thought of what fate awaited me. There was no escape, only despair, and uncertainty loomed in the air like a thick fog. As quickly as it had come, the euphoria of my daydreaming was gone, replaced with a chilling fear that seemed to consume me from within. I closed my eyes again, hoping against all hope that somehow I could make it out alive with my baby safe inside me.

A sharp pain erupted in my arm, and I scrambled to keep my balance - almost losing consciousness again. The person who had broken my arm stood there, their face twisted with rage.

I wanted to scream at them, tell them they had no right to do this to me and that I would never forget this moment, but all I could do was stare in shock at the cruel injustice of it all. My arm throbbed painfully, and I found myself wishing for a miracle – something that could bring justice against this person's actions so that no other innocent life ever has to face such cruelty again.

A sudden kick to the stomach sent me falling to the ground in agony.

The searing pain was unbearable, and I could feel the warm blood flow pouring from my legs as consciousness began to slip away. Death seemed like a welcome relief compared to the torture they put me through, and I found myself praying that everything would go away. All I wanted was peace — an end to this nightmare that had become my life. I cried in agony. The pain was so unbearable.

I lost track of time. My entire body throbbed with searing pain as I felt my consciousness slipping away. The last thing I could make out was a dream of Richard's voice calling out to me, begging me to stay with him. Tears streamed down my face as I realized this might be the end for me. But even in the depths of despair and agony, a spark of hope still shone within — that somehow, some way, I would be able to protect my baby from all the darkness in this world.

Then everything went black, and a deep sleep engulfed me like a comforting blanket.

26

As I slowly regained consciousness, I felt disoriented and couldn't recognize my surroundings. My eyes slowly opened, attempting to adjust to the bright fluorescent lights above. I realized I was lying in a sterile hospital bed, the sharp smell of antiseptic filling my nostrils. Gradually, the fog began to clear, and I recognized the face of the person hovering above me — Henry. His expression was a mix of relief and worry, but his tender touch as he stroked my hair provided comfort.

He immediately called out to his father, exclaiming with relief, "Dad, she's awake!"

Richard stood over me in an instant. His face beamed with a mixture of joy and relief and deep exhaustion. It looked like he hasn't slept in days, with stress visibly written on his face.

Then it all came back to me. He had found me! I was not dreaming, and it was his voice! He softly touched my face, afraid that even those soft touches would hurt me.

"Hello, beautiful," he smiled, attempting to soothe me. He took my right hand in his, giving it a gentle squeeze. My left hand was in a splint. "I was terrified that I might lose you."

My body felt heavy and unresponsive as if I were trapped in some sort of nightmare. I tried to sit up, but an excruciating pain surged through my chest and legs, causing me to gasp and fall back onto the bed. The sudden movement made me aware of the bandages wrapped around my ribcage and the cast encasing my right leg. "Darling, it's alright," Richard whispered softly. "You need to rest, and we'll take care of everything else."

Fragments of memories began to resurface — dark, terrifying images of being kidnapped and brutally beaten. Panic surged through me, and I instinctively reached for him. My heart raced as I waited, fearing that my captors might still be lurking nearby. "You're safe now," Richard reassured me.

Suddenly, a doctor and a nurse clad in scrubs entered the room. The doctor, donning navy blue scrubs, flashed me a warm smile and inquired, "How are you feeling?" Without waiting for a response, he proceeded to examine my pulse and peered into my eyes with an intense flashlight, momentarily blinding me. Meanwhile, the attentive nurse adjusted the various monitors surrounding me.

As I clutched Richard's hand, my eyes implored him not to abandon me. Sensing my unease, he smiled reassuringly and whispered softly, "I'm right here, darling."

Summoning my strength, I managed to utter, "Hurt, all over."

"You've been asleep for nearly two days," the doctor informed me, concern lacing his voice. Turning to Richard, he added, "Her vitals are stable and looking good."

Looking at Richard, I gripped his hand tightly, my eyes welling up with tears. "What about our baby?" I asked, my voice barely above a whisper.

Richard kissed my hand gently and tenderly, his eyes filled with sorrow and love. His touch upon my lips was soft, understanding, and filled with the depth of his own grief. At that moment, I knew we had lost our precious little one, and I could feel the tears streaming down my face. The doctor and the nurse left us alone to give us space and privacy as we confronted this most difficult moment.

As I looked deeply into Richard's eyes, I knew he was also grieving the loss of our baby. Despite his pain and anguish, he was there for me, offering comfort in every possible way. He whispered tenderly, "I'm so sorry I wasn't there for you sooner." He spoke words of love and care, his voice hushed and full of emotion, as tears swelled in his eyes.

In that moment of unspeakable grief, silence enveloped us. Time stood still. The outside world faded away — as if it no longer existed. We held each other close, cherishing our little time together with our unborn child. Richard's comforting touch and loving words were a source of solace, a ray of light in the darkness surrounding us. But I also knew that this tragedy had forever broken a part of me, a part that could never be fully repaired.

Then Richard broke the silence in the room. "When you get better, I will take you back to Paris — our happy place. I will buy us a house and build you a writing salon. Oh, we can even set up your own publishing house," he said, his voice filled with hope. I almost laughed, aware that he was attempting to lift my spirits and maintained a strong facade for my sake. However, I knew his heart must have been aching from the moment he entered the room. The sight of me lying here, frail and hooked up to countless machines and monitors, must have been devastating for him. The once vibrant and lively person he had fallen in love with seemed to have disappeared, replaced by this vulnerable version of myself.

Henry entered the room, reminding his father of my need to rest and that the doctors would return soon. "I'm sorry, Hope," Henry said.

I knew he felt guilt for what his mother had done to me, so I took Henry's hand in mine and gently squeezed it as if to say, "It isn't your fault." He looked at me, grateful yet saddened by the situation we were both in.

Before long, the familiar doctor and nurse reappeared in the room. They diligently checked my vitals once more, adjusted the IV drip, and administered a new medication to aid in my recovery. As the sedative effect of the drugs began to take hold, I felt the comforting presence of Richard by my side.

Sensing that I was drifting off again, Richard leaned in and gently pressed his lips to my forehead, leaving a tender kiss that enveloped me in warmth and love.

"Rest now, darling," he whispered softly, his voice filled with love and concern.

Through my tears, I pleaded, "Don't leave me," filled with fear and loneliness. Richard reassured me with a promise of never leaving my side. "There's someone who would like to see you when you wake up, and your mother will be here in the morning," he said softly. "She booked the earliest flight she could find."

With his reassuring words, I allowed myself to surrender to the soothing embrace of sleep.

———

I woke up with a start, my scream echoing through the room. It was still dark outside — I had no idea what time it was or how long I'd been asleep. Richard hurried to my side, grasped my right hand, and gently kissed my forehead, reassuring me of his presence. Despite being in my hospital gown with tubes extending from my arms, I felt scared and terrified at that moment.

He knew why I had screamed. The nightmare had brought back memories of what happened to me in the barn house. Though he could not take away the pain from that night, Richard's presence was enough to keep any future danger at bay. Whispering softly into my ear, he reassured me, "You're here. You're safe." "

My heart sank as I remembered the events of that night. My tears blended with my anguish, and I screamed, "My baby, Richard! They killed my baby!"

I could feel Richard's anger and frustration coursing through his veins, yet he remained composed. He wanted to protect me, not add to my anguish by allowing his rage to manifest. "Let me deal with her, with them. But my job right now is to see that you recover completely. I will deal with all of these later. I added security outside and in the corridor. No one ever comes near you again." I felt secure and protected once again in his arms.

The doctors entered the room, ready to administer medicines to calm me down so I could pass into slumber again.

"Please don't let them make me sleep again," I pleaded with Richard through my tears. He cautiously held my right hand, the only part of my battered body he could touch. His gaze locked intently on the doctors, silently pleading with them to help alleviate my distress.

"If we don't put you to sleep, the pain will continue to worsen," one of the doctors explained gently. On morphine already, I felt like I was barely surviving — and that was with the drug in my system to help suppress my pain. Despite my fear of closing my eyes and succumbing to the nightmarish dreams that awaited me, I knew it was necessary if I wanted any chance of recovery.

But the fear of returning to my nightmares was too much to bear, and I choked out my plea to Richard, "I'm so scared to close my eyes!"

Richard spoke to the doctors in a firm and direct tone, "Can we do without it? Give her some time to recover from her nightmare. I will call you the moment she feels any discomfort." The doctors agreed, understanding that I needed time to heal from the traumatic experience.

Once they left, Richard moved to sit by my bedside, carefully cradling my head with a tenderness that conveyed his unspeakable love. His voice was filled with emotion as he whispered, "You scared the hell out of me, my darling."

"How did you find me?" I asked anxiously.

He recounted his frantic search for me when I hadn't returned home. "At first, I thought you'd simply lost track of time at a museum or library, and when your phone became unreachable, I began to worry. Then the police arrived at our doorstep, inquiring about you. Someone from the bookstore you visited reported a potential abduction. One of the book vendors recognized you and claimed they saw you being forcibly pushed into an unmarked van."

Richard went on, "The police emphasized the importance of finding you within 24 hours, but they couldn't find any leads. I was advised to contact the U.S. Embassy, as you are an American citizen."

"The police said they weren't optimistic about finding you within 24 hours. The CCTVs couldn't capture the van's whereabouts," Richard explained. "I realized then that we might not find you in time. So, I called Oliver, hoping his connections could help me locate you quickly. Without hesitation, he personally contacted the U.S. Ambassador to the UK. He reached out to his old colleagues, connected with underground contacts, and sought assistance from people across the city," Richard shared with me. "Those who owed him favors pitched in as well, working tirelessly to find you before it was too late. He even utilized resources that were previously unknown to me, exhausting every possible avenue to ensure your safe return."

"Where is he?" I asked, my voice shaking.

"He's camping outside your room," Richard replied. "I asked him to come back when you recover, but he insisted on waiting for you."

My eyes pleaded with Richard. "I want to see him," I whispered.

Richard sighed before replying, "On one condition — I don't want to leave your side. And promise me you'll take it easy and tell me if you start feeling pain again." Relief flooded my body as I nodded, eager to see my dad.

Richard never left my side. Instead, he pulled out his phone and called my dad. "Oliver," he said into the receiver. "She wants to see you."

My father walked into the room. His shoulders slumped with exhaustion. However, his face was filled with relief at the sight of me. His walking was slow and deliberate, as though he wanted to savor every moment of this reunion. He stopped a few feet from me and examined my features with something like reverence.

I saw a mixture of emotions flicking across his face as I looked into his eyes. His wide eyes revealed a deep-seated relief, while a slight smile tugged at the corners of his mouth, hinting at a long-lost joy. But there was also a deep sadness, a pain stemming from seeing his daughter overwhelmed with grief and loss. His eyes seemed to long for something that could never be regained, and his lip quivered slightly as he struggled to hold back his emotions. At that moment, he appeared defeated, yet an unmistakable strength emanated from him, a proof to everything he had endured and overcome.

"How are you feeling, Hope?" His fists clenched tightly as he spoke, radiating a fierce resolve you could feel from across the room.

"Scared and hurt," I replied, tears streaming down my face. Richard held me even closer, cautious not to touch my bruised body, while my dad approached and tenderly took hold of my hand.

His eyes burned with an intensity that was both intimidating and reassuring. He seemed to radiate a power that belied his age — a reminder of years spent as a protector, determined to look after those he cared about no matter the cost. Every inch of him expressed his commitment to safeguarding me, even if it meant going against the most daunting odds. There was something unshakeable in the way he held himself, standing steadfast in the face of danger and turmoil.

Looking at me with unwavering determination, he said, "They won't get away with this. I promise you that. Emilia will spend the rest of her life in prison, and those men will never see the light of day after the trial." He fixed his gaze on me, and with an unwavering voice, he made it clear that he would never back down when it came to protecting me and ensuring justice was served. His words were a comfort and a source of strength, assuring me he would be there for me no matter what it took.

My father looked at Richard and said, "I added private security." His gaze returned to me, giving me a kind yet firm look. "Just go back to sleep, I will return tomorrow at noon, and your mother will be here in the morning."

Richard nodded. "I will arrange for airport pick up, Oliver," he said.

My dad shook his head and met my eyes again. Something was reassuring in his expression; I knew he wasn't going anywhere until he felt sure of my safety. "Let me take care of that," he said firmly, looking back at Richard. "Your job is to stay by her side."

He softly touched my face and kissed the top of my head before stepping away. "Dad, thank you for helping Richard find me," I said through tears that refused to stop falling down my cheeks. He just smiled back at me with an assurance that could only come from a loving father, then stepped out into the hallway and shut the door behind him.

The pain reliever was slowly wearing off, and the unbearable pain of the night's events began digging its claws back into me. Richard saw my discomfort and stepped in before I could try and put up a brave face.

"This is enough for tonight," He said softly. "Let's have the doctor administer your pain reliever."

I looked at him with worry in my eyes. "What if the nightmare comes back?"

He gave me a reassuring look, his voice firm yet gentle as he spoke. "I'm just right here. I will never leave your side." Before I could respond, he had already pressed the button beside my bed to call for help.

The doctor arrived shortly with a kind smile as she approached me. She moved around the bed and started to prepare my medication, explaining what each step was for as she went along. After a few minutes, she helped me take the medicine and reassured me that it would help me fall asleep faster. I nodded gratefully in response and watched her leave.

Almost immediately, I felt the effects of the pain reliever and could feel my body start to relax. With Richard sitting beside me in silence, I drifted into a restful sleep until morning.

———

My eyes scanned the room, looking for Richard — but instead, the face I saw belonged to Henry. He had tied his blond hair into a neat ponytail, and his boyish face looked tired. "He went to the hotel to change," he said with gentle concern in his voice, "he didn't want to leave your side, but I convinced him to freshen up because you would never let him go when you woke up." His care touched me deeply, reminding me I was not alone.

"Henry, thank you for being here," I said, grateful for his presence.

"Of course, you're family, Hope." I raised my arms, difficult to do as they were encased in a cast, urging him to come closer so I could hold him. He softly cradled my head in his arms, kissing my forehead.

"I'm glad you're safe," he whispered. "Dad will never forgive himself if something happened to you — I've never seen him so angry. When he saw you lifeless in a pool of blood, he almost lost it," Henry said sadly. "Your immediate condition is the only reason he didn't kill my mother on the spot. I know he will never forgive her, and neither will my grandmother."

"I'm sorry, Henry," I said softly.

"He said these wounds will heal, but he's worried that those people — including my mother — will break your spirit. He said you wouldn't be the same Hope we used to know." His voice was heavy with sorrow, and his hold tightened around me as if trying to protect me from further pain.

I wanted to put on a brave face for his sake, but the sorrow in my heart was too strong — tears overflowed as I spoke. "I tried so hard to protect little bean, Henry," I sobbed. "I don't know how to process this grief. It's like a part of me was taken out and replaced by a big black hole."

The pain was overwhelming, and no matter how hard I tried, the emptiness kept growing until it almost swallowed me whole. Henry held me close and stroked my hair silently, giving me all his strength. His presence was like a lighthouse in the darkness of my grief, guiding me back to shore. But still, no matter how much he comforted me, it didn't fill the void that the loss of my child had created.

Suddenly, the door opened, and my mother stepped inside. Henry moved away to give her space. I wasn't prepared for her reaction when she saw me like this. "Oh, sweetheart!" she cried as tears filled her eyes. "I will kill those people who did this to you," then she locked eyes with Henry. "I'm going to start with your mother!"

Henry shook his head and put a hand on her shoulder. "Debbie," he said firmly, "you need to fall in line. Plenty of others are ahead of you in this, including my father, who already has a headstart by ensuring my mom was locked in jail." He tried his best to soothe my mother's anger and fear.

I could see my mother's gentle expression as she began speaking. "Your father briefed me on the way here from the airport," she said. My heart warmed to hear her say that she had forgiven him for all his mistakes, considering how he and Richard left no stone unturned just to find and save me. Henry slowly exited my room, and I gave him a reassuring smile — one that was meant to express both my gratitude and sorrow.

My mother's phone started ringing, and she answered it. "Hello, Richard," she said. "Yes, she's awake. She's fine." I could hear the anger in her voice as she listened to whatever he was saying on the other end of the line. "Just make sure that bitch rots in hell!"

"Mom, let me talk to Richard, please," I asked her. She hesitated for a moment before handing me the phone.

"I'm sorry, darling, I have to take a quick detour and talk to my barristers," Richard said on the other end of the line. "This will give you some private time with your mother. I'll be back as soon as I can."

"Barristers? What does that mean?" I asked.

"They're lawyers, but here in the UK, we refer to them as barristers," he explained.

"Okay," was all I could say in response.

"I love you," he said softly. Those words meant so much to me, but this pain kept me from expressing my feelings to him. He must have sensed my hesitation and ignored it as best he could — just like always. "Just rest, darling," was his final message before disconnecting the call.

Mom never brought up the topic of the baby. I could only assume that my father and Richard had likely already told her, as she seemed to know all the details.

We talked about her new life in California with Steve's new firm, and she seemed surprised at how well-off my father was. "I know he's rich," she said, "but not that rich!" She laughed, and I couldn't help but smile back. With Mom around, it was easy to forget my loss and just focus on the moment. She always knew the perfect thing to say in any situation. Today, she had made it clear that she was here for me.

The doctors and nurses returned for their daily rounds shortly after. "Hi, Hope. How are you feeling? I'm Dr. Ann Gibson, one of your primary physicians." She glanced at my medical chart and smiled reassuringly. "Your recovery progress is going well. Due to the severe injuries and loss of your pregnancy, we'll need to perform a D&C as soon as you're strong enough. This procedure will remove any remaining tissue from your uterus."

I nodded, managing a weak "Okay." My mom held my hand tightly, understanding that I was once again confronted with the most heartbreaking aspect of my ordeal. The medical staff checked my cast, examined my IVs, and adjusted something on the monitor beside my bed before leaving us alone again.

Not long afterward, Richard returned. Mom made up an excuse to return to the hotel near the hospital to freshen up and rest a bit — she was giving us some privacy. "I'll be right back," she said before kissing my cheeks and touching Richard's arms. Then she left the two of us alone.

Richard's lips met mine in a tender kiss, the first since my kidnapping. He held me with the gentle but unwavering grasp of someone who never wanted to let go. We remained like that, wrapped in each other's embrace, for what felt like an eternity. Eventually, Richard cut through the silence softly, asking me how I was doing. Despite the unshakeable pain and exhaustion, I reassured him I was holding up okay. His expression was genuine concern, mirroring the sadness and worry that filled my heart.

He began to update me about the lawyers' plans and how we would proceed with the case against Emilia and her goons. "But we'll talk more about the plans when you're better," he said reassuringly.

He then asked if I wanted him to read some of my books to me. I smiled in appreciation, knowing that this was his way of trying to distract me from the pain while keeping my spirits up. We spent some time reading. He read, I listened, and sometimes laughed over some jokes. Although I wasn't faring well physically, I felt a sense of solace knowing that Richard was there with me during this difficult period.

———

On my fifth day at the hospital, I awoke to loud voices arguing in the room. My parents were debating with Richard about my legal case against Emilia.

"Debbie, I trust our legal system just as much as you do in America. Emilia will be facing trial soon. The police have found compelling evidence linking her to the crime," Richard argued firmly.

"Richard, forgive me if I am not confident. That bitch used to be your wife and is still the mother of your son. I can't help but think that your team is open to an out-of-court settlement," Mom countered skeptically.

"Deb, I won't allow that!" my dad interjected angrily.

"Jesus, Debbie! How can you entertain that thought when you know how much I love your daughter?" Richard exclaimed passionately, his voice laced with concern and fury.

"Mom, Richard," my voice was almost a whisper.

Instantly, Mom rushed to my side, and so did Richard. They both looked relieved to see me awake again. I looked at my mother, fondly reminiscing. "Mom, do you remember when I came home with a broken wrist because I punched someone for calling me a bastard? I think I was five years old then; we were in the playground," I laughed softly, remembering the silly incident.

"You brought me to the hospital to have my wrist fixed, and I clearly remember what you said about not using my hands and instead picking something to punch those kids with. You raised me to be independent and never back down from anyone who tried to hurt me," I added warmly.

I looked at her determinedly. "This is one of my biggest battles, Mom. I will not allow anyone, including Richard, to influence how I deal with them," I said firmly.

Mom interjected and explained, "I was suggesting to your father that we consider filing the case in America. I'm not as confident in the British court system, and you're still half-Asian. This country can be prejudiced against non-whites."

Reacting with anger, Richard lashed out, "This is absurd, Debbie! Emilia is already in custody. The police have gathered necessary evidence, and the prosecutors are preparing to file formal charges against her. My legal team is working round the clock collaborating tirelessly with the solicitors handling the case preparation!"

I then shifted my gaze to my father, standing at the foot of my bed. He remained quiet and calculated while everyone else was tense due to our heated discussion. Taking a risk, I addressed him directly by saying, "Dad?" Of all people in this room, it was unexpected that I was turning my trust to him.

My father cleared his throat before talking, "If I were to decide, they would not see a day in court." He looked at Richard sternly and said, "Can you bear to see that, Richard? Can you look into Henry's eyes after you allow someone to decide his mother's fate? He will never forgive you. He will never forgive Hope."

"That is not fair, Oliver," Richard said meekly.

Dad pointed at me and said firmly, "Look at her. Is there fairness in what happened to her? She lost her child, your child! It pains me to see her not grieving properly because you were there and being who she is and her love for you. She can't show it. She can't grieve because she doesn't want to hurt you even more."

Richard held my right hand and kissed my fingers. His face was filled with anguish and pain as he said, "My darling, tell me what you want."

I felt selfish for not seeing Richard's grief. He lost his child, too. I wanted to comfort him but couldn't because of my sorrow. Then I looked at my parents and said softly, "Can you leave us alone, please? I just want to talk to Richard first."

Richard's embrace was warm, but I felt a deep sorrow emanating from him. His chest heaved as he struggled to speak, but all he could say was, "I'm so sorry, my darling…"

His voice trailed off, and I saw tears in his eyes. I wanted to cry, too, but I knew that we both needed to stay strong for each other. So with a heavy heart, I pulled away and looked into his eyes, my brimming with sadness. "It's ok," I said softly. "We'll get through this."

I asked him to sit behind me so I could rest my head on his chest. This is how we talk and comfort each other. I leaned back into Richard's embrace, feeling the warmth and comfort of his arms around me. His heart beat steadily against my back as I relaxed, listening to his steady breaths and relishing his closeness. His lips gently brushed softly against my hair before he leaned down and tenderly kissed my mouth. His kisses lingered for a moment, each like a prayer that we would never have to be apart again.

I looked into Richard's eyes and told him how much I loved him, how important he was to me, and how my heart ached for all we had been through. He held me carefully as he kissed me again, more intensely this time, as if seeking reassurance of the depth of my love for him. Despite my broken body, I kissed him back passionately, I wanted him to know that I would always be there by his side no matter what happened.

At that moment, my heart was overflowing with emotion. Love and security battled against sadness and fear as I clung to Richard in our embrace. I felt safe and content in his arms, yet scared of losing myself and who I am. I could feel the power of our connection pushing away any doubts I had, reassuring me that we would always be together no matter what happened.

"I never fell in love until I met you. I promised myself I would never allow myself to fall for someone and end up like my mom. She dedicated her life to raising me alone," I said as Richard listened closely. "But with you, Richard, it was magic!"

All my fears and doubts about love slowly disappeared as Richard smiled against my hair. "Being with you is the happiest moment of my life. Making love with you is everything I ever dreamed of and more.

When I saw those two lines on the pregnancy test, I was overwhelmed with emotion. We were creating something beautiful, something that came from both of us." Tears welled in my eyes as I spoke, overcome with the moment's intensity. There was something special between us that could never be broken or taken away, no matter what happened.

I looked up into Richard's eyes, trying to find the words that would express how sorry I was. It felt wrong to apologize for feeling hurt and scared, but he deserved more than that. "The past few days, you had been so gentle and caring with me, taking every step carefully not to upset me further. Yet, I had forgotten about your pain in all my selfishness." I sucked in a deep breath before I continued speaking, willing myself to make the right words appear. "I'm sorry, Richard...I'm sorry for not seeing that you were hurting, too."

Richard's voice was soft as he spoke, but his words cut me deep. "I had let you down when you needed me the most, and it haunted me to know...just being with me caused you such pain." I looked into his eyes, knowing he wouldn't accept my comforting words. His voice was thick with sadness. "Everything you're feeling is because of me, and I deserve the consequences."

I tried to reach out and hold him, wanting to offer some kind of comfort. But I knew that whatever I said at this moment could only hurt him further, so instead, I looked away. The silence was heavy as I processed all of the feelings we both had. So I stayed quiet, hoping that if I gave him the right amount of space, he would understand what I was about to say and do.

I looked down at my left hand in its splint, a stark reminder of Emilia's cruelty as she viciously broke it and brutally forced the ring off my finger. Richard noticed my gaze and seemed to understand what I was thinking. He gently took my hand and said softly, "Don't worry, we'll get you another one. The insurance will replace it."

"No. Not yet," I said, looking up at Richard. He studied my face, carefully assessing what I was about to say. Before he could speak, I stopped him with a finger on his lips.

"My love," I began, my voice soft but filled with emotion. "I'm not ending things with you. I just feel like I need some time to process everything on my own and find myself again. I am so broken, and while you've helped me pick up the pieces, I don't think I can fully heal with your constant presence hovering over me." Richard's face froze, he heard the desperation in my voice.

"I want to do things like walk around or ride the subway without security or the paparazzi trailing me," I went on. "I want to be able to say something without worrying if it will end up on the front page or social media. I need to feel like my own person again, and I hope you can understand that."

Richard looked at me sadly, understanding my desperate plea. He could sense how much I needed to escape the public eye and live as I wanted without fear of scrutiny or judgment. "I know I can make these go away," he said softly. "We have more money than we'll ever spend in our lifetimes. I can always take you away from all this."

I smiled sadly at him. "No," I replied, shaking my head. "That's who you are — acting, directing, producing; it's your life just as writing is mine."

"I can't lose you, too, Hope," he pleaded, his eyes shining with emotion. "I can't. I need you more than ever."

"I know," I whispered. His words touched my heart, and I felt a warmth spreading throughout my body. "And I need you, too. But sometimes, we must take time apart to find ourselves — to gain the strength we both need."

"I'm not leaving you," I assured him, taking his hands in mine. "I just can't be held back by all of this — by the public scrutiny or expectations that come with both of our lives."

Richard nodded sadly, understanding my decision but still longing for me to stay.

"This isn't permanent. I want you to take a step back for Henry." I pleaded.

Richard shook his head. "Henry is an adult," he said firmly. "He can handle this."

I couldn't help but feel a twinge of frustration, but I pushed it aside and continued. "If we're going to be family, then I don't want him to feel abandoned because of me. That's why I need you to repair your relationship with your mother, so she'll accept me despite everything that happened."

Richard was quiet for a moment, deep in thought. Then he looked at me, "If you want space, I will give you space. I can start filming in Ireland, and I won't take you with me, but please stay until you recover fully. I will talk to Oliver to meet our lawyers so they can take over. Don't shut me out of your life completely. I still want to hear your voice," he said, squeezing my hand lightly. "And I don't want you to date anyone."

I laughed, "Of course. My heart belongs to you." I took Richard's hand and placed it on top of my belly, the place we touched when we used to talk to our little one.

Richard whispered softly, "When you're ready, we can start over and build something even stronger." I nodded quietly, my heart feeling heavy with emotion. As I looked deep into Richard's eyes, I only wanted to hold him closer and never let go.

27

The days in the hospital passed slowly, but each day brought a small sign of progress. This morning, I woke up to find that the IV tubes and catheter had been removed from my body, and for the first time since I arrived, I was feeling more and more like my old self. I was able to eat a normal breakfast. My meal of soup, cereal, and toast was simple, but it tasted better than any meal I had ever eaten before.

I received even more good news during today's doctor's visit: they will remove the cast on my arm. Although the one on my right leg remains, I knew it wouldn't be long before it, too, was gone. The wounds and bruises were starting to fade, bringing a sense of hope and healing to my body. Although the road to recovery may still be long, I was grateful for these small victories that brought me one step closer to being my old self again.

My father and I delved into the details of my legal case against Emilia, discussing the necessary preparations that needed to be made. His tone was serious, never breaking eye contact with me. "This is going to be a long battle," he said sternly. "But I assure you, she will spend the rest of her life in jail. And even if, by some miracle, she manages to get out, I will make sure she doesn't see the light of day as soon as she steps out of prison." His unwavering commitment to ensuring justice was both heartening and terrifying, a reminder of the depths of his love and protection.

I knew he wasn't making idle threats. He asked me if I wanted this to go away instantly because he could make that happen. He can ask someone to do it and make it appear as an accident or suicide out of depression. But I told him I wanted to do it legally, not just for me but for Henry. He nodded in agreement and began to outline exactly what I needed to do. As we talked through the options, both of us had a newfound sense of resolve — this was something that I had to do, something that could help bring resolution.

"It's important that you understand," my father said, his voice serious but kind. "You don't have to be at every court hearing. The lawyers will take care of it. All you need to do is make sure the facts are correct, and they'll handle the rest. But," he added, raising a finger in warning, "you must appear for your final testimony. They must hear all the details in your own words." I nodded in understanding, taking in my father's advice as if committing it to memory. I had to do this — something I had to see through — and with my father's help, I felt more confident than ever before that I would succeed.

We discussed the strategy further over lunch. Eventually, we worked out an actionable plan. My father clapped his hands with a determined smile and declared: "Let's show them what we can do!"

Upon entering my hospital room, my mother began discussing the preparations for my journey to the airport. "Your doctors mentioned that you'll be traveling with the cast on your leg, which needs to remain in place for another five weeks. They've already coordinated with your medical team at New York-Presbyterian Hospital," she clarified.

"Wait a minute! Does this mean I'll have to stay in another hospital once we arrive in New York?" I asked uneasily.

"No," my father reassured me. "Though I must admit, I'd feel more at ease if you were in a hospital. However, knowing your preferences, I don't think you'd agree to that," he said with a gentle smile.

My mother chimed in, "The care you'll receive in New York is for outpatient purposes. You'll require various therapies and regular visits to monitor your cast until you've made a full recovery."

The thought of leaving London and Richard behind was nothing short of heartbreaking. As my mind began to wander, I could no longer hear what my mother was saying; her voice faded into the distant background. How did this nightmare come to be? This city could have been my second home, and I even pictured myself with Richard and our little bean shopping at Harrods during Christmastime. But instead, this city broke me.

"You will gain invaluable experience from this," my father said, sensing the shift in my mood. "When you're fully recovered, I want you to see how our businesses operate on a global scale. Not only will you get to see the business I've built in Asia, but you can also help me establish a global office in New York. It's the perfect opportunity for you to learn more about international business and build your network."

While these prospects were something to look forward to, I wasn't quite ready for them. All I wanted was to forget this nightmare. I understood that my father was trying to open a new world for me to explore, hoping that it would help me move past the horrors of the last few weeks. "Thank you, Dad," I said softly, a faint smile appearing on my lips. "But writing is what I want to do — it's all I've ever wanted to do since I was a kid. Don't you see? I've got a break to carve my name, which could be my chance to make a name for myself in the publishing world."

My mother offered a gentle smile and nodded in agreement. "Your father is right, sweetheart. This change in environment will be beneficial for you. I understand that there's a lot to absorb at first. Still, you possess your father's unwavering determination and ambition, as well as the tireless work ethic of your grandparents," she said, her voice brimming with pride. "As the sole living heir to Ortega's legacy, it's only fitting that you eventually inherit what they've worked so diligently to build. The time has come for you to delve into this new world and begin mastering the complexities of the family business."

Dad quickly pointed out the obvious, "Exactly, Debbie. I think it would be a shame to miss out on such an amazing opportunity, Hope, especially one that can potentially bring you so much joy and fulfillment." He looked at me sincerely as if to assure me he understood. Then he turned to my mother, "Let's not rush her," my dad said. "I want her to recover fully, get back on her feet, and if it means focusing on finishing her book and publishing it, let her."

I nodded in agreement, my heart full of gratitude for my father's understanding. "Thank you," I said softly, the words carrying all the emotion in my heart.

He smiled knowingly and patted my hand. "I've been there, sweetheart," he said fondly. "I know how important it is to follow your dreams and make your path in life."

My mom nodded, took my hand, and looked at me lovingly, "How's your heart?" She was referring to Richard.

I sighed. "It still hurts," I admitted, my voice catching in my throat. My mother gave me a warm hug, and I let out a shuddering breath, grateful for her understanding.

"It will get better with time," she said softly, patting my back gently. "Focus on yourself and your work — that's all that matters now."

My heart felt heavy with the weight of my separation from Richard. I had thought we would be together forever, and now it seemed our time together was ending. Tears pricked my eyes as I remembered all the special moments we shared, all the laughter and joy that had filled our days. Even though it was difficult, I knew I had to find a way to move on and face life without him, even if just for a while.

My mother smiled comfortingly at me as she shared the good news that I would be officially discharged from the hospital tomorrow in time for our departure to New York. "Your dad and I need to arrange something with your lawyers. Will you be all right if we leave you alone tonight?" She could sense my reluctance to part with Richard despite my firm decision to give our relationship a breathing space. She seemed intent on giving me some space for us to have a private goodbye. Her thoughtfulness touched me, but a lump began to form in my throat, knowing that our time together was almost up.

I quickly checked my watch when my parents left, realizing Henry should be out of his classroom by now. My heart raced as I dialed his FaceTime and waited anxiously for him to pick up. A wave of emotion swept over me as he answered the call, and all I could do was muster a shaky "hello."

"How are you doing?" Henry asked me. "I heard from Dad that you are leaving tomorrow."

I smiled warmly at him. I replied. "Thank you so much for being here with me."

"Hey, it's the least I can do for my stepmother," he joked, eliciting a laugh from both of us.

"Don't you dare call me that!" I gently protested, feeling the warmth of our familiar banter returning to our conversation. Our friendship had been through a lot with his mother, but knowing that nothing could ever change our bond was reassuring.

"Take care of your Dad for me, okay?" I pleaded, tears welling up in my eyes.

"Of course," Henry replied softly. Even though it was hard to say goodbye temporarily, he understood why I had to do it. "I know that Dad loves you, but he also knows that this will help you get through all the bad stuff and process it better." His voice was tinged with sadness as he spoke.

"I love him," I said, almost to myself, feeling an overpowering sadness as the reality of being away from Richard settled in. My heart ached at the thought of missing out on precious moments with him, but I knew that this was something I had to do.

Henry and I talked for a while longer on lighter topics, like my plans to publish a book and my freedom to ride the subway again without worrying about paparazzi trailing behind us. We both acknowledged that this wouldn't be easy as long as his father was in the film business.

Our conversation gradually wound down, and we promised each other to keep in touch via FaceTime, and we'll feed the ducks in Central Park when he visits New York. Finally, the call ended, leaving us both feeling slightly better than when it started.

I was about to drift off to sleep when suddenly I heard a familiar voice whispering my name. I opened my eyes, and there he was, Richard, standing at the foot of my bed. He was wearing a light blue shirt neatly tucked into his tailored charcoal grey pants. I couldn't help but smile from ear to ear. He had a bouquet of white tulips in his hand that he placed gently on the bedside table before sitting beside me. It was a lovely gesture; he knew how much I'd always loved them. I pulled him towards me, wrapping my arms around his neck as I looked deeply into his blue-grey eyes. "Kiss me, Richard," I said softly, and without hesitation, he leaned in and sealed our lips together in a passionate kiss. All of the love and longing that had built up during our brief separation came out with an intensity that could only be relieved by this moment of pure bliss. His hands brushed against my face gently and lingered for what felt like an eternity before finally breaking away from each other.

"Hmmm, how could anyone refuse such an enticing invitation, particularly now that your arm is finally free from the cast?" Richard mused, his smile widening as he tenderly took my left hand and pressed gentle kisses on each of my fingers, lingering deliberately on my ring finger. With a playful glint in his eyes, he leaned in close and captured my lips in a passionate kiss. His hands roamed along the contours of my back, drawing me closer as I melted into the moment. His left hand moved on the side of my breast. His thumb made feathery brushes across my nipple, partially covered with a thin hospital gown. Everything around us seemed to disappear, and all that remained was us — lost in this moment of pure bliss as we parted and looked into each other's eyes.

"Please…" I don't even know what I was asking in my current situation. But Richard understood it very well. I could feel a wave of embarrassment wash over me. I wanted nothing more than to be in his arms and have him kiss me again, but my current physical state made that almost impossible.

He looked at me intensely and smiled, his eyes filled with understanding as he looked around the room before gently whispering to me, "Darling, you know how badly I want you…but not here." His gaze focused on my casted legs, adding, "And in your current condition, it's too tempting — but safety first." He kissed my lips again before pulling away with a mischievous grin, adding softly, "Besides, I want those legs wrapped around me." We both shared a giggle as we embraced each other.

I looked up at him. My heart filled with longing as I said softly, "I'm going to miss kissing you."

He met my gaze and replied, "Believe me, I'll miss it, too. I'll miss waking up to the scent of your hair, how you somehow manage to take up more than half of the bed, and your irresistible habit of making love at the break of dawn." Suddenly, his expression shifted as he recalled something important. Reaching into his pocket, he pulled out two gleaming keys and presented them to me. "You left these in our top drawer – you'll need them when you get home," he said, revealing the keys to our penthouse.

"I'm planning on moving back to my apartment, Richard," I informed him.

"You can't move there in your current condition. You'll need weeks before you can walk on your own again. That place is too cramped for wheelchairs, and the lift is unreliable. The penthouse, on the other hand, offers both space and accessible facilities. Plus, Leticia and Jeffrey are there to help you."

"I can't, Richard. That place just reminds me of you and us," I protested.

"I think you've forgotten that it's already yours," he gently reminded me.

"I know. But staying there won't do me any good. I'll be reminded of you every second. I can't sleep in our bed knowing your scent still lingers there."

"I understand, which is why I'm trying to persuade you to reconsider," he said with a playful grin. "I don't want you to forget about me."

"How could I ever forget you, Richard Collins!"

He chuckled and planted a tender kiss on my lips. "At least hold onto the keys."

"You know I can't!" I insisted.

But Richard fixed me with a determined stare and replied softly, "Please, keep them. If the day comes when you find yourself missing me, you can retreat to the penthouse and call me. I promise I'll board the first available flight to New York."

Tears welled up in my eyes as I asked quietly, "Will you wait for me? Until I find myself again?" He pulled me close and replied firmly, "I will — I'm not going anywhere." A wave of relief passed over me, and I buried my head in his chest, comforted by the warmth of his embrace.

"I made a quick detour to an old bookstore on my way here, and look what I found!" he exclaimed, pulling a book from the brown paper bag. It was a copy of Stephenie Meyer's *Twilight*. I laughed so hard that I momentarily forgot about my aching ribs. "Let's have some fun reading this," he chuckled.

"I was twelve years old when that movie hit the theaters. I was one of those people who eagerly waited in line just to see Robert Pattinson," I said with a proud grin.

"Really? You were a fan of Robert Pattinson?" I could tell he was teasing me. "You know, I actually auditioned for that role."

"Seriously?"

"Yes, and for Harry Potter, too. Sadly, I was seemingly the only British actor of that time who wasn't in that film. Almost everyone else was part of it," he lamented with exaggerated sadness.

"Oh, poor you," I responded dramatically.

Richard cradled my head against his chest and began reading. His voice was soothing, and he often punctuated his thoughts with a broad grin, making me chuckle. The night was usually filled with comfortable silence, interrupted only by the occasional sound of Richard turning a page or laughing at something amusing I had said.

"I don't understand why girls like you back then were so enamored with this concept of sparkling vampires. It's ridiculous...sparkling vampires? What happened to the classic vampire with fangs and blood, seducing innocent women?"

"Hmm, says the man who auditioned for that role," I retorted, and we both burst into laughter.

We occasionally made light-hearted predictions about what would happen next in the book, and Richard continued to poke fun at the vampire characters. As the hours passed, the gentle rhythm of Richard's breathing, synchronized with mine, lulled me into a peaceful slumber. My head nestled against his chest, and we snuggled together in blissful harmony.

———

I woke up to medical staff bustling around my room as they did their final rounds. They declared me fit to travel, albeit cautiously, and I thanked them for their care and attention. As they left, I noticed the extra security details roaming the corridors — it was clear that they were looking forward to a return to their normal and peaceful routine.

I then asked my mother, who was busily packing my bags, "Mom, where is Richard?"

"Sweetheart," she replied, smiling, "He left before you woke up."

He had left without saying goodbye. He knew we both hated goodbyes, so I assumed he wanted me to happily remember our last night together. That one night of comfortable silence and playful debates. Other times we would drift into banter, all while cuddled up together. Even now, after he left, I could still feel his gentle touches that lingered in my heart, making me smile as tears of joy trickled down my face.

My mom walked towards my bed and pulled me into a tight embrace. "I'm so sorry, sweetheart," she said softly, wiping away my tears with her thumbs. Her warmth enveloped me in a comforting cocoon, and for a moment, I felt safe.

"It's all gonna be okay," she said as she held me close.

Letting out all the emotions building up inside me, I whispered, "I love him, Mommy."

She helped me get dressed, looking at me with a reassuring smile. As she finished doing up my shirt, I heard the sound coming from outside and knew it must be my dad. Taking a deep breath, I wiped away my tears.

As my dad's security detail gathered our bags and escorted us to the basement parking lot, I made a quick trip to the nurses' lounge to thank everyone who had cared for me for the past few weeks. One of Dad's security lifted me off my wheelchair and seated me at the back of a huge black SUV. Shortly after, Dad emerged from one of the elevators and rode in a separate car.

The ride to Heathrow Airport was quick and peaceful, allowing me to reflect on the roller coaster of emotions I had experienced over the past weeks. I couldn't help but feel overwhelming sadness. Despite my nightmare, this city gave me beautiful memories of my life with Richard.

We arrived at the airport and passed through immigration without any trouble. The uniformed officer smiled at my passport before stamping it and sending me on my way. As my mom pushed my wheelchair to the tarmac and not the usual gate, I looked at my dad, and he smiled with pride, "The Ortegas don't fly commercial." My eyes widened as I saw a gleaming white jet waiting on the runway. The pilot warmly greeted us as we made our way toward the private jet. "Welcome aboard!" he exclaimed, a smile stretching across his face. I could hardly believe it — just moments ago, the idea of flying home with my family seemed like an impossible dream. But now, here we were, about to take off and head home.

With my family's help, I settled comfortably into the plush leather seats, marveling at the magnificent view outside the windows. The beauty of the sprawling clouds and endless skies was breathtaking, and I couldn't help but grin from ear to ear at the realization that I was living a moment I thought impossible.

As soon as I was comfortably seated, Dad handed me a rectangular box and kissed me on the forehead. He left to give me some privacy, and I opened it to find a Tiffany box with a white envelope addressed to me in Richard's handwriting. My heart leaped at the sight of it — there was still one last message from him before we had to depart. I carefully opened the envelope, cradling it close to my heart as soon as I recognized Richard's familiar handwriting. I read it with trembling hands, taking in every word and feeling each emotion course through me.

My Darling Hope,

The sun was about to break from the horizon, and I still couldn't find the right words to express my love for you. All I could think of at that moment was how much more time we could have spent together exploring this world with each other.

Our days of bliss were fleeting, and it torments me to know that our goodbye must come soon. Although we are apart now, I will never forget all the memories we made together. They only made me fall deeper in love with you, and it's something that is irrevocable.

The thought of us being apart is unbearable - every second feels like an eternity - yet I know this is just another one of life's challenges we must overcome to find your way back to me. And when the right time comes, nothing will stop me from slipping your ring back onto your finger like how it was before. In the meantime, here is something to remind you of our life together — a reminder that I'm with you always, no matter what.

Until then, remember what I said — no matter how far away we are from each other, I will always be there for you, waiting for the moment we can reunite again.

Your love,
   Richard

With tears streaming down my cheeks, I opened the Tiffany box. Inside was a beautiful personalized charm bracelet crafted with gold, silver, and diamonds. Each charm on the bracelet represented a special part of our love story. There was a gold leaf for fall, a snowflake for winter, a flower for spring, and the sun for summer — the four seasons of the year reminding me we'll be together throughout the years and whatever season in life we'll go through. Then there were symbols of our journey together: a vintage film camera, a book, the Empire State Building, a tulip, the Eiffel Tower, a bottle of wine, Big Ben, a palm tree… and a tiny angel made of gold.

As I held the charm bracelet in my hand, I marveled at the thoughtfulness behind Richard's choice of charms for me. Each one held a special meaning, representing small snippets of our journey together. And to my amazement, he had even remembered to include one for our little bean — a reminder that he was always with us.

Gazing at the bracelet, I felt as if I was looking at our own little constellation of memories and love. Each charm sparkled and twinkled in the light, symbolizing a significant moment we could hold onto forever in our lives. Richard's gesture was a beautiful reminder of just how much he loved me and the lengths he would go to make me feel cherished and adored.

As I closed my eyes, an overwhelming sense of longing enveloped my heart while s our plane glided into the sky, accompanied by the sun's gradual descent toward the horizon. The fleeting moments we shared will forever be etched in my mind, for no amount of time could ever erase them. As I watched the sun slowly dip below the horizon, I silently said my goodbye with one last tear rolling down my cheek.

28

After a long journey back to New York, I finally settled back into my old apartment. The hustle and bustle of the city below welcomed me like a long-lost friend. Salem was understandably angry at me for leaving him alone with Richard's housekeeper while I was gone. But his grumpiness quickly faded away when he realized it was me, and I was back for good, snuggling up to me like we were friends reunited again.

My father tried to persuade me to move to a much bigger place. He offered to buy me a comfortable house or an apartment with all the modern amenities, but I refused his offer. I explained to him that rent here was still much more affordable for me than a mortgage, plus I didn't want the responsibility of being tied down with property taxes and maintenance costs. But my father kept pushing me by saying that I didn't need to refuse something just because it cost more. I didn't mention that I actually owned a penthouse in Upper East Side, a gift from Richard.

On the other hand, my mother had been worried and borderline paranoid after the incident in London. Even though I insisted I would be alright, she wanted to stay by my side for a few days until my full recovery. No matter how often I assured her everything would be okay, she still wouldn't leave. Finally, after two days of persistent reminders from my stepfather, she agreed to go home — but only after making me promise to call her every day.

I was grateful for my parents' unwavering love and support, but I was used to living independently. Salem had difficulties adjusting with Mom around, so he stayed at Charlie's downstairs most of the time. My dad, however, implemented full security details around me —at least, they're just shadowing me, and I don't get to see them.

Veronica kept me informed and updated on all the news surrounding the crime committed against me and my baby. She gave me detailed accounts of everything reported in the tabloids and on social media, including photos of Emilia in mug shots, Richard's temper tantrum in the courtroom, and Henry's sneaky visits to the hospital. Even though these reports were difficult for me to hear, it was comforting to know what was going on and to be able to counter any false or inaccurate statements that might have been circulating. Dad and Richard also managed to keep my privacy intact by not allowing any compromising or current photos of me to be released. The security in the hospital was not only there so no one else could harm me further but also to keep out the paparazzi.

I found myself feeling constrained by the rigid confines of my plaster cast, unable to roam freely and explore as I once had. However, as time progressed, I came to understand that there were alternative methods for venturing out without jeopardizing my recovery. At home, I used crutches and walking sticks, which allowed me to traverse short distances when required.

Although I longed for the expansive living space of our penthouse on the Upper East Side, complete with a chauffeur and housekeeper to attend to my needs, I found solace in the coziness of my modest apartment. Its compact layout ensured that everything I needed was within arm's reach, making it the perfect sanctuary for my current circumstances.

It was an exciting journey exploring different ways for me to move around even when my leg was still healing in a cast. Eventually, as the days passed, I could move more freely as my leg became stronger until, one day, the cast finally came off.

As I was recovering in the hospital in London, Jenna took it upon herself to care for my manuscript. She worked closely with my book agent, and together they worked hard to make sure everything was ready for publication, just waiting for my approval on the cover artwork. I had intended to avoid setting foot in Richard's place on the Upper East Side, so Jenna and I met somewhere near my apartment instead.

I spent my first week getting acquainted with the place again — from walking around my old neighborhood to catching up with friends I'd missed. Being in this familiar city was bittersweet, yet feeling like a stranger all over again. With the cast finally off my leg, Mavi took it upon herself to assist me in gently reintegrating into my physical routine through soothing yoga sessions. Naturally, I continued attending the hospital for my biweekly appointments with my team of physical therapists, making good on the promise I had made to my parents to prioritize my recovery. However, I remained steadfast in my refusal to engage in regular sessions with a psychiatrist. The prospect of discussing the traumatic events that transpired during my time in London was not something I was ready to confront just yet.

Erin and Charlie were incredibly supportive, going above and beyond to ensure that I was comfortable and well-fed during my recovery. They didn't let me fuss over cooking meals, instead opting for fresh food deliveries and homemade dishes. Their selflessness and care made all the difference in the world, and I felt grateful for their constant presence as I regained my strength.

Even though I'm miles away from him now, mornings are still hard — I missed Richard every day. I knew he remained in Ireland, in the middle of his filming project. He had departed as soon as I left London, and true to his word, he refrained from calling or visiting me until I signaled that I am ready.

His commitment to honoring my wishes only deepened the void created by his absence, leaving me longing for the day when I would finally feel ready to reconnect with him.

Henry and I kept in touch often through FaceTime, and it was through him I found out that Richard colored his hair blond for the new role.

After weeks of paparazzi following my every move, I eventually managed to get some peace. It felt like they would never leave me alone, but after a while, they were tired of tailing me and finally backed off.

I was relieved to finally have some privacy and the freedom to go about my life without having cameras up in my face all the time. It had been a long journey, but I could finally breathe a sigh of relief that it was finally over.

As the days become shorter and the temperatures begin to drop, the leaves transformed to vibrant colors, from bright reds and oranges to yellows and purples. A crispness in the air can only be found during this season — a special feeling that brings a sense of cozy nostalgia. From hot apple cider and pumpkin-spiced lattes to crunchy fall foliage and warm fireside gatherings...there's no denying that autumn was on its way.

———

As the highly anticipated release date for *Back In Time* drew near, the marketing and PR teams worked tirelessly to ensure the TV show received the attention it deserved. To build excitement and anticipation, our teams utilized various promotional tools, such as trailers and posters, and boosted social media engagement across multiple platforms.

One highly engaging tool was the active involvement of Brittany and the rest of the cast on their Instagram and Twitter accounts. With frequent behind-the-scenes shots, they successfully allowed their followers to feel like they were part of the production process.

In a curious twist of events, the production management team discovered I was the daughter of the film's executive producer. They promptly included me in the email group intended for management only. This allowed me to gain an exclusive glimpse into the ins and outs of the post-production process and marketing and publicity activities and plans.

After a few days of trying to dodge Yumi's invitation, I finally gave in and agreed to meet her for lunch at The Grill on Park Avenue. This exclusive venue had been previously out of reach for me. As I walked in, I was amazed by the restaurant's mid-century-inspired decor, featuring bold geometric patterns, rich textures, and warm colors. The spacious dining area was well-lit, with comfortable leather banquettes and chairs adding to the upscale and refined ambiance.

As Yumi arrived, I could tell that she had put some thought into her outfit, with her bright red lips and perfectly matching fingernails adding an extra touch of elegance to her look. I wish I could be that attentive to dressing up, too, as I looked at my white shirt tucked neatly in a charcoal pencil-cut skirt. She took the seat opposite me, and as she looked over the menu, I couldn't help but feel a little apprehensive about what we would discuss.

As I perused the menu, our waiter was already at Yumi's side, waiting for her order. Yumi opted for an oyster and shrimp cocktail and requested the sommelier's recommendation for a wine pairing. She then proceeded to order her main course, which was steamed branzino.

When Yumi turned to me, my mind was still awash with memories of my first encounter with Richard, when I had an oyster and wine for the very first time. It took me a moment to collect myself before I answered her. "I think I'll go for the black truffle ravioli, please," I said, still slightly lost in thought.

After ordering our meals, Yumi wasted no time in revealing the purpose of our lunch meeting. "I have good news and bad news for you. Which one do you wanna hear first?" she asked.

"Give me the bad news first," I replied hesitantly.

"I need to pull Richard out of Dublin for *Back In Time* promotion," Yumi revealed. "He'll have to attend rounds of shows and press conferences both here and in LA."

Yumi told me that my father had advised her to discuss the matter with me first, although he was okay with shelving the project and losing money as long as it didn't cause me any trouble.

Feeling a bit overwhelmed, I took a moment to gather my thoughts before asking, "I don't have to be there, right? I'm just the screenwriter after all."

"You have to be there being one of the executive producers, as your father's name shouldn't be on any Hollywood projects."

I couldn't help but feel a bit anxious about this development. Despite my concerns, I knew that Yumi had our best interests in mind and that we would find a way to make this work.

"You are the sole heir of Oliver, whether you like it or not. You need to step up and take responsibility so suck it up." One thing I don't like about Yumi, she's used to get her way, and she's using that with me. I couldn't help but feel frustrated by her response, as she seemed to be dismissive of my efforts and hard work.

Feeling defeated, I asked sarcastically, "What's the good news then?"

"Your father is buying a building in Manhattan as one of the companies' headquarters, including the film company, which is yours, by the way. We can expand to publishing books and maybe you can consider working with big tech for database and access of writers to pitch their books for Hollywood movie or television adaptation."

"Is that good news to you?" I asked. I couldn't help but feel a bit ambivalent.

"Yes! Look, Hope. You can't deny your birthright. You are wrong if you think you don't want it or deserve it. Your father made sacrifices in the past and until now to secure your future, even in several lifetimes."

As the sommelier poured our drinks, Yumi reminded me once again that I needed to act the part of being Oliver Ortega's daughter and Richard Collins' fiancée and that I needed to dress accordingly. "I know your better clothes are in Richard's apartment, I can have the 'twin goons' collect them, or we can shop together," she said firmly.

"Now, I understand why you are my father's shooter," I said.

"Good! Then let's eat."

Feeling a mix of anxiety and resignation, I took a sip of my drink and tried to focus on the positive aspects of the situation.

29

Autumn, New York

The return of autumn in New York City marked a significant shift in the city's energy. The leaves on trees turned vibrant shades of orange, red and yellow, painting a beautiful backdrop against the city skyline. The sun's light was warm and soft, casting long shadows across the streets as the cityscape becomes drenched in a golden glow. As the pace of life in the city began to slow, people started to spend more time indoors, savoring the warmth of their homes and the company of loved ones. I loved how the city's energy shifted from the hustle and bustle of the summer to a more relaxed and reflective one.

Autumn will always be my favorite season — the mood is more intimate and comforting. I took a deep breath as I stood in my favorite running spot at Central Park. The carpet of fallen leaves covered the ground. The sun beamed down on me as the breeze picked up and carried around the scent of pumpkin spice latte from nearby cafés. I took a moment to appreciate this moment — soon, I'll be able to ditch this cane and return to my usual running stride.

Same time last year, my life was a completely different world. I was just an ordinary girl trying to find her spot in this seemingly crowded space. In the span of a few short seasons, my life took an incredible journey from someone who dreaded the days going by to someone who was now financially secure for multiple lifetimes. I loved deeply, but I was hurt more than I could have imagined, too.

Gaining so much and losing what mattered most — these drastic changes happened in the space of just four seasons and will stay with me forever. But no matter how far I go, the autumn air will always bring back memories of where I started and everything that had changed since then.

With trembling hands, I touched the angel charm on my bracelet — one that I never took off. A single tear rolled down my cheek as I whispered, "I remember you every day, my little bean." Then I walked slowly, this time going back home. I know the 'twin goons' are following me discreetly. So I just learned to accept their presence. It was one of my father's non-negotiables for allowing me to still live in my apartment.

———

When I arrived home, I found a package waiting for me. As I opened it, I was immediately struck by the beautiful artwork on the cover of my book. The design was simple yet incredibly powerful in conveying the emotions behind the writing. Against a backdrop of light blue watercolor, a single white tulip stood in full bloom. Next to it lay a lone petal adorned with a shining golden angel charm against its snowy white surface. The whole image was incredibly moving.

As my finger hovered over the charm, I felt myself slipping further into a downward spiral of loneliness. The pain and sorrow of losing my little bean before he even stepped into this world were incredibly overwhelming, and I tried to sweep my feelings under the rug in the hopes that the pain would somehow disappear.

Although my medical team in London recommended that I see someone to process my trauma and grief, and my parents begged me to see a therapist — with my father even attempting to get me one of the best in the city — I found it difficult to face the complexity of emotions that came with such a loss. Instead, I took care of my body and spirit as part of my healing process. I engaged in self-care activities like yoga and meditation, and once in a while, I allowed myself to seek moments of happiness and joy, even amid grief.

As I looked at my book cover, memories of my ordeal in London flooded back to me, and all the emotions I had suppressed came rushing to the surface. I wasn't prepared for this sudden rush of feelings, and I felt overwhelmed and unsure of how to move forward.

Without a second thought, I reached for my phone and dialed Richard's number. He answered almost immediately, not even allowing the first ring to complete. His voice was laden with concern and worry as he asked, "Hope, are you okay?"

I didn't need to say anything as my sobs filled the air. He just listened quietly and patiently, knowing that's what I needed more than anything.

It was as if he could feel my pain through the phone. His calming presence grounded me and made me feel like I wasn't alone in my grief. Even though I knew he couldn't take away my pain, just hearing his voice was enough to ease some of the burden.

"It hurts, I'm feeling it now, Richard," I cried desperately. I slumped my body on the floor and pressed both hands on my stomach, hoping to feel something, anything that I used to have.

"Please let me come to you now. I can take the next available flight," he said.

"No, Richard... I can't," I cried, and let out all the emotions I had been holding back. He remained a steady presence on the other end of the line. He didn't offer advice or try to fix the situation. He simply listened and let me express the full extent of my pain.

Richard had the unique ability to make me feel protected and at ease with just his presence, and this time was no different. His silent understanding gave me the strength I needed to confront my emotions and move on from them. But this wasn't fair to Richard, and I knew that as he silently listened to my sobs. Even in the midst of my anguish, I couldn't help but feel guilty about burdening Richard with my pain. He, too, carried his own grief over the life that was taken away from us.

As I struggled to regain my composure, I took a deep breath and said, "I'm sorry, I have to go." I could feel more tears choking my throat as I pushed the end call button. Despite my desire to hold onto him and let him fix everything, I knew deep down that I had to face my emotions in my own way and in my own time.

I let myself curl up on the cold floor. For weeks, I had been dodging my issues and keeping myself busy, but tonight, I finally allowed room for everything to sink in. The love, the loss, and the raw hatred for the one who had caused it all. Emotions swirled around me as I wept until dawn, knowing that Richard had stayed on the line until he was certain my storm had run its course.

I felt as though the world had shifted beneath me tonight, and nothing made sense. All around me were reminders of what I had lost —

memories of Richard and I planning to decorate the nursery and choosing names. Silently, a river of tears flowed unchecked as I mourned for the baby that was never born. A tide of sorrow and longing washed through me, and it seemed like no amount of time or space would ever lessen its intensity.

I was desperate to believe there was still love — a light that shone on despite it all and kept me going when everything else felt too heavy to bear. And although my heart ached with loss, I knew that somewhere amid my pain, this love still existed — a reminder that even in the darkest moments, there is always hope for healing and growth.

As dawn began to break, I knew that the healing journey would be a long and often painful one. For so long, I had been dodging my emotions and keeping myself busy, but now I finally gave myself permission to grieve. Allowing myself to feel the pain and loss was a crucial first step.

30

In the next few weeks, I have two significant events happening in my career — the release of our new TV show, *Back in Time,* and the launch of my long-awaited book, *Fleeting Embers.* At the same time, Jenna has already finished writing the sequel to her book and sent it over for me to start working on the script for season two. Down in Los Angeles, Brittany and Richard will also be making waves with a series of TV and podcast appearances to promote the show.

As excited as I am for all these upcoming events, I couldn't help but feel a little anxious at the news of Richard's imminent arrival in New York. The thought of seeing him again brought a mixture of emotions — from joy and anticipation to fear and uncertainty.

Tonight was my regular ladies' night with Erin and Mavi at Erin's bakery. As usual, we gathered around her kitchen counter to sample whatever new baked goodies were leftover today and some pampering packs for Mavi's Yoga store. I got them VIP Broadway tickets. I finally ditched my cane. Mavi recommended I needed to level up my yoga classes. Both were pestering me if my father was still single and what type of women he liked. We all laughed at the prospect of any of them becoming my stepmother.

Erin turned to me and mentioned casually, "Hey, did you know that Richard and Brittany are about to appear on ABC in just a few minutes? Do you want to catch the segment?"

At first, I considered declining, but then I remembered how supportive my friends are of this project. "Sure, let's take a look," I smiled.

Within moments, Erin turned on the large-screen TV in the kitchen just before the three hosts introduced Richard and Brittany. Even through the screen, Richard looked impeccable. His crisp white shirt was neatly tucked into a pair of grey pants, highlighting his vibrant blue-grey eyes and infectious smile. I can't help but be drawn in by his charisma, which seemed to shine even brighter in the spotlight of the television studio.

As Richard began to speak, the audience in the TV studio was captivated by his deep British accent. It was smooth and velvety, filling the room with sophistication and elegance. He was effortlessly charming as he discussed the new TV series we all poured our hearts into. Every word he uttered seems to hold weight, and it was evident that the hosts were just as enamored with him as the studio audience. I can't deny that even I was caught up in his spell. It was impossible not to be charmed by his accent and the easy confidence when he speaks.

Watching the rapport between Richard and Brittany on-screen, it was clear that they made the perfect match. It was apparent that they developed a strong camaraderie over time, which only added to the chemistry between their characters.

One of the hosts jokingly asked Brittany if she was ever attracted to Richard, but she quickly shut it down, reminding everyone that he's very much engaged and in love with someone special.

I froze. I knew they were advised not to mention my name in any interview, so I waited with bated breath to see how they'll handle the follow-up question regarding Richard's love life. Brittany grinned mischievously and motioned to Richard to give her his phone.

Richard hesitated, shaking his head in mock refusal, but eventually handed it over. Brittany laughed as she saw the wallpaper. I knew it was the picture of the two of us that he'd posted on my Instagram, the one that announced to the world we were together. "See?" she said, holding it up to the camera.

"This guy is head over heels in love with this girl," she quipped before explaining how actors can have real love lives while still having romantic on-screen chemistry. The audience applauded, appreciating the honesty and authenticity that Brittany and Richard have brought to the show.

I watched as Richard and Brittany continued to charm the audience with their wit and warmth. I was grateful to both of them for putting so much effort into making *Back In Time*. They also gave credit to all people who poured their energy into it, especially those behind the scenes, the ones who worked tirelessly to bring the project to life. The cameramen, the writers, the sound engineers, and all the other unsung heroes who helped create this world.

As the interview drew to a close, I felt a sense of calm wash over me. Looking at Richard onscreen now, I can feel the ache inside me beginning to subside. The black hole of emptiness that had once consumed me was slowly dissolving, replaced by a growing sense of peace.

Glancing over at Erin and Mavi, I can tell they had a lot on their minds, but they kept their thoughts to themselves for now. They knew the unspoken rule — until I find myself again, Richard remains out of sight.

I appreciated their unwavering support and understanding. It was comforting to know that my friends won't judge me for needing time to heal and find my bearings again.

As the credits rolled onscreen, I stretched my limbs and let out a contented sigh. "Thank you for watching that with me, guys," I said, a warm smile spreading across my face. "It means so much to have you by my side through all of this."

Erin wrapped her arms around me in a comforting embrace. "We've always got your back, baby girl. You know that."

"I know," I replied softly, reaching out to take Mavi's hand and drawing her into our circle of affection. We stood there, hugging each other in a rare moment of silence, which was unusual for us, given our penchant for lively conversation. Moments like these served as a poignant reminder of the true essence of friendship and love, and why they were worth every effort to protect and cherish.

31

After months of hard work, my first book, *Fleeting Embers*, was finally making its debut at the press launch. This moment marked a turning point in my life, a culmination of my efforts and dreams. A mix of emotions filled me as I prepared to share my creation with the world. A big part of me still longed for my little bean, who inspired me to do it. Around this time, he was supposed to come out into this world and into my arms.

I felt emptiness engulf me. I wished more than anything that my little bundle of joy was with me, but I knew that he would always be a part of my story, and he will always be my motivation to keep moving forward. And Richard, who gave me the greatest love story, was thousands of miles away. I couldn't help but feel the weight of the distance between Richard and me. I had never imagined that loving someone so deeply would also mean hurting so much. But I learned to find peace in the midst of the pain. I focused on living in the moment and cherishing the love we had created. I knew that it wouldn't be easy, but I also knew that our love was strong enough to withstand anything.

Flipping through the pages of my book, a sense of pride and joy washed over me. The hardbound and Kindle versions looked beautiful, but the gorgeous cover drew me to the book. Its glossy sheen shimmered in the light, and every intricate detail stood out against the snowy white petal, including that beloved golden angel charm. I remember when I chose that design — it captured my heart, and I knew it had to be the one.

I turned to the dedication page.

To Richard, my greatest love of all.

To my little bean, you will always be in Mama's heart.

No matter how many times I looked at this book, each time felt like a special moment shared between me and them. That's why every time someone flips through its pages, I hope that my words will connect with their hearts just as I hope that someone's story will connect with mine.

32

Today was the big day.

The news of the special book-reading and book-signing event at Barnes & Noble in Manhattan last week had spread rapidly throughout the city. As the event drew closer, my excitement and nervousness grew simultaneously. At the outset, the intention was to focus on book readings and signings. However, my publisher and agent proposed incorporating a press launch to amplify the publicity surrounding the event.

Though initially reluctant, I eventually conceded to the idea, aware of the fact that it could potentially garner even greater interest in the event and, by extension, my book. Nonetheless, I stood my ground, asserting that this occasion was primarily intended for readers and not an exclusive press event where they receive advance copies. Despite agreeing to the press launch, I couldn't help but feel uneasy, as the lingering thought of the event devolving into a chaotic and overwhelming spectacle weighed heavily on me. After all, I remained Richard Collins's fiancée, and the press's fascination with our relationship had yet to wane.

Regardless, I prepared for the event with both excitement and trepidation, determined to make the best of whatever came my way. I was especially looking forward to meeting my readers, signing their books, and sharing my story with them.

The days leading up to the launch gave me plenty of time to worry —

would the press be understanding or antagonizing? Would I keep my composure during their questioning? No matter how anxious I felt, I knew one thing for sure: this book launch was worth putting up with the stress beforehand.

Every achievement came with its own challenges and uncertainties, and I knew this book-reading event was no exception. Despite my desire for everything to go smoothly, I understood there were no guarantees. Nevertheless, I was determined to trust myself to handle whatever came my way — the good and the bad — and to take each moment as it came.

I reminded myself that this was a moment I had been waiting for, the opportunity to share my work with readers, and I would not let my nerves get the best of me. Instead, I would focus on enjoying the experience and connecting with those who supported me. Despite the unease and nerves accompanying the event, I was excited to see where this achievement would take me.

As I prepared for my book launch, a wave of sadness washed over me. Both of my parents were unable to attend the event. My mother was sick with the flu, and my father was likely somewhere overseas, tending to his business empire. I didn't bother to invite him, knowing that he had more pressing matters to deal with.

At that moment, I turned to Salem, the bundle of black fur sleeping soundly on my bed. I gazed into his sleepy eyes and whispered, "I wish I could bring you with me." He licked my hand to reassure me that everything would be okay.

Although I felt a pang of sadness at not having my family with me, I took solace in the fact that I had Salem by my side. His quiet presence and unconditional love served as a source of strength and comfort, reminding me that no matter what happens, there will always be someone who has my back.

With a long, deep look in the mirror, I saw the transformation that had taken place: no more designer clothes and camera-ready hair. I was ready for my book launch as Hope Williams, writer and ordinary girl living in a small apartment with her cat, not celebrity fiancée. I wore fitted jeans tucked into black boots, a navy blue turtleneck sweater, and light makeup. My messy bun was bundled securely with my bangs casually falling over my forehead —a look that felt like it had been made just for me.

I touched my earrings, the gift from Richard on our first dinner in Paris, and caressed the charm bracelet he had given me. I wanted parts of him with me today and these will have to do.

———

When I arrived at Barnes & Noble, there were dozens of people inside — press and readers alike — and a line of excited people stretching around outside of the bookstore. It was an amazing sight to see, and it sent a surge of excitement through my veins, but I felt nervous at the same time.

Inside the bookstore, my books were arranged carefully atop a large table in the center of the room. The display was inviting and intricately designed, with tulips and other decorations placed beautifully everywhere. Looking around, the atmosphere in the room was electric — people were excited to be there, and they seemed eager to hear what I had to say.

"Congratulations, sweetheart. I am so proud of you," said a warm voice behind me. When I turned around, there he was — my father standing tall in his pinstriped black suit.

He came here on this special day. He knew how important this launch was to me. Without a word, I embraced him tightly; joy and pride burst in my heart.

My father kissed my forehead and urged me to move forward and meet the other guests. He whispered, "We'll catch up later." He had taken time out of his schedule to be there meant the world to me.

As soon as I stepped onto the platform for the book reading, my jitters faded away. I selected a few chapters to read. Everybody was quite mesmerized by my narration as I read the last part, a poem dedicated to little bean. I heard sighs as I read and I knew then my words had moved my readers.

Love that blossoms like a rose,
Petals unfurling, heart exposed,
Fragrant, sweet, a tender pose,
A beauty that never fades, it grows.

But sometimes love can turn to pain,
The rose withers, the petals wane,

Heartache grips, its bitter refrain,
As loss grieves, the tears remain.

Yet even in the depths of sorrow,
Love endures and shines tomorrow,
Memories forever in our marrow,
A light that guides us through the hollow.

For love and loss, forever entwined,
The sweet with the bitter, the heart aligned,
A beautiful tapestry, to remind,
That love and loss, forever bind.

When I closed the book, my audience erupted in applause and cheers. Questions began to fly from all directions, as everyone wanted to know what would happen next in the lives of the characters they had come to love. It was amazing to see how invested readers had become in the story, and it filled me with a great sense of pride and accomplishment. I knew that my book had impacted these people's lives, which was a feeling unlike any other.

Then the press began firing questions related to my personal life.

"Hi, Hope, Jenny from *The New York Times*. We've noticed that you're no longer wearing your engagement ring. " My heart began to race. She had brought up a topic I wasn't ready or willing to discuss. I took a deep breath, trying to steady myself. It was an uncomfortable truth but knew I could not ignore. Even though it was a personal and private matter, being in the public eye meant that my personal life was not entirely my own. I knew I had to handle the situation with grace and tact, no matter how difficult it might be.

Before I could reply, another news network piped in. "Hope," the journalist asked. "What happened to the engagement? Are you and Richard still planning on getting married?" I took a deep breath and replied with the spiel my publisher's PR team told me to say, knowing that any answer I gave could potentially make or break my relationship with Richard.

"I'm sorry, but I cannot comment on my personal life," I replied, my voice steady but firm. "What I will say is that Richard and I are on good terms and are focusing on our respective careers at the moment."

I hoped that my response would be enough to quell further speculation and put an end to the invasive questioning. But another press pushed for another follow-up question, "So, is the engagement still on?"

An expectant silence enveloped the crowd, the stillness so deafening that it felt as though time itself had come to a halt. Every pair of eyes was fixated on me, eagerly awaiting my answer.

Suddenly, a familiar voice filled the room. "I'm dying to hear the answer to those questions, too," the voice declared with unabashed curiosity.

It was Richard! His deep blue-grey eyes never left mine. His now sandy blond hair was neatly combed back, and he wore a warm, inviting smile. His broad shoulders seemed to exude confidence and radiated an aura of calmness as he emerged from the back the audience and walked toward me. Dressed in a crisp white shirt and navy blue fitted slacks, his captivating smile never faltered, and his gaze remained fixed on mine. The room fell into a shocked silence as he stepped forward, produced a small velvet box from his pocket, and said, "Hope, let's put these rumors to rest. Will you wear this ring again?"

As he came to stand before me, he knelt down and looked up at me with such love and adoration that it took my breath away. The rest of the room seemed to dissolve, leaving only the two of us standing beneath a spotlight of pure bliss.

I felt the warmth of his hands in mine, the spark in his eyes reflecting the depth of his emotions. My heart raced with excitement and joy as he awaited my response. Overwhelmed by emotion, tears streamed down my face as I whispered the word that would bind us together forever — "Yes!" I sensed a profound, unbreakable bond between us, a connection destined to last a lifetime. For those moments, we were the only two people in the world, basking in the glow of each other's love.

Richard slipped the ring onto my finger, and I marveled at its beauty. It symbolized our love, filling my heart with pride and happiness. He then gently kissed my wrist, his lips brushing the golden angel charm that rested on my pulse. It was an intimate gesture that spoke volumes about the depth of our love. Looking into my eyes with longing, he whispered, "I love you, Hope Williams." Richard rose to his feet and swept me into a passionate embrace, our lips meeting as the room erupted around us in applause and shouts of joy. Every fiber of my being was alive and electrified with love.

His lips were tender and gentle, yet filled with a passionate intensity that left me breathless. I wished the moment could last forever, as if time had come to a standstill and we were the only two people in existence. In that instant, I knew without a doubt that nothing could ever separate us – our love was an indestructible force, destined to withstand the test of time.

* * *

My dearest readers,

As I write this dedication, my heart is filled with gratitude and love. This book would not have been possible without many incredible people's unwavering support and inspiration.

Firstly, I want to thank my editor, Frances Amper-Sales, who has been my guiding light throughout this journey. Frances, you pushed me to step out of my comfort zone, take risks, and trust my voice. Your insights, feedback, and encouragement have helped shape this book into something extraordinary, and I am forever grateful to you.

To my cheering squad, Erika Dela Cruz and Merle Victorino, who helped me shape the characters and storyline during those endless nights and countless bottles of wine. Thank you for being my sounding board and my constant source of motivation. Your wisdom and hilarious anecdotes have kept me going through the ups and downs of writing.

To my two darlings, Luis and Julia, you are mommy's strength to capture the beauty and complexity of true love in my writing.

Finally, to my partner in crime, Carlos, who has held my hand and my heart through every chapter, every sentence, and every word of this book, thank you for being my constant muse and source of love. You are my happily-ever-after, prince charming, knight in shining armor, and your love has inspired me to write stories that celebrate the power of love and the beauty of human connection.

To all of you, my readers, thank you for taking this journey with me. I hope the love story of Richard and Hope brings you joy, laughter, tears, and renewed faith in the transformative power of love. May we continue to write, read, and live our love stories, and may they never be far from our hearts and pens.

With love and gratitude,

Justine

ABOUT THE AUTHOR

Justine Castellon is a brand strategist with an innate ability to weave compelling narratives. She seamlessly blends her professional insight with her passion for literature. Her literary works include romantic drama novels—**The Last Snowfall, Gnight Sara / 'Night Heck,** and **I Love You Sunday Sunset**. With her ability to tell stories that linger long after the last word, Justine leaves a mark not only in the world of branding but also in the hearts of her readers.

Fall in love with these 3 charming romance stories from Justine Castellon

🌱 FOUR SEASONS

A struggling New York writer's dreams come true when a chance encounter with a Hollywood star shoots her into a glittering world of romance and fame. But, as love and illusions shatter, she must rebuild her life and rediscover her own voice in the aftermath of heartbreak.

❄️ THE LAST SNOWFALL

A writer-turned-heiress marries a British Hollywood star, only to be swept into a high-stakes world of love, betrayal, and buried secrets. As ghosts from the past threaten her marriage and power struggles consume her father's empire, she must confront the ultimate question: how far will she go to protect the life she's built, and at what cost?

🌙 GNIGHT SARA/'NIGHT HECK

In a bustling New York City café, amidst the noise and chaos, two souls, a young copywriter and a reluctant heir, find a unique sanctuary. This romantic drama delves deep into the complexities of friendship, self-discovery, and the choices that define our lives.

www.justcastellon.com

www.ingramcontent.com/pod-product-compliance
Lightning Source LLC
Chambersburg PA
CBHW020905200626
46814CB00001BA/182